'ANTIGUA, PENNY, PUCE'

Robert Graves was born in 1895 at Wimbledon, son of Alfred Perceval Graves, the Irish writer, and Amalia von Ranke. He went from school to the First World War, where he became a captain in the Royal Welch Fusiliers. His principal calling is poetry, and his *Selected Poems* have been published in the Penguin Poets. Apart from a year as Professor of English Literature at Cairo University in 1926 he has since lived by writing. His bibliography published in 1965 credits him with 114 heterogeneous books; but the score is now 120. His historical novels include: *I, Claudius*; *Claudius the God*; *Sergeant Lamb of the Ninth*; *Count Belisarius*; *Wife to Mr Milton*; *Proceed, Sergeant Lamb*; *The Golden Fleece*; *They Hanged My Saintly Billy*; and *The Isles of Unwisdom*. He wrote his autobiography, *Goodbye to All That*, in 1929. His two most discussed non-fiction books are *The White Goddess*, which presents a new view of the poetic impulse, and *The Nazarene Gospel Restored* (with Joshua Podro), a re-examination of primitive Christianity. He has translated Apuleius, Lucan and Suetonius for the Penguin Classics, and compiled the first modern dictionary of Greek mythology, *The Greek Myths*. He was elected Professor of Poetry at Oxford in 1961. He has made his home in Majorca since 1929.

ROBERT GRAVES

'Antigua, Penny, Puce'

PENGUIN BOOKS

Penguin Books Ltd, Harmondsworth, Middlesex, England
Penguin Books Australia Ltd, Ringwood, Victoria, Australia

—

First published by Constable 1936
Published in Penguin Books 1947
Reprinted 1968

—

—

Made and printed in Great Britain by
Cox & Wyman Ltd,
London, Reading and Fakenham
Set in Monotype Garamond

CONTENTS

CHAPTER I

'OUR STAMP ALBUM'

'*ANTIGUA, penny, puce.*' The eye dwells on it excitedly, and a flood of memories and conjectures surges into the heart. For is not Antigua a British colony? And are not most of the classic rarities in the world of stamps early British colonials? And besides, one penny being the commonest denomination of British colonial stamps, is it not clear that the stamp in question had something very remarkable about it to justify it as the subject of a book? Perhaps what marked it out from all others like it was its puceness – its unique puceness? The solemn ring of the word 'Antigua' and the pretty alliteration of 'penny puce' will also have been noted, rightly, as elements of narrative importance. Had the phrase been 'Turks Islands, 1881, one shilling slate blue, with the error TRUKS', the psycho-sensual impact would not have been anything like so strong, in spite of the high desirability of errors and in spite of shilling stamps being nearly always priced higher in stamp catalogues than penny ones of the same issue. But, of course, there are no alternatives to the truth. The truth is that the stamp which gives the title to this story was (though a few philatelic purists clung obstinately, for years, to the more conventional term 'purple-brown') *Antigua, 1d., puce.* The circumstances did not allow it to be anything else. 'Turks Islands, 1881, one shilling slate blue, with the error TRUKS', would not have made even a good newspaper caption. Do you not see what we mean? The only sure way to spot the winner of the Derby is to look down the list of runners on the morning of the race and then imagine the headlines in the evening papers, putting yourself in the position of their millions of eager readers. If you do this with complete impartiality, eliminating all personal bias in favour of names which happen to have particular significance for yourself, there is always only one possible horse; back it heavily! The soundness of the principle can be proved after every race. *Sunstar's Great Derby. Call Boy Wins in a Canter. Windsor Lad's Triumph. Who backed Felstead? Mahmoud makes*

History. You are forced to admit that no other names would have answered. So with this postage-stamp, headlined in the World's Press again and again – a predestined winner.

Antigua, penny, puce. And though it is only into the heart of the ordinary *man* that the flood of pent-up memories and conjectures is expected to surge, the ordinary woman too must inevitably have a recrudescence of feeling on seeing him, after all these years, flush with emotion at the mention of a wretched, perfectly useless postage-stamp. For every ordinary man is a schoolboy at heart, and every ordinary woman a schoolgirl. All British schoolboys of a certain age collect postage-stamps, or at least all schoolboys whose parents have a little money; below a certain social level the collecting instinct must, we suppose, be satisfied largely with cigarette pictures and gift-coupons. Schoolgirls, on the other hand, except perhaps at those freak schools which are claimed as faithful replicas (with the substitution of net-ball for boxing and conduct marks for the birch) of the old foundations where boys of the moneyed classes rag gentlemanliness into one another under the pleasantly lax supervision of a scholarly staff – schoolgirls do not go in for stamp-collecting. In fact, they usually despise the pursuit, which is not direct and personal enough to satisfy them emotionally: if they collect anything it is signed photographs of famous actresses and actors. But they have brothers, and brothers collect stamps. So in the holidays they very often consent to lend a hand in the game. They rummage in bedroom drawers, and in the parents' writing-desks, and in boxes in the attic, and sometimes make quite useful hauls. The brothers are touched and gratified. Schoolgirls are not interested in stamps, agreed, but – this is the important point – they are undeniably interested in their brothers' preoccupation with stamps. What is it all about? What is the sense of it? They behave just as if they were in love with their albums.

As a reward for the spoils that she has brought him from places where he would never have had the moral courage to rummage himself, the brother one day instructs the sister in the mysteries of his craft. He explains to her, in a trembling voice, the fine differences between this stamp and that, the exquisite care that must be taken in the handling and mounting of specimens, and the relations of rarity, genuineness and condition to market-value. She listens to him with well-acted attention and will even sit patiently through further lessons on the subject of surcharges, watermarks and rouletting. But little or nothing stays in her memory. For she is not studying philately itself, but only, it must be repeated, the behaviour of a boy who has fallen in love with his stamp album. This is why, after a time, he becomes so impatient with her and decides that he has been wasting his time. She is apparently of inferior intelligence and, in the language of his recent geometry report, 'woefully lacking in concentration; shows gross carelessness'.

'Didn't I tell you only this morning,' he groans, 'that the 1894 issue has *two* of those wavy what's-his-names on it, and the 1895 has only one? And now you've gone and mixed both lots up together and it's going to take me simply *hours* to sort them out again.'

She is tactful and answers gently, 'Oh, I *am* so sorry. How very stupid of me! Let me sort them out myself. It will be good practice, and it won't take me a moment.'

So they get on all right together until she does something tidy but quite unforgivable, like breaking up a rare block of unused Newfoundland five-cents into its constituent parts and putting each one neatly in the centre of one of the little oblong cages ruled in the album. He goes red and white with rage when he discovers what she has done. He catches her by the hair and pulls her about, and only a sudden recollection that it is cowardly for a boy to assault a girl, especially a sister younger than himself, restrains him from doing her any serious injury. She cries, but more from excitement than pain. To think that he could go so raving mad about a trifle like that! Why, he made far less fuss, in fact hardly any fuss at all, that day she accidentally spilt a whole tin of green paint on his jacket. She would have been furious if it had happened to her. Boys are like that about all clothes except their Sunday ones. They treat paint-spots and blood-stains and barbed-wire rips as honourable scars of battle. He only called her a clumsy little fool, and actually laughed. But now, just because she neatly separated those four stamps . . .

When he lets go of her hair she behaves with dignity. She

does not throw an ink-pot at him, or even at the stamp-album. She says nothing at all, but goes slowly out, crying into her handkerchief. It is only when she reaches the door that she turns round and says that, for this, she'll never go *near* his horrible stamps again or ever do anything more to help him. He laughs scornfully. '*Help* me, indeed!' But the door has shut, so he can't say all that he was going to say. He mutters it to himself. He is very angry still, but growing a little uncomfortable. He shouldn't have done anything so ungentlemanly as to pull her hair. She is quite capable of going to Father and making a row about it; and if she does, Father is sure to take her side.

He tries to busy himself sorting his swaps and making sure that they really are all swaps and not varieties that deserve a place in the album. But he can't concentrate. He is ill at ease. He keeps on muttering under his breath about her stupidity and meddlesomeness, and makes up a sort of defence for himself in case Father comes in with his customary: 'My boy, it appears that you have behaved like a brute to your little sister . . .'

He'll answer: 'My dear Father, of course I'm sorry I lost my temper, but you know about stamps, and if *you* had an unused block of Newfoundland five-cents, and someone, without saying anything to you about it, wantonly came and tore them all apart I bet you'd be as annoyed as I was. Besides, I didn't really hurt her.'

He need not worry, because she has not gone to Father, who would only make things worse, but to Mother. These two talk the matter over together sensibly, with a certain amount of indignation, but a lot of laughter too. In the end some money changes hands in a conspiratorial way and the girl says, smiling, 'All right, darling, if you think it's the best way. Thank you ever so much. But all the same, I don't see why he should be *rewarded* for pulling my hair.'

'Think it out, my dear,' Mother answers.

She thinks it out. That evening after a silent tea she gets up from her chair and goes round the table to where her brother is sitting, moodily crumbling up the shell of his boiled egg. 'Take that,' she mumbles in a voice apparently intended not to be heard by Father, who is reading the evening paper, 'as a cure for your beastly temper. But I meant what I said about never helping you with your collection ever again.'

He glares at her, but then he examines the packet she has thrust into his hand. His face changes. What she has given him is that packet of fifty Central American stamps, priced at 3s. 6d., which he has coveted so long. It has been displayed in the side-window of the local newsagent's and at least forty of the fifty will go straight into the album. The collection is very weak in Central American stamps. But he doesn't like to accept a present given in that spirit. He says so, in a semi-hostile voice.

She laughs, a little hysterically: 'I don't collect stamps. Let's throw them away, then.' She takes them from him and marches over to the fire. 'Like me to burn them?'

He jumps up hastily. No, that's not what he meant at all. He only meant . . .

She begins to cry a little and he feels an utter cad and tries to comfort her, but she won't be comforted. Father now realizes that something is happening and puts down the paper. But Mother gives him a look which means that it is the best, perhaps, not to interfere – let them settle it between themselves. So Father says nothing and finds his place again in the news, wishing that quarrels weren't so frequent between his only son and daughter.

The only daughter now understands perfectly what Mother meant by giving her the three-and-sixpence and warning her, 'Don't let him know that it isn't what's left over from your birthday money.' She is getting a good deal of enjoyment out of the situation and will get still more before she has done. She goes out of the room and draws her brother after her, upstairs into the linen-room, where she allows him to work himself into such a state of contrition and self-reproach and gratitude for her sportsmanship in not telling Father that he ends by offering to share his stamp-collection with her.

At this memorable declaration she stops sobbing, tearfully accepts his clumsy caress and asks whether he really means it. Of course he means it, and she says how sorry she is that she ever accused him of being selfish about his collection.

'You mustn't call it "*your* collection" any more,' he says

magnanimously, stroking her hair. 'It's *our* collection from now on.'

'You're a really darling brother,' she cries, and they go downstairs again, hand in hand, where Father says how pleased he is that they have made up their quarrel, like sensible children.

That it is now 'our' collection affords her far more opportunity than before for observing his behaviour in regard to it. He is really extraordinary sometimes, she decides. For instance, when his boy friends come to the house to look at the album and do some swapping it is invariably 'my collection'. And yet he seems to expect her, as a matter of course, to spend all her pocket-money, and all her birthday and Christmas money, too, in completing broken sets of stamps or finding at least one representative for every out-of-the-way island or state for which provision is made in the album – Heligoland, Thurn and Taxis, Portuguese East Africa. 'Our collection is worth pounds and pounds now,' he gloats. Then, though it is 'our' collection, she is apparently forbidden to have any opinion of her own about its arrangement, and she mustn't put in her oar when he's busy swapping – it puts him off.

'But you tell such whopping lies about the valuableness of the swaps,' she says. 'I really don't think it's fair. You swapped that torn Barbados stamp which I mended with a little bit of a common French stamp, and pretended that it was in perfect condition.'

'Well, *he* told lies too. And if the Barbados twopence had been in perfect condition I wouldn't have swapped it for his Malta half-penny surcharged.'

'But we hadn't got the Malta half-penny.'

'I know, but it's only catalogued at fourpence, and the Barbados is catalogued at one-and-six.'

'One-and-six, unused,' she corrects him. 'Only three-pence, used.'

'Well, anyhow, I thought it was one-and-six,' he says gruffly.

What cheats boys are! They even try to cheat their own consciences. Next he gives her, as a sort of favour, the task of writing to distant relations – Cousin Eric, a mining engineer in

Bolivia, and Aunt Nellie at the British Legation in Persia – to persuade them to send stamps. 'Ask them for high denominations, unused, and tell them to put as many different low denominations as possible on the envelope. Those will be useful as swaps. But put it in a PS after a nice long letter full of news or they'll think you're writing just to get the stamps, and then they won't be bothered to answer.'

'No, PS's are too suspicious-looking. I'll put it in the middle. I'll say that they're for you, because you're ill in bed. You won't mind my saying that, will you? I mean it's just the sort of thing you'd say yourself in a letter.' There is a hint of nastiness in her voice.

'I *was* ill in bed last week,' he says, looking down and shuffling his feet. Boys hate to be involved in a lie by someone else. They like to invent their own and somehow square it with their confused memory of what really happened on such-and-such an occasion.

She is also expected to ask all her girl friends, at any rate the ones who happen to have nobody in their own family who collects, to rescue all foreign stamps from the waste-paper basket for her. 'Even if they seem quite common ones, tell them. There might be a new variety among them, or even an Error. Errors are frightfully valuable.'

But she will not, of course, allow herself to be put upon in this way more than serves her purpose. For example, she will arrange that she gets her birthday and Christmas money in kind, not cash; and though, for tactical reasons, she will allow her brother to call it 'my collection' in front of his friends, she will take it out of him afterwards in a variety of ways. She will say, one morning, for instance, 'I'm using our stamp-collection this morning. It's my turn.'

'What are you going to do with it?' he asks suspiciously.

'Oh, nothing.'

'What do you mean – "nothing"?'

'Nothing much.'

'You're not going to move any of the stamps about, are you?'

'But you've told me dozens of times that I mustn't do anything without your lordly permission. *You* can do anything you like, it seems, but I'm not even allowed to take stamps out and hold them up to the light to look at the watermarks.'

'You'd tear them; that's why.'

'Who tore that Seychelles stamp last week?'

'It was your fault for breathing so hard over my shoulder. Now listen, are you or are you not going to move any of the stamps about?'

'You've told me not to.'

'I know, but are you? Yes or no?'

'Guess.'

'Yes?'

'No, I didn't say "yes", I said "guess!"'

He runs out of the room and collides with Father, who catches hold of him. 'Where are you charging to so blindly, my boy?' This gives her a chance to slip past and get upstairs first. She knows that he was going to rescue the album and hide it away, so that she shouldn't get a chance of handling it that morning. He's caddying for Father, who is playing against Sir Reginald Whitebillet, a retired shipbuilder and senior partner of the Whitebillet shipping-line founded by his grandfather.

Father holds him in spite of his wrigglings to get away. 'I asked you a question. I expect an answer. Where are you charging to so blindly?'

'Only upstairs, to get my stamp-collection.'

'But you can't want your stamp-collection this morning? We've got to be at the Club House in a quarter of an hour.'

'I just wanted to look at it for a moment.'

She comes in with the album at this point and sits down with it on her lap, daintily, in the easy-chair by the fire.

'Well, you can't, my boy, that's all. There's no time. You've not even got your boots on yet. And I want you to scrub my balls for me. They're upstairs in the drawer of my dressing-table.'

'You know you always have new balls when you play with Sir Reginald.'

'He may not turn up. He had a touch of rheumatism yesterday. In case he doesn't, I want my balls scrubbed, do you hear? Now cut along and don't argue.'

He goes out of the room, grimacing threateningly at her over his shoulder. She says: 'Father, I'm going to study our stamp-collection this morning. It's so seldom I get it all to myself. It's supposed to be ours, but he never lets me touch it when he's not about. And really I am very careful with it.'

'I'm sure you are, my dear.'

'Father, have you remembered your long-distance glasses? The ones you've just put into your pocket are your reading-glasses.'

Father is most grateful. If she had not noticed the mistake he would have found himself at the first tee without a chance of beating Sir Reginald, who is certainly not a man to wait about while the Parson sends back to the Vicarage for his glasses. And when Father plays Sir Reginald there's money on the match. If Father wins, Sir Reginald pays five shillings to the Organ Fund. If Sir Reginald wins, Father contributes five shillings to the Otter Hounds. Sir Reginald is not a church-goer, and Father has disapproved of otter-hunting ever since the hounds killed some pedigree Bombay ducks of his and the Hunt Committee, presided over by Sir Reginald, questioned the pedigree when he put in a fair claim for damages. So the match is always fought as keenly as if the Royal St Aidan's Gold Cup were at stake. Father usually wins, but only by a couple of holes. The wrong glasses would have given Sir Reginald a lead of five holes before a caddy could have fetched Father the right ones. So she is in a strong position, sitting there with a magnifying-glass in her hand, carefully studying stamps. If there is a last-minute attempt made to rob her of the album Father will have something strong to say.

So the brother spends a wretched morning on the links, imagining all the terrible things that she may be doing to the album – *his* album – while he is away. He keeps on handing Father the wrong club, which makes Father cross, because he is losing. When eventually he gets back home (without his glass of ginger-ale, because when Father loses he doesn't stand treat), he runs ahead up the drive to see what damage has been done. She is not in the room where he left her with it, but there it is on the table by the window and – horrors! – a pot of gum by the side of it, and the gum-brush, wet, balanced on the cork! She can't have been so mad, surely? She can't have been *gumming* stamps in, instead of putting them in with neat little hinges of transparent sticky-paper?

The gong goes for lunch, so he can't spend more than half a minute going through the album for evidence of her criminality. He finds nothing. But there's no time to examine every page. He's late already and has to wash his hands first.

His suspense is prolonged. He finds her at lunch, sympathizing with Father over his defeat and asking him what happened at the Third, and the Fourth and the Fifth and the Sixth. He doesn't dare interrupt. Father is furious with him already for his inattentiveness on the links. It is only when everyone else has finished his soup and Mother reminds Father to eat his, and to 'tell us the rest afterwards', that his sister turns to him; 'I had a lovely morning with our stamps. I learned such a lot.'

'What were you doing with that gum?' he roars at her.

'Gum?'

'Yes, gum! You had the gum-pot out.'

She pauses for a moment, as if puzzled. 'Oh, yes, the gum. I was using it for gumming down the cloth on the back cover. There was a little tear in it.'

'You swear you didn't use it for anything else?'

'There was nothing much else to use it for, was there? You surely didn't want me to gum the stamps down for fear of burglars?'

Of course the gum-pot was put there just to frighten him, and of course she hadn't really spent the whole morning with the stamps. As soon as they were out of the house she went off to the boxroom and practised acrobatic dancing for a couple of hours. Then she came downstairs and read *Three Men in a Boat*.

But he doesn't know this. As soon as lunch is over and grace said he runs to the album and spends the whole afternoon looking it carefully through to see what tricks she's been playing on him. He feels that there's some trick, by her manner. He finds nothing. That makes him still more suspicious.

CHAPTER 2

AT THE PICTURE GALLERY

THE hypothetical brother and sister about whom the first chapter was written were, in real life, named Jane and Oliver. Jane was eleven years old, and Oliver twelve. Their father, it will have been grasped, was a country vicar; but it should be added that their mother was a marquess's daughter who had decided to marry him when he was private chaplain at the Castle, and had done so wholly against the wishes of the family. (The circumstances will be given later.) The date in 1919 on which Oliver agreed to share the collection with Jane is not now precisely known, but it appears to have been about two months after Germany signed the Versailles Peace Treaty – let us say August 28th. By then food-supplies were almost normal again and chocolates and bull's eyes could be bought at the village sweet-shop. Happy holidays for sugar-stinted children! Happy times for stamp-collectors, too: queer provisionals, airmail covers and cachets, and stamps of wholly new countries!

Every ordinary man will have forgiven Oliver for pulling Jane's hair in his just rage at her meddlesome and undeniably stupid act of separating a block of four Newfoundland five-cents, mint, of a quite early issue – 1897, say – just because it looked tidier to have each stamp in a separate oblong! And he will have made out a good case for Oliver's continuing to think of it as 'my album', considering how little, it seems, Jane knew or cared about stamps and how little money, it seems, she contributed to the improvement of the collection. And every ordinary woman will have congratulated Jane on her cleverness in getting a strategical hold over her brother. Every ordinary woman will realize that Oliver's selfish and masterful behaviour called for whatever punishment it was in Jane's power to administer; and, if she laughingly calls Jane a little beast, she will use the word in a complimentary sense. A little beast is a creature who had a superiority in cunning over a little brute.

The average man will continue his train of thought with

increasing self-justification, recalling stories that he has heard of the wives of numismatists who officiously remove the exquisitely aged emerald-green patina from unique Green coins with metal-polish and emery-paper, and soon have them shining like Guardsmen's tunic-buttons; and of wives of bibliophiles who remove the original wrappers and neatly cut the pages of virginal first editions. And the average woman will continue her train of thought, too, but in a more personal way; connecting the story of Oliver with some experience of her own with a father or husband or brother, some typical masculine behaviour on his part over a car, or a radio set, or a week-end cottage.

Our next view of Jane and Oliver is a great many years later. Jane is now twenty-six and Oliver twenty-seven. They are standing side by side in front of a large oil-painting in a rather second-rate London art-gallery. The picture, which suggests the work of a competent Royal Academician of twenty or thirty years ago, is called 'The Stamp Collector' and was, as a matter of fact, painted in the spring of 1920 by Sir Luke Salmon, R.A., an old friend of their father's. It is past one o'clock, so there are few visitors about, which seems to make the coincidence a very striking one indeed: for these two have been on the coolest of terms for four years now, and here they suddenly meet without prearrangement in front of a very dull picture in a gallery which, in the ordinary course of events, they would never have thought of visiting. But it is really no coincidence at all, except for the fact that Mrs Trent, who is wardrobe-mistress at the Burlington Theatre, of which Jane is now actress-manager, happens to have a flat immediately opposite the entrance to the gallery. She was rung up early this morning with: 'Do me a favour, Gwennie, dear. Keep a watch on the picture-gallery this morning and if you happen to see my brother Oliver go in, phone me at once.'

Mrs Trent was recovering from influenza and was delighted to have something to occupy her morning. As soon as she spotted Oliver she phoned Jane, who was inside the gallery only a minute afterwards. Jane lived just round the corner.

'Hullo, Jane.'

'Oh, hullo, Oliver. You saw the paragraph in the *Observer*?'

'No, I always read the *Sunday Times*.'

'And I always smoke Gold Flake. I suppose you still always smoke Players?'

'Don't let's quarrel, child. All I meant was that I didn't happen to see anything in the *Observer* about this "Twentieth-Century Conversation Piece Exhibition", or whatever its pet name is, because I don't read the *Observer* and never did; but that, on the other hand, there was a very full notice of it in the *Sunday Times*. It mentioned the picture. It said what a charmingly English piece of work it was, and then something nice about Father having been the man who made St Aidan's famous, so I thought I'd stroll along and have a look at it. I never saw it finished before. You remember, it was at the end of the Easter holidays, and I had to go back to my prep school, so Sir Luke painted me first and put you and Father in afterwards. And then when it was exhibited I had measles, and they sent me abroad to that school at Geneva to get well. So I missed it.'

'Well, I saw the *Observer* notice. The *Observer* is always very sound on pictures. In fact, on most things.'

'You think so?'

'Have a cigarette.'

'Not if it's a Gold Flake.' Here Oliver felt in his pocket for his cigarette-case and found it empty. 'Damn,' he said, 'I'm afraid it will have to be a Gold Flake. Or anything with tobacco in it except, perhaps, one of those "Havana Resurrections". Did you read about that case? Disgusting.'

'Many worse things can befall a gentleman than to be reduced to smoking Folly's Havana Resurrections.' She gave him a Gold Flake. When he had lighted it she said, 'I suppose you realize that we aren't allowed to smoke here?'

'Why the devil didn't you say so before?' He snatched it out of his mouth and dropped it on the floor, crushing the lighted end with his heel.

'Because I supposed you realized.' She took a cigarette for herself and asked him whether he had a match.

He was angry and began to expostulate. 'I'll be bothered if I'll give you a match.'

'Then I suppose I'll have to use one of my own.' She began smoking. 'They can't do more than call your attention to the

"No Smoking" placards, and then you say politely, "Oh, I'm sorry" and ask where you should put the stub. That always makes them feel awkward. But unless they have actually seen you strike a match it's usually some time before they notice that you're smoking. You get the first few puffs. It's the first few puffs of a cigarette that taste the best. Or that's my experience with Gold Flakes.'

'I do think you women are immoral.'

'Especially the daughters of the clergy. But isn't it a splendid picture? Doesn't Father look smug? Anyone would think that he had spent the whole day visiting the aged sick, organizing Bands of Hope, writing sermons for three months in advance, helping the sexton dig graves, training the bell-ringers, disciplining the churchwardens and reforming the village drunkard. Back he comes, weary, but indefatigable in the Cause, and after a frugal supper pulls out the old Morris chair, cooks up a blackened briar, and helps his little son arrange his stamp-album. The little son's album. *Not* the album held in joint ownership by his little son and little daughter – was I really made to wear such an awful frock as late as Easter, 1920? I don't remember it – but the album owned by his little son, The Stamp Collector.'

'I rather thought you'd bring that up.'

'Considering that the title of the picture conveys a maliciously false impression, it would have been gracious if you had brought up the subject yourself, especially as it still seems to be on your conscience after all these years.'

'It isn't on my conscience. What do you mean?'

'Don't contradict yourself. You said a moment ago that you thought I'd bring it up. That could only mean that you thought I had a legitimate grievance against your hoggish behaviour in those days, the sort of grievance that no decent woman would care to abandon even after a long term of years. And that this grievance might be associated in my mind with your similar hoggish behaviour in 1930.'

'If you mean our difference of opinion over Mother's things, that is something I refuse to discuss. I'll discuss the stamps, if you like, though. How should I have graciously introduced the subject of the ownership of the album? Should

I have apologized for my stubborn possessiveness? You know perfectly well that, except for the merest legal fiction . . .'

'No, I didn't mean you to humiliate yourself. But you might have introduced the matter in an indirect way. You might have said something like this: "Poor Father, our stamp-collection meant a lot to him, didn't it, Jane? He pretended that it was rather beneath his dignity to play at stamp-collecting with us, but he got a lot of fun out of showing off his knowledge and pretending that he was as expert as we were." At any rate, something tender like that, containing the words "our collection".'

'*We* never became experts! *You* never learned a thing about stamps! And I don't at all like the way you talk of Father. I think it's a very good portrait of him, and shows him just as he was – a jolly good sportsman.'

'That's what I mean. All that poor Father ever thought about was golf.'

'He did his job decently. More than decently. St Aidan's wasn't a slum parish or a place that went in much for religion. Most of the village people were Chapel, anyhow. He conducted the necessary church services, and he prepared candidates for confirmation, if there happened to be any, and then there were marriages and baptisms and funerals . . .'

'And visits from the Bishop.'

'Yes, why not? Visits from the Bishop.'

'The Bishop was always swinging a club at St Aidan's.'

'Why shouldn't he? Nearly the entire population of the diocese was Chapel, if it comes to that, except for the gentry and their hangers-on. And he liked a round of golf as much as Father. That's one of the reasons he was so popular. The present Bishop is a Hebrew scholar and sticks frowstily in his study, mucking away at midrashim, whatever *they* are; and Church attendance has now hit a new low, I hear. Besides, Father had made St Aidan's the best links for a hundred miles round. It's all very well your sneering at Father, but he did a jolly sight more for his parish than ninety-nine out of a hundred other vicars can claim to have done for theirs. He built up the Royal St Aidan's Club from nothing. He was President for fifteen years – in fact, he only resigned so that the Prince could

be asked to be President and it could be called The Royal St
Aidan's. And he was one of the original four members. The
first Club House was that tin shed, the old caddy-shelter; now
it's not even good enough for the caddies – they have an army-
hut all to themselves with a wash-room and a bagatelle-table.
And the new Club House has a ballroom, and a cinema and a
bathing-pool, and lockers for about a thousand members, and
a landing-ground for planes. I was there the other day. It
quite amazed me. Look at the prosperity Father brought to the
place! St Aidan's used to be nothing but the quarries and a
few farm-houses and an occasional summer visitor. Now it's
all golf. And the hotels that the golf has brought along. And the
bathing, which was made possible by the road that the Club
built across the sandhills. And the tennis, of course. There's
never been any genuine unemployment in St Aidan's since the
golf started. And at least ten ex-caddies have become golf-
professionals. Charlie Evans – remember him? – was runner-up
in this year's Open Championship. St Aidan's is one of the
richest villages in the country now.'

'I like bishops to be bishops and clergymen to be clergymen,
not jolly good sportsmen or chairmen of local chambers of
commerce. I admired the Chapel people for breaking our
windows when Father came out strong for Sunday golf.'

'Oh, *did* you? And I suppose you approved of the Wesleyan
minister's protest?'

'I think it was the bravest thing I ever saw in my life. A man
who can lie all day on the first tee of a famous links in the form
of a cross, feet neatly together and a Bible in each of his out-
spread hands, and get away with it, too –'

'I call it a positively blasphemous act.'

'Father would never have had the courage to do a thing like
that for the sake of championing sound Church doctrine. Not
to save his life.'

'Father believed in the Church's moving with the times. And
what good did it do the man to make a fool of himself?'

'He forced them all to drive off from the Ladies' tee that
Sunday – even Sir Reginald. I call that something.'

'We seem to be on the verge of a row. Let's stop in time.
Tell me, what did your *Observer* have to say about the picture?'

'Well, it said that the grouping was a happy inspiration and that the characterization was strong and the brushwork bold, but that the chief interest for the general public would lie in the somewhat supercilious-looking little girl who is leaning over the table on the right, toying with a pair of tweezers; for she has grown up to be none other . . .'

'Than yourself, in fact.'

'Than myself. If you ask me, I think that your *Sunday Times* fell down rather badly on that news-story. Mentioned Father but left me out. Tell me, Oliver, what's become of our collection?'

'I've got it in my flat somewhere. And it's not "our collection" now, please. I've had it in my possession for fifteen years, so you've lost your shadowy title to it long ago. I'm keeping it for my son – when I marry and have a son.'

'You've not had it in your possession for fifteen years. It was in Father's charge until four years ago. And I want half of it for my daughter – when I marry and have a daughter.'

'Go on wanting. It's my collection. I began it. I paid for practically all the most valuable stamps in it. I knew most about it. You were never really interested in stamps, and, what's more, your daughter won't be either, and you know it. You've just started this out of nastiness. You were always a little beast.'

'And you were always a little brute. And I'll tell you something, my ugly Nollikins: just for losing your temper and making a public exhibition of us in a place where *I* have certainly been recognized, even if you haven't, I am going to insist on having my half of that collection of ours. And you're going to come to my house, or else I'm going to your flat, and we're going to work through that album, page by page and side by side, each extracting one stamp in turn. And every stamp that I take you're going to feel like a tooth drawn from your head. And I'm going to watch your face carefully to see which stamps you most hope I won't take, and then I'm going to take them. See?'

'No, indeed I don't see. And I'll tell you something now, my fine sister Jane. You got your claim to half my collection by sharp practice. I once asked Mother, long afterwards, if you had really been decent enough to spend the remains of your birthday money on buying me that packet of Central American stamps. And from the way she smiled . . .'

But Jane had heard enough and was walking away. Oliver went a few paces after her, trying to finish his sentence, but realized that he was behaving in an undignified way in public – there were now two other visitors in the room. So he came frowning back to have another look at the picture. With Jane next to him he had not been able to take anything in. Damnation and everlasting plague to Jane! How she had the nerve . . . He mechanically pulled out his cigarette-case, opened it and felt for a Player, his eyes still fixed on the portrait of Jane. Innocent little darling she looked. Took everyone in.

An attendant touched his elbow. 'No smoking allowed in the gallery, sir.'

'I wasn't smoking,' said Oliver irritably. 'And I can't. I've got no cigarettes. Look! And why didn't you stop the lady who was with me from smoking? You passed by three or four times.'

'Well, sir, as an admirer of Miss Palfrey, I own I turned a blind eye. And who wouldn't? No offence to you, sir, but though it's my duty to point out the notice to visitors who happen to forget where they are, I don't think that in the exceptional case of a visit from Miss Jane Palfrey – and so few people about, too – I don't think, sir, that it's my duty to detract from the pleasure of her visit, if you understand my meaning.'

'Miss Palfrey isn't Royalty.'

'Not exactly, sir, but in the same way, for example, as the general public wouldn't like to see me calling the attention of His Majesty the King to the notice, if he happened to light a cigar, so they wouldn't like me to ask Miss Palfrey to put out her cigarette. And I'm sure the Trustees themselves, if they were in my place . . .'

'Come, come,' said Oliver, 'aren't you rather exaggerating her fame? Personally, I don't admire Miss Palfrey much – not all that much, I mean. But I'm her brother you see. That's what distinguishes me from the general public.'

The attendant was impressed. 'Oh, sir, if I'd realized that you were her brother –'

' – you'd have been far more polite. You'd have waited until you were really sure I was going to smoke and then you'd have said, "Excuse me, sir, but I'm afraid I must ask you not to smoke in the gallery," and then you'd have chatted with me for a bit, and in the end you'd have hinted how much you'd appreciate it if I could persuade my sister to sign a photograph for you some day. I know you people. Isn't that correct?'

The attendant owned that it wasn't far out. 'For myself, of course, I wouldn't think of asking such a favour; but for my son, that's different. I heard my son Harold say, the other day, that he would give his ears for a genuine signed photograph of Miss Palfrey's. She's not like the other ladies of her profession, you see. She doesn't sign her name for any Tom, Dick or Harry. In fact, there was an article in one of the Sunday illustrateds the other day by her, "Why I don't give away autographs." Very amusing and sensible bit of writing, I thought. Consequence is that a Jane Palfrey autograph – a genuine one – is about the rarest on the market, I understand. And signed photographs don't exist.'

'Why do you say "on the market"? Is your son a dealer in autographs?'

'He collects, sir. It's the fashion. He tells me he's lost interest in his stamp-collection lately. He collects signed photographs of actresses and actors and so on; for a girl he's sweet on, I suspect. Sixteen years old, nearly seventeen. In the highest class at St Mark's College, down at Hammersmith. Was that a Stanley Gibbons album in the picture, sir? My boy's is a Stanley Gibbons, too; 1916 edition. I used to collect stamps during a long spell in hospital on my back in the last half of the War. Very interesting I found it. My boy Harold's added a lot to the album. One day, no doubt, he'll marry and pass it to *his* son. But about the smoking, sir, I'm sorry . . .'

'No, no, that was quite all right. A compliment to my sister. I understand perfectly. It's what the general public would have wished. But, about that autograph, Mr . . .'

'Mr Dormer.'

'The fact is, Mr Dormer, I don't see how I can help your son to fill that distressing gap in his collection. I can guess how he feels about it as a collector; and I'm sorry for him. But as you have reminded me yourself, Miss Palfrey doesn't go about distributing signed photographs to the crowd like advertising leaflets.'

'Exactly, sir. But, pardon me, I thought that perhaps as her brother . . .'

'That's what they all think, Mr Dormer, and they are all wrong. Good morning!'

'Good morning, sir! I sincerely hope I have given no offence?'

'No offence at all, Mr Dormer.'

He collected his stick from the cloak-room attendant. Visitors were obliged to leave sticks and umbrellas at the cloak-room for fear they might poke holes in the pictures with them. Perhaps that was why they weren't allowed to smoke. Might feel tempted to burn holes in the pictures with a cigarette. And yet they didn't search one for fire-arms or bottles of vitriol or razors. Inconsistent.

He said something like this to the cloak-room girl, but she answered, 'Oh, no, sir. It's the insurance company. They won't insure the pictures if there's smoking. Mr Dormer has to be pretty hot about it. Why, only yesterday there was the Home Secretary here and his wife and the Governor of the Bank of England. The Home Secretary pulled out a pipe, but Mr Dormer was on him like a flash.'

Oliver thought: 'So Jane's more important than the Home Secretary, the Home Secretary's wife and the Governor of the Bank of England, all three in conjunction, is she?'

The cloak-room girl was saying proudly, 'We had a most distinguished visitor in, just now – Miss Jane Palfrey. Did you see her? She's the little girl in the picture called "The Stamp Collectors".'

'Collector, not Collectors.'

'Yes, sir. She must have come in for a peep back into her past. *The* Jane Palfrey, you know, sir.'

'*The* Jane Palfrey!' Oliver echoed in ironic ecstasy. And then turning away abruptly, muttered to himself with increasing scorn: 'But surely not *the* Jane Palfrey – not *my* sister – not *that* highly intelligent, grey-eyed, black-souled, acrobatic, aristocratic snake in the grass!'

CHAPTER 3

SABOTAGE AT THE VICARAGE

THAT was a Monday and by the first post on Tuesday morning a letter came from Jane. It said:

17.9.34

Dear Oliver,

I meant what I told you in the gallery. On Thursday afternoon, the 27th of this month, at four o'clock, unless I hear that you prefer some other day and time, I shall be at your flat with a stack of envelopes and a pair of tweezers. The tweezers are not merely for toying with, this time, but for removing alternate stamps from the pages of our collection; and the envelopes are for putting the stamps in, when removed, according to countries. You may keep the album itself. It was a Christmas present to you from Mother, so that 'seems fair. If you persist in your refusal to give me my rights in this matter, I shall sue you. And as I have a better case than you and as I can afford a better lawyer than you, and as the sympathies of any decent judge will inevitably be on my side, I advise you to be sensible and make me very welcome at 4 o'clock on Thursday, the twenty-seventh, at your flat.

Love (conditional on your complaisant behaviour),

Jane

At the top of the letter was a printed heading, Jane having for the moment run out of private stationery:

from

JANE PALFREY, AMALGAMATED,
THE BURLINGTON THEATRE,
W.I.

Oliver's face hardened. So she had not just been trying to take a rise out of him? Meant it literally, did she? He would be utterly and completely blasted if he allowed Jane to remove a single stamp. He'd make a point of being out on Thursday. Or . . . Well, perhaps it would be better to be in and face her and tell her what he really thought of her. She had dashed away yesterday without giving him a chance to characterize her

behaviour in really frank and stinging terms. In general his
regard for women was high, though obviously there were
few things that they did as well as men, but they certainly had
a very low level of sportsmanship. In fact, the more gifted they
were – and Jane really was a very clever woman, he had to grant
her that – the worse sportsmen they seemed to be. If Jane had
been his brother, not his sister, and a dispute had somehow
arisen between them as to whether the album was his own or
whether it was a joint possession, the affair would have been
settled without any fuss. First of all they'd have tossed as to
whether it was really entirely his, or whether only half was
his, and then if he'd lost the toss they would naturally have had
the collection valued by someone mutually agreed on, and he'd
have cheerfully paid her half what it was valued at, and so
kept the collection intact. The suggestion that a carefully
organized stamp-collection should be picked to pieces in the
manner she suggested was shocking. As shocking in its way as
Solomon's judgement about cutting the child in two. More
shocking, because Solomon didn't really mean it, and Jane did.
And Solomon proposed to halve the child with a single clean
blow of the sword, not to pick it to pieces with tweezers.

When Jane was a girl she would never spin a coin to decide
a disagreement about anything. 'I leave nothing to chance,'
she would say coldly. Once, as children, they had got caught in
a mist on the hills behind St Aidan's. They reached a fork in
the road and argued as to which turn led home. He proved to
her logically that the left-hand turn was the proper one to take.
He said: 'See that pine-tree? It had moss on one side. Pine-
trees have moss on the north side because the sun doesn't
shine from the north, so it's damper on that side. Well, St
Aidan's lies west from here. So this left-hand road is the one to
take, see?'

She said: 'I don't care about moss and north and west and
all that clever Boy-Scout-lost-in-the-Jungle talk. And I'm not
going by this road, whatever you say, because it looks wrong to
me. I'm going by the other.'

He called her an obstinate idiot. 'Why, it leads up, not down!
We're about a thousand feet above sea-level already. We don't
want to get any higher.'

She said: 'I tell you, I don't believe in your road. It hasn't a this-way-to-St Aidan's look about it. It probably leads to a deserted quarry.'

Then he offered to toss for it, and she refused. 'I'm going this way and if you care to come with me you can.' He knew that if he came home without her he would get into an awful row for deserting his little sister in the mist and exposing her to attacks by tramps and so on; so he had to go against his better judgement. As a matter of fact, her road *had* taken them home all right. It went uphill for a few hundred yards and then swung round downhill in the direction he had logically deduced was the right one. So obviously the road he had wanted to take would have been a short-cut. A few weeks later they came to the same spot. There was no mist, so he took the other turn just to prove to her that he was right. The road did rather tail off, after reaching a barn, and lead through a somewhat boggy meadow, and he had to climb a few walls, but in the end he struck the proper road again. In triumph he waited for her to come up. He waited and waited and she didn't come, so he decided that just to tease him she had run as fast as she could and got ahead of him. So he hurried on to catch her up. But he couldn't see her anywhere down the road, even when he came to the place where one had a clear view for a mile. So he waited again, and then went back in case she'd twisted her ankle or something. But she wasn't there. He found her at the Vicarage some hours later; she had got a lift home in the car of the quarry-inspector. It had never occurred to her to wait for him at the end of the short-cut. Said she knew about the boggy meadow and all the high toppling walls that had to be climbed over – she had tried it herself once one day when he was caddying. Jane was mean. Brilliant, but mean. No sporting sense at all.

Acts of sabotage were her speciality in those days. Perhaps the worst thing she ever did was to hide one of his football-boots on the day of the St Aidan's–Port Hallows match. Only one football-boot, not both. And he had to play in borrowed boots, and of course nobody can play football in any pair of boots but the ones he has been carefully breaking in since the beginning of the season.

He was centre-half, and centre-half has more running about to do than anyone on the field. The trouble was that his foot was a very broad one and ordinary eights were too tight for him: he always wore broad eights. So he had to manage with a pair of nines, and stuff the toes with cotton wool. He never actually traced the theft of the boot to Jane, but it could only have been her doing. They had had a row just before the match. She had wanted to go shopping at Port Hallows that afternoon, and he had protested at breakfast that it would look very queer for her, as Father's daughter and his sister, to be seen taking a ticket to Port Hallows on the day of the match. He was quite right, too, because the occasion was really a most important one. It was during the six-months' quarry strike of 1925. There was no football played in those parts before the War: the only sport was cock-fighting – in secret hollows far back in the hills, with scouts thrown out to warn against the approach of the police. When the War ended, the St Aidan's quarrymen who had learned to play football in the Army formed an irregular sort of club; but it was not until the strike, when they got bored by doing nothing, and two cock-fighting mains had been broken up by the police, with heavy fines following, that they took up football seriously.

Father, who had a strong political sense, realized that un-employed quarrymen striking for higher wages and shorter hours would not feel very well disposed towards a rich and Royal Golf Club, even though it brought prosperity to the district and had employed them, when boys, as caddies. He therefore prevailed on the committee to rent the footballers the field at the back of the Club House for three afternoons a week at a nominal rate. St Aidan's then challenged Port Hallows to a match on the new ground; the workers and capitalists of St Aidan's being thus momentarily united in a common cause. Oliver and the son of the Golf Club Treasurer, who had kept goal for Repton, were invited by the quarrymen to play for the team. Oliver was in his last year at Charchester and had been playing regularly for the School Second Eleven. He hoped to play for the First Eleven after Christmas, when the School centre-half would have left.

Naturally Father insisted on Jane's putting off her shopping

visit to Port Hallows until after the match; though she declared
that it was absolutely necessary to get some trimming there for
a dress she was wearing at the garden-party the next day.
Father was firm. He said, 'My dear girl, when you come of age
you can do as you like, I suppose. But until you come of age,
and afterwards too, if you are still under my roof, there will be
occasions when I shall have to insist, as a father, on your pre-
serving the social decencies. This is exactly such an occasion.
Oliver and I expect to see you on the touch-line this afternoon,
watching him doing his bit for St Aidan's.'

She got up from the table, dropped Father a deep curtsey
and recited with downcast eyes:

Good my Lord,
You have begot me, bred me, lov'd me: I
Return those duties back as are right fit.

Cordelia, in *King Lear*. And Father looked amused, so he had
grinned too. She wheeled round on him: 'Do you bandy looks
with me, you rascal?' It was so sudden, it quite startled him.
He shouted, 'I won't be recited at, d'you hear, you cheap
School of Dramatic Art actress!' 'Nor tripped neither, you
base football-player,' she hissed, pulling his chair over backwards, and *exit*. That was from *King Lear*, too, he had found
since.

Jane was nearly seventeen then, at a now-defunct School of
Dramatic Art at Bristol. It was a grievance of Jane's that
Father would not let her study in London, because the fees
were higher there. Jane had protested that they were not so
high as the Charchester fees. Father's point was that it was more
important for his son to have a public school and University
education than for his daughter to take an expensive course in
dramatic art: it was nine chances in ten that she would marry
young, and then the money would be wasted. Jane couldn't
see this: thought money should be spent according to natural
talent, not sex – as though *he* had no natural talent.

Anyhow, Jane went off leaving her bacon and eggs untouched. When someone rises suddenly from the breakfast-
table because of a quarrel and leaves her food untouched, it has
a most depressing effect on the rest of the family, even if she is

obviously in the wrong. The eggs get cold and stare greasily at you, and the bacon gets cold and grins greasily at you. In any ordinary scene of this sort – they were not infrequent – Mother would have waited a couple of minutes and then taken Jane's breakfast up to her workroom (the old Nursery) for her to eat there; but on this occasion she did nothing of the sort. She did not even allow a dish-cover to be put over the plate to hide it from people in the bread-and-marmalade stage. At the time he thought that Mother was being stern, seeing Jane's behaviour in the right light, refusing to indulge her. But she was, he saw now, secretly siding with her – enhancing the dramatic effect of the empty chair, the untouched food. And Jane must have gone straight to his bedroom and thrown the football-boot out of the window. It was found, some weeks later, embedded in the lavender-hedge. Jane said that he had thrown it there himself in the very early morning – at a cat. Pretty weak!

It was a ghastly match. The Wesleyan minister who had protested against Sunday golf refereed. He was the only referee whom the rival teams could agree on as likely to be impartial: he had a chapel in both districts. His real game was Rugby (he was from Pontypool); so they had taught him a few Association rules that morning. 'Don't tell me too much, boys,' he laughed, 'or it's going to spoil your game.' St Aidan's had an old feud with Port Hallows. It dated from a fishery dispute early in the nineteenth century, in the course of which a St Aidan's man had killed a Port Hallows lobster-poacher with a boat-hook and had subsequently been sand-bagged in a dark lane close to his own cottage. Father said that he hoped the feud would now be sublimated into sporting rivalry on the football field. Yes, a ghastly and incredibly foul game. Tripping, hacking, handling, charges in the back, fisticuffs, everyone off side. The sportsmen of Port Hallows had turned up in their hundreds to see fair play. They occupied one touch-line, five deep; St Aidan's held the other. The County police were there in force and made several arrests in the course of the afternoon. 'Up the Boat-hooks!' 'Up the Sand-bags!' 'Do 'em in, boys!' 'Smash 'em!' 'Scrag 'em!' The minister only used his whistle when the ball went off the field and wasn't immediately kicked back by the crowd, or when it went between the posts. If it went between the posts it was almost always a goal, however it got there. If there was a free fight between players he would rush into the thick of it and grab at the ball. 'Gently, boys,' he would shout, 'it's only the Reverend Jones!' He would then kick into touch and blow the whistle; and the game would go on.

Jane was on the touch-line, shouting enthusiastically. 'Oh, *come on*, St Aidan's, do something!' For Port Hallows was leading by two goals (one glaring off-side, and the other accidentally put through by a St Aidan's back when the ball was stone dead). And, 'What's wrong with you halves? Centre-half, you're not feeding your forwards properly!' She always chose a lull for shouting 'What's wrong with you halves?' And the crowd would take up the cry. But in the first place the forwards were never in a position to take a pass, and in the second he couldn't control the ball properly with his boots. The ground was rough and he was always tripping up. He shouted back at the crowd: 'Someone stole my boots. I can't play in these.' They roared with laughter at him. St Aidan's equalized shortly after half-time with first a timely fist-through, and then an immensely high punt by the Reptonian, which found the Port Hallows goal-keeper not at home – drinking something out of a bottle close to the corner flag. How wild the Port Hallows men were! Just before the end, when the score was still two all, Oliver took advantage of a pause in which two Port Hallows men were carried off the field with kicks on the head – thus reducing the sides to eight men apiece – to change into golfing shoes. That was much better, but he hoped nobody would notice the spikes. Then the Reptonian came up forward and he and Oliver immediately dribbled through with quick neat passes, and the Reptonian shot a perfect goal. 'Off-side!' bawled the Port Hallows crowd. And the referee gave it off-side! They immediately repeated the performance: another goal, also disallowed! Then the whistle blew for time – five minutes too soon – with the score still at two all. The minister was quite frank about it after-wards. It was to the public interest that neither side should win; and for the Reptonian, a mere guest of the team, to have shot more than one goal would have made a bad impression in the countryside, he said.

Oliver had got a black eye from a Port Hallows forward who charged him with raised elbows, and his feet were so chafed by those boots that he was lame for days. And soon after, when he happened to be walking through a back street in St Aidan's where quarrymen lived, a woman shouted to him derisively out of a window: 'Oh, *come on*, centre-half, why don't you feed your forwards?' That made him angry. He replied: 'Feed them yourself, curse you; feed them on coke!' That nearly started a riot. A big quarryman, an old-fashioned Socialist, caught him by the coat-lapels and wanted to know what the Devil he meant by swearing at respectable women, and how would *he* like to see his children starving before his something eyes for want of a something bit of something bread and butter? The last thing he heard as he broke and ran was the jeering 'Who stole centre-half's kick boots?' A most unpleasant incident, altogether.

As for Jane, not only had she been complimented by Father for the encouragement she had given the side, but she had contrived to get into Port Hallows by car the same evening, just before the shops shut. Because Father himself had to go. It was Saturday and his spare pair of glasses were at the optician's at Port Hallows, having the hinge of a side-piece mended, and now his regular pair were found broken on the floor of his study. Apparently the window had blown open, for all his papers were on the floor, too. He needed his glasses to read his sermon with. He knew the service off by heart, but he had to read his sermons, and he couldn't read without his glasses. Father belonged to a sermon club (just as some people belonged to a gramophone-record club) run by a retired clergyman. One sent in sermons and got other people's old sermons in exchange: an old sermon in one parish is always new in another a reasonable distance away. It saved a lot of time. Of course, nobody was supposed to know about this, not even the churchwardens, and nobody would have known, but for Jane. She found out that when Father was supposed to be composing his sermon he was only copying out one preached by someone else, and putting it into slightly different language as a disguise – like schoolboys who have used a crib for preparing their Latin translation and don't want the master to know. Dear old Father, he was a schoolboy to the last. And a real good sportsman, too.

The Sunday after the match Jane said at lunch, 'You used "according to the light of Holy Scripture" three times in your sermon today, Father, and it's an expression you've never used in a sermon, or out of one, in the whole of your life. It's a borrowed sermon, isn't it? Own up!' Father was taken off his guard and mumbled: 'Well, what with breaking my glasses and one thing and another, I really didn't have time to make it my own.' And Jane sneered: 'So *that's* your private word for the process, is it? – take someone else's sermon and "make it your own"? Those packages that you are always getting from Peterborough or sending back to Peterborough – sermons aren't they? I've suspected it for months.' Rough on Father. He did occasionally write a sermon of his own, but he wasn't a man of the pen; writing came difficult to him, some-how, though he was a fluent talker. Besides, the Royal St Aidan's always kept him busy with committee meetings and he often had to be acting-Secretary, because the Secretary drank. Father wasn't lazy: far from it.

In any case, it seemed perfectly clear now that Father's broken glasses were more sabotage on Jane's part. Jane would stick at absolutely nothing if she was crossed. And now, with this vile letter, she had sabotaged his breakfast, and his good humour for the next three or four days at least. But for once he intended to hold his own; and more than hold his own.

CHAPTER 4

THE ZINC-LINED TRUNK

OLIVER'S flat was at the very top of Albion Mansions, a seven-storey red-brick Victorian-Gothic pile close to Battersea Park. He was quite comfortable there, though a little self-conscious about living on the wrong side of the River. He liked being high up, and it was cheap, and he could take his dog for walks in the Park. He used to explain to his friends that a pleasant flat in an ugly building has charms that a pleasant flat in a pleasant building cannot equal; and further, that his was one of the few places in the neighbourhood with a view that did not include Albion Mansions. The joke was not original; it was first made by some Paris painter who took rooms in the Eiffel Tower, but it passed as new among his friends (all right-side-of-the-river men). As for his flat's being pleasant, it was at least tidy, commodious and in safe taste. The School and University group that hung on the wall proved him never, after all, to have reached more than the Second Eleven at Charchester, but to have played for his College team at Oxford (one of the smaller colleges), to have been vice-president of his College Debating Society and to have belonged to a College drinking-club called 'The Church Wardens'. His bookshelves suggested that he had taken Modern Greats, that he had also been interested in modern poetry of the safe sort during his Oxford years, that he had been a foundation member of the Book Society, that he was an admirer of the works of Eric Linklater, Mary Webb, Henry Williamson, Joseph Conrad, W. H. Hudson, the Powys brothers and Sheila Kaye-Smith. Apparently he also had a partiality for early Italian pictures; the four Medici prints which alternated with the College groups, and with two panoramic photographs of Alpine scenery, each showing distant climbing-parties roped together, were all early Italian subjects. Musical too, perhaps; there was a guitar-case in a corner. The furniture was solid, but indefinite; the curtains, of olive-green rep, faded at the folds. The ornaments on the mantelpiece were a carved wooden chamois, which worked in with the Alpine photographs; and some Venetian blown-glass animals and a piece of carved lava from Vesuvius, suggested that he had seen some at least of the early Italian paintings in their native setting. 'A good all-round man' was what Oliver liked to be considered.

Breakfast had been cleared away and he was busy unpacking a small zinc-lined trunk in front of the window. He was looking for the stamp-album of which so much has already been written. It was right at the bottom, he seemed to remember. On top, carefully packed in tissue-paper or in old-fashioned leather cases, were the things that had caused his quarrel with Jane four years previously. Really choice things – which, if they had been arranged about the room, would have made it look much more than the room of a good all-round man. Three obviously genuine seventeenth-century Dutch miniatures; two original Rowlandson caricatures, in colours, representing scenes in a French barracks; a carved ivory Madonna with Child, probably fourteenth-century French; a *Book of Hours*, also fourteenth-century French; a fine silver pyx, English pre-Reformation; and a first edition of Spenser's *Shepheardes Calender*. But as soon as he had found the album, back they would go into the trunk. It would never have occurred to Oliver to substitute the Dutch miniatures and the Rowlandsons for College groups, Alpine scenes and Medici prints; to put the Madonna on the mantelpiece, first removing the chamois; to set the pyx in the corner-cabinet in place of the silver cup he had won at Charchester in 1923 for coming in second in the Under-Sixteen steeplechase; to put the Spenser and the *Hours* in the bookshelf along with his other books. No, it would never have occurred to him, even if he had been convinced of the honesty of the woman who cleaned the flat, and the friends who visited him – but he was a suspicious fellow – and even if he had felt that these precious objects were as much his own indisputable and inalienable property as were the chamois, the College groups, the Medici prints, the silver cup, the carved lump of lava, and of course the stamp-album. Actually he could not quite feel them his own. The zinc-lined trunk was rather a private museum to be opened perhaps once a year, no more. The museum pieces had an embarrassing history: one might indeed say that they were only on loan.

Mother had married Father strongly against the wishes of her family, the Palfreys. (Oliver was a Price; so was Jane originally, but she had adopted Palfrey as her stage name, which Oliver had always thought rather in bad taste.) The Marquess – Babraham was the title – had refused to settle any money on Mother, though he was extremely rich as modern marquesses went. So when she had just turned twenty-one she revenged herself by carrying off as many family heirlooms – from cabinets in the drawing-room, shelves in the library, obscure corners of the picture-gallery and the gilt case in the Chapel – as would pack into the single handbag with which she escaped from the Castle early one morning, never to return, leaving a short note to that effect on the hall-table. Besides what remained in Oliver's possession, there had been a number of gold and silver Greek coins, and some exquisite old French enamelled snuff-boxes. Mother had sold these, discreetly, to American dealers and bought clothes with what they fetched. They were not of any sentimental value, merely forming part of collections made by her grandfather and a great-uncle.

Oliver had not even known of the existence of the remaining treasures until March 1930, when Father, on his death-bed, had given him a key and told him to fetch them from the deed-box in the attic where they were stored. It had been difficult for Father to talk about them, quite apart from the severity of his illness. He finally managed to explain: 'My boy, your mother, as you know, was a remarkable woman in many ways. She came of an old, rather queer family. These things really belong to Babraham Castle, but your mother always refused to return them; she felt herself morally entitled to some small share in the estate even though she had quarrelled with her father. I urged her repeatedly to send them back – it was always a great anxiety to me that the Marquess might sue her for their recovery. But she said that he was not likely to notice that they were missing, and I comforted myself with the thought that, even if he did, the loss would probably be blamed on one of the servants.'

He then asked Father whether he wished the things returned

to the Castle, but Father said that it would look rather odd to
do so – putting a smirch on Mother's memory, as it were.
By this time the loss had probably been forgotten. Besides,
the coins and snuff-boxes complicated things awkwardly:
if Oliver returned only some of the missing objects he might
be asked for the return of the rest. Better to keep everything.

Father had gone on: 'But, above all, I don't want Jane to
be told the history of these treasures. You know the great
esteem that she had for her mother. And we can't very well
entrust them to her, or any part of them, without telling her
their history. And then she might be tempted to sell them by
public auction, and the auction-room experts would be sure
to recognize the pyx and the Spenser, and she would say that
they were her mother's and came from the Castle; and then that
would get into the papers, and the present Marquess would
be sure to see it, and then the fat would be in the fire. It is my
express wish, Oliver, that you keep all these things in your
own possession, for a time at least.'

Mother had died three days before this, from eating some of
the same tainted oysters that he had, and Father only lived two
days more. Jane was away in America at the time, so Oliver had
to do everything himself. When Jane came back, almost the
first thing she asked was what had become of the things Mother
had looted from the Castle: she wanted her share. He was
astonished that she knew, but she explained that Mother had
told her about them years ago. She had opened the deed-box
with a skeleton-key one day while looking for stamps (Edith
Whitebillet had made her a set of skeleton-keys for rummag-
ing), so she knew about them even before Mother told her the
story. For her share she demanded the pyx, and the *Shepheardes
Calender*, and the *Hours*. He could have the Rowlandsons, the
Madonna and the three Dutch pictures, which did not interest
her so much and were more in his line.

He was infuriated by her self-assurance and greed and the use
of the word 'looted'. He told her that it was Father's dying
wish that the whole collection should remain in his possession,
because she could not be trusted not to sell them. She did not
make a fuss, though, as he had expected her to do. She only
said, 'But they weren't Father's to dispose of, and you know

perfectly well which of us two would have got them if Mother had said anything about them herself.'

He said: 'I think Father knew more about Mother's real feelings than you.'

And she answered: 'Father wasn't altogether honest with himself about his own feelings, so how could he be sure of Mother's?'

Then he told her that Mother (who had not made a will) had said, 'All my personal things go to Jane.' But the objects in the deed-case weren't Mother's personal things – they were Palfrey heirlooms to which she had no right.

'So you actually mean that you are going to hang on to them?'

'Yes, for the present.'

'Very well, I refuse to take part in a vulgar squabble about family property, with Mother and Father hardly cold in their graves.'

He winced and said, 'I think that you take the prize for vulgarity. "Cold in their graves" is the sort of expression a charwoman might use.'

She let this go by, and went on coolly: 'Mother always said that you were a crook by nature, but that it would probably take a long time to come out, because you were so hopelessly public-school.'

He retorted angrily that if Mother had really said that, it came very badly from her, after having let them all down by playing the thief herself.

Jane smiled cruelly and said, 'Perfect. That's what you were bound to say. A typical Price pronouncement. Now, if you still wish to keep those Palfrey things, after having admitted that you think Mother had no moral right to them, keep them! Have it on your conscience that Mother was a sneak-thief and that you are a receiver of the swag. Respect poor, honest Father's dying wish! My God, Oliver, I do think you are an unspeakable character.'

He said, 'You are not going to have the things, that's all.'

'Well, brother Oliver, if you won't, you won't and I'm certainly not going to the police about it. I shall leave you to your crook's conscience, and an everlasting good-day to you!'

He had not seen her since then, not until yesterday, in the gallery.

Oliver unwrapped the *Hours. Horae Beatae Virginis Mariae. In usum Parisiensem cum Calendario.* He gloated. Vellum. Must be worth pots of money. Illuminated initials in gold on grounds of blue or magenta – no, it wasn't magenta, properly speaking; magenta was a nineteenth-century colour. Call it damask-rose. And the curious little miniatures of medieval life painted in the margin: hawking, husbandry, the coronation of a king, the Feast of Pentecost, the miraculous draught of fishes, Job with his tiresome boils, a court lady walking in her flower-garden with a book in her hand – probably this very book – and her little dog chasing an enormous butterfly. The rose, the lily, the gillyflower. The court lady was not unlike Mother, with her long fingers and long straight nose and abstracted expression. He had never understood Mother. She belonged to quite a different world from his.

The question again presented itself: what to do with the things? The present Marquess, a third or fourth cousin, was not yet born at the time that Mother had gone off with them; he was an Australian and had only been discovered after six months' steady advertising for him in the Colonial newspapers. It would be absurd to make him a present of them. Most unlikely that a man like that would have any feeling for the beautiful in art or literature. He seemed only interested in polo, and kept the Castle permanently shut up except for a week or two every year in the shooting season. This *Shepheardes Calender*, now. 'Conteining twelve Aeglogues, proportionable to the twelve monethes. Entitled to the most noble and vertuous gentleman, most worthie of all titles both of learning and chivalry, Maister Philip Sidney.'

> Goe, little booke! thy selfe present
> As childe whose parent is unkempt . . .

Nay, stay, little booke! What's the use of cloystering yourself – thyselfe – agayne in the darke and mouldie bibliotheca of Babraham Castle? Bide here in the pleasaunt loftie Mansions of Albion, hard by the Cittie of London.

He wrapped it up again, grinning, and opened the russia-leather case, to have a look at the pyx. He wondered what it was worth. His college at Oxford had been Roundhead during the Civil Wars, and so had not melted down its plate, as all the Cavalier colleges had loyally done to help the King pay his armies. Consequently there were still some wonderful old pieces in the strong-room. When he was up, the Warden and Fellows had sent for an expert from Christie's to value them. The old manciple had shown the expert a silver pyx, not unlike this, but had been unlucky enough to drop it on the floor and dent it. The expert said cheerfully: 'Well, that's two hundred guineas off the value for a start!' Oliver forgot what the reduced value was that the expert set on it. Several hundred guineas, anyway. Of course, there may have been something unusual about its chasing which this pyx hadn't. The same, too, with the Spenser: its sale-room value would depend on whether it was really a first edition or only a pirated second, and whether supposing that it was a first edition, it had such and such 'points' about it – the misprint 'sweare' for 'swaine' in the third aeglogue, the broken colophon after the introductory epistle, the omission of Hobbinoll's *Embleme*, and finally (joke coming!) the curious insertion found in the Speechly Hall copy, advertising Rowland's Macassar Oil – forsooth and bah! The absurd value that bibliophiles set on original advertisements! Father had some first editions of Thackeray – *Vanity Fair*, *Pendennis* and *The Newcomes*, but the dealer would only offer him ten pounds for the lot. He said: 'They'd be worth a fiver a volume if the original advertisements were there.' Probably only a trick on the dealer's part, though. Tricky gang, dealers. Simple fellow, Father.

At last, working slowly through successive layers of the past, he came on the stamp-album. His dear old stamp-album, its broken spine patched with transparent gummed paper, its gilt lettering tarnished, its corners battered. 'Oliver, with love from his Mother. Christmas 1918.' The familiar Great Britain representation, beginning with the first postage-stamp ever issued – the 1d. black. What was that stupid story in 'French without Tears'? About a certain *Monsieur A. qui désirait plus que tout autre chose un timbre-poste noir pour la gloire de sa collection philatélique*. The author misunderstood Monsieur A. as wanting just any black stamp – as opposed to red, green, blue, orange, bistre, magenta or dandy-grey-russet stamps, of which he had plenty – and not caring what the condition or catalogue-value might be, so long as the colour was correct. Monsieur B. was a rival, and Monsieur C. had the very stamp they both wanted. It ended in Monsieur A.'s death. Must have been written by a woman – Jane always liked stamps more for their colour than for their rarity. After Great Britain, British Colonies. His set of British North Borneo animal stamps – complete. Two complete sets, rather, one used and one unused. 'I suppose Jane with her tweezers thinks that she's going to break both sets. Jane's entirely wrong.' Europe. Here was that Spanish *dos reales* of Queen Isabella: quite a rare stamp, swapped with someone at his prep-school for a nearly new cricket-ball. Catalogued at 15s.

At this point something slipped out of the album: an envelope. He picked it up from the floor and at first couldn't place it. The stamp was Antigua, and above it was written, in ink, 'Recd. April 6, 1866'; and below it, in faint pencil, 'Insufficiently stamped. Collect.' Then he remembered that Jane had enclosed it to him in a letter when he was in his first quarter at Charchester. After his measles and two terms at that funny school at Geneva he had gone to Charchester, and had naturally taken his stamp-collection with him, expecting it to be greatly admired and prepared to do brisk business with the swaps he had collected in Switzerland. But a former prep-school friend called Hazlitt warned him, the first day, that stamp-collecting 'wasn't done' at Charchester. It was considered a kid's game. Oliver protested that he knew a fellow at Westminster who collected, and was in the First Eleven there, too. Hazlitt said that if the 'Wesser fellow' was a First Eleven blood, naturally he could afford to be as kiddish as he liked. It proved that you were a real blood if you behaved like a kid at times. Besides, Wesser wasn't Charchester. He doubted whether even a blood would dare to collect stamps at Charchester. So he advised Oliver to give his album in charge of the matron instead of keeping it in his locker in the junior common-room. Someone might find it and tear it up for scent at the Founder's Day paper-chase – the fate of two or three new boys' albums in the last few years. And not to let on that he had ever collected stamps, or they'd all think him a mother's darling, plus cursed idiot.

When he had spent about three weeks at Charchester, mostly in revising his vocabulary – at Charchester one wasn't allowed to say 'chap', one had to say 'fellow', and one was laughed at for saying 'bally ass', instead of 'damned fool' or 'cursed idiot', and so on; and revising his values – at Charchester it was considered disgraceful to do more work than just enough to satisfy one's form-master, and honourable to cheat, and bad form to discuss one's family, and so on; well, when those three uncomfortable weeks had been got through without much discredit, he had a letter from Jane with this Antigua envelope enclosed. She said that a friend of hers who wished to remain anonymous had acquired it from a source which wished to remain anonymous, and that she had looked it up in her friend's cousin's big catalogue and it wasn't listed, so it must be frightfully valuable. There had also been an exciting letter in the envelope all about a shipwreck, but she wouldn't send it now because it was upstairs and she was in a hurry for the post. It had something about the stamp in it.

If he wanted to see it, she'd send it next time she wrote. She hadn't taken the stamp off the envelope because it would be more valuable like that, wouldn't it? The address (Mr Frederick Young, last heard of in Canterbury Settlement, in the care of Messrs. John Whitebillet and Sons, Parliament Street, Liverpool, England) was written in such an old-fashioned handwriting and the paper was so yellow and the ink so faded that nobody could dare to say that the stamp wasn't genuine.

He had not read Jane's letter at once, because he recognized her handwriting and did not want anyone to read over his shoulder. Besides, there was a bulge in it which he guessed, rightly, was an assortment of stamps. So he went to the lavatory and read it there. He did not know what to do with the stamps; he was ashamed to bother the matron again. He must think of a safe place to hide them. That night he put them in the frame of his mother's photograph which he kept by his bedside. He didn't even look to see whether they were stamps that he had not already got in the collection. He persuaded himself that they did not interest him, that stamp-collecting was a kid's game.

Powerful thing, the Public School Spirit. Something very primitive about the demands it made on one. At Charchester there were two words, *fas* and *nefas*, which one learned the moment one went there. *Fas* was what you were permitted to do, *nefas* was what was forbidden. It was *fas* for a boy in his second year at the School to wear black socks with a coloured clock, but *nefas* for a boy in his first year to wear anything but plain black socks. Not until one's third year was it *fas* to wear really coloured socks. It was *nefas* for anyone to smoke or get up a sweepstake until his fourth year. Smoking and sweepstakes were both against official school rules, but school rules had no relation to *fas* and *nefas*. Certain things were only *fas* if you were a blood, such as wearing a butterfly collar and light-grey trousers and walking arm-in-arm with other fellows. To be a blood meant getting into the First Eleven at cricket or football. The fact that you were in the Sixth Form and had won a University scholarship, or that you had represented the School at Aldershot in the Public Schools boxing competition, or that you were in the School racquet pair, or captain of the shooting six, or that you could give any of the masters a couple of bisques at golf and beat him – as Oliver himself could, even in his second year – did not make you a blood. It had to be either football or cricket; and it had to be the First Eleven. Second Eleven in both did not make you a blood. Oliver had never become a blood. It still rankled. Hazlitt, who was Captain of Football in his last year, had kept him out of the team from personal spite. Hypocritical about it, too. Told him that it would look like favouritism to put a School House man into the vacant position at centre-half when there were two or three fellows from other houses who were just about as good. And then gave himself away by playing centre-half himself and bringing in a new man into his own position as right-half. *And* played shockingly badly. Never fed his forwards. A lot of shouting and a few melodramatic tackles, but no real work.

For a blood, everything was *fas*. If he professed a whim for collecting Baxter prints, airing political prejudices, or burning incense in his study that whim would be held sacred. It was his privilege to be eccentric. Indeed, his dormitory-house expected him to be eccentric, to demonstrate his freedom from ordinary social taboos. It rarely happened, however, that a blood succeeded in being really eccentric. The fact was that for all these years he had been concentrating solely on proficiency in games and on cultivating so consistently modest and decent a deportment that no member of any selection committee could possibly say of him (in the school dialect), 'I bar that man: he advertises', or 'I bar that man: he stinks'. Still, he had to have some slight peculiarity, nuisance-value, to impress his bloodhood on the house. He might perhaps devote all his leisure time to attaining solitary expertness with a hunting-horn, bagpipes, a lasso. A less energetic or less gifted blood would perhaps buy a set of classical gramophone records and make his fags play them over and over to him during meals, and throw loaves of bread and lumps of sugar at anyone who dared to interrupt the music by moving his chair, coughing, or rattling his cup and saucer. 'Uncle' Hazlitt, for example, went in for china pigs; he used to arrange them in quaint positions on a baize card-table. The fags had to dust them twice a day and serenade them once a week with a song he taught them, called 'A Jolly Old Sow Once Lived in a Sty'. If they laughed, he beat them with a single-stick.

It had been Oliver's dream for nearly five years to become a blood. His whole school-life had been lived in that dream. In those first weeks at Charchester he had deduced from the talk going on around him that, if he was to succeed in life, he must let no interest whatsoever compete with games. Games-success led to bloodhood. Bloodhood seemed the necessary goal to reach before becoming a member of Parliament or a financial magnate or a major-general, or a success in whatever career he might choose. It did not occur to him to doubt that all doors flew open to bloods on their leaving school – why else was the whole system allowed to revolve on the central fact of bloodhood? It was a natural deduction to make. Charchester education was either 'Classical' or 'Modern': the Classical was a mere exercise-ground for the wits, the Modern the same thing in disguise – dead modern subjects instead of dead Greek and Latin. It was something to be got through somehow, part of the system, and (on the admission of the masters themselves) irrelevant to the ordinary practical business of life. 'What I like about Lucretius,' his form-master once confessed, 'is that the substance of his writing is, to all intents and purposes, negligible. Read him in search of knowledge or good sense and you are misinformed and mis-directed at every point. But ah, what noble nonsense! Con-centrate on the *manner*, gentlemen, and forget the matter.' Games were the only serious activity going on and were, moreover, compulsory. Apart from grumbling small talk about the badness of the food or the insanity of the staff, and boasts about how little schoolwork one had contrived to do, there were only two permissible topics of general conversation. One of these was games. And about the other you had to be careful, because the House-master used to wander about in felt slippers.

At his prep-school, which was 'advanced', things had been entirely different. There one was encouraged to read good books and understand something about politics, and there was a farm attached to the school where one learned about animals and chicken-keeping and fruit-trees, and each form had a garden, and there were dancing lessons every Saturday in the winter term, with pupils of a neighbouring girls' school as partners, and a carpenter's shop, and a printing press on which the school magazine was set up by the boys themselves. There was even a game organized by the Headmaster in which one watched the stock-market and speculated in mythical millions; but one had to justify one's investments by some statement in writing as to why one thought that they were secure. (A boy called Guldenstein always won. He got tips from his father. Oliver suspected that the Headmaster arranged the game in order to get Guldenstein's father's tips himself.) Once they held a mock-election, properly conducted in every detail. He stood as an independent Conservative and nearly got in. But at Charchester all that interesting pseudo-adult life had come to a sudden paralytic stop. In his letters home Oliver did not attempt to convey the tremendous change that he was experiencing in his general outlook on life, except by giving no news except football news. Jane wrote to ask whether the stamps had arrived safely and what he thought about them, especially the Antigua one. She enclosed a few more. He wrote back, perhaps a little stiffly, that he didn't collect stamps any longer, and told her, in what was intended to be a joking tone – but unfortunately letters don't convey a joking tone, there being no punctuation marks available except the note of exclamation, which leaves too much to the intelligence – that he had left all that sort of thing behind him at his prep-school. She missed the point and wrote him a beastly letter, headed: 'An Address to a Public School Man by an Admiring Younger Sister.' Jane at thirteen years old was a frighteningly precocious child. He had kept the letter to complain about it when he got home. Here it was, in the album:

> The Vicarage,
> St Aidan's
> *Oct. 27th, 1912*

Honoured Brother,

Now that you have suddenly come to man's estate, by the grace of the Lord, and in the words of the Holy Apostle Paul have 'put away childish things', your obliged sister grieves for the loss of an innocent and sportive playmate; yet rejoices to have won, in his stead, a wise counsellor and protector – one, moreover, skilled in the ways of the world, ripe with the wit of the age, altogether *à la mode*, and with his brow shaded with a thousand green leaves of Academia's laurel – you conceited prig, you – you idiotic showing-off sham, pretending to be too rottenly superior to carry on a correspondence with a little pigtailed girl out of your babyish past! You wait until you come back for the hols – I'll teach you your place in the home! Just try out that haughty manner at the Vicarage and see what happens!

Therefore believe me, wishing you God's blessing and all good increase, Honoured brother, your very affectionate, humble, dutiful and obliged sister,

> Jane Elizabeth Palfrey Price

He got the letter on Sunday on his way to early Holy Communion. The Bishop had confirmed him just before he went up to Charchester. Holy Communion was voluntary. Not many fellows attended it, but religion was one of the few questions left open at Charchester. If a Carcestrian chose to attend Holy

Communion nobody either sneered or applauded: it was, indeed, *nefas* to discuss religion in public, unless you happened to be a blood. He was very glad indeed that he had got up for Holy Communion this morning, because the rest of the House was still in bed and nobody but the House-butler had handled the letter yet, and Jane had actually dared to address the envelope to '*Master* Oliver Price, c/o Dr Grant, The School House, Charchester', exactly as if he were still at a prep-school! She knew very well that at Charchester or any other decent public school even new boys were, as a matter of courtesy, addressed as 'Esq.' and not put in care of anyone but themselves. It was hitting below the belt. She could be as nasty as she liked inside the letter – that was only between him and her – but to make a public scandal of it by writing insults on the envelope for anyone to read and rag him about, that was beyond a joke.

At Charchester it was *nefas* to talk of 'hols' when one meant 'vacations'. That *vacation*, therefore, he and Jane were hardly on speaking terms. It was a great temptation, now that he was home again, to slip back into his old ways of thinking and forget that he was a Carcestrian, and in the School House too. But apart from sorting the stamps which Jane had sent him and putting the few that were any good into their proper places in the album, as a mere matter of routine, he conscientiously refrained from stamp-collecting. So it was a very boring vacation, with nothing to do on wet days but read or play patience. Next quarter – it was *nefas* to say 'term' at Charchester – he would no longer be a new boy. It would be his duty to warn new arrivals from the prep-school that stamp-collecting wasn't done by Carcestrians: it wasn't *nefas* exactly, only kiddish . . . Still, he would have liked to know about the Antigua stamp. He had thought of writing up to Messrs Stanley Gibbons about it, but restrained himself; it was certain to be quite common, just accidentally left out of the catalogue, though he certainly had never seen a specimen of it before. Anyhow, it obviously wasn't safe for him to mess about with philatelic firms. They might send him circulars at Charchester, which he would have to explain away. Jane didn't show him the shipwreck letter, and he was too proud to ask to see it.

Oliver held the envelope up to the light for another good look. Not a very nice-looking stamp. The common Antigua, one penny, young Queen's head in various shades of red, was much more dignified. This was an ugly sort of brownish-purple – 'puce' was probably the word, though Messrs Stanley Gibbons did not use it in their catalogues, so far as he could remember. But then he did not know any other stamp of exactly this queer colour – and it had a ship and a lighthouse awkwardly placed, left and right, below an octagonal medallion enclosing the Queen's head. He picked up the catalogue and turned to *Antigua*. He found that the early one penny, red, was issued at various dates between 1862 and 1876. 'Rose-mauve', 'Dull-rose', 'Vermilion', 'Lake', 'Scarlet', 'Lake-rose'. Various perforations from 'Rough perf. 14 to 16' to $12\frac{1}{2}$ and '14'. Various watermarks – 'Small Star' and 'Crown CC'. Catalogue value from 12s. to 35s., unused according to water-mark and perforation. From 4s. to 15s., used. The most valu-able variety was an imperforate stamp, catalogued at £12, used. But no puce. No mention of ship and lighthouse. The postmark on the letter was 'A02' without a date. There was also a very faint red cancellation which he made out to be that of the shipping company which carried the letter to England.

'Antigua, one penny, puce,' Oliver muttered to himself. '1866. Perforation 14. Watermark not visible. Would have to steam the stamp from the envelope. Prefer not to do that yet. Will investigate the matter tomorrow. Might just happen to be worth a few pounds.'

We apologize for having written at such length about *fas* and *nefas* at Charchester; but their formative influence on Oliver's character cannot be over-emphasized. And about bloods; but if Oliver had somehow managed to get his First Eleven cap it would have made a vast difference to his subse-quent outlook on life, and this story would have taken, we think, an altogether calmer and happier course.

CHAPTER 5

JANE'S RISE TO EMINENCE

It must not be assumed that Jane was prompted by mere petty spite when, meeting her brother Oliver in the picture gallery, as if by accident, she roused in him such strong feelings of anger and resentment. She had, of course, a definite grudge against him in the matter of the Palfrey heirlooms, and there was no redeeming memory of childhood – no single occasion when Oliver had behaved with spontaneous generosity to her – to tempt her to forget it. Stupid Oliver. He had always suspected her hidden hand, most absurdly, whenever anything went wrong for him. Brooded over it, too. That Port Hallows football match, for instance. The truth was that she had heard him crash the window open the night before the match and hurl something at a cat, swearing foully; and when next morning he accused her of stealing one of his boots in order to spoil his game, she simply hadn't felt like suggesting that he should search for it in the garden. But she would not now be troubling to raise the ghosts of the past if she did not have a definitely constructive purpose. Petty spite was not Jane's way. Though Oliver was quite unaware of it, she had a professional reason for spending so much time on him. Acting on behalf of Jane Palfrey Amalgamated, she was taking careful notes of his gestures and behaviour, with the intention of communicating them to a member of her theatrical company who went by the name of Owen Slingsby. An explanation of this will be given in due course. It is enough for the moment to state that Jane had a permanent company of players under contract to her at the Burlington theatre – five of either sex. The men were 'The Squire', J. C. Neanderthal, Roger Handsome, Owen Slingsby, Horace Faithfull. The women were Doris Edwards, Leonora Laydie, Madame Blanche, Nuda Elkan, Fairy Bunstead. Occasionally she engaged extras, but seldom. These players, originally chosen by Jane as forming, together, an almost perfect compendium of dramatic character, acted under her direction in a number of stock dramas, modern

comedies and topical revues, and had become the darlings of
London. Jane was generally regarded as the most talented
actress of the post-war era, but it was almost never now that
she made a personal appearance on the stage; except at rehearsals, demonstrating brilliantly to her people how each
part should be played. Those who were privileged to watch
made her name legendary: ah, if she could only be persuaded
to return to the boards!

The reader has every right to ask how it came about that
Jane, at the age of only twenty-six or so, had risen by her own
unaided efforts to her present eminence as a public entertainer.
We shall explain at once; but 'unaided efforts' is perhaps an
over-statement. Edith Whitebillet, Jane's partner and girlhood
friend, had from the start put her technical inventiveness at
Jane's disposal, and later a deal of money. Jane was not
beautiful in the stage or screen sense, it was generally agreed.
She never had any of that mute apple-blossom-in-April charm
that is of such service to young actresses who do not quite
know their jobs yet, nor did she cultivate that haunted look
of lost innocence that, to many theatre-goers, spells the grand
style in actresses of experience. She was on the tall side, strongly
but gracefully built. Her eyes were grey, her hair was parti-
coloured – corn colour shading in patches into brown. She
held herself well and had long aristocratic fingers and a long
aristocratic nose like her mother's. Oliver, by the way, had
taken after his father in almost every physical detail – the same
round head, round shoulders, broad thighs, square hands,
snub nose, fair hair, pale eyebrows, clerical chin and clerical
grin. Only his eyes were blue, like his mother's, and his skin
delicate, and he had inherited her extreme fastidiousness about
clean linen (he had a fresh set of underclothes every day), her
passionate love of concert music, and her remarkable memory
for cards. Not that these characteristics will come up much
in this story: but such was Oliver. Speaking of cards, he bore a
remarkable facial resemblance to the Knave of Spades, except
that the moustache he affected was not quite so twiddly, nor
his eyes so large.

And here we may take the opportunity of also giving a
portrait of Edith Whitebillet, the third of the leading characters

in our story. (The fourth is the Marquess of Babraham.) Edith was dark-haired, brown-eyed and rather sallow. She had a friendly, good-humoured face behind the dreadfully powerful spectacles that she always wore, and a thin but well-proportioned body. She was very shy and stuttered slightly. Her father had never been able to forgive her for not having been born a boy. That she had exactly the sort of brains that would have made her an outstanding success in his own trade of ship-building, if he had considered it a suitable trade for a girl, was what annoyed him. He felt no such resentment towards Edna, her twin sister. Edna was pretty and brainless: as a boy she would have been useless to him. Edith was always begging him to send her to an engineering college, and used to read the technical reports that came to him from the White-billet yards on the Clyde with rather more attention and interest than he could find time to give them himself. Wireless was her speciality. Sir Reginald had an engineering workshop at the end of the garden, built when he first settled at St Aidan's; but golf, otter-hunting and other local interests occupied him more and more. Edith gradually moved in. Sir Reginald employed a man to keep the machines and instruments in order, and Edith's occupation of the shop kept the fellow up to the mark. So he pretended to be unaware of her activities. When he felt like doing any experimental work himself he could always turn her out.

Edith had loved and admired Jane from the start. Jane soon came to have an affectionate respect for Edith, though science and mathematics, Edith's principal interests, meant nothing to her. There was little show of friendship between Whitebillet House and the Vicarage, but as children Jane and Edith used to meet regularly down at the beach, with an alternative rendez-vous, for rainy days, at the Free Library. Jane used to set Edith little problems of invention to work out for her: a book-rest, so that she could read in her bath and turn over the pages without wetting them, a goffering machine for the frills of a ballet dress, improvements on the metronome she used while practising her dances, so that she could set it to work in any musical time, single or compound, and even arrange beforehand for it to accelerate, slow down or change the time after so many hundreds of ticks. There was no nonsense about Pure Science with Edith; she liked working towards a prescribed practical end. And she was the first person, besides the Mrs Trent mentioned in the second chapter, whom Jane took into her confidence about her theatrical ambitions, and who was invited to act as a stage-hand when Jane was trying something out with the help of her toy theatre.

Jane had always thought in terms of a theatrical company consisting of herself in multiplication, all the parts played by Jane Palfrey. She would perform painstakingly in front of a pier-glass, now as this character in a play, now as that, and the toy theatre was useful as a reminder of what every member of the cast was doing at any given moment. Mrs Trent once suggested that Jane should form a company of boys and girls from the village and rehearse a play for Christmas; but Jane said that Father would insist on making an in-aid-of festival of any show she put on, and probably try to boss it himself, and that, anyhow, she was teaching herself how to act, not the whole of St Aidan's.

Edith, who moved the paste-board figures about under Jane's supervision, said one day (it was the summer of 1923), 'Wouldn't it be more fun to have these people moving by themselves, instead of having to shove one's hand in among them? And speaking for themselves, too?'

Jane said, 'Oh, marionettes! You can't do much with them, and the movements are so jerky. And the strings are the devil to manipulate. And ventriloquism is just like bad acting.'

Edith explained: 'No, I meant robots – life-sized robots, probably of rubber and steel, controlled by wireless and activated by this new phototropic principle – you know, it's derived from a study of how moths' wings react to candle-light. It ought to be possible. And no need for ventriloquism, either. With wirelessed gramophone records you could make them really talk. But they'd have to move their lips in a convincing way and be able to dance about rubberily. I'd love to try it. You could even get on the stage and act along with them. There would have to be two sets of robots, one life-size and the other a tiny set attached to a sort of keyboard. Someone behind the stage would manipulate the tiny set by touching various buttons and switches on the keyboard, and the big set would respond sympathetically. There would have to be what is called 'sensitivity-locuses' on their joints: the relation of the sensitivity-locuses would be what counted. Facial expressions would be complicated: to work out the proper position for each facial locus and find different formulas for, say, a scowl or a leer or a grin would take a lot of doing. But nothing's impossible. And all the voicing could be yours – I have found out an amusing way of converting a woman's voice on the gramophone into a man's. You could sing choruses with yourself – in soprano, contralto, tenor and bass.'

'You're quite mad,' said Jane. 'But I give you leave to try. If you get any sort of results I'll take you into partnership and we'll make our fortunes.'

'I'll want five years,' Edith said, 'and a great deal of money. But I'm afraid I can't expect Father to buy all the materials I'll need. I'm lucky to have the shop and a good technician to help me. Jenkins is surprisingly good.'

'That's all right,' said Jane. 'I'm not quite sixteen yet and I'll need five years to learn my side of the job properly. We'll get the money somehow. Are you on?'

They shook hands. It sounded a fantastic scheme, but they both took it perfectly seriously, and when there is complete confidence between two young and capable people and they suddenly shake hands on a bargain of this sort it may easily happen that they will overcome all obstacles and make a great success of their undertaking. We shall see how it worked out.

First, then, Jane persuaded her father to send her to a school of dramatic art. That sounded respectable; it was a useful way of gradually accustoming him to the idea of having a daughter on the stage. And at least it got her away from home, though as we have seen he could not afford to send her further than that place at Bristol, where the training was indifferent, except for a good singing teacher. But, being Jane, she picked up a lot of useful knowledge, especially out of school-hours. Mrs Trent had given her an introduction to the stage-carpenter of a local theatre, and the stage-carpenter's wife knew the landlady at the hostel where Jane stayed, and persuaded her to overlook Jane's frequent absences from the hostel after hours. Jane secured a free pass to the theatre and used to watch night after night how the audience reacted to different sorts of bad acting. She took notes and expanded them into generalizations which she then tested. When she went to London she would have the opportunity of making further generalizations from watching the audiences' reaction to better acting.

Mrs Trent, it must be explained, had once been Gwennie Pope, the music-hall favourite of the nineties. At the height of her popularity she had married a rich Canadian and gone to live in British Columbia. Ten years later he lost all his money and she fell ill and lost most of her looks, and then he killed himself and she drifted back to England and took a small cottage at St Aidan's. Nobody knew that Mrs Trent was really Gwennie Pope and it was best to say nothing about it. The Chapel people were taught to regard all stage-players as sinful; and, though the gentry had no such prejudices, Gwennie Pope did not propose to invite their pity by reminding them of her former triumphs. She came to the Vicarage every Friday morning to sew. For an ex-music-hall favourite, she sewed very well. The only person at St Aidan's who knew her history was Jane. Jane used to sit and talk to her while she sewed, and one day a story that Mrs Trent told her set her mind working. She read carefully through several old bound volumes of the *Illustrated London News*, comparing the portraits of smiling stage favourites with Mrs Trent's solemn mask, until she finally tracked her down. Mrs Trent tried to deny that she was Gwennie, but Jane soon forced the truth out of her, promising not to reveal her identity even to Edith. In return, Gwennie, who had for years been longing for a confidante, secretly taught her to dance, and told her scandalous anecdotes of stage and society that she had kept bottled up for twenty years. Gwennie had been for some years on intimate terms with Jane's grandfather, the Marquess. 'A real gentleman', Gwennie called him. Gwennie had been in ballet, pantomime, musical comedy, was once an expert in the can-can, kicking higher and faster than any woman of her size in England or France, had dined more than once with the old King of the Belgians, and one night had been privileged to share the honours with Lily Langtry at —'s. Dan Leno and Phil May had both been in love with her, and Sir Henry Irving had once given a champagne picnic on the River in her honour. She could remember Marie Lloyd as a madcap girl, 'up and down the City Road, in and out The Eagle'.

'I was a regular trouper, my dear, born in my mother's dressing-room while we were on tour. It was at Coventry I believe. We carried our theatre about with us – of the sort that we used to call "Portables". There aren't any such now. They were just planks of wood, numbered and fitted together into a full-sized hall, with stalls. I played my first part at four years old. I was Little Willie in *East Lynn*. And oh, how respectable we were, too! I remember going to Paris as a little girl with Barnes' troup, and dear me, how shocked I was that the French girls wore no tights! As for rouge or lipstick, off that came as soon as my part was over: only very naughty women wore them off-stage.'

Gwennie was a good teacher and Jane an apt pupil. Gwennie had once had a friend, a French girl, who specialized in Eastern dances and taught her how to wriggle her body about in an unnaturally snaky sort of way. Gwennie said that in her day this was supposed to be the height of immorality and that she had been blamed for making friends with the French girl, but nowadays nobody thought anything about it: it was part of proper artistic dancing, and Jane had better learn it. Jane learned it, her childish innocence of expression increasing the sinister effect.

Jane was at the school at Bristol for three terms and was then expelled, for inattention, insubordination and exercising a bad influence (as a strike-leader) on the younger girls. Her father made this expulsion an excuse for forbidding her to go on with her studies, and found her a job as secretary to an old friend of his, a professor of economics at London University. She pretended to be quite willing to do what was expected of her, because it gave her a ticket to London and some new clothes. But she resigned a fortnight later and disappeared. She found a job in the dressing-room of a suburban variety theatre and kept her eyes and ears open. She sent post-cards home every now and then from various parts of London, and once called on an uncle and aunt to reassure the family that she had not got caught up in the white-slave trade. But she never let anyone know where she was or what she was doing, except Edith, with whom she communicated regularly through Jenkins.

Then she got a trial engagement for a week at the same theatre, to fill in an unexpected gap, with a sketch called 'Practising' – just a schoolgirl and a piano, with acrobatic absurdities. It went quite well, and through it she became connected with a provincial circuit. The gags were new, and the timing and the general principle of the thing were carefully worked out from her notes. She wore a carroty wig, altered the slant of her eyebrows and widened her mouth. She called herself Doris Edwards at this time. Her next character was Madame Blanche, a blowsy woman who monologued in a flat humourless voice and explained that she ran a home for lost dogs: there was a good deal of *double entendre* about this home, and in one town protests were made by the Purity League and the number was taken off. She then became Leonora Laydie, a woman of society who sought adventure in the underworld. Jane used genuine criminal types as her assistants in this act. Leonora's plights and perils went so well that any ordinary person would have stuck to her. But Jane did not wish to get into a groove, so her next turn was as Nuda Elkan, the exotic dancer. Jane had studied all the ways in which, while keeping technically within the letter of the Lord Chamberlain's regulations about nudity on the stage, one appeared, most of the time, to be wearing absolutely nothing at all. Jane was not lasciviously inclined, but she had no romantic sense of modesty: she wanted to know how to get an audience sweating hot and cold, and she wanted to make the experiment herself. Nuda was an Eurasian, which meant a blue-black wig and walnut juice. When Edith wrote to ask, 'Why Eurasian?' Jane replied, 'Because everyone likes a brown egg to his breakfast.'

Nuda retired when Jane had sufficiently studied the mechanics of sex-appeal and collected a stupendous fanmail, including proposals of marriage or worse from rich rayon-manufacturers, officers of the Royal Horse Guards, Egyptian princes, Negro tenors and the like, and surprised the world by her inaccessibility. Nuda was never seen dining in the gossip columns of the daily Press, and even refused to take a stall in the Theatrical Benefit Bazaar. Leonora Laydie was there instead. In an interval of the Nuda period, which brought in a great deal of money and helped Edith over a difficult part of her researches, Jane experimented with an act which she called 'The Barber's Pole'. She needed foils again, and picked out three men from the queue at a Labour Exchange, warning them that if they tried to act with originality she would fire them at once. One was an ex-seaman of the United States Navy but a Huddersfield man; one had been dismissed from the Corps of Commissionaires for negligence; the third had been a cook in the Black Watch (Royal Highlanders). She had a few copies of the book of words printed, so that when Edith's robots, for which *The Barber's Pole* was written, were in working order, her hirelings would not dare to take the act round the halls on their own. They did dare, as a matter of fact, at Portsmouth; but Jane sent the police after them.

The Barber's Pole was composed on the principle that women would be interested to know just how their menfolk behaved when they were by themselves. Jane took the part of a youth, the Barber's new assistant, and went by the name of Roger Handsome. M'Ostrich, the Squire and J. C. Neanderthal were the names of the customers. The Barber was getting married that morning, so could not attend to them. Young Handsome, left in charge, tried to reproduce his employer's confidential patter, but the men took little notice of him and kept up an old-fashioned semi-indecent conversation, intended to be over his head, in honour of the Barber and his bride. M'Ostrich (the Black Watch man), who was having his very stubbly beard shaved, did most of the talking. The dreadful insipidity and crudity of his jokes was the chief point of the sketch. J. C. Neanderthal (the ex-seaman), a lusty rogue and rather drunk, talked about horses and women in such a way that one could never make out which was which. The Squire (the ex-Commissionaire) was a respectable old gentleman who nevertheless chuckled a good deal at the others and finally joined in with naughty Edwardian club-man's wit. The climax of *The Barber's Pole* comes when someone rushes in to say that M'Ostrich's wife has been killed in a street-accident. Immediately the whole atmosphere changes from obscenity to piousness. M'Ostrich remains to finish his shave, because only one half of his face has been done, and weeps bitterly. The others comfort him. Handsome is greatly affected and work proceeds slowly. Then it turns out that it wasn't M'Ostrich's wife at all, but his mother-in-law. So everyone is himself again, and when Handsome unwittingly says something to the point the customers hail him as a pretty smart lad and admit him to their unsavoury society.

Mention was made in a previous chapter of Jane's reading *Three Men in a Boat*. It will have been supposed that she read it merely for amusement. Jane read practically nothing for amusement; nearly everything was for information. To record a brief dialogue between her and Edith: Edith said one day to Jane, 'I don't think jokes are funny, do you?' Jane answered seriously, 'No, I don't think they are, really.' Edith, a scientist, could not believe in jokes as objective phenomena. Jane meant that jokes were part of her professional stock-in-trade, something to break down the audience's self-possession with, not to laugh at. Jane thought *Three Men in a Boat* an important book, written by a man with a remarkable instinct for his public. 'Popular humour cannot aim too low,' she once wrote to Edith. 'Jerome K. Jerome was one of the few English humorists who has ever realized this. (Surtees was another.) Jokes about cheese and stuffed trouts in riverside inns, and seasickness. But these jokes need a background of really sickening sentiment. The older and more awful the jokes, the more cloying must be the accompanying treacle.

Night's heart is full of pity for us: she cannot ease our aching; she takes our hands in hers, and the little world grows very small and very far away beneath us, and, borne on her dark wing, we pass for a moment into a mightier Presence than her own, and in the wondrous light of that great Presence, all human life lies like a book before us, and we know that Pain and Sorrow are but the angels of God. From *Three Men in a Boat*.

'But he was a good technician. At first he introduces this sort of rhetoric ironically, and cuts it short with a bathetic remark from Harris or George. Then gradually he gives sentiment equal standing with farce. A good bit of farcical business is the dead dog that drifts down the river just after they have made tea with river-water. Three chapters later it is a dead girl who drifts down the river.

She had loved and been deceived, and her family and friends had closed their doors against her. Left to fight the world alone, with the millstone of her shame around her neck, she had sunk ever lower and lower. For a while she had kept both herself and the child on the twelve shillings a week that twelve hours' drudging a day procured her. . . .

'It needs courage – courage and perfect shamelessness. Dickens had both. *Pickwick Papers* is built on the same principle of opposites. For example, those dreadful ins erted *Tales*– "The Stroller's Tale", "The Convict's Return", "A Madman's Manuscript", "The Old Man's Tale"; presumably honest reminders to the reader that life had its screams of terror as well as its screams of laughter. Really, just the simplest melodrama.

"Father – devil!" murmured the convict, between his set teeth. He rushed wildly forward, and clenched the old man by the throat – but he was his father; and his arm fell powerless by his side. The old man uttered a loud yell which rang through the lonely fields like the howl of an evil spirit. His face turned black; the gore rushed from his mouth and nose, and dyed the grass a deep dark red, as he staggered and fell. He had ruptured a blood-vessel; and he was a dead man before his son could raise him.

'It isn't parody. Certainly not. Dickens did just the same sort of thing in his serious work. He knew he could not try his public too low.'

So in *The Barber's Pole*, Jane explained, the grief expressed by M'Ostrich for his poor wife must be real grief, and the Squire and Neanderthal and Handsome must be perfectly whole-hearted in their sympathy. And at the end Handsome must be left alone in the Barber's shop to sing a sentimental song beginning, 'As his fond wife lay dying,' which has not the faintest possible snicker it it – and must carry the audience with him. 'You see, Edith, the public has been taught to believe that life is like that – laughter and tears going hand in hand – and thinks that a man who can make you cram your handkerchief into your mouth for laughter and then make you pull it out again to wipe tears of sympathetic grief from your eyes is a genius. He's not that, really. He's either a howling cad or an experienced professional entertainer. Or perhaps both. What was Dickens? It is better not to say. To breathe a word about Dickens is like sitting down when the band plays "God Save the King". Nobody has really read Dickens, just as nobody really knows the words of "God Save the King".'

Late in 1928 Edith wrote Jane a long letter, confessing to failure; the robot-job had proved too hard for her. There was more difference than she had thought possible between the job of directing a torpedo or plane by wireless, and the job of directing the movements of a life-sized dancing doll. She had succeeded in activating them phototropically, but could so far only just manage to control the leg and arm movements of a single doll, and even then the control was always breaking down. And she hadn't been able to make it sing convincingly. The most honest thing was to let Jane know at once that a full troupe of robots was quite out of the question. She hoped Jane would forgive her for having let her down, but if there was anything she could possibly do to make up for her failure. . . . Of course, if Jane thought that she ought to go on with her experiments, she would. But it was a most dishearteningly slow job and fearfully expensive, too.

Jane answered that it didn't really matter at all, because scientific novelties were pretty boring, really, and nobody could be expected to go and see a robot-show more than once, out of curiosity. And she had a new idea now, by which the beauty of the robot-idea, which was the perfect subservience of a company of actors to the manager, could be translated into terms of flesh and blood. It was an extension of her *Barber's Pole* method. She would build up a company of actors none of whom had any ideas about their job except what she drilled into them; they would be made to realize that they were persons of complete insignificance except as members of *her* company. At the least sign of self-assertion on their part out they would go. If they obeyed her implicitly they would have a most sumptuous time, excellent pay and plenty of applause. A new sort of slavery. There were lots of people who would thoroughly enjoy being slaves; lazy people. The only real argument against slavery was that *occasionally* you got misfits – slaves who ought to be masters and masters who ought to be slaves. She would transfer to the women the separate female personalities that she had built up herself in the last year or two; and transfer to the men the *Barber's Pole* male personalities, enlarged and improved. And create one or two subsidiary characters of either sex. So she counted on Edith to help her run their theatre when the time came, and meanwhile to study all the latest innovations in stage-machinery, lighting and so on, so that their show would be absolutely up to date. She had her eye on The Burlington, the lease of which expired in a couple of years. Meanwhile she would go on tour in America. Nobody had a right to settle down seriously to the theatrical business without first spending at least six months in America. American audiences taught actors to feel absolutely at home on the stage. It was always 'Make yourself at home' with Americans.

CHAPTER 6

JANE PALFREY AMALGAMATED, AND FOLLY'S RESURRECTIONS

WHEN Sir Reginald Whitebillet died, towards the end of 1929, Edith and her twin, Edna, inherited his huge fortune. Edith at once let Jane know that as soon as she wished to take over the Burlington Theatre lease the money was there. Jane replied, the sooner the better: by the time Edith had thoroughly modernized the building and got her revolving expanding-and-contracting stage in position, the company would be ready to take the boards. She kept her word. They signed a forty-year lease and also a formal contract as business partners, with heavy penalties provided should either of them fail in her obligations. The distribution of work and responsibility was as follows: Jane was responsible for supplying suitable plays, training players, designing costumes and scenery, seeing that performances were punctually and professionally given, and for all advertising and publicity. Edith, for the stage-machinery and stage-hands, for the attendants, dressers and cleaners, for the refreshment-bar, for the supply and upkeep of costumes and properties, for the box-office, and for all general business in connexion with rates, taxes, insurance, police regulations and those of the Lord Chamberlain, L.C.C. by-laws and so on. Edith had far more money invested in the business than Jane, and Jane in consequence drew only thirty-five per cent of the net takings. A number of able assistants were engaged, among them Jenkins as chief electrician and Mrs Trent as wardrobe-mistress; and when the Burlington opened on December 10th, 1930, it was voted not only the handsomest and best-equipped theatre in London, but the friendliest and liveliest house of entertainment in the entire British Empire.

The company was organized on the lines that Jane had outlined in her letter to Edith. The actors and actresses were under contract to Jane to perform their parts exactly according to her instructions, without the least improvisation or amendment, and – a novel clause – to adopt, for all social purposes, while in her employment, the names and personalities she allotted to them for off-stage use. The salaries were extremely high and, after a year's loyal service, members of the company were entitled to a small percentage of the box-office takings. But a breach of the contract made them liable to instant dismissal.

Jane had by now elaborated her argument as follows. 'An actor, in order to achieve any success in his art, must be able to adapt his voice, gestures and facial expressions to those of any stock part within his acting range. A professional villain must be ready, if called upon, to represent Uriah Heep, Caliban, Bugs O'Gorman the gangster, Black Will in *Arden of Feversham*, Mr Hyde. Uria Heep must not chew gum, spit, juggle with a sawed-off shot-gun or jerk out wise-cracks from the side of his mouth; Bugs O'Gorman must not wash his hands with invisible soap, screw his body about, speak in a whine, or silently shake his fist at a closing door. So much is elementary. Nevertheless, theatre-goers' (Jane argued) 'are not interested in Uriah Heep, or Bugs O'Gorman, *as such*. It is the highest common factor of all these villainous parts, namely the personality of the actor, his natural off-stage existence with all its individual human detail, that makes the real appeal. But acting is a purely imitative art, and the qualities that make an ordinary, efficient actor do not make an interesting off-stage character. It is too much to expect from an actor, first, absolute subservience to a stage part and then, independence and initiative in private life. Most actors are either hopelessly frivolous and light-headed as private characters or hopelessly dull and respectable.

'Obviously, therefore, the discipline that they get in the theatre under a capable manager who refuses to be bullied by their vagaries and their self-importance ought to be applied to their private life, too. They ought never to be allowed to get out of the theatrical trance induced in them by the footlights and the curtain; but should be given an adequately dramatic life to live off-stage as a credit to themselves and their profession. An actor should be grateful for having this load of responsibility taken off his shoulders. If he isn't grateful, he is fit for something either better or worse than acting. And the fact that the off-stage personality is not his own, and yet all the personality that he has, is bound to induce a proper humility in him towards his employer. He will know that the moment he walks out of the company where he has been enrolled, say, as J. C. Neanderthal, he is nothing. He has no name to sell to a rival theatrical concern, for J. C. Neanderthal's role and name will immediately be allotted to someone else. I expect to find no greater difficulty in recruiting suitable actors on these terms than the Police find in recruiting suitable constables. There is the same handicap in each case: never being wholly off duty, and having to keep up one's professional dignity all the time. But glory, too. And glory cheaply earned. It is an easy job being a policeman and an easy job being an actor. All you need is lack of imagination, a good presence, and a good memory. Besides, I shall do all the publicity for my people myself.'

Yet Jane, it will be seen, had set herself a complicated task. She had first to invent the appropriate off-stage personalities for her company of ten, complete with circumstantial private histories, temperaments and mannerisms. Then she had to find ten actors who roughly fitted these personalities and were ready to be them just for the fun of the thing, and/or because they were tired of their own dull selves. Finally, when these personalities had become second nature to them, she had to teach them how to let second nature shine through their stage performances.

Where did Jane look for these actors? At first her search was haphazard, but one day she had the excellent idea of consulting Dr Marcus Parmesan, the celebrated ethnologist, neurologist and alienist, to whom Edith gave her an introduction: he specialized in the study of hypnotic subjects and split personalities. Dr Parmesan was greatly impressed by Jane and delighted at her offering to find profitable employment for a few at least of the 'interesting but socially maladjustable' people whom he used as laboratory specimens. 'I have far more than I can deal with,' he said, 'so you can take your choice. I think, Miss Palfrey, that you have stumbled upon a most plausible answer to a question that has been exercising thoughtful psychologists for some years now, the question of the increased occurrence in civilization of these morbid types. The view, I mean, immediately suggested by your inquiry – namely, that the racial sub-consciousness, aware of the approaching age of perfect leisure that will follow the mechanical solution of the major material problems of life, is now evolving patently theatrical types which will be of service to mankind when the Theatre becomes, as it is bound to do, the central activity of civilized life.' He promised her his whole-hearted support: he would recommend her to the relatives of his patients as a most responsible employer. Jane liked Dr Parmesan, except for an annoying habit (common to his profession) of shooting sudden looks at everyone who visited him, even Jane herself, whenever they did or said anything that was not completely dull and behaviouristic. Jane had to pull him up sharply once or twice, but he was still, at this time, sane enough to be grateful to her, not offended. (In the end, however, he had to be put under treatment with a colleague who was in not quite so advanced a stage of *psychiatrosis* as himself.) He let Jane into many of his professional secrets and even allowed her to have the Madame Blanche she wanted, though this was the celebrated Miss B., his prize exhibit, about whom so much has been written and in so many different languages by professional and amateur psychologists all over the world, since 1912 when Dr Parmesan first reported on her case in the *British Psychological Reports*. Miss B. had six distinct, unrelated personalities, which could be switched on or off at will – a great asset to Jane when casting, because all six characters had different accents and styles and were all quite stageable.

Jane Palfrey Amalgamated had been in existence for four years now and only five alterations had been made in the original company: the first Leonora had not been satisfactory, nor had the first two Neanderthals, and two Doris's had left to get married. But it was eighteen months since there had been a change, and the troupe had taken so kindly to their personalities that Jane had eventually permitted the seven originals to change their names by deed-poll to the ones she had given them, though of course on condition that if they ever broke their contract they were to change them back again. They all lived in a big house together and were very comfortable; and no lunatic with a natural obsession that he was Henry VIII, a parrot or the prophet Elijah ever made so good a job of it as they did of their artificial obsessions that they were exactly what Jane had told them they were: for she had been careful to give them roles that were easily within their power to live up to, as most lunatic roles, including the three that we have just instanced, are not.

J. C. Neanderthal was always cast as the villain; but in private life, Jane decided, he was not a bad fellow, though notoriously unreliable in money matters and usually scrapping with Leonora Laydie (in private life Mrs Neanderthal). He was a devoted uncle to Leonora's niece Doris, and a keen, if foolhardy, yachtsman. His secret ambition was to be elected a member of the Royal Yacht Squadron, but nobody could be found to sponsor him. He was known to have contributed letters to the *Spectator* and other journals on the subject of smoke-abatement. Jane made him walk with a hardly perceptible limp (infantile paralysis), wax his moustaches and affect a deer-stalker hat and a loaded walking-stick. His mannerisms included a careless flick of his fingers and a jolly toss of his head when he was talking big, a habit of examining his finger-nails when he was not telling the truth, and of putting his hands stiffly behind him when he was crossed. On the stage he played a silent little tune with his fingers – on his knee, or a table – whenever he was about to do something dreadful. He was a finger-drummer in private life, too. During the War, Jane alleged, he had been in the Kite-balloon section in the Ypres sector, but had fallen into the River Yser from the height of two hundred feet and had been invalided out with the rank of major. He was a North of Ireland man, in spite of his name.

As *Jane Palfrey Amalgamated* became more and more famous, further details of the private lives of the company were made public. Roger Handsome had been married and divorced four times. On one occasion, according to Jane, the co-respondent (no, that's the wrong word; co-respondents are, technically, male only; we should say 'intervener' or 'woman named' according to the moral indignation of the lady in question) was the wife of a foreign ambassador and the case was heard in camera. At present he was fixed up with Nuda but the public hoped that he would return to Doris, who had been his first and third wife and during the last proceedings expressed willingness to give him just one more chance. Owen Slingsby was known to dislike Handsome intensely, and had once publicly threatened to horsewhip him if he did not break off his connexion with Doreen, Slingsby's seventeen-year-old sister. (She was a talented girl who was expected to join the company, but was not long afterwards reported to have committed suicide in pathetic circumstances.) Slingsby was a comparative newcomer, having taken the place of the M'Ostrich character, who had been getting on Jane's nerves. A Scottish humorist is all right on the variety stage, but cannot hope to be the permanent comedian of a West End theatre; Jane realized that she had made a mistake in stabilizing him. She now had it bruited that his wife had died in a boating accident on the Norfolk Broads and that in consequence he was losing grip and taking to solitary whisky drinking. She made him give up golf and allowed no new witticisms of his to be circulated. His stage performances grew more and more ragged until Jane decided that the time was ripe for killing him off. One morning, after a foggy night, the public learned that his car had collided with Charles I in Whitehall. It was hinted that it was not altogether an accident. The theatre was in mourning for three nights. Fairy Bunstead, whose mother came from the West Highlands, wrote an obituary poem in synthetic Scots which appeared in a special Burlington advertisement. Even Nuda, who had always disliked M'Ostrich's sentimentality and religious morbidity, came into line by wearing, in her next dance, a glittering black arm-band on her otherwise severely uncostumed person.

Owen Slingsby was a more complex character than M'Ostrich and needed a good deal of slow building up. Jane worked out his history in loving detail. He had been successively a boy evangelist, a temperance worker, an elementary schoolmaster, a ship's steward and a salesman in a Bond Street picture shop, before he rose to be M'Ostrich's successor. He wrote, too, in an amateur way. He was now supposed to be hard at work on a first novel; first novels are always semi-autobiographical, so one would soon know even more than one knew now about Slingsby's past. His talk and mannerisms were taking on a satisfactorily distinctive tone, and Jane always kept him in the height of fashion. She had decided that he would be revealed in his novel as the natural son of the golf-professional at a fashionable links and the Club-house caretaker's sister. But Slingsby's real secret (though he did not know it himself and nobody knew it but Jane) was that, though totally different in outward appearance, he was in character and mannerisms the living image of her brother Oliver. In fact, Jane used to ask herself, during her development of Slingsby as a permanent member of her company, exactly how would Oliver behave in such and such circumstances.

Jane's old note-books and her unrecorded memories of Oliver provided material enough to work on, but she was conscientious, and there were certain irritable movements of the hands and head that she was not quite sure about. She wanted to get them exactly right. 'The Stamp Collector', if she could catch Oliver in front of it and tease him a little, would almost certainly bring them out, she thought. And she was not disappointed. Before she left the picture gallery she had made a mental note of all the salient points; and this would have been the end of the incident for her, if it had not entered her mind on the way home that a joke was a joke, but that Oliver ought really not to be allowed to behave so abominably, and that as a matter of principle, rather than for the fun of it, she must be prepared to stand by her threat to dismember the stamp collection.

Jane instituted weekly practice hours for her company to keep them up to the mark. They came to regard her with much the same childish awe that they had felt for Dr Parmesan. Indeed, though Jane was no psycho-analyst, her process was much the same as his: making them believe in what they knew to be false. Shorthand minutes were kept of these hours, by Miss Hapless, Jane's secretary, and copies later distributed among the company. From one of these minutes we extract the following:

The Squire: Good morning, Miss Palfrey. Take a pew, won't you?

Jane: Be yourself, Squire! Edwardian familiarity is not Edwardian courtesy. 'My *dear* lady! This is indeed a pleasure,' is your cue. Then you bumble about fussily with cushions and say, 'So we are about to embark on our hebdomadal *tête-à-tête*, are we? Well, well, well.'

The Squire: I understand. . . . Miss Palfrey, I am, I confess, still a trifle hazy about the early events of my life. Perhaps you will be able to put me wise. . . .

Jane: Not so bad, Squire. But if you must use a phrase like 'put me wise' you must underline it, by saying, 'in the language of the cinema, ha-ha,' or 'as our American cousins have it, ha-ha.'

The Squire: Precisely, precisely. All apologies, my *dear* lady!

Jane: You were, don't you recollect, expelled from Eton, sacked from Harrow, bunked from Wellington, kicked out of Marlborough; but Charchester (my brother's school, by the way) succeeded in making a man of you. All that happened to you there was that you were superannuated.

The Squire: True. Trouble at a crammer's and then I was sent down from Oxford.

Jane: That's right; and failed to satisfy the examiners at Cambridge.

The Squire: Cambridge: that's where my yarn of the confoundedly impudent gyp comes in, is it not?

Jane: Correct. And at Oxford there were those midnight orgies in the Park Road Museum with Banbury cakes and audit ale, and a party of jolly girls from Reading.

The Squire: I get you – ah, 'as our American cousins have it, ha-ha!' From that point onward my memories are relatively clear. I took a medical degree, did I not? but was struck off the rolls.

Jane: Ah, I should say 'the medical register'.

The Squire: Precisely, precisely.

Jane: Don't overdo the 'precisely', Squire.

The Squire: I went into the City and was soon hammered on 'Change. Then I left England, with a contingent of other old

sheep of black family – I should say black sheep of old family –
and became first a colonel in the Army of the Empress of
Madagascar who was engaged in a little war with the French,
and then a boatswain in a gunboat of the Spanish navy. During
the Spanish-American War, I take it.

Jane: Correct. By the way, do you remember how you came
to leave the Empress's service?

The Squire: Drummed out of the Army, was I not?

Jane: Drummed right out, and the Spaniards later piped
you ignominiously round the Fleet.

The Squire: *But* –

Jane: But –

The Squire: BUT on my return to England, penniless and
without a friend in the world, I met, at a pro-Boer rally in
Hyde Park, the most adorable, virtuous, wealthy . . .

Jane: Etc., etc.

The Squire: So this paragon, etc., etc., consented to marry
me, in spite of all, and we spent two blissful years together,
until that fatal day on a Leicestershire hunting-field . . .

Jane: I am not at all satisfied yet with the way you manage
your monocle. When you feel tears starting to your eyes, for
instance, you should remove it.

The Squire: Dear me, how right you are! But one last
question: what am I to say if they happen to ask *why* I was
expelled from Eton, sacked from Harrow, bunked . . .

Jane: You grin in an embarrassed way, wave your hand
vaguely and say: 'Oh, *not* the usual thing, my dear fellow, ha-ha,
not the usual thing.'

A valuable and inexpensive form of publicity came from a
new method of advertising that Jane initiated. Other theatrical
stars wrote only in praise of silk stockings, cigarettes, whisky,
cosmetics and the like; but the stars of Jane Palfrey Amalgamated always had something cruelly double-edged to say about
even the most reliable proprietary goods. A novelty. They were
soon accepted by the millionaire companies as licensed Royal
jesters: their impertinent remarks were a tribute to a commercial glory which was no longer in need of flattery, being
supposedly enthroned in the hearts of the people. Jane supplied

the copy, and a gifted caricaturist of her own. For example: Leonora Laydie, disdainful in evening gown, making a grimace at the advertised cigarette between her fingers – 'Why do I go on smoking these gruesome gaspers?' The company's courteous comment: 'Leonora Laydie having her little joke.'

It now remains to explain the reference made by Oliver, in the art gallery, to a brand of cigarettes called 'Folly's Havana Resurrections'. Oliver sneered; Jane defended. The story of their manufacture is worth telling. When Jane first moved to London she had to keep herself, on a very small weekly wage, and she also had it on her mind that Edith badly needed money for her experiments. Edith had spent all her savings and a small legacy from an aunt and was now being forced to pawn her jewellery. Jane thought: 'We want regular money from some source or other. We don't want to borrow. It must be something commercial. Commercial and very simple. I'll do the organizing part. Edith will think out a process. Some new process for providing something that everyone wants to buy, cheap. I'll know I'm on the right track if I find some simple way of making a fortune with only one technical drawback to it. It will be Edith's job to remove the drawback.'

One night, just before she resigned from the dressing-room to go on tour as Doris Edwards, Jane was tidying up the dressing-table after the show was over – this was included in her duties – and noticed for the first time what a remarkable number of cigarettes got smoked, or half-smoked, in the course of an evening's performance. She began counting the stubs on the floor and the dressing-tables. At a rough estimate, three hundred stubs. The sweeping woman would save them, perhaps, for her husband to smoke in his pipe. That would keep the husband busy. Three hundred stubs were the equivalent of about twenty-five pipefuls. Then think how much the audience smoked. There must be thousands of stubs left behind every evening. The perquisites of the cleaning women? Cigarette tobacco wasn't supposed to be much good in a pipe, so perhaps the husbands rolled the stuff into cigarettes again. Disgusting to smoke tobacco that somebody else had already mouthed. But waste not, want not! (Some cheap brands of marmalade were said to be made out of orange peel left lying about in waiting-rooms and railway carriages.) But, of course, a heavy smoker who couldn't afford . . .

And then Jane found herself muttering aloud: 'But why leave the stubs to charwomen's husbands? There's a fortune in them. Why not make them up into cigarettes and sell them, at threepence a packet of ten, to needy smokers? With mouth-pieces, to make them sanitary, and cellophane wrapping? And a good proprietary name?' Jane now had the very idea she was in search of. She knew it was the right idea as soon as she tried rolling some of her own stubs in a cigarette paper. The cigarette didn't taste bad as soon as she got it going, but it had a stale smoky smell beforehand – the sort of smell any cigarette has when it goes out and has to be relighted. This was the technical snag that Edith must overcome. Edith wasn't a chemist, really, but she could be counted on to find out all about tobacco and how to recondition it, and to invent a cheap cigarette-making machine.

She wrote to Edith that very night and two days later Edith answered:

> Whitebillet House,
> St Aidan's,
> *October 3rd, 1926*

My Dear Jane,

It can be done, I think. I'll list all the points. A cigarette made out of cigarette stubs has a higher percentage of toxic factors than an ordinary cigarette, but I have spent a morning in the Free Library looking up the whole question of what one may legally put into a cigarette and what one may not, and I don't think that an Excise inspector could prosecute one on the charge of making cigarettes out of cigarettes. It is not as though one added molasses or hashish or anything. I suggest a piece of cotton-wool in the mouthpiece to draw off some of the extra toxins which as you probably know are nicotine, ammonia, pyridine and pyridine derivative, cyanides, sulpho-cyanides and arsenic. The smoky taste of which you complain comes chiefly from the burnt cigarette paper; but in spite of what people say, I find in a recent issue of the *Journal of the American Medical Association* a report by Drs Flight and Maffett on the toxins of cigarette smoke, to the effect that 'the products of the cigarette paper may be eliminated as offending mediums.'

I am now making experiments in reconditioning with a vapour which counteracts the stale smell and sterilizes the tobacco – in case the Ministry of Health, or whoever it is, turns nasty – which then has to be dried out again. I am trying to find the simplest process, the sort of process that will only need a gas-ring, a kettle and a couple of biscuit tins. You can count on my getting the solution before the end of the week. Full instructions about times, temperatures, etc., will be supplied.

As for cigarette-making machines, it has occurred to me that it might be best to use something quite small and primitive, worked by hand, that you could employ cheap female labour on. I introduced the topic casually at dinner last night – it was an Otter Hound night – and Dr Parmesan, the neurologist, who was there, said that when he was in Cuba (studying nystagmus among the sugar workers), where everyone makes his own cigarettes, he bought a little machine which turned them out quite nicely, and one could get ready-made tubes with stiff mouth pieces from the tobacco shops, or else roll the papers oneself on a little stick. He said that one forced the tobacco in, instead of folding the paper round the tobacco (which is the usual principle of cigarette rolling machines). This morning I went over to Port Hallows and borrowed it, because he doesn't use it any more. You see, in Cuba one smokes loose fairly dry tobacco, not long shredded moist tobacco like the English sort; and he doesn't find it practical in England because when one rams English tobacco into the tube the ramming makes it cake too hard in the cigarette. However, I took the thing home and this afternoon I've been experimenting with it. It consists of a small metal cylinder, jointed longitudinally, which you open and lay the tobacco in, then close up again and slip a catch over to keep it firm. Then you insert one end of the cylinder into the paper tube and push the tobacco down the cylinder into the tube with a metal ramrod.

The problem is how to prevent caking. Probably the solution is not to have the tobacco too moist, and after laying it in the cylinder to press it down flat with the side of the ramrod. It still cakes slightly but not so much, and one can ease it up the tube with a twiddle of one's fingers. I also tried mixing dry cigar tobacco with the stub tobacco to make it cake less – I broke up a Havana cigar of father's – and the result was quite good. Couldn't you get damaged cigars cheap, to mix in with the stubs? I am sending the little machine; you'll undoubtedly be able to get duplicates in London. I was slow at first at the job of making cigarettes this way, but I calculate that after a steady week at it a moderately capable woman could make one hundred and fifty to two hundred an hour, rising to three hundred after a month or two. I am now working out what is technically called the 'occupational usus' of the machine: the quickest, most energy-saving way of manipulating it, every movement worked out so that the whole sequence is a perfectly rhythmic process, as natural as breathing and eventually, of course, done in time with the worker's breathing. What takes longest to learn is how to grab the exact amount, no more and no less, of tobacco required to fill a single tube. And how to hold the clip ready, in the little finger of the left hand, while busy with the cylinder, the tobacco, and the ramrod. I have worked out a nice movement of the fingers for laying the tobacco evenly, just flush with the top of the cylinder.

You will have to get the cigarette tubes ready-made. The diameter of the tubes should be .95 cm. I suggest that you get plain tubes with mouthpieces and then insert in the mouthpiece of each a pellet of the special cotton-wool which I am at present experimenting with. I must now dress for dinner and shall write again tomorrow. Keep me in touch with your end of the business. How will you ensure a regular supply of stubs? How will you put the cigarette on the market?

I am delighted to hear that you are getting on so well with 'The Squire' in your barber-shop sketch. Since you asked me, I turned the dictaphone on under the table at the Otter Hound dinner, as soon as we ladies rose and went old-fashionedly away, leaving the gentlemen to their port. I have just tried the record out. Most of it is too obscene for your purpose, probably, but I think there are a few good Edwardian sequences that the Squire will be able to employ without getting you into trouble with the Lord Ch.

Yours always,
Edith

Jane's part of the business was to get hold of the raw materials as cheaply as possible; to rent a dry basement and engage four handy girls to work in it; and to build up a trade connexion with small tobacco shops, public-houses and coffee-stalls in the poorest part of London. To be brief; she leased a basement in a street off the Edgware Road and engaged four girls to learn the trade, paying them twenty-two shillings a week as a minimum and then raising this to thirty as they grew expert. She bought the stubs from the cleaners at seven big West end cinemas, paying a pound-note for every twenty pounds' weight of stubs. She used to explain that she was collecting them for export to Russia. She employed one woman in a separate establishment, paying her thirty-five shillings a week, to sort the stubs, cut off the blackened ends with a clipper and strip away the paper. The tobacco was then teased out into a loose heap and conditioned according to Edith's formula. Jane herself brought the finished product along to the filling factory. She did not wish the filling girls to know that it was made of stubs: she told them that it was salvage from a warehouse fire. This was also the story she told to the retailers to whom she sold the finished product; she had to account somehow for the low price at which she offered it – threepence halfpenny for a packet of ten. It went very well indeed, for Jane gave the retailers a commission of three farthings a packet, which was high, and these Resurrections were quite a good smoke if you did not know what they really were. Jane put in the broken cigar tobacco as Edith advised: she could buy it cheap, as it was an almost useless by-product of the tobacco trade now that there was so little demand for it from snuff-takers: they used once to buy it and grind it down into snuff. The mouthpieces were popular: with a mouthpiece one can smoke a cigarette down to the last crumb of tobacco, and that means a lot to needy smokers. The cellophane was a great recommendation too: any product wrapped in cellophane looks completely hygienic, however insanitary the conditions under which it was manufactured, however dirty the fingers that did the wrapping. The girls soon grew very quick at filling the tubes, working up to two thousand a day each.

It may be interesting to give an account of sales and a rough summary of expenses in August, 1927, the third month of Jane's venture, when she had taken on several new hands, improved the occupational usus, engaged a capable sales-agent, extended her sources of supply and moved into larger premises. The tubes had 'Folly's Havana Resurrections' printed on them in gold and were of quite good paper.

EXPENSES

	£	s.	d.
Wages, insurance, etc.	70	0	0
Agent's commission on sales	18	0	0
Rent, light, rates, etc.	18	0	0
Tobacco, stub and cigar	91	0	0
Paper tubes, wadding	32	0	0
Conditioning	10	0	0
Cellophaning	44	0	0
Delivery	27	0	0
Incidentals	7	0	0
	£317	0	0

TAKINGS

From 48 thousand packets of 10 cigarettes,
at 3½d. a packet, less retailers' commission
at ¾d. a packet   £550   0   0

Net profit   £233   0   0

By the sixth month her expenses had risen to £460, but the
net profit was £346; she now had a capable forewoman
and two excellent sales-agents. The business was practically
running itself. By the end of the year she had coaxed sales up
to £800 a month, which gave £473 net profit, and then she
sold out. The price was £9,000, which was not high considering
the volume of business and the possibility of its extension to
the provinces, but Jane had a feeling that, if she did not get
out, somebody would soon prosecute her under the Adulter-
ated Tobacco and Foodstuffs Act or whatever it was; or that
the Tobacco Trust would find her a nuisance and push her off
the market. Nobody had discovered her secret yet, because she
continued to be the only link between the stub stripping and
conditioning department and the filling department. But any
day it might get out and that would be the end of Folly's
Havana Resurrections. It may be asked how it was that, since
every wholesale tobacco transaction had to be reported and is
officially recorded, and Government excise and licensing
officials are so hot on infringements and evasions of the Tobacco
Regulations, Jane managed to get away with it for so long.

But 'The Government doesn't aim at controlling *everything*,' as a friendly ex-excise inspector had once told Jane over a free bottle of whisky. It was just a matter of neat book-keeping, and knowing how to keep quiet. And luck. Jane had for once to admit the element of luck into an undertaking of hers – perhaps because it was an undertaking that she didn't feel very personal about. Luck (we may say fancifully) felt itself honoured, and proved a loyal partner. And there was no law, so far as Jane's legal adviser could discover, against making new cigarettes out of old ones, *per se*, always supposing that the original cigarettes had already paid duty. But it is best to indulge us in this part of the story and ask no further questions.

The buyer took over the policy of the business together with the stock, staff, premises and good-will, and did very well out of it, setting up branches in Liverpool, Manchester and Glasgow, clearing double what he paid Jane before he sold out to another buyer four years later. The third buyer tried to increase profits by using old cigar butts, instead of clean broken cigar leaf, and did not condition the tobacco properly either. His failure to be as discreet as Jane got him into great trouble. Fortunately Jane's name was not mentioned in Court, only the name of the second proprietor. The case had just been heard at the time that Jane and Oliver met in the gallery, and Oliver spoke without the slightest knowledge that Jane had ever had anything to do with the business, so discreet had she been.

CHAPTER 7

EDITH AND EDNA

JANE used to say that it was a mistake, in telling a story, to tell too much at a time. One should follow a single theme as far as it takes one, and only when it begins to get entangled with a second theme should one leave it to bring the second theme up to date. Jane's chief criticism of Oliver's first two novels (foreign travel and Riviera life) when she had read them in typescript – and they never went any further than that – was that he got all his characters too soon off the mark. She told him that he should introduce them one by one, not throw a great dinner party on the first page and expect the reader immediately to master the identity of everyone present and pigeonhole all the various scraps of conversation for future reference; especially when on this or that nuance, belike, the fate of the story would turn.

Oliver said stiffly, 'An author has a right to expect perfect attention from his readers.'

Jane replied, 'A reader has a perfect right to shut up the book and say, "I can't be bothered".'

Oliver said, 'I don't write for that sort of reader and I don't encourage him to read my books.'

Jane asked, 'Oh, indeed, and whom do you envisage as your public?'

'The intelligent man or woman.'

'You mean to say that you think your novels are contributions to literature?'

'I intend them to be. I don't write them merely for money.'

'That explains things. A writer has to make up his mind in which of three ways he is writing: there are only three ways. The first way is to give the public what it wants, just as it wants it – the method of the popular entertainer. Then there is the way of writing without any consideration for the taste of the public; and not complaining if the public is ungrateful. That, speaking as a public entertainer, I must call the method of the eccentric. I admire the conscientious eccentric as much as

I do the conscientious popular entertainer: I like to see things published occasionally that are completely unreadable. But you, Oliver Price, are the third sort of writer, the sort that tries to feed the public what he thinks the public will think it ought to like because it's just a little superior. You're the sort that says, "I don't write merely for money," meaning, really, "I don't want to choose between being either famous in the present or else famous in the future. I want it both ways." For which, Brother, both the intellectual reader and the ordinary vulgar reader will unanimously despise you.'

This was in 1929, just before Jane went to America. We have now followed the Jane and Oliver theme to a point of familiarity, and can go back to become better acquainted with Edith and her twin, Edna. Except for Edith's wearing glasses, and being slower in her movements, and stuttering, they were as like one another, superficially, as twins are expected to be. But they seemed to have little in common, either mentally or emotionally. Edna was not interested in science, only in sport: at the age of sixteen she took charge of the Otter Hound kennels and acted as whip. She won the Ladies' Gold Medal at St Aidan's three years in succession, played a superior game of tennis and used to race at Brooklands. Everyone was in love with Edna, but few dared to propose to her, because of her goddess-like attainments. Oliver fell under her spell, and was profoundly wretched about it. As a tennis and golf player he was not in Edna's class. He followed hounds religiously because of her, but without any instinct for otters. He had no accomplishment to set against her Brooklands triumph; he would have taken up flying, but he was ham-handed and a bad mechanic and, anyhow, could not afford a plane. However, Edna was always very nice to him, as she was to everyone, so he did not lose hope. Because Edna read a good deal in her spare time, Oliver determined to be a successful novelist and attract her attention to himself that way. Jane guessed Oliver's secret and told Edith about it in confidence.

The story now becomes complicated. For Edith, stupid girl, had allowed herself to fall in love with Oliver. Jane was not so bright as usual: she did not realize that when Edith looked unhappy at the news she was not merely expressing sympathy for Oliver as having been made wretched by a member of her family, and deploring this as a possible cloud over her friendship with Jane. It is always difficult for a girl like Jane, who knows a brother's shortcomings only too well and is not sentimentally inclined herself, to realize that her otherwise level-headed and reliable girl-friend can have gone all soft about the fellow. What Edith told Jane was that she was sorry for Oliver, because she knew that Edna was determined to marry someone really famous and really rich. 'And I feel responsible in a way,' Edith said, 'for Edna. I mean, I'm her twin, and I can't bear all the havoc she causes in young men's hearts. I wish she'd hurry up and get married. Poor Oliver, will he ever get over it?'

At last Edna married, and the lucky man, Freddy Smith, an ex-rowing blue, whom Oliver knew at Oxford, was neither particularly rich not particularly famous. His cachet was being a big-game hunter: he had once killed two elephants with a right and left. He danced badly, ran a stud farm somewhere in Wiltshire, and was a second cousin. Oliver was properly disgusted. He tore up Edna's photograph and seriously thought of destroying some love poems he had written about her.

This had happened just before his parents' death and his quarrel with Jane, and Jane had written him a letter about it. She had tried to cheer him up by saying that Edna had deliberately chosen the dullest man of her acquaintance to marry: she had suddenly gone Victorian in the super-fashionable modern style and was planning to settle down in a red-brick farm and have lots and lots of healthy, strong, stupid, respectful children who would call her 'Madam' and their father 'Sir' and sew samplers, spin tops, tie kettles to the tails of cats, and read *The Pilgrim's Progress* and *Josephus* on Sunday afternoons, sitting in a row on the horsehair sofa in the best parlour. 'I think you can congratulate yourself on not having become Edna's mate. Victorianism is not really a joke: it gets you.'

So far, so good. But then there came the quarrel. And Oliver, who had a great desire to marry and have a son, began to look around for a suitable mother for him. This was not a Victorianism, but (according at least to the Parmesan school of thought) a sign of a well-known pathological condition: he wished to be a person of importance! At Charchester, it will be remembered, he had never quite been a blood, at Oxford he had just missed a First in Classics and a half-blue at golf; and the tutoring jobs that he had taken on since, while giving him free travel abroad, a luxurious existence, and the acquaintance of rich and prominent people, had not done much to increase his self-esteem. He had written those two novels about Riviera life and 'scrapped them both and was not so sure whether his third, now half-finished, would turn out to be quite the masterpiece he intended. As the head of a family he could, however, surround himself with an atmosphere of local but very real importance, especially if he married a girl with money, and so became free of the humiliation of having to eke out his living by occasional tutorship. Unfortunately, he could not find the right girl. If she had both money and looks she aimed higher than a mere tutor, even though he might be a good sportsman, an Oxford graduate, the grandson of a Marquess and a promising novelist. But it took a lot to discourage Oliver. He proposed no less than four times between 1929 and 1934.

At St Aidan's, in 1925, while his passion for Edna was still young, Oliver happened one day to be going for a walk in the sand-dunes. He had a cold, otherwise he would have been bathing with Jane, Edna and Edith. But he thought it best just to go for a walk. They were all in the water when he arrived at the hollow between two dunes where they had been undressing. Suddenly a violent breeze sprang up and blew sand into his face, temporarily blinding him. He turned his back to the wind and walked away in the direction of home. Something white went flapping along at his feet. He grabbed at it, and after removing the sand from his eyes, which were watering painfully, looked to see what it was. It was a sixpenny notebook. On the left page were a number of diagrams and mathematical jottings, on the right were notes, which he naturally expected to refer to the diagrams. But they did not. They proved to be a sentimental diary.

SUNDAY THE THIRTEENTH

Saw O. in church. I have quite a good view of him from our pew, but can't get him in full profile unless he happens to move his head. However, if his pew were in line with ours, I'd always be tempted to turn round and steal peeps in his direction, and then someone would be sure to notice.

It would be difficult to excuse Oliver for going on, and reading the Monday entry. The first three lines of Sunday should have been enough to tell him that this was something very private, and that it was dishonourable to read another word. The best case that can be made out for him is that he had a cold, and his eyes were hurting. Morality is with many people a matter of being in good health and in full possession of their faculties. Some slight physical incapacity or disorder, and at once they slip into error and even into infamy. Ask any morbid psychologist – Dr Parmesan for example – and he will confirm this with a thousand instances. It may be further suggested that he thought, perhaps, that it was Edna's diary not Edith's (they both wrote in a round, bold hand); and nobody would blame a lover for taking advantage of a windy accident to discover what the girl he loved really felt for him. But that plea cannot be allowed. If Oliver originally began reading the notes under the impression that they referred to the diagrams, then he must have known that it was not Edna's but Edith's note-book. It may, of course, have been that he hoped to come across some side reference to Edna's feelings for him. If this was so, he was sufficiently punished for his curiosity.

MONDAY THE FOURTEENTH

Have been so tempted to tell J. about it, but I don't think she'd sympathize, and anyhow what good would it do? If he's in love with E., as Jane swears he is, I obviously mustn't complicate things for him or for J. Lucky, lucky E. When E. talks about him in that patronizing way of hers it makes my blood boil. Thank God that I can get on with my work in the shop and shut it all out of my mind most of the day. The nights are the worst.

He took the book back to where the girls' things were lying, peeped over the dune to make sure that they were still in the water and had not seen him, and then walked rapidly away. Naturally, he told nobody about the incident and tried to forget it honourably. But he could not help behaving in a

rather embarrassed way with Edith when next they met, and
cultivating a rather fine consciously charming style with her –
the sort of manner that a fox-hunting squire jogging along in
hunting pink to a meet might show to a poor female relation
pedalling alongside on a bicycle. But if Edith knew that he was
in love with Edna, Edna must know too. Hence her queenly
off-hand style. Edith on an old push bike, he on a fine horse, but
Edna at the wheel of a supercharged sports car going by him
like the wind. Dust and the fumes of her exhaust and his
horse bucking under him. Couldn't he make some sort of use
of Edith's feelings for him? If he pretended to be in love with
Edith, would Edna be jealous? No, Edna would just laugh.
Besides, Edith was such a friend of Jane's. It wasn't safe to
use Edith as a tactical convenience.

Jane noticed his changed manner with Edith, and taxed
him with it, in front of their mother too. 'You did show off
this afternoon, Oliver,' she said. 'Anyone would think that
you were trying to captivate poor Edith's girlish heart.
What's the game?'

He flushed, growled unintelligibly at her, and walked out
of the room. After that he avoided meeting Edith and, if they
did meet, merely took off his hat, smiled faintly and walked
on; and at church was careful not to be so generous with his
profile as before. He had the satisfaction of knowing that
Edith's disappointment and distress would make her very
poor company for Jane.

He told himself that he was sorry for Edith, but after all was
it his fault? He had not asked her to fall in love with him, had
he? Jane had told him to stop being nice to Edith, and Jane
was supposed to be Edith's best friend, so he had taken her at
her word; if Edith was feeling unhappy, that was Jane's look-
out. And he played his hand very well.

Edna met him alone in a secluded lane one day. 'Oliver,' she
said, 'I have reason to suspect that you are in love with me.'

He did not know what to answer. He was trying to make a
fitting declaration when she cut him short. 'In that case, what
I have to say will make sense to you. It's about Edith. I have
also reason to suspect that she's in love with you. She doesn't
know that I know. And I think that she's kept her infatuation

for you concealed from Jane. I accidentally happened to read
a few words in a diary she keeps. Someone called O is suddenly
being very stand-offish to her and she is miserable about it, and
wonders whether you have been hearing any scandal about her,
or something. Have you?'

'N-no,' said Oliver, thoroughly uncomfortable.

'Well, I want to find out just why you are playing the cad.'

'I'm *not* playing the cad! It's only that I suddenly felt that
she was in love with me, and I wanted to make it quite clear
that I wasn't in love with her. Of course, I think she's a very
nice person, and all that!'

Edna made a few thoughtful strikes, forehand and backhand,
with the tennis racquet she was carrying. 'Well,' she said slowly,
'I think you're a great fool, Oliver, to behave like this. After all,
Edith and I are twins and she's been a damned good friend to
me. It means, of course, that I shall have to retaliate. Next time
we meet I cut you dead. To make it quite clear that *I'm* not in
love with you.'

Oliver shouted indignantly: 'I think it was extremely cad-
dish of you, if you ask *me*, to take advantage of information that
you got by reading someone's private diary. You say you read
a few words accidentally, but you seem to have read at least a
couple of paragraphs.'

Edna nodded indulgently: 'Yes, the eye does slip down the
page quickly, doesn't it, when one's interested?'

Oliver said, 'If you try any retaliations on me, Edna, I shall
tell Edith that you have been reading her diary and that you
told me what she felt about me. It will please her, won't it?'

Edna's eyes narrowed. 'That would be a nice honourable
public school thing to do, wouldn't it?'

Oliver grew bold. 'It's all your fault. I'm in love with you
and have been for years and you don't give a hoot for me, and
now I'm supposed to be awfully pleased and honoured because
Edith keeps a sentimental diary about me. I keep one about
you, if you'd like to know.'

'I know already. That's why I have been as nice to you as
I have. I thought it was sweet of you to keep a diary about me.
I'm a decent sort of person. I don't behave as you do to Edith
in just the same circumstances.'

'How do you know I keep a diary? You're bluffing.'

'Who wrote, for whom, and on what occasion, the following lines:

> To thee, when to the socket burns
> The candle, nightly my heart turns.
> Those dear proud hands, and dear proud eyes . . .?

By the way, haven't you electric light upstairs at the Vicarage?'

'My God, has Jane been at my diary? I'll absolutely kill that woman!'

'Everyone reads people's diaries when they are left lying about. Human nature. Now, Oliver, be sensible. It was quite a nice poem, candle and all, and I won't mind you being in love with me if you behave decently to Edith again. Just decently. I don't expect you to transfer your passion from me to her . . .'

'That's nice of you,' Oliver cut in bitterly.

'But don't be so utterly selfish, or the whole thing is going to end very unpleasantly for all of us. I forbid you to let Jane know that you know that I know that she's been reading your diary. That was a confidence and I shouldn't have broken it. But behave decently, and I'll be as nice to you as I can.'

Oliver said, 'All right, it's a bargain. Give me a round of golf this afternoon, and let me come to tennis on Wednesday. And . . . and . . .'

'And what else?'

'And may I kiss you now?'

'If I do let you, you'll have to be exceptionally nice to Edith.'

'I will. I swear I will. I'll even let her kiss me if she asks.'

So the bargain was sealed. Oliver, in the vain hope of another kiss from Edna, behaved very nicely to Edith, though not too nicely. Edith continued to be in love with him, and Jane was unaware of the complicated drama that was going on about her. Edith was apparently so wholly wedded to science, and Oliver so obviously a boor and clown that the very suggestion that Edith could fall in love with him would have seemed farcical. Jane had a theory that the test of good stage farce was its impossibility in real life. This theory blinded her to the fact that in real life impossible situations do occur. As when early in the afternoon of September 19th, 1934, Oliver, emerging from the picture gallery full of rage against Jane, happened to see someone going up the steps of the house opposite, recognized Edith and took a sudden resolution.

CHAPTER 8

PHILATELY AND DIDYMOLOGY

JANE arrived at Albion Mansions on Thursday, September 27th, not at four o'clock, as she had arranged, but at half-past three. She did this partly because, if Oliver had decided not to be at home that afternoon, he would be likely to hang on as long as possible so as to avoid the feeling that she had entirely spoilt his afternoon's writing for him. (Oliver used to boast that he did his best work between lunch and tea.) In that case she ought to catch him just coming out. But, if he had decided to be there, by arriving before the proper time, she would take him off his guard. She might even catch him at some last-minute tampering with the stamp album – removing whole pages of stamps, for instance. She told her chauffeur to drop her at the corner. If she wasn't back by a quarter past four, he could go away and she would come home by taxi.

The lift was out of order, but Jane did not mind stairs. She only paused at the sixth storey, and then not for breath but because she heard Oliver's voice through the open door of a flat called 'Mr Algernon Hoyland'. Mr Hoyland was introducing Oliver to some name she did not catch (and which is immaterial to the story) and apparently thought that Oliver and the other fellow would be glad to meet each other, because, he said, they were both interested in modern drama. Jane listened for a few moments more, just to satisfy herself that Oliver was settled there for a bit, and then went softly upstairs.

Good, Oliver had left his door open and, better still, all his keys, in a bunch, were hanging from a latchkey in the lock. People who live on the seventh storey of mansions where the lift is out of order are inclined to be careless. She went straight in, and immediately began looking for the bathroom and a soft cake of soap. But before she identified the bathroom she found something that suited her purpose even better – several packets of chewing gum on his bedside table. She was soon chewing hard and, just as a neighbouring clock began striking the third quarter, she finished her task of taking impressions of all Oliver's keys. She then put the moulds in cold water in the bathroom washbasin to harden them, and made a rapid survey of the living-room.

On the table lay a paper bag of biscuits, a small pot of cream and a carton container with cakes from a local tea-shop. So Oliver had decided to be hospitable, had he? Now why? And there on the sofa, where he had apparently been studying it, was the stamp-album. She picked it up. 'Oliver with love from Mother, Christmas 1918.' She hurriedly turned over the pages. No tricky work, apparently. Odd. It wasn't like Oliver to yield the battlefield to her without a struggle. Perhaps he would try to negotiate; he might even suggest some agreement about the heirlooms on condition that he should keep the stamps. After all, the heirlooms were of no use to him: he was too much of a coward either to sell them or display them.

On the sofa, too, was her recent note to him. She seized it and put it safely away in her handbag. There was nothing remarkable about this perfectly rational action, was there? Yet Dr Parmesan, the neurologist, etc., was professionally delighted a few days later when he caught her similarly sneaking an old letter from herself to him out of the letter rack on his consulting-room desk. He pronounced it to be a highly significant atavistic impulse, and quoted the anxiety felt by the savage inhabitants of some Melanesian island, lest they have by chance left a few hairs, the paring of a finger-nail, or the fragment of a pubic leaf lying about: they fear that someone may find this 'dirt' and use it to make magic against them. Atavistic fiddlesticks! Nobody liked to see an old letter signed by herself hoarded by the addressee after it has outlived its immediate purpose of conveying a message: and Jane did not trust Dr Parmesan more than any other witch doctor. Besides, in the case of this note to Oliver, it would, as it turned out, have been very dangerous to have left it with him: it would undoubtedly have figured in a later chapter, and embarrassed Jane considerably there. The remarks about lawyers and judges, we mean.

On the side table were two books. One had a piece of blotting paper as a marker and the other a packet of chewing gum. Odd again. He had, by the look of things, been reading when he had been called downstairs. But instead of leaving the books open – both the windows were closed, so there was no danger of the pages blowing over in a draught and his place getting lost – he had closed them guiltily with the first objects that came to hand. More chewing gum. Must be trying to stop smoking by the chewing method. Naturally she looked to see what the books were. One was *Studies in Didymology* by John Sinclair, M.D., and the other was *Sex and Inheritance in Human Beings*, a translation of some thumping German work. Nine hundred closely printed pages. Jane did not have time to do more than skim a few lines of each book at the places marked, and took in little. But both seemed to be about the occurrency of twins. In the German book she noticed that the words 'identical twin' were constantly repeated; they struck her as a rather silly expression. A mistranslation perhaps. If two twins prove to be identical, then there is only really one of them. But if there are really two, then they are not identical. Quite. She heard Oliver saying good-bye on the landing downstairs, quickly returned to the bathroom to rescue her moulds from the basin, wrapped them in a spare handkerchief and put them safely away at the bottom of her handbag. When Oliver turned up, followed by Kate, his bulldog bitch, she was back in the sitting-room, looking out of the window.

She greeted him. 'Hope you don't mind, I've been washing my hands in your bathroom.'

'How long have you been here?' he asked suspiciously.

'Just arrived this second.'

'Oh, good! Pretty punctual, aren't you? I was borrowing a teapot from the man below me. Then a friend turned up and I had to be polite. Glad you didn't have to wait long, and sorry the lift isn't functioning, and all that. Tea now. I won't be a second. Meet Kate. Nice girl – too nice, in fact. Chums up with anyone in trousers. Courteous to women. Dotes on children.'

While he was boiling the kettle and arranging the cakes and biscuits on plates with elaborately hospitable gestures, Jane asked him: 'What's Did . . . Didymology, Oliver? It's a new one on me.'

He spilt some biscuits on the floor and answered indistinctly, as he stooped to pick them up: 'Oh, that? That's a book I got to look up something in a thing I'm writing.'

'No answer to my question.'

'Well, you know that St Thomas was called "Didymus", don't you? It's in the Bible. . . . Well, "Didymus" means "twin" – it's Greek for "twin".'

'I don't follow.'

'A novel I'm writing. About a fellow who's a twin and there's a doubt as to whether he or his brother is born first; and that's important because there's a title that goes to the one who . . .'

'So you bought *Studies in Didymology*, and *Sex and Inheritance in Human Beings*, to boot, in order to find out?'

'I wanted a general grasp of the subject of twins.'

'Thorough, very thorough,' said Jane, mentally noting valuable Slingsbyisms, and let the matter pass.

Oliver made the tea and poured it out. 'Are you ready with your tweezers, Jane?' he asked in forced friendliness, and then: 'Cream? Sugar?'

Jane produced the tweezers. 'Eyebrow tweezers really, but they'll do. No, no cream and no sugar, thank you. Sorry!'

'Right, let's get to work!'

'That's the spirit. Shove over the album! I think the best way will be for me to put a mark against the ones I choose, and you to do the same, and then at the end of every page I'll take mine out and put them in an envelope. I've got envelopes.'

'As you please.'

'I bet you've been looking at the catalogue steadily for the last two days to see which are the most valuable.'

'Yes, why not? But I won't offer to lend it you. It would delay us too long.'

'That's all right. I think I remember the ones you used to be most proud about. Come on – you can have first choice.'

So they started at Great Britain. Oliver put an *O* against the 1884 £1 brown-lilac and Jane a *J* against the 1887 £1 green, and then Oliver chose the 2d. blue 1840, and Jane the 1d. black, and so on down the page. They finished Great Britain and turned over to Antigua. It was Jane's turn.

She said, 'Antigua! Hullo, Oliver, where's that Antigua stamp on the envelope?'

'Which stamp on what envelope?'

'The one I got from Edith and sent you at Charchester.'

Oliver assumed a puzzled look. 'I *do* remember vaguely. It must have slipped out. It wasn't gummed in, you see.'

'Are you telling the truth?'

'If you start cross-examining me in that offensive way I'll shut up the album and heave you out of the room. I've been too damned nice to you as it is.'

That guilty glare: perfect. And the inept slap of the thigh. And then reaching for a cigarette, and remembering (evidently) that he had decided to stop smoking, and chumping chewing gum instead. Slingsby, you'll be a better man for all this.

What she said was: 'All right, I was only asking. But that's my choice. Go on.' She purposely missed a turn. Oliver was so keen on an Antigua 1s. mauve, unused, 1884, that he did not notice it.

It was six o'clock before they reached Venezuela, the last South American country, and Jane rose to say good-bye. There had been a slight incident among the Spanish Colonies. Jane noticed that the pair of unused Puerto Rico 5-centimos stamps, with the head of King Alfonso as a child on them, had become separated. 'Talking of didymology,' she said, 'how did these twins get separated?'

He tried to bluff. 'You separated them yourself,' he scoffed. 'Don't you remember the row we had about them at St Aidan's? That was the unfortunate incident that prompted my offer to share the album with you.'

'Yes, I remember the row, but those were Newfoundlands.'

'No, they weren't. They were Puerto Rico.'

'Newfoundland five-cents.'

'Puerto Rico, five-centimos.'

'Newfoundland.'

Oliver said: 'Answer me this: would it be like *me* to separate a rare pair of stamps?'

Jane said pacifically: 'There's something in that.' But her suspicions were thoroughly aroused now. Oliver was playing some sort of trick on her, she couldn't quite decide what. For the present she pretended to believe him. She turned the subject: 'What's the title of your novel?'

'I'm not quite sure. It's a historical novel which centres in the Diet of Worms. Interesting period. Probably I'll call it "The Diet Decides".'

'Ambiguous. Sounds like a study in the effect of starchy foods on –'

'Or . . . perhaps something with "Worms" in.'

'I know, teacher! Apples! But how do the twins come into the Diet?'

The apple joke was neatly calculated to his rudimentary sense of humour. If he had made it himself he would have roared with laughter and stored it up in his memory as one of the few occasions when he had really been on the spot. But as it was Jane's joke, and Jane was his enemy, a strained look came into his face, the look of a man with a grudge fighting against his own sense of humour. 'The twins have nothing to do with the Diet,' he pronounced.

'Oh, haven't they? Poor little blighters!'

Oliver somehow found this dreadfully funny too, and exploded into a loud crowing laugh; then remembered himself, tried to turn it into a cough, blushed, and said gruffly: 'We're wasting time. Let's go on.'

Jane tried (on Slingsby's behalf) to draw him out on the subject of novel-writing – how he got inspiration, whether he planned ahead to the end of the story or just let things happen naturally; and why he preferred writing in green ink – she had noticed green stains on a piece of blotting paper. But he was guarded in his replies, and when she went away shepherded her carefully out of the room, standing between her and the side-table as if to prevent her from touching the Twin books.

At the door Jane paused. 'Well, good-bye, Oliver, and thank you for a nice tea. You've not sprinkled arsenic on the cakes, have you? Or dropped strychnine in my teacup? I didn't expect you to give up those stamps so easily. An obscure tactical move, perhaps? There's something, isn't there? Own up! I know that sheepish guilty grin . . .'

He slammed the door in her face.

Jane's intention had been to return the stamps to Oliver, if he behaved decently about them: she didn't really want the things. But the slammed door decided her against any such gesture; and when she arrived home she examined the stamps carefully. There was something wrong about them. What? The Puerto Ricos for a start. Why separated? And now she remembered that the Edward VII 1s. stamp had originally come off a sheet of brown paper in a trunk in the Vicarage attic; and it used to have a very ugly blurred postmark on it. Now it was much paler and was lightly postmarked *Hull*. And the French 10-centimes of Napoleon III ought to have a slight tear at the left-hand bottom corner, but instead it had a slight tear at the top. She pondered for a few minutes and then called her secretary.

'Miss Hapless, I want you to do me a favour.'

'Yes, Miss Palfrey.'

'Secure a London Trades Directory and look up the principal stamp dealers. I believe there are some firms that have stamp auctions at regular intervals. Those are the ones I want. Then write as follows, to each in turn: "Dear Sirs, I am a specialist in the stamps of Antigua and should be obliged to hear from you whenever you have any outstanding philatelic rarity of that country for sale." Sign it, "M. Hapless". You don't mind doing that, do you?'

'Not at all, Miss Palfrey. My brother used to collect stamps once and I used to help him. I remember he had a pretty pinky-red unused Antigua stamp, with Queen Victoria as a girl on it. It was my favourite of the whole collection.'

'Excellent. By the way, what happened between you and your brother over that album?'

Miss Hapless grinned a little. 'As a matter of fact, he lost his temper with me one day for making a mistake. He pulled my hair.'

'The brute. And you?'

'I bit him in the leg.'

'Wrong tactics. Frontal assaults are tempting, I admit, but the indirect approach is what wins wars.'

'I don't understand, Miss Palfrey.'

'Well, the correct move would have been to draw off to a

flank and buy him a three-and-sixpenny packet of fifty Central
Americans, present him with it, and then run upstairs to the
linen-room in tears. The military decision would have been
reached in the linen-room.'

'I'm afraid I wasn't much good, as a kid, at turning the other
cheek. In fact,' Miss Hapless admitted shyly, 'I never enjoyed
anything so much in the whole of my childhood as the feeling
of my teeth well fixed in my brother's leg. But we were the best
of friends after that.'

The above conversation has been recorded to forestall the
foolish objection that there are no nice, natural, straight-
forward characters in these pages. Those who raise the objection will only mean, of course, that they don't like the resolute
cunning way in which Jane pursued a quarrel; and that they
are cheated of a natural sympathy for Oliver because he was
such a swine too. Here then, we offer them Miss Hapless.
What's amiss with her? Miss Hapless behaved as naturally and
straightforwardly as anyone could wish; but what's her story
worth? Nothing. Examine it: stamp-album, quarrel, hair
pulled, leg bitten, best of friends ever afterwards. Nothing.
Yet we are pleased to incorporate it as the didymous dermoid
growth in the main body of this fully developed story, just to
show that we are not prejudiced.

That night at supper after the show Jane told Edith:
'I've collected a lot of excellent new Slingsbyisms this
afternoon.'

Edith asked, 'Where?'

'Oh, I happened to meet an accidental Slingsby type at tea
and he turned the stuff out for me like a dictaphone. I noted
down five or six sequences. For instance. . . . But first you must
make a joke: it's part of the gag.'

'Me? I . . . I never made a joke in my life.'

'Well, say something mathematical or scientific and I'll
pretend it's a joke and then, when I answer with a Slingsbyism,
you say: "Oh, haven't they? Poor little blighters!" Got that
straight?'

'Yes, but I don't see . . . Would a multiplication table do?'

'Yes, or a bit of poetry even. The first thing that occurs.'
Edith said:

And yet no force however great,
Can stretch a cord, however fine,
Into a horizontal line
That shall be absolutely straight.

Jane twitched her mouth convulsively, swelled her neck muscles, frowned, glared, and said in an uncanny imitation of Oliver's voice, 'The twins have nothing to do with the Diet.'

Edith gagged gravely: 'Oh, haven't they? Why not?'

Jane uttered a frightening bass noise that ended in a squeal, squirmed, choked, recovered and finally said: 'That's that. Like it?'

'It's awful. What is it?'

'Only a Slingsby hearing a joke that isn't his own.'

'I do wish you wouldn't do sudden things.'

'Yes, it's pretty horrible, isn't it? But I'll give you a worse one – a Slingsby making love. Based on deduction only, mind. Like gauging the volume of a man's affections by the ratio of the height of his instep to the length of his shoe. But don't let me confuse you. Here goes!'

Jane got up from her chair, lurched towards Edith with compressed lips and hands clasped under chin (a trick that Slingsby had long ago borrowed from Oliver), then, with eyes intently fixed on Edith's, suddenly gripped her shoulders and barked: 'Do you hear, Edith! You know you want me – you always have. And now I want you! Silly one, you can't pretend that you're calm. You can't not want me to Embrace You.'

Edith burst into tears, screamed and ran out of the room.

Jane ran after her. 'Oh, Edith, I'm so sorry I frightened you. It was only supposed to be one of those ridiculous Slingsbys, anyhow.'

Edith dived into the bathroom next door and banged the door after her. She gasped through the keyhole: 'I hate you, I hate you, I hate you! N-*nothing*'s s-sacred to you.'

Jane felt very bad about it, but thought it best to leave Edith alone to bathe her eyes and recover. She went to look for Mrs Trent. 'Oh, Gwennie dear, what have I done? Without thinking much about it, I tried out a Slingsby gag on Edith and she rushed away, and now she's shouting that she hates me.'

'What sort of gag, my dear?'

T—D

'Only a Slingsby in love.'

'Oh, Miss Jane, you couldn't have chosen a worse subject.'

'Why, Gwennie?'

'Because Miss Edith has been acting a bit queer for the last few days, haven't you noticed? And if I know the signs . . .'

'Gwennie, you don't say so! But whoever can the man be? It's not one of the company, it it? That would be too grotesque. *Do* tell me, Gwennie, that it's not our Slingsby.'

'No, I'm sure it's not. But do you realize that she's twice been out to lunch and once to tea with those Stefansson friends of hers?'

'Who? Those scientific people in South Kensington? Yes, I think she said something about some short-wave experiments that Dr Stefansson was making. I didn't pay much attention. But he's married and *not* very attractive.'

Mrs Trent said slowly, 'She's not been herself, really, since two Mondays ago, the day Mr Oliver had that chat with her.'

'*What*! Oliver had a chat with Edith? How? What about? Why didn't you tell me before?' Jane started shaking Mrs Trent in exasperation.

'Oh, Miss Jane, please don't! Please have patience! I'll tell you. It was on Monday, after you left the picture gallery. Mr Oliver saw me at the window, and waved to me. And then he crossed the street towards the house. I thought at first, "he's coming to see me," and then I thought, "no, he's just crossed the road to buy some cigarettes at the shop next door." He disappears. Half an hour later in he comes for a chat. I have always had a warm corner in my heart for Mr Oliver, you know, my dear. He reminds me so of your father, who was a very kind man in his way, only very childlike. He says that he spotted Miss Edith just coming into the house and caught her on the stairs and took her for a walk in the Park – and would I forgive him and that he's come instead of Miss Edith, who's gone home for her lunch. I say, "Well, I forgive you. But it's a long time since you went out walking with Miss Edith, isn't it?" And he smiles and says: "Yes, Mrs Trent, that's true. The fact is, that I'm writing a novel, and there are scientists in it, and I don't want to get my details of the conversation wrong.

The only person of my acquaintance who's a scientist is Miss Edith. So I've been getting some material from her."'

'Funny sort of novel my brother seems to be writing. Diet of Worms, twin noblemen, and modern scientists. And why didn't you tell me, Gwennie? I thought you and I had no secrets from each other. Edith and Oliver arm in arm in the Park! It would have been the headline of the week.'

'Because he asked me not to, my dear. He said that he didn't want Miss Edith to be embarrassed by your knowing that he's been out walking with her. Thought that you might misunderstand him as trying to speak against you behind your back, when all he wanted was information about the conversation of a couple of scientists.'

'Did you believe him, Gwennie?'

'One never quite believes Mr Oliver, does one, Miss Jane? But I thought no harm of it. So Miss Edith didn't mention his visit to you, neither?'

'She hasn't said a word. And what's more, I'm not going to pump her. Well, what do you make of it? Do you think that she's meeting Oliver at the Stefanssons' every day now – helping him to fill his notebooks with yards and yards of genuine conversation?'

' – Oh, and there was another thing. Yes, that's right about twins. . . . Said he was interested in the subject of twins for his novel. And, by the way, could I give him details about Miss Edith's and Miss Edna's birth?'

'What sort of details?'

'What sort of twins they were.'

'Don't understand. "Two girls" was the correct answer, wasn't it?'

'No, it was more complicated than that, Miss Jane. He wanted to know whether they was "identical twins" – whatever that may be. I told him that the only person who could know was Old Rose, the village midwife at St Aidan's. I happen to be in touch with Old Rose's son, and I told Mr Oliver that I'd get hold of her address and write to ask. And then I'd let him know. He tipped me a pound note "to cover expenses", he said, and it was then that he asked me, "Please, Mrs Trent, you won't tell my sister I've been here, will you?"'

'Gwennie, you old double-crosser! Bought your silence with a pound note, did he? And now you've told, after all.'

'I couldn't hurt his feelings by refusing it, and my first duty is to you, my dear. So none of your teasing. Well, today Old Rose's son comes and tells me that his mother is dead. Died last winter . . .'

'One moment, Gwennie. This sudden interest of Oliver's in twin births may be a clue of the greatest importance. I must find Madame.' She hurried off.

After a time she came back and said to Mrs Trent: 'You still have a warm corner in your heart for Oliver, have you, Gwennie?'

'Yes, Miss Jane.'

'Then slosh buckets of iced water all over it, Gwennie. Oliver's a low-down, stinking, perfectly unspeakable . . . ugh!' Jane was nearly weeping.

'Oh, honey, what's wrong? What has he done? I don't . . .'

'Gwennie, I'll tell you. The bounder is thinking of marrying our sweet innocent Edith. He may even have arranged it already. But Gwennie, take thy pen and sit down quickly and write as follows to the ruffian. Say: "Dear Master Oliver, Old Rose tells me that the two little darlings came wrapped up in the same parcel. She says she can't remember any more about the case, except that they weighed six pounds, two ounces, a-piece. Hoping you are well, etc., etc., Yours respectfully." – Signed'

Mrs Trent stared, but Jane said, 'No, I'm not mad, only very, very upset. Write that letter, dear Gwennie, and ask me no questions. Post it at once. Perhaps Edith isn't lost to us yet.'

Jane wrote a letter herself:

September 28th, 1934

My Dear Oliver,

Nice of you to give up the stamps so willingly, and I shall overlook your final brusquerie which was forgivable after the strain of being quite pleasant for nearly two and a half tortured hours. . . . Perhaps some other day you'll give up Mother's things also. It was too much to expect of you in a single afternoon, so I did not mention them today. By the way, I've just heard a bit of news about an old flame of yours: Edna. She's just this moment telephoned Mrs

Trent. She says she expects a baby in March. Isn't that splendid for her? They had almost given up hope.

Affectionately,

Jane

Edith apologized to Jane, saying that she had been over-working and that she hadn't meant what she said. But all the same, she wished that Jane could invent another male character to take the place of Owen Slingsby. He was the only member of the company that she couldn't get to like. And she didn't think that the audience liked him either.

Jane accepted the apology graciously, but told Edith that Slingsby was as unquestionably the most popular actor they had, as Doris was the most popular actress. 'We'll put it to a straw vote, if you like.'

Edith couldn't bring herself to say that she had at last realized that Slingsby was Oliver; which was what she really meant. So there was an uncomfortable silence. Jane broke in by asking: 'Are you going to the Stefanssons' again today?'

'Yes, why shouldn't I?'

'Why on earth? I only asked.'

Another silence. As Edith evidently was not going to say anything more, Jane went away.

That evening Mrs Trent remarked: 'Something's happened to Miss Edith this afternoon, by the look of her eyes.'

Jane said: 'Poor, foolish Edith! What helpless toys of fate people are when they're in love. Do you know what's hap-pened? Well, I don't either exactly, but I think I can reconstruct it. Oliver was to be there at the Stefanssons', or wherever the rendezvous really is, but he wasn't. And why? Because he's got my letter.'

'What letter?'

'Telling him that Edna was having a baby.'

'*Is* Miss Edna having a baby?'

'Not so far as I know. But I told him so. So he'll send Edith a note regretting his absence and telling her a gallant lie. If I know my Oliver, he's probably told her that he can't marry her after all, because if he did they wouldn't have any children; leaving Edith to suppose things about him.'

Mrs Trent looked so bewildered that Jane took her into her

confidence. She said that when she had consulted Madame Blanche, who understood these things (her fifth personality having assisted at several births in its time), Madame explained that if two children of the same sex arrived 'wrapped up in the same parcel', they were called identical twins; but if they came in separate parcels they were ordinary twins.

'So I asked Madame's fifth personality: "But what's the difference? Are identical twins peculiarly attached to each other? If one had a toothache, does the other feel it? Or what?" And she said: "No, Miss Palfrey, it's not that, though I *have* heard that identicals have an unfortunate habit of falling in love with the same person. It's this: if they're girls, only one of the little darlings can ever hope to become a mother." So *now* you understand it all, Gwennie.'

'I'm beginning to see, Miss Jane. Mr Oliver wants children, and if Miss Edna has a child, then Miss Edith can't hope for one, if she marries. So Mr Oliver's calling it off with Miss Edith.'

'Flawlessly stated, Gwennie, so far. But there's one thing more. Do you know *why* Oliver wants children? Or, more precisely, why Oliver wants a son?'

'Why?'

'He wants a son to bequeath his wretched stamp-album to. I can't think of any other reason. He can't want to perpetuate his features or character, can he?'

CHAPTER 9

THE LETTER TO
BROTHER FREDERICK

A WRETCHED situation developed. Edith went about pale and silent; inefficient, too, in her various theatre duties. If she had been Jane's employee Jane would have sacked her. If she had been Jane's employer Jane would have resigned. But being a partner. . . . And Jane felt guilty, in a way, though she had acted from the most charitable motives in saving her from Oliver. Who would have thought that any self-respecting adult woman could possibly have taken it so hard ? Was it not obvious to Edith that Oliver was a monster ? Or did he fascinate her just because he was a monster, as scientists fall in love with quite revolting phenomena ? She tried to cheer Edith up by indirect means, but it was a heart-breaking task and in the end she got bored and angry.

Then Mrs Trent managed, after several attempts, to coax Edith to tell her what was really wrong with her. Edith wept, but afterwards said she felt much better. Her story was that she had met someone (she did not mention his name) at the Stefanssons' who had fallen in love with her; and she with him. And he had proposed, and she had accepted. And then he had suddenly called it off. He wrote that he had been to a Harley Street doctor to get overhauled, and it appeared that his heart was so bad that he might die at any moment. So he didn't think it fair to keep her to her promise and begged her to forget him. 'But he would always, always treasure her memory for the few more months he might live. And etcetera and etcetera.' Mrs Trent finished indignantly.

'He deserves to be smothered with damp dishcloths. You didn't say anything to Edith, did you ?'

'Nothing about twins or nothing. I only tried to comfort her, and said that doctors often made mistakes and that maybe her young man would get better and propose again.'

'You did wrong, Gwennie. Very, very wrong. You have undone a lot of our work. Now she'll go round torturing herself with faint hopes until Oliver dies – which, the Devil knows, may not be for seventy years or more.'

'What about finding some other young man for her?'

'You mean that a girl who can fall in love with Oliver could surely be made to fall in love with almost anyone? On the face of it, a sound argument. But Edith is fearfully loyal. No, no, Gwennie. He's been too clever for us.'

'Then let's tell her the whole story.'

'Worse. She'd merely get evidence that she wasn't an identical twin and then he'd marry her and she'd never forgive. This is terribly serious, Gwennie. It's the end of the Burlington if the marriage comes off.'

'Well, she can't go about like this, can she, Miss Jane? It's killing her. And it's bad for business too. Dispiriting.'

Then one day Edith seemed suddenly very much happier. Not entirely happy, but quite human again – she went about humming hymn tunes. Jane felt a great load lifted from her mind. Edith had evidently fought a great battle and got herself under decent control again. The next thing that happened was that a copy of the *Western Sentinel* came for Mrs Trent, who liked to keep in touch with St Aidan's affairs; and there was 'O. Price, handicap 2' playing in the mixed foursomes of the St Aidan's November Golf Meeting and O. Price also playing in the men's doubles at the St Aidan's Covered Courts Tennis Tournament, and O. Price addressing the Quarrymen's Artistic and Literary Society on 'The Trend of the Modern Drama'.

The question that arose was how to break the news to Edith that Oliver's heart was apparently in perfect working order; or whether it was wise to tell her. It might be a shock for her to realize that she had been fooled, Mrs Trent thought. But Jane decided that it wouldn't kill her. So would Gwennie please leave the *Sentinel* open in her room with Oliver's name starred in the margin with blue pencil, as if by some friend of the family at St Aidan's? So that was done. And Edith noticed the name. But her only comment was a mild, self-possessed: 'Mr Oliver seems busy, doesn't he?' No emotion, no irony. Neither Mrs Trent nor Jane could make head or tail of this. Jane said: 'Perhaps she'd got someone else in mind, after all.' Mrs Trent thought not.

At last Mrs Trent, poring over the *Sentinel* in the wild hope of finding a clue to the problem, unexpectedly found one. She noticed that Mrs E. Smith, handicap plus 2, was also playing in the mixed foursomes. Mrs E. Smith was Edna, so they both saw all.

Jane groaned. 'Oh, what a mess I have made of this. It never occurred to me that Oliver would see Edna – and no sign of any baby on the way. So he's probably written to Edith that he's been to another Harley Street specialist, who thinks that the first fellow may have misread the X-rays. And that he's going to go on playing games as if nothing was wrong and trust to luck. And that perhaps then. . . . Temporizing until he's sure that Edna isn't really having a baby. Oh, I wish to Heaven I had left the whole business alone! I felt bad enough before; I feel worse now.' Jane's reconstruction of Oliver's actions was correct to the smallest detail; but it must be remembered that she had made an extensive psychological study of him while building up Owen Slingsby's character.

Miss Hapless told Jane that she had been sent two or three notifications of the occurrence of rare Antigua issues, but none of them was the missing stamp. Jane now remembered a bundle of letters from her school days put away somewhere in a writing-desk. When Edith had given her the Antigua envelope for the stamp-collection, the original letter had still been in it. Rather an exciting letter, so she had not thrown it away. It might be in that bundle still.

Yes, here it was. She uncreased the thin sheet of paper and began to read.

Steam-packet *Phoebe.*
Off the coast of the Island of Antigua
March 1st, 1866

My Dear Brother Frederick,

This is the first Letter you have had from me for a Heap of Years and unless God has reserved a Miracle for me, it must be the Last Letter I shall pen to any Soul in this mortal Life. My Vessel lies in Chancery between two Sunken Rocks but Half a Mile from the Coast, though what with the Violence of the Sea that Distance might well be a 1000 Miles. I am alone in the Ship. The Crew and Passengers took to the Boats, though much against my Counsel, for I knew that no Boat could live in that Sea, and were immediately hurled to Destruction. Among those who perished before my Eyes were the Incoming Governor and his Wife, poor Lady. So I have purchased a Half Hour or happen a whole Hour of Life more until my poor *Phoebe* goes: her After Part is slowly breaking up.

Well, then, Dear Brother Frederick, this is to grip your Hand, as it were, and say God Bless You, and that I have left all my earthly Goods to you or your Heirs, which is not Great Riches indeed but ne'er the less a Tidy Sum, and all sealed and safe in the Charge of the Whitebillet Packet Line at their Head Office at Liverpool, together with my Last Will and Testament; to whom I have wrote another Letter reporting the Loss of Vessel and Crew, which I have consigned to a Separate Bottle from the Bottle I shall consign this Letter to, and blaming the Loss on the Absence of a Light House on a certain most Perilous Headland and on Uncharted Rocks. And look you at the Postage Stamp, dear Brother, which I shall fix on the Envelope of this letter from a Consignment in my Safe of new Postage Stamps for the Antiguan Post Office. Observe a Vessel and a Light House. They should by rights have built the Light House first and printed the Postage Stamp arter. Then happen their Postage Stamps would have reached St John with their Gum unlicked by Father Neptune and the Mermaidens, and their new Governor no Corpse. And I have wrote to tell them where to make Enquiries for your present Whereabouts, being last heard of in Canterbury Settlement in the year 1849.

I have just quit my Cabin to cock an Eye at the Sea. The Waves are frightful, but I reckon my *Phoebe* will hang together a Couple of Hours longer: so shall now ease my Heart writing to you, dear Brother, of Old Times. My Heart flies back to the Moor, with the Red Legs in the Marshy Parts and the Marigolds and Larks singing overhead and the great Flocks of Geese at Pasture. And I remember, Dear Brother, how you saved my Life at the Stank that Day as I was pulling Pussy Willows and in I went and under. And I remember that mighty Perambulation of fully 1000 persons of every Age and both Sexes, in which I took Part, Ducket in Hand, at your Side, destroying Fences with the Best, though but 6 Years of Age at this Time. And you and Uncle Will and 40 more trussed up and carried off in Wagons by the Yeomen to Jail, and my Tears. And that great Battle at the Fair, how the Brick Bats flew, and I with a Cobble Stone struck the Lieutenant's own Horse and made him Rear up and Cast his Rider. And at the Turn to the Jail, Great Deeds and Cudgel Play, and you freed and the Yeomen themselves trussed and carried in the Wagons before the Mayor. And I remember that Dark Month that separated us and how Heavy was my Heart while the Oddy Bells rang: 'Hang Sam Gomme, Save Will Young!' It was Common Talk that Uncle Will would hang, spite of all the Bells and you to be Transported for Life though but a Lad of Fourteen. But the Magistrates was in Terror of the Mob, and back you came together safe and sound arter but 2 Months in Jail. Yet you swore that England was no longer the Land of Free Men and you would push your Fortune beyond the Sea. And presently you kissed me Goodbye and gave me a Shut Knife as a Keepsake, for which I gave you a Copper Cart Wheel in Exchange, lest Love be cut between us, and I never saw you, Brother, again, though dearly I loved you; and myself I left the Moor so soon as ever I was of Age and took to the Sea, and our Ways have lain apart. I laid out a Sum afore I left England last for the Tending of our dear Parents' Graves close by the Church Gate: that much Care is off my Mind.

So now Goodbye, Dearest Brother Fred, and God Bless You and Yours and that you may enjoy Health and Wealth and marry another Good Woman like the One you told me was took from you, and that you may be blessed in Children, and that you and I may one Day meet in the Other Land is the Wish of

> Your Truly
>
> Affectionate Brother,
>
> Tom,

Who now consigns this Letter to the Mercy of the Waves

A copper cartwheel was one of those George III twopenny pieces, wasn't it? But what were Duckets and Stanks and Oddy Bells? And – one moment – where was that album? A funny coincidence: there was something about 'Save Will Young' in one of the pictures there. 'Miss Hapless, please get me that Victorian costume album!'

Now, Jane had just bought an album containing early Victorian costume prints. She wanted it for a strange show that she was putting on at the New Year (1935) called 'Victorian Paradise'. In the album were pasted a number of miscellaneous pictures of the years 1830 to 1840, and one of these happened to be a hand-painted woodcut of a young countryman in a smock holding a banner on which was inscribed, 'Save Will Young'. This was what Jane wanted. The doggerel legend underneath ran:

The web-footed men to the Fair are come,
To save Will Young and to hang Sam Gomme,
The D. . . . e of M. . . . gh's Yeoman they
Are trussed in wagons with ropes of hay.
The Mayor has given his word, has he,
That Doomsday Book shall respected be.
Against Enclosure we Swains will fight,
For Freedom was ever the Briton's right.

Evidently the same story. Jane wondered where it had all happened. There were plenty of clues in the letter, but no geographical names to go on, unless 'Oddy' was a place, and none in the picture either. But the Duke of Marlborough lived at Blenheim Palace near Oxford, so possibly it was somewhere in that region. On the other hand, Oxfordshire wasn't a county of moors or marshes. And who were the web-footed men? The young countryman in the cut, she noticed, had webbed feet like the fat goose beside him.

But since it seemed an altogether unimportant problem to solve, and Jane was extremely busy with 'Victorian Paradise', she let it stand for a while. It will be mentioned again later.

The next step in the story is Jane's engagement of Adelaide Moon. This was a young Australian dancer who came to see Jane one day. She said that she had noticed that last month, when Nuda had the 'flu, Nuda's understudy wasn't at all up to the mark. Adelaide danced well and seemed full of ideas and had once had an advertising job on the *Sydney Bulletin*; Jane engaged her in the double capacity of understudy for Nuda and assistant in the publicity department. Adelaide had been living in Hammersmith with a brother who had now returned to Australia, so she was quite alone. Jane found Adelaide a good-hearted, capable, tidy girl and gave her a room in her house. She was one day explaining to Adelaide that all the members of the company were ready to give signed photographs of themselves to the public at the usual half-crown fee (the proceeds going to the Royal Actors' Benevolent Fund) – but not herself. She made absolutely no exceptions to the rule.

Adelaide said, 'I know that, Miss Palfrey. But I've got one.'
Jane asked: 'One what?'

'Photograph of you, signed, one.'

'There's not such a thing in existence.'

'Isn't there, Miss Palfrey? The friend of mine who got it for me swore it was dinkum. It's a very early one, of course. It's you way back in 1923 and it's signed: "Much Love from Jane."'

'*What*? In a Columbine's get-up, with a wand?'

'That's it.'

'You say a friend got it for you. Do you mind very much telling me your friend's name?'

'No, that's all right. His name's Dormer. He's a student at St Mark's College, Hammersmith. He thinks he's in love with me, the calf. And me nearly two years older than him and earning my own living. Poor Harold.'

'Has he told you where he acquired that photograph?'

'No, I asked him, and he looked sort of proud and mysterious and said he couldn't tell. Did he steal it, or something? Harold would swim the Atlantic in a pair of football boots if I asked him to. He knows I collect signed photographs of famous actors and actresses and he's got me a good many rare ones. I reward him for every one he gets me, poor Harold. He got a specially hard hug for yours, 'cause it's unique, isn't it?'

Jane said: 'Yes, I had it taken while I was at a school of so-called dramatic art at Bristol, and signed it for my mother. My mother's dead. Someone must have stolen it from her things. I had forgotten all about it.'

Adelaide promised to ask Harold, again, how he had got hold of the photograph. She did so the next day. Harold couldn't be persuaded to say much, beyond admitting that he had swapped his stamp-album for the photograph. He said that his father would be furious if he found out, because it contained a number of stamps he had collected when on his back in hospital during the War.

Jane said to Adelaide: 'Tell Harold to write a letter to whomever it was with whom he had made the swap. Tell him to say that his father is furious at his having sold it, because he (the father) wanted it to stay in the family; but that he (Harold) will return the photograph, if he (the other fellow) sends back the album. Force or coax Harold to do this, Adelaide.

More depends on it than you think. Then show me the letter
Harold gets in answer. The answer will be "no". But never
mind: I can't tell you how important it is!'

'This won't get Harold into trouble?'

'No, indeed. Not a hair of Harold's head shall be harmed.'

'I suppose Harold will expect another reward for this.
Poor Harold, I don't like giving him false hopes.'

So Harold wrote the letter that Adelaide dictated and promised to hand over to her any answer that came. Harold said,
'If the photograph was stolen, he had no right to ask me not to
give him away; he was trying to make me a receiver of stolen
goods. Besides, I'm doing it for you. I'd do anything for you,
Adelaide.'

The letter that Harold wrote to Oliver was worded very
piteously, and Oliver, who had the same fatherly sentiment
about keeping stamp-albums in the family as Mr Dormer had,
was touched. In reply he said how sorry he was that he could
not return the album in the same state as it had been when he
had bought it; that he was sending it, with a different set
of stamps in it, but quite valuable ones. He regretted that the
original set had been disposed of. And Harold need not
trouble to return the photograph.

When Jane read Oliver's letter she offered Harold ten pounds
for the album and the letter; which Harold was very glad to
accept. So Jane got the album and, as she had expected, it was a
Stanley Gibbons album with a cover just like Oliver's, only
a little cleaner. The cover had become detached from the book
along with the fly-leaf – 'Harold with love from Dad'. Harold
said that it had not been like this when he sold it. And the
stamps in it were the very ones that she had gone over with
Oliver – the ones that Oliver had himself chosen! He had not
even taken the trouble to rub out the *O*'s and *J*'s.

So! So! Painstaking Oliver! It was easy to see what he had
done. He had swapped this album with Harold for a purloined
photograph, then he had somehow filled it up with a set of
stamps in exact duplication of the ones in his own (or rather
'our' own) album – which must have cost him quite a lot of
money. And then he had temporarily given Harold's album
the cover and fly-leaf from 'our' album and let her imagine

that she was picking the real collection to pieces, while all the time ... Why couldn't he have removed the stamps from 'our' album and put the new set in their place; why borrow another album just for that? Undoubtedly because 'our' album was too sacred to be played about with like this, even for a day. Emotional. And ingenious. She rather admired him for the fight he was putting up. And how had he come across Harold?

Jane knew everyone in London worth knowing and among them was 'The Emu', or Henry Palfrey, eighth Marquess of Babraham, her third cousin. He was a fine, long-legged, good-natured Australian, who seemed to have few interests in life beyond horse racing, shooting and having a good time. He had unexpectedly succeeded to the title in 1930, while apprenticed to a firm of Sydney solicitors. One day he happened to meet Jane and Adelaide at a dance; and Jane decided that Adelaide, who was a very smart girl, was just his sort. She said to Adelaide: 'I'll ask Babraham to join our publicity department and then you and he can see more of each other.' To Adelaide's delight The Emu accepted. Adelaide had long planned a marriage into the peerage as the social climax of her dancing career, and it had always worried her that the peerage was so stiff and British. Whereas The Emu was at once a dinkum peer and a dinkum Australian. Ideal. They got on very well together and put a lot of gay zeal into publicity doings. For example, Leonora and J. C. Neanderthal borrowed Babraham Castle and gave a great house-party there at Christmas. The highest in the land were invited and a great many of them accepted, because they foresaw high jinks. No one was disappointed. Stolen pearls. Everyone suspected and searched. The thief unmasked (the Squire, of course) but forgiven in the proper Christmas spirit. An alarm of fire. Hauntings in the West Wing. In short, a round of thrills, expertly organized by Adelaide and The Emu. At the Boxing Day shoot, J. C. Neanderthal surprised everyone by bringing down far more birds than anyone else, including a carrier pigeon with a mysterious message round its leg which nobody succeeded in deciphering before the party broke up. The papers did it justice. The adventures of the Company were a standing feast in the Press, and in every decent British home.

All this time Jane behaved to Edith as if there were nothing wrong between them, and Edith had by now regained full control of her work. But it was clear that Owen Slingsby was getting more and more under her skin; she cut rehearsals as often as she dared. Jane therefore accentuated Slingsby's Oliverisms: either she would cure Edith of her infatuation or she would force the matter to a crisis. But nothing happened. New Year came, the new show went down very well and was booked up for two months ahead.

And then at last Miss Hapless had a letter from Messrs. Harrow and Hazlitt, of the Argent Street Stamp Auctions (founded in 1878, by appointment to H.M. the King of Egypt and H.H. the Maharaja of Ophistan: Cables: 'A WATERMARK, LONDON'). It reached her on the afternoon of February 11th, eighteen days after it had been posted. This was because she had been away in Switzerland for ten days (on special leave to visit a consumptive brother), and the letter had been forwarded to her there just a day too late. The porter at her hotel in Switzerland was careless about sending letters on: it had been lying about there all that time. What Messrs Harrow and Hazlitt had to say was as follows:

Dear Sir,   *Jan. 23rd, 1935*

We are pleased to inform you that a postage stamp of the greatest beauty and rarity will come under the hammer at our auction room in the sale commencing at 2 p.m. on Tuesday, February 12th. The stamp in question is a totally unrecorded issue of Antigua, the country in which we understand that you are a specialist: a purple-brown, one penny denomination, Young Queen's head *upon an octagonal tablet, flanked with ship and lighthouse,* lightly cancelled, 1866. Perforation 14. Watermark Crown CC. The stamp is in situ on its original cover (cover slightly creased) and in irreproachable condition.

May we respectfully suggest that should you favour us with your presence on the above date, you will arrive no later than 1.30 p.m.? The philatelic world has already expressed the greatest interest in this grand stamp, seats cannot be reserved, and our accommodation is not unlimited.

> Yours obediently,
> Harrow and Hazlitt, Ltd

M. Hapless, Esq.

'All girls who collect stamps are honorary Boys, you see,' said Jane. 'Dear Mr Hapless, please acknowledge the favour of their kind advice. And put me through at once to my lawyers. Not the theatre's lawyers – my own ones, this time. I only hope it's not too late to act.'

CHAPTER 10

THE FIRST AUCTION

LET us deal openly with the reader. Let us assure him or her at this point that the Antiguan stamp was literally unique. The rest of the consignment had gone to the bottom, never to be recovered. No others of the same issue were ever printed. The bottle containing the letter that Captain Tom Young had written just before his death to the owners of the Whitebillet Line, reporting the loss of the *Phoebe*, had never reached the shore. The stamp on that letter – if one was in fact affixed to it – had therefore been irrecoverably lost. We may say more: nobody in this story will be found contesting the authenticity of the stamp; no other example, used or unused, will turn up; nobody will try to forge a copy, nobody will even try to steal the original. There will be no murders because of it, and the services of Scotland Yard will not be called upon. The nub of the whole business remains what it was: a long-protracted and hard-fought conflict between Jane and her brother Oliver, of which the possession of the Antigua penny puce stamp has become the symbol. And it will be only fair at this point to move from Jane's camp back to Oliver's, so as not to draw the sympathies of the reader too strongly over to Jane's side. The view that Oliver was an unspeakable cad is Jane's – not necessarily ours. A great many readers, on hearing Oliver's case, may range themselves solidly behind him. We have our own private verdict, but are officially neutral and are doing our best to poise the scales of justice evenly.

First of all, then, about Oliver and Edith. Granting Oliver's view of Jane as an ambitious, unprincipled, heartless creature who had done him many a bad turn and deserved no mercy from him, his actions are perfectly explicable. He could not marry Edna, because she had married someone else; and there was nobody else for whom he really cared. Yet there were things about Edith that reminded him of Edna, and some years ago Edith had been in love with him, he knew, and probably still was. Edith wasn't at all a bad sort in her quiet, humourless way. He was sorry for her, too. In her partnership with Jane she must feel absolutely stifled – kept so busy at the theatre, in mere routine work of stage upkeep and accounts and so on, that she had no time for the scientific research that was her real work. Whereas, he and Edith could live very happily together – Edith had lots of money and no idea how enjoyably money could be spent. Weaning Edith away from Jane would be rather a heroic action, like rescuing a lovely maiden from the enchanted castle of an ogress. (Quite apart from the revenge – Oliver counted on Jane's feeling completely lost without her slave.) He thus made out a good case for himself, and was altogether serious in his intentions towards Edith. He almost persuaded himself, even, that he was in love with her, though Oliver at the age of twenty-eight was no longer romantic, and ready to express the view – to Edith herself – that the most successful marriages were founded on mutual respect and community of interest rather than on physical attraction. Edith's loyalty to Jane he found the most difficult element in the situation. But he was careful to say nothing outspokenly nasty about Jane in Edith's presence, as if all the ill-feeling were on her side; and though he mentioned Jane's curious behaviour in the matter of the stamp-album he left Edith to draw her own conclusions about it. Edith thought it very fine of him to have given up the stamps without a struggle, as he let her believe he had.

Then came that jolt, the news that Edna was having a baby. He had to give up the idea of marrying Edith. For Oliver had old-fashioned moral views about marriage. He agreed with the Prayer Book that it was 'ordained for the procreation of children', and when it seemed as if Edith, not Edna, was the twin who was doomed to barrenness, not even the glory of the victory over Jane could persuade him to go on with it. The deceit was not cruelly intended: Oliver was merely rather unimaginative and the weak heart was the first plausible excuse that occurred to him. And if it had been Edith who had cried off because of a weak heart, Oliver would have felt no hesitation in looking for someone else; so it never occurred to him that Edith could suffer greatly on his account. He must face the question practically. He had to get out of it somehow and he did not want Edith to know the real reason: it might depress her.

By the way, we do not guarantee that there is any biological warrant for this theory of the necessary barrenness of one or other of a pair of identical human twins. We could find no mention of it, for example, in our edition of the *Encyclopedia Britannica*, nor even in the two medical books consulted by Oliver. We do not know where the theory originated. All that matters to us is that it is widely current and that Oliver, Madame Blanche's fifth personality and, as it proved, even Edith, believed in it. The doctors whom we have questioned invariably reply: 'I'm afraid I'm only nose, ear, and throat,' or 'Sorry, but I'm only a G.P.,' or 'I don't suppose anyone really knows. Accurate statistics would be hard to come by. Of course, as you are aware, in the case of guinea-pigs . . .'

As for the stamp-album fraud: Oliver felt himself completely justified in this and had enjoyed, with no sense of guilt, the delicious irony of swapping Jane's photograph for the stamp-album that would assist in Jane's defeat. Oliver was not a particularly greedy character. That he was indeed capable of considerable generosity has been seen by his return to Harold of the album without asking for the photograph back: especially as the stamps that remained in it after Jane had removed her choice were more numerous and more valuable than the original Dormer collection.

We already know more or less what happened at St Aidan's in November when he met Edna, looking as usual, taking violent exercise as usual and playing bridge at the Club House every night with a whisky and soda at her elbow. Early in December, on his return to Town, Edith told Oliver that she thought, from something that Jane had said, that Slingsby was intended to be a caricature of him. Of course that made Oliver really wild. He could hardly wait until the New Year. He then attended the first night of *Victorian Paradise* to see whether he could fasten on any particular phrase or gesture as libellous; but there was nothing. He would only make himself ridiculous if he sued. So he again pretended to be magnanimous, and Edith, who was as hopelessly in love with him as ever, was now convinced that he had all the right on his side. She was going to tell Jane that she *insisted* on Slingsby being abolished. But Oliver said, 'No, wait! We'll get secretly married one of these days and face Jane with the accomplished fact, and then *I'll* talk to her, as your representative. After all, you have the controlling interest in the Burlington, haven't you? You can jolly well force her to take Slingsby off.'

'I can't marry you before next October, darling, I'm afraid,' said Edith. 'In October, 1930, I promised Jane I wouldn't marry anyone for five years.'

'Oh, nonsense!'

'I promised. We both agreed not to marry. It wouldn't have been fair on the theatre.'

This was on Sunday, February 10th, 1935, some weeks after Oliver had assured himself that his heart was perfectly all right. He had gone, he told Edith, from one end of Harley Street to another and now everyone gave him a clean bill of health. The fact was, that Edith had told him that Edna was going big-game shooting in Africa. Nobody goes big-game shooting if they intend to have a baby almost any day; so, clearly, Edna had made a mistake. He dismissed the suggestion that Jane could have worked out about his twin-dilemma and that she had deliberately invented a baby for Edna. He was sure, to start with, that Mrs Trent would not have told Jane about his inquiries, especially after getting that handsome tip. Mrs Trent was a good sportswoman. And again, if Jane *had* somehow guessed about the twin business and *had* invented Edna's baby, then as soon as she'd seen him sheer off from Edith she'd have told Edith at once what the game was, and it would have put him in a very ridiculous light with her – pretending to have a weak heart in order to escape marrying! No, Jane could know nothing.

At one-thirty on the following Tuesday Oliver completed his usual lunch of cold meat, salad, pickles, Dutch cheese and bottled beer, locked up his flat and went out. His mind was on his novel and he walked in a brown study to the nearest taxi-rank: 'Hazlitt and Harrow, stamp auctioneers, Argent Street. I don't know the number.' The taxi-man drove off. They passed the Marquess of Babraham strolling towards Albion Mansions, and it is a curious fact that although Oliver did not then know

The Emu by sight, there was an expression on his face that made him say half in earnest to himself: 'That fellow looks like a crook. I hope he's not going to slip up to my flat and sneak off with my silver cups.'

The Emu had been assigned a task which he was to perform at precisely two o'clock. Jane had told him that it was of the utmost importance and that if he brought it off she would reward him even unto the half of her kingdom; and appealed to his sporting instincts, and assured him that he was perfectly within his rights. The only thing he had to remember, for Heaven's sake, was to get rid of that bunch of keys as soon as possible. They were evidence against him, and her.

The Emu was wearing rubber soles and gloves. He looked up at Albion Mansions. It seemed a terribly tall building to burgle. Not that he was instructed to steal anything. Jane had assured him that it wasn't necessary. What she had said to him was this: 'Emu, dear, I want you to do me a service. Do you know my foul brother Oliver, by any chance?'

'No, I can't say I do. Didn't know you had any surviving kin.'

'All the better, then: he won't recognize you.'

'When?'

'On Tuesday at two o'clock.'

'Why?'

'Why is too long to answer, but I'll tell you where and how. You go to a place called Albion Mansions, near Battersea Park. Number 27, at the very top, left, lift not working. And you take this bunch of keys and go boldly in: this one is the latchkey. And somewhere there'll be a zinc trunk, in some boxroom or what not. One of these is the key to it: I don't know which. And in that zinc trunk there'll be a book called *The Shepherd's Calendar*, spelt all wrong; and in it will be a big Babraham Castle book-plate with a shelf number. And what you do is to have ready with you another Babraham Castle book-plate – send for one from the librarian, but be sure to get a new one with your own name on, not my grandfather's, and date it August, 1935. You lick the book-plate and stick it in, over the other one; then you put everything back in its place and steal away, whistling insouciantly.'

'Oh, and if I'm caught by someone?'

'You won't be.'

'But if I am?'

'You aren't doing harm, tell them.'

'What about the keys?'

'Oliver lent you them to fetch something for him.'

'How do you know Oliver won't be about, himself?'

'I have heard on good authority that he has a date at a stamp auction in Argent Street.'

'And if he changes his mind? If I get in and he comes seeping back? What then?'

'Throw him out of the window.'

'Seriously?'

'Emu, I swear that it's all right. But if the worst comes to the worst, tell Oliver I sent you. He'll believe *that*, never fear.'

'I'd not like to drag your name into the business, Jane.'

'Very charmingly put, Emu. But the worst won't come to the worst. All the same, better not be caught with the keys on you. If arrested, swallow them, like the good emu-bird you are.'

'There won't be any burglar alarm?'

'I don't think so. Oliver is a novelist and in constant terror of someone's stealing his ideas, but I don't think he'd go to the length of a burglar alarm. Oh, there's a bulldog there, I ought to warn you.'

'Fierce creature?'

'Not at all. The silly over-bred sort. Chums up with anyone in trousers, according to its owner. Answers to the name of Kate.'

'I like this job less and less.'

It was now five minutes to two. It occurred to The Emu that the sooner he started, the sooner the job would be over. This Oliver what's-his-name – not Palfrey – must be well on the way to the auction now. He located Number 27 of the Mansions and went briskly and noiselessly upstairs. No door opened. He thought that he must be pretty near the top when he came to J. V. Clogg, I.C.E., left, and Mrs John Beaver, right. But above J. V. Clogg lived one Herbert Anstruther, Esq., and above him one Mr Algernon Hoyland. By the time he reached O. Price he was panting, and dripping with sweat.

He knocked. No answer. Again. No answer. The key was a bit stiff in the lock, but he managed to trick it. And went in, leaving the door open in case that bulldog bitch happened to go for him. Where was she? She woke up, came waddling out of a corner and gave him an uncertain but not hostile look. He greeted her affectionately and introduced himself with a biscuit and a large lump of Oliver's cheese. She slobbered over him, evidently deciding that he was an old friend whose smell she had somehow forgotten, and then returned to finish her nap in the corner. All clear, so far.

Stuffy sort of room. Like a doctor's waiting-room. Still, a guitar. The Emu could strum a guitar himself. He felt a bit of an outsider boring in here with a bunch of false keys. But Jane. . . . And then again Adelaide. Adelaide was a fine girl. A real bit of old Australia. So he fossicked round for the zinc trunk and at last discovered it in a sort of cupboard in the bathroom. He found the key that opened the trunk and messed about a bit and came across a book. It wasn't a calendar but something in Latin, so he left it alone. And then another, but it was only a stamp-album. So he had one more shot and got the right affair this time (badly spelt, so it must be the fellow), licked the book-plate, slapped it in on top of the old one, a trifle crooked, tidied the trunk, locked it again, shut the cupboard door. He felt that he had done well.

A childish tune came into his head. He began humming:

> I am on Tom Tiddler's ground
> Picking up gold and silver.

He made a closer survey of the sitting-room. A pile of manuscript written in green ink lay on a side-table. He had a look at it. Appeared to be a novel. The Emu had never seen a novel in the making before. It fascinated him. He read a sentence.

'Nay,' cried the good bailiff of Hochschloss, 'all folk who journey through this bailiwick must first drink the health of my Lord the Duke: in mead, be they poor; in good Rhine wine, be they of the better sort.'

'My oath,' commented The Emu.

A shadow fell on the page. He looked up and there was a young, thin man with large round spectacles and an inky forefinger. 'What do you want?' The Emu asked pleasantly, speaking first.

'Oh, I'm Hoyland, from below. Came to borrow some cigarettes. Where does Oliver keep 'em?'

Emu replied: 'I don't know this Oliver; or where he keeps his cigarettes. Never seen the man in my life. But they told me he was a novelist, so I broke in to pinch a few of his ideas. Been casting my eye over this stuff – and listen, you tell this Oliver when he comes back that he needn't worry.'

Hoyland said, 'What name shall I say?'

'No name. Or, say "Operator Eleven", if you like. There's a whole gang of us. The publishers employ us to steal ideas. They fit us out with gum-shoes and send us round to this promising author and that. It's just a precaution – in case there may be some new idea about that ought to be exploited commercially. But there never is. Well, I must be moving now. By the way, you an author too? Yes, I spotted the ink on your finger. They all have it, except the sort that use typewriters. Perhaps one day I'll pay you a visit when you're out and you'll come back and find an idea gone.'

Oliver's cigarette box was empty, so The Emu gave Hoyland a couple, and a light, and everything passed off nicely. 'Don't tell old Oliver,' he said. 'Actually I'm a pal of his from number 23, top right. I climbed up here to borrow a whisky and soda, found him not at home and the door unlocked, entered, helped myself and got entranced in his novel. I felt a bit of a rabbit when you came in.'

'I won't say a word.' They went down together and exchanged a cheerful farewell at Hoyland's door.

When Oliver returned, three hours or so later, he may have noticed vaguely that the door was open, but was too flustered to be sure that he had slammed it to when he went out. And everything seemed exactly as he'd left it.

An account follows of why Oliver felt flustered. The taxi had dropped him at the Argent Street Stamp Auction Rooms at 1.30 or so, and he had squeezed in through a bit of a crowd at the door and just managed to get the last vacant chair. There must have been two hundred and fifty people present. It was a long room with huge windows at both ends, and at one side, and long narrow green-baize-covered tables running parallel with each other down the whole length of it. At the auctioneer's end these tables were connected by a red-baize cross-piece. This was the show table on which, Oliver's neighbour told him, the stamps to be sold would be laid. The auctioneer's rostrum commanded the show table; to one side of the rostrum was a writing-desk. Behind the tables, along the walls, were five rows of seats, in tiers, on the non-window side, and on the window side three untiered rows. Match-boarded walls. Brown linoleum on the floor. No pictures except, over the door, a framed steel-engraving of some early Victorian person whom Oliver guessed, rightly, to be Sir Rowland Hill (1795–1879), the inventor of Penny Postage and thus the godfather of Philately.

At the back of the hall, facing the rostrum, was a mixed set of chairs, evidently collected from neighbouring offices because of the unprecedented demand for seats; it was on one of these that Oliver sat. More and more people came in, and stood about in corners. At five minutes to two the doors were closed. Oliver looked about him. First, the people sitting along the tables. Irregular-featured men, mostly of middle age. Some of them with soft hats, which they had laid on the table in front of them; some of them with bowlers, which they had pushed on the backs of their heads. The soft-hatted men smoked pipes, the bowler-hatted tended to cigarettes and cheroots. Collectors and dealers? They were sitting there turning over the pages of the General Collections about to be sold, puffing hard, peering through magnifying glasses, and measuring perforations with pocket gauges. Extreme quiet reigned.

'Who are those people at the other end of the hall?' Oliver asked his left-hand neighbour, a Lancashire man, in the subdued tones that one uses to a guide in a cathedral.

'Commission agents: they buy stamps on commission for absent gentlemen.'

'Oh, thanks.'

A fog came up, so the curtains were drawn and the lights switched on. They were green-shaded lights and the room began to look very pretty. Four little girls in green uniforms appeared. The people in the tiers of seats behind were a

mixed set, like the chairs. Many of them ran to shag and
tweediness; some might have been City clerks, from their
clothes. Few women. Three, to be exact. A gaunt, hyper-
tweedy one with horn-rimmed spectacles, possibly the owner
of a Borzoi; a nun with a very heavy gold cross; and a securely
veiled youngish woman in deep mourning.

Oliver asked his neighbour: 'Many nuns come here?'

'Not many, in my experience. I understand that the lady
yonder is the Superior of a convent down in Surrey. They
found a packet of old letters from a sister foundation in Italy.
Mr Harrow went down to have a look at them, and lo and
behold! the most beautiful collection of Tuscany 1851–52
and 1857–59 and a fine lot of the 1860 issue! What a stroke of
luck, eh? The gem is a 2-soldi brick red, with spacious margins,
and *value tablet inverted* – what do you think of that? It'll not
go for a penny less than five hundred quid.'

'Plenty of romance in stamp collecting,' said Oliver sen-
tentiously. 'Now the nuns will be able to afford rubber hot-
water bottles, and cocoa after compline.'

Enlarging on the phrase 'plenty of romance', the Lancashire
man told Oliver his own story in a hoarse whisper. It began:
'I started literally on a shoe-string.' He had evidently told it so
often before that he could no longer succeed in making it sound
very credible. Charabanc accident at a level crossing, racing
gentleman terribly injured, first aid administered by Lancashire
man, racing gentleman's gratitude and last words 'Mustapha
Bey, a cert for the 3.50 tomorrow.' Mustapha Bey, backed with
Lancashire man's last tenner acquired by selling a fine old
grandfather clock, romps home at 33 to 1. Lancashire man
thereupon buys up a derelict mail-order stamp business at
Leamington. 'That was eight years ago. I started on a shoe-
string and now I have sixteen young lady clerks under me.
Smart lasses, too. Enjoy their work. Every sort of customer
from dukes and earls and honourables down to prison warders.
My biggest business is with boys' preparatory schools on the
South Coast. My son Bob used to travel in sports accessories –
cricket bats, boxing gloves, footballs, and so on. Still does a
bit of that, does Bob. But his principal job now is scouting
round for me. Gets pally with the school porters and finds out

from them who's the school cricket or football captain. Then we write the lad a polite letter asking him to become our agent. Enclose sheets of stamps on approval. He gets 20 per cent profit – that's to say, more like 5 per cent net, because he has to take it in stamps, you see. Does champion business with elder lads who want a position in the team, and with kids who want to chum up with him. Human nature, you see. Are you a schoolmaster, sir, may I ask? We have many good customers among that profession.'

Oliver hated being taken even for a private tutor.

'No,' he said evasively. 'I'm in cheese. That's to say, a cheese taster. I started literally on a cheese rind.'

On his right an old clergyman was reading a catalogue and grumbling in dry whispers at the new fashions in philately. 'Official air-mail stamps, by all means. Duly accredited, I mean. Must move with the times. But cachets and covers, no! Semi-official issues, still less. No right to be offered in these rooms. Look here: "First aerial delivery, 1913. Robert Sinclair Tobacco Company. Sinclair vignette. Block of ten, mint." Can't call those *stamps*. Might as well take the bands off cigars and call them stamps.'

His neighbour, another clergyman, replied:

'I'm afraid, my dear fellow, that you'll think me very much of a Simon Pure, when I tell you that practically no stamp issued later than the year of the Great Exhibition has any aesthetic appeal for me whatsoever. I specialize in the archetype and grandmother of all stamps – the Penny Black of 1840 – and have made a lifelong though perhaps (some cavillers might say) over-sensitive study of its glorious range. For relaxation I collect somewhat more modern philatelic examples, chiefly first issues of other lands, with a tender leaning towards the British Guiana 1850 "circulars". But that's an expensive hobby. Expensive.'

The Lancashire man nudged Oliver. 'See who's sitting at the end of this table?'

Oliver saw. 'That aged fellow with the rheumy eyes and the wispy beard?'

'Yes, that's him, that's Sir Arthur Gamm, prominent member of the Royal Philatelic Society. It's seldom you see

him in the rooms these days. He's a sick man. He'll be after
that surprising Antigua, purple-brown, I reckon.'

Oliver said 'Puce', rather curtly.

'Officially purple-brown,' the Lancashire man replied softly
but insistently. 'Puce isn't a philatelic term.'

'*Un*officially purple-brown, *officially* puce. It's *my* stamp, it's
unique, I reserve the right to name its colour.'

Oliver spoke with warmth and several people turned
round, rather shocked; but a moment later the clock chimed
two and a stout, fair young man bounced in, threw a compre-
hensive smile towards the soft hats and bowlers at the tables
and mounted his rostrum with speed. Oliver expected everyone
to stand up as they do when a judge enters Court, but nobody
stirred. Behind the auctioneer came a girl clerk, in green,
like the others, who slipped into the desk at his right and
snatched up a fountain pen.

The auctioneer began without the least preamble, in
fluent and unemotional tones, 'Lot 1, general collection in
Improved Album: ten pounds, guineas, fifteen; eleven pounds,
guineas, fifteen; twelve pounds, guineas, fifteen; thirteen
pounds, guineas, guineas, thirteen guineas.' Bang! 'Name, sir,
please.' It was a very correctly dressed little Japanese who got
it, and the way he had been nodding his bids reminded Oliver
of a toy he once had; only it was a Chinaman, not a Jap. The
Jap was handed the album by one of the green girls, made her
a charming bow, swiftly counted out thirteen pound notes and
thirteen shillings, and darted for the door. Time, one minute.
Always first off the mark, the Japs.

The bowler hats did most of the bidding for the general
collections, which came first. Nods, winks, forefingers.
'They'll take them home,' Oliver speculated, 'and break them
up into exciting packets of 100 British colonials, all different,
5s., 50 Central American, 3s. 6d., and so on, for schoolboys
to buy with their birthday and Christmas money and tips from
uncles. And the schoolboys will persevere and build up
valuable collections of catalogue value amounting to fifty
pounds or more, and then gradually lose interest, but hang on
to them until perhaps their first year at the Varsity (where one
always runs into debt) and then they'll send them here for sale

to Japs or chaps in bowler hats – who will buy them for a mere thirteen guineas, guineas, thirteen guineas, bang! and carry them home to break up once more into exciting packets for schoolboys. *Le cycle du timbre-poste.*'

The Lancashire man secured the largest and cheapest lots. 'I can do with any amount of sixpenny-packet stuff. Got to keep my lady sorters busy. And there's many a silver spoon found in a dustbin.'

'Lot 24, various British colonials on album sheets, including St Helena first types: New Brunswick first types; Turks Islands; St Christopher, Gambia, St Vincent, Cape of Good . . .'

'Good God!' cried Oliver under his breath. 'It can't be.'

But it was. He hadn't somehow made the connexion before. Yet the man Hazlitt, of Harrow and Hazlitt, Ltd., was none other than that swine 'Uncle' Hazlitt, the football captain who had jockeyed him out of his place in the Charchester team – the same Hazlitt, in fact, who had warned him gruffly in his first week at Charchester: 'Stamps are *nefas* here, you blasted new boy,' or words to that effect. That Hazlitt who used to tell *him*, Oliver, that he was eating too much and getting out of condition. That Hazlitt who proved his bloodhood by collecting china pigs. That very Hazlitt, as fat as any 'Jolly Old Sow' now, with a potty little hammer in his hand, selling stamps all afternoon to Japs and chaps in bowler hats and old Sir Arthur Gamm, by damn, with the rheumy eyes and well-gnawed beard. Well, of all the unlikely freaks of fate!

The nun was busy with her beads as lots 38 to 50 drew nearer: her Tuscany rarities. These and some other issues of Italian States had been put into the sale out of the usual order as a courtesy to the Italian bidders present. An important reunion of London Italians was taking place that afternoon at half-past three. The nearer clergyman grumbled audibly at this. 'What right, what moral right, has Italy to thrust herself forward to the head of the alphabet, at the expense of Afghanistan, Albania, Alsace-Lorraine . . .?'

The further clergyman answered, epigrammatically: 'To an Italian, sir, the "I" takes alphabetical precedence! The Fascist fallacy!'

Oliver smiled scornfully; his love of Italian art had made a

Fascist of him. (That was another thing Jane had against him, for some reason or other.)

There was a respectful hush as the green girl carried the brick red gem for inspection down the left of the room, up and down the aisle between the tables, back up the right of the room. It looked importantly minute in the centre of a huge sheet of paper. Hazlitt rapped. Bidding started at twenty guineas and dealers and collectors alike soon abandoned their pretence that they didn't really want it. Bids jumped five pounds at a time; within half a minute Hazlitt had brought the price to three hundred. There it stuck, but at the last moment old Sir Arthur raised his handkerchief to his nose, and it was clear that he meant business. A formidable opponent, but the two soft hats who had been making a private quarrel of it since the two hundred and fifty mark were not abashed and drove him up to three hundred and fifty, where one of them, who used a modified Fascist salute for his bid, fell out. Sir Arthur Gamm at four hundred and ninety pounds shook his head, gravely smiling at the soft hat and handkerchiefed at a bound to five hundred guineas. He got the thing. Soft hat shrugged.

The nearer clergyman whispered, 'Sir Arthur lords it over all the Italian States, and refuses to be dispossessed.'

'All the same,' thought Oliver, 'it's easy money for old Uncle Hazlitt. Twelve and a half per cent on five hundred guineas is roughly, well, let me see, it's over sixty quid! Sixty quid in about two minutes! No wonder he's got so fat.'

About twenty people went away at this point, Italian specialists, and there was a scramble for their vacant seats. Three o'clock struck, and then, from a door behind the girl clerk, in came another green girl with a rattling trolley of tea in white cups. It reminded Oliver of Crewe railway station and made him feel rather train-sick. Each saucer contained two dry biscuits; there was nothing to pay. Both clergymen took tea and so did the Lancashire man, and one bowler hat. Nobody else. Hazlitt had accepted a cup first of all, to make everyone feel at home, but paid no further attention to it.

Oliver was forced to admit that Hazlitt knew his job. He never missed a wink or twitch, and in announcing his wares calculated the stress very exactly; he had been duly respectful in alluding to the *tablet inverted* of the Tuscany brick red. Oliver felt that when the penny puce, Lot 74, came up it would be in competent hands. He had always wondered what point there had been in the creating of Uncle Hazlitt and now it was clear. God moved in a mysterious way His wonders to perform. Uncle Hazlitt had been created expressly for the purpose of, in the first place, plaguing him, Oliver, at Charchester and so fortifying his spirit against the shocks of post-academic life, and, in the second, of auctioning this stamp in a highly professional style and bringing him, Oliver, great sacks of coin to cheer his soul withal. After that Hazlitt would probably be allowed to die off.

Sometimes Hazlitt would make a bid himself from written instructions sent him by absent clients. At one point a telegraph boy arrived with a telegram which the girl clerk opened and laid beside Hazlitt on the rostrum. In some cases, Oliver suspected, Hazlitt made forcing bids which had no authority behind them: the notes that the girl clerk handed him might easily be bluffs.

Lot 72. Bang! Lot 73. Bang! An impressive pause. Hazlitt cleared his throat. 'Gentlemen – ah, and ladies – you will pardon me, I hope, if I break with the traditions of this room and record with what emotion I announce Lot 74. When this wonderful little gem was first brought into our research department, the senior partner of the firm very appropriately quoted the words of the American humorist, Bret Harte:

> Do I sleep? Do I Dream?
> Do I wander and Doubt?
> Are things what they seem,
> Or is visions about?

Lot 74. Antigua: one penny, purple-brown, Young Queen's Head.'

'Puce,' interrupted Oliver, firmly.

There was a gasp and a titter.

But Hazlitt continued smoothly: 'Purple-brown or puce, whichever pleases the gentleman most. A rose 'neath any other name, you know. . . . Lot 74. Antigua: one penny, *puce* or purple-brown, Young Queen's head on octagonal tablet, with ship and lighthouse design, 1866, is a unique and hitherto unrecorded stamp. Not merely an unrecorded variety, but an early stamp of wholly unknown design and yet of unimpeachable genuineness. An ironical note is struck by the pencilled message on the cover: 'Insufficiently stamped. Collect!' It will be recalled that in those distant days it cost sixpence to convey a letter from Antigua to these shores: 1d. was the denomination for island use only. Researches have shown that the vessel which was carrying a consignment of some hundreds of sheets of this design struck a rock and went to the bottom off the coast of Antigua, in March, 1866. How this particular specimen came to survive the wreck and to be handed in at the Post Office of St John – for it bears the familiar cancellation A02 – is not known. It is likely to remain one of the great Mysteries of the Sea. Beautiful condition, original cover entire, with the certificate of the Royal Philatelic Society. What a lot!'

'Good stuff!' muttered Oliver.

'And now that I have wasted your time by this little outburst, gentlemen, I shall venture to save what I have wasted by starting the bidding at a price worthy of the occasion. I make an opening bid of fifteen hundred pounds.'

Startled by the figure, nobody made any move for a few seconds; then a soft hat cocked a finger, a bowler who had hitherto been inactive twitched an eye, and the struggle had begun. Up and up.

'Two thousand one hundred – and twenty-five – and fifty – and seventy-five – two hundred – and fifty – and seventy-five – three hundred . . .'

Three thousand, and four bidders still in. At four thousand, three. At four thousand, five hundred, a slight weakening. A bowler fell out. Soft hat versus the remaining bowler. 'And twenty-five. And fifty. Going at four thousand, five hundred and fifty . . .'

Oliver had noticed that it was considered good form for the people not bidding to look away, so as not to confuse the auctioneer, but now all necks were craned, like a crowd watching a street fight.

T—E

'Six hundred,' said the soft hat, and the bowler had to return to the charge.

At five thousand, intense excitement. Bowler wins. 'Going, going . . .'

A gleam of white from an unlooked-for quarter. 'Sir Arthur Gamm,' the Lancashire man gasped. 'Crikey! Now we're in for a fight.'

'One hundred – and fifty – two hundred – and fifty –'

'Five hundred,' said the bowler out loud, hoping to end the matter.

'And six hundred to you, sir,' rejoined Sir Arthur tartly.

Bowler was weakening. 'And twenty-five,' he switched.

'And fifty,' Sir Arthur handkerchiefed.

A bustle at the door. A seedy-looking man in a wet mackintosh came swiftly in with something in his hands, something in a long envelope. The girl clerk tried to intercept it, but he brushed her aside and thrust it into Hazlitt's hand, mumbling something.

'An outside bid, by Jove!' said the further clergyman, with a faint whistle, like that of a sleepy canary.

Hazlitt tore open the envelope while the whole room glared and gaped. Then he smiled significantly at the intruder: 'Thank you, sir. I bid six thousand pounds,' he announced quietly.

Sir Arthur turned white. Yet he struggled gamely on. 'And fifty!'

'I bid seven thousand pounds,' said Hazlitt in the tones of one who will not permit contradiction. The bowler grinned. His instructions had been not to let Sir Arthur get the stamp. Sir Arthur's handkerchief trembled, checked, was still.

The stamp was knocked down to the unknown bidder for seven thousand pounds.

The rest was mere anti-climax. The room emptied of all except a few bowler hats and a soft hat or two. Sir Arthur Gamm staggered away disconsolately. The Borzoi woman and the woman in mourning remained. The Borzoi woman bid excitedly up to twenty-five shillings for a Labuan Surcharged or something, failed to get it, dashed out chattering. The bowler hats were active but bored. Hazlitt had returned to his dry style. Lot 203 ended the show, with Oliver still sitting in a golden dream.

Seven thousand pounds, less commission. Over six thousand pounds clear. Six thousand fine rustling pound notes, all for a potty, soppy little bit of coloured paper, not a square inch in total acreage. What couldn't he buy or do with six thousand? Would he have to pay income-tax? Would he . . . ? And then the thought constantly suppressed, constantly recurring: 'Jane will read about this in the papers – can't miss it. *I* don't care.'

Hazlitt slowly climbed down from his rostrum. The two were alone in the room now, but for the green girls and some-one settling a small debt at the desk. And the woman in mourning sitting immovably in her seat. Must be a pretty woman, by the by. Neat ankles, well-cared-for hands. But rather muscular calves, like a dancer's.

He saluted Hazlitt. 'Hullo, Uncle, didn't realize you were you. Pretty smart bit of work this afternoon, eh?'

Hazlitt looked at him for a moment, waited for the customer to finish settling his debt and then said, without holding out his hand: 'Yes, Mr Price, pretty dashed smart. And now what are you going to do about it?' He held out a document.

Oliver was nonplussed. 'Eh?'

'Read this.'

'What is it? The seven thousand bid, isn't it?'

'Seven thousand bid, hell! It's an interlocutory injunction to prevent us selling that stamp; because someone swears it isn't yours.'

'But you've sold it, haven't you?'

'To O. Price, Esq. A formal way of withdrawing a lot without offending either the highest bidder or the owner. But we'll not be hard on you: we'll charge you no commission on the sale, only a fee to cover advertising and my services, and those of the staff. A fiver will probably be enough. Oh, and there's the insurance.'

'But . . . it's my stamp, no question about it.'

'Tell that to the High Court Judge.'

'Or at least I'm selling it on behalf of . . .'

Hazlitt turned his back, to give the clerk some instructions.

Oliver's voice trailed away. He picked up the injunction and read it dully:

In the High Court of Justice, King's Bench Division

Between JANE PALFREY, PLAINTIFF,

AND

Oliver Price, and Ernest Harrow and Thomas Cobleigh Hazlitt trading as Harrow and Hazlitt, DEFENDANTS.

Upon hearing Counsel for the plaintiff, and upon reading the affidavit of Jane Palfrey filed the 12th day of February, 1935, and the plaintiff by her said counsel undertaking to abide by any order the Court or a Judge may make as to damages in case the Court or a Judge shall hereafter be of opinion that the defendant has sustained any, by reason of this order, which the plaintiff ought to pay:

IT IS ORDERED AND DIRECTED that the defendants Ernest Harrow and Thomas Cobleigh Hazlitt trading as Harrow and Hazlitt, their agents and servants and every of them be restrained and an injunction is hereby granted restraining them and every of them from selling, offering for sale, or in any way disposing of or imperilling the adhesive postage stamp referred to in the claim endorsed on the writ of summons herein until after the hearing of a summons returnable on the twentieth day of February next. And it is further ordered that the plaintiff be at liberty to issue and serve a summons for that day to continue this injunction and that the costs of this application be reserved.

Dated the 12th day of February, 1935 . . .

So that was what an injunction was like, was it? He'd always wondered. Just as he had always wondered what a stamp auction was like. Pah! The Devil fly away with all injunctions and all stamp auctions. With them and every of them!

He went out slowly. The woman in mourning went out too. It was dark now and raining hard. A taxi cruised past. Oliver hailed it. The woman hailed it. Oliver gallantly opened the door for her. She got in and said: 'Burlington Theatre, please.' And then to Oliver, 'Thank you, Oliver, that was very considerate of you'.

Jane!

Always Jane.

And that fat pig Hazlitt, the man who . . .

And Jane.

CHAPTER II

BEFORE THE TRIAL

THE next day Oliver asked Edith whether she had noticed a paragraph in the papers about the auction of an Antiguan stamp. She hadn't.

'Well, it happened to be the one you once gave Jane for my collection. Do you remember? On an envelope? Saying you wanted the source to be anonymous.'

'Oh, yes. I stole the letter from Father's papers. I had a feeling it was a valuable stamp.'

'That's all right. He never noticed the loss, did he?'

'No, but still . . .'

'You did intend it for me, not Jane, didn't you, darling?' (He managed to call her 'darling' now quite easily.)

'Jane had asked me for stamps; but I should never have stolen if it hadn't been for you – it seemed so exciting doing it for you.'

'That's just what I thought,' said Oliver triumphantly. 'Well, Jane suggested dividing up my collection by each of us taking a stamp in turn – I told you about that, didn't I? And I let her do it, Heaven knows why, because, though I had once allowed her to call the collection "ours", it was really entirely mine, as you know. I did all the work on it and spent all the money. I suppose I was "too hopelessly public-school", as Jane puts it, to stand up for my rights. But before we started I removed the Antigua stamp out of harm's way. I felt she had even less right to it than to the rest of the collection. I mean, it was a definite present from you to me. Well, by a bit of bad luck she must have had advance news of the auction, so she had an injunction served. It arrived in the middle of the bidding, and the auctioneer had to withdraw the stamp. Naturally I felt an awful fool.'

'Oliver! Does this mean Jane will sue you?'

'I'm afraid it does. It'll look pretty bad in the papers.'

'I'll beg her not to.'

'Jane has a spite against me: she wouldn't listen to anything you said. It's much better if you keep out of this, Edith. Promise me you won't mention the matter to her in any way! She'd guess our secret if you did.'

'O Oliver, can't we tell her everything? I do hate this hole-and-corner business.'

'Not yet, darling. It would make things far worse than they are. We must wait until she sues me and then surprise her by your giving evidence on my side.'

'O Noll, darling, I don't want to do *that*.'

'Look here, Edith,' Oliver said roughly, gripping her shoulder, 'you love me, don't you? You're not going to let me down? Jane will sue me, anyhow – whether she knows about you and me or whether she doesn't. And if you don't stick by me now I'll lose my case and be publicly declared a common thief.'

Edith looked miserable. 'You know very well I love you. But I don't believe Jane's as heartless as you say. If I told her that you and I were going to get married . . .'

'If you tell her that, everything's over between us,' Oliver threatened. 'Now be sensible, darling. You'll have to give evidence in any case. If you don't come forward on my side, Jane's lawyers will subpoena you to witness for her and trick you into saying things against me. Much better if you volunteer evidence on my behalf.'

'What do you want me to say?'

'If you tell the literal truth they'll twist it against me. The best thing is to tell a near-truth which will have the effect of literal truth. It's like, well, if one wants to see a faint star clearly with the naked eye one looks not quite directly at it, so as to avoid the dull spot on one's retina, and then it shows up. But stare straight at it and there's a blur.'

Edith, like many scientists in love, was easily convinced by a false analogy. She said resolutely, 'All right, darling, if I must. I see what you mean, I think.'

'I want you to say that you didn't actually *give* me, or Jane and me, the stamp. It wasn't yours to give. You just sent it me as something interesting to look at when I was away at school. And that when I came back for the vacation I forgot to return it. And that recently I came across it when I was thinking of selling my album, and showed it you. And, it being yours now, you authorized me to sell it for you. Do you mind saying that?'

'It isn't true. I *did* intend it as a gift. Can't I say that I found it lying about the house and gave it to you and Jane *then*, but that it wasn't mine, so the gift wasn't valid? And when you pointed the stamp out to me the other day I said that, really, I ought to make a formal presentation of it to you, since it *was* mine now as Father's heiress? That I didn't mention Jane, thinking it all rather a joke, but that none the less I did definitely give it to you?'

'Not a possible defence. The Law would say: you gave it to Jane and me, and your father didn't dispute our title – perhaps not knowing we had the stamp, but as I say, not in fact disputing our title. That it remained Jane's and mine – as you know, possession is nine points of the Law – and it's been in our undisputed possession since 1921. Whatever you say your intention was then is what you'll have to stand by now. At this late hour you can't say that you gave it to only me, if you also say that originally your intention was to give it to Jane and me.'

'But my inner intention *was* to give it to just you, because ... because I was in love with you.'

'If you told that story, the Law would probably say that you had to abide by your intention as originally expressed, which was that Jane and I should own the stamp jointly.'

'It I'd only realized ...'

'So now, if you love me, or even from a common sense of fairness to me, you'll get me out of this hole by saying that you only lent Jane the letter, to read, and said that I might be interested in the stamp on the envelope. You expected both to be returned. It doesn't concern me whether Jane ever returned the letter or not, but what does concern me is that you should say that I did eventually return the stamped envelope. And that you asked me to sell it for you.'

'I'd do anything for you, Oliver, you know. If you really think it's honest.'

'It Jane had played the game there'd be no need for slightly colouring the facts. But she hasn't.'

So he made Edith sign a document, antedated to June 23rd

1934 (which was several weeks before his meeting with Jane in the gallery), giving him authority to sell on her behalf, 'a stamped envelope postmarked A02'. That would put him right with Hazlitt and be valuable evidence at the trial.

'I don't like doing this at all,' Edith sighed.

Harrow and Hazlitt wrote to Jane's lawyers, saying that they had offered the stamp for sale in good faith and that the sale had been commissioned by Mr Oliver Price of 27 Albion Mansions, Battersea, on behalf, he now stated, of a third party. And that the stamp had been withdrawn from sale by Mr Price himself.

When his own injunction was served on him, Oliver, who did not like wasting money on lawyers and felt himself capable of conducting his own case, wrote to Jane's lawyers as follows:

> 27 Albion Mansions,
> *Feb. 20th, '35*

Dear Sirs,

The stamped envelope is not Miss Palfrey's and she knows it, and it never was. It was never even mine, so I could not transfer to her a title which I did not possess. That's logic, isn't it? The stamped envelope to which she alludes was not included in the division of the collection. I had previously been authorized to sell the stamp by the real owner, whose name however I am not at present permitted to divulge. Miss Palfrey can sue if she likes. She will only lose her case, and I advise her not to do so, because if she does she will make herself publicly ridiculous.

> Yours obediently,
> Oliver Palfrey St Simon Price

Edith did not say a word. And Jane was firm in her resolution not to say a word to her about either Oliver or the stamp. But Jane was genuinely puzzled. The 'real owner' could not be Edith, because Edith had unquestionably given her the stamp for the collection – she couldn't deny that.

She told Mrs Trent: 'I think he's perhaps trying to bluff me by pretending that Edith is prepared to perjure herself for his sake in the witness box. Thinks that a sense of public decency will prevent me from suing him if there is a risk of creating a stink by having my partner appear as a witness against me. That's dangerous, though. How is he to know that private decency will keep me from questioning Edith? He has no sense of private decency himself. Perhaps the real owner is someone else. Perhaps it's Edna. Perhaps all Sir Reginald's papers were left to her and Oliver was genuinely selling the stamp on her behalf. Or perhaps the owner is the whole Whitebillet Company, not a private person at all. But no, then they'd not use Oliver as a go-between. Oliver couldn't possibly have routed out the descendant of the original addressee, could he? That's whom the stamp belongs to really, I suppose, if there *is* such a person. No, that's impossible. I've got the letter and the only clues are in that.'

She decided to sue and risk it. 'Some dirty work is bound to be revealed at the trial. That's all I care about. I want Edith to realize what sort of a rogue she proposes to marry.'

'But suppose they get married before then, my dear?'

'They can't, Gwennie. I haven't told you about that, but it's as follows. When Edith and I entered into partnership in 1930 my lawyer and hers agreed that neither of us should marry without giving the other six months' notice. At least, not until October 15th, 1935 – under stringent penalties. Edith knows that. Anyhow, she can't get married for six months from now, and by that time the trial will surely be over and she'll have seen Oliver for what he really is. So I think it's safe enough. If she's taken Oliver into her confidence, he'll advise her not to expose herself to the said stringent penalties. They involve the forfeit of a lot of money, and Oliver's after her money, of course.'

Jane had a sudden thought. 'Edna's safe among the lions and zebras in Kenya, by now, isn't she, Gwennie?'

'Oh, yes, my dear. She sailed the first week of January, I believe.'

'Then I'm very worried about Edna, Gwennie.'

'Why, my dear?'

'She's never been quite herself since her accident.'

'What accident? I didn't hear of any accident.'

'Listen, Gwennie. Poor Edna, last October, slipped on the stairs, fell and hurt herself, and that's why her baby wasn't born. She shouldn't have played golf and tennis at St Aidan's only a month later. Edna's very careless of her health, you know.'

'But there wasn't a baby!'

'No, she slipped on the stairs.'

'I mean. . . . Oh, Miss Jane – you're very wicked, you're teasing me again. Meaning, I suppose, that I'm to spin that yarn to Mr Oliver?'

'Yes, Gwennie, that's exactly it. Except that I want you to let him know indirectly, somehow.'

'That's going to be difficult, isn't it?'

'It's got to be done. Whom do you know at St Aidan's who would tell Oliver? It has to be someone whom he'd believe, and also someone who's willing to tell lies for you.'

'The only person who answers that description is Mrs Harris, the Club House caretaker. What's more, she wrote to me that she's coming up to London soon to do a bit of shopping and will call in to see me. I don't think she'll refuse to undertake the job for me. I once arranged something rather border-line for a daughter of hers.'

'Splendid. There'll be nothing peculiar in her calling on Oliver at his flat, will there, and giving him a packet of St Aidan's gossip?'

'No. And she would have privately heard about Miss Edna's accident from the village nurse who attended her?'

'Make it so. Mrs Harris must get him to swear not to mention it to a soul. That will prevent him from comparing notes with Edith. He'll wonder why Edith didn't tell him.'

Here chance intervened. Two or three days later Edith had a cable: 'FREDDY BADLY MAULED BY LION LITTLE HOPE EDNA.' And the same day it appeared in all the newspapers, headed 'SAFARI TRAGEDY: Captain "Freddy" Smith Mauled by Lion.' Gangrene had set in and the 'little hope' seemed Reuter's view as well as Edna's. Just before lunch that day, Mrs Harris called at Oliver's flat. She told him about Edna's accident, making him promise to let it go no further, because if anyone knew that the village nurse had given away a professional secret she would lose her job.

'God!' he said. 'How disastrous!'

'Yes,' said Mrs Harris, 'I knew you'd be sorry for the poor dear. I remember you were a bit sweet on Mrs Smith in the old days, Master Oliver.'

At this point the telephone bell rang. Oliver got up to answer it, his brains churning. It was Edith, to tell about Freddy and the lion.

'It will shatter Edna,' Edith sniffed. 'She'll *never* marry again. And nothing at all to show for her marriage – I mean, no babies.'

'God, how disastrous!' he said again, and then, in a telephone whisper, 'Excuse me, I've got friends here. Meet me as usual and we'll talk it over.'

By this time everyone knows Oliver well enough to be able to guess with fair accuracy what he was thinking. His first thought was neither for Edna nor for Freddy nor for Edith, but for Oliver. He cursed himself for having disbelieved the story about Edna's baby and for having in consequence got compromised with Edith. He couldn't honourably retreat now. And besides, he was so deeply involved in his struggle with Jane that he could not risk giving up Edith, his most valuable ally.

And his second thought? Has anyone guessed that yet? His second thought was that if Freddy died, which he would not regret in the least, having been madly jealous of Freddy and hated him with the peculiar hatred of an Oxford aesthete for an Oxford hearty – and Freddy, playing with Edna, had once driven into his three-ball match on the links at St Aidan's, with only a perfunctory 'fore!' though the other two balls were Father's and the Bishop's. ... Well, if Freddy died, Edna would be a widow, and it was Edna whom Oliver really wanted, always had wanted. And now it was clear that, after all, Edna was the one who could have babies. Edith was a barren stock, in Queen Elizabeth's words.

They met at four o'clock, as usual, at the Stefanssons'. When they were alone, Edith shyly leant against Oliver. 'O Noll, you can't think what it means to me to have someone to share my worries with.' She burst into tears.

Oliver stiffened. 'Yes, rotten luck,' he forced out. Oliver, as he bitterly reminded himself, was too hopelessly public school to do anything so ungentlemanly as to fling her aside and tell her for the love of God to stop crying down his neck.

Poor Oliver, poor Edith, poor everyone!

He persuaded Edith that she ought to go out to Kenya at once. Edith thought this so noble of him – wouldn't he be terribly lonely without her? And another thing was: could Jane possibly manage alone?

Oliver said that Jane would jolly well have to manage, so Edith flew to Port Said the next day, where she picked up a Union-Castle liner and reached Nairobi just as Freddy took a turn for the better. He had refused to let them amputate his injured leg and the gangrene gradually drained away. He was perfectly fit again in four months.

Meanwhile Jane put The Emu in Edith's job; he did creditably under her supervision. But Jane was overworked. It was lucky that *Victorian Paradise* was still playing to good houses. And when the run came to an end she could put on *Hamlet*, which had been in rehearsal a few months before, but had been postponed when Jane had the Victorian idea. Jane grew very fond of The Emu, and one day took him into her confidence about the whole Oliver-Edith-and-Antigua entanglement, incidentally showing him the shipwreck letter and the 'Save Will Young' cut.

The Emu asked her all sorts of intelligent questions. At last he said: 'Do you mind if I take a typed copy of this letter?'

'Type away. But why?'

'Just an idea. Forget it. If nothing comes of it, nothing's lost.'

'Emu, are you heart and soul with me in this war with Oliver? You haven't the slightest reservations? No pity on his behalf, no feeling that I'm being a beast?'

'No, Jane. It's just the way I'd have played the game myself, if I had your brains. I've never met your brother, of course, but he doesn't seem quite human, does he?'

'Human, all too human.'

'Well, you know what I mean. Churchy, and at the same time a bit of a welsher. Not one of *us*, in fact.'

'I accept the amendment. Yes, he's somehow missed the Palfrey strain in the family blood-stream. I got it all.'

Oliver wrote to Edith at Nairobi. He felt he had to write. He wrote how lonely he was, but that she must stay away as long as was necessary – and have a good rest.

Edith was back in April. She was looking unusually pretty,

and had done her hair in a different way and was dressed very
becomingly. Edna had given her a very good time and lectured
her on her appearance and told her to stop at Paris on her way
back and put herself in the hands of Molineux, or someone,
and engage a French maid: for what was the good of having
lots of money if you went about looking like a first-year
Polytechnic student?

She said how glad she was to be back. Funny, that when she
was away it was always St Aidan's she thought of as home, not
London. She'd never forget St Aidan's. 'I still send birthday
presents to Jenkins, and Mrs Harris of the Club House.'

'And old Rose, too, I suppose,' Oliver said politely. 'Nice
old thing.'

'O no, Noll, didn't you hear? She died over a year ago.'

'Are you *sure*?' Oliver exclaimed, sitting up. 'She actually
died over a year ago?'

'Yes. I heard from her son.'

'Oh, I *am* sorry,' Oliver said, covering his surprise. 'Dear
ugly old thing!'

'She helped Edna and me into the world,' said Edith with a
sad smile.

Oliver gulped. 'Tell me, Edith – idle question, but anything
to do with you, of course, interests me in a special sort of way –
do you know whether you and Edna were identical twins or
ordinary ones?'

Edith laughed. 'The ordinary sort, darling. Were you worried in case you and I mightn't have any children?'

Oliver pretended not to understand. So Edith explained the
penalty of being an identical twin, and said that, as a matter of
fact, if she had been one she would have considered it only
honest to tell Oliver the moment he had proposed; because
the fact that Edna had been married so long without having
children wouldn't necessarily have meant that she was the
unlucky one: it might have been some incapacity in Freddy.
No, no, they were ordinary, perfectly separate twins, Edna
and she.

Oliver said: 'I didn't like to mention it before, but I heard a
rumour that Edna was going to have a baby last year, but that
something went wrong.'

'Who on earth told you that?'

'Oh, just St Aidan's gossip.'

'It's an absolute lie. I mean, Edna would certainly have told me about it. She tells me *everything*.'

So the whole aspect of things changed for Oliver. He now congratulated himself on having done the decent thing by Edith. He even asked her to take off her glasses, so that he could see her eyes better; and she did so, and he kissed her with genuine ardour. . . . They agreed to get married as soon as the Antigua case was over.

The next day he gave her part of his novel to read, and Edith, who was not very sophisticated, thought it wonderful; she had hardly read a novel in her life. She told Oliver that it reminded her of *Ivanhoe*. Oliver looked rather offended. 'But much, much better, of course,' Edith added quickly.

Then there was a play that Oliver had written. It was a political satire, all about Fascists and Communists in a place called Angletania, which was really England. Edith thought that very good, too, and said that Oliver ought to get it staged as soon as possible.

'It's been turned down by four managers,' said Oliver.

'They're all hopelessly the same, won't try anything new. Of course, they all agreed that it was dashed good stuff – I'll show you some of their letters – but what's the use of that?'

'If only there wasn't this row with Jane,' Edith sighed.

'Jane! I wouldn't trust a play of mine to Jane if she went down on her knees for it,' Oliver exclaimed.

Jane said to Mrs Trent: 'I can't understand it. Judging by the golden daze in which Edith is going about, Oliver seems to have swallowed all his prejudices against a childless marriage.'

Mrs Trent said: 'Well, I don't know, my dear. Miss Edith's certainly far better groomed than what she was, and that may have made all the difference to Mr Oliver. But on the other hand it may be that he's hanging on to her only until this case comes on, and then he'll develop another bad heart.'

'You mean that he's counting on Edith to back him up in some lie, Gwennie?' It was the first time that Jane had allowed herself to voice such a suggestion, even for the sake of immediately repudiating it as scandalous and incredible.

'That's my instinct, my dear.'

'Well, I believe Oliver capable of any evil work or renegade dealing, but Edith is far too straight a person to allow herself to be involved in a lie, however much in love she may be. If I thought she was, I'd chuck up the theatre and get me to a nunnery, soured for life.'

'And Mr Oliver would gladly step into your shoes. If he marries Miss Edith, that's exactly what he'll do. He'll make Miss Edith put up the money to buy you out, and *then* you'll see! O. Price handicap 2, manager of the Burlington Theatre – astrakhan collar and all.'

'Gwennie, is this a wild fantasy, or is it based on anything solid in the way of fact?'

'Well, my dear, Mr Oliver writes plays, doesn't he?'

'Does he?'

'Yes, he distinctly mentioned plays to me that day he tried to pump me about the twin business. And he's got just the neck for an astrakhan collar.'

'Gwennie, Gwennie, you must learn to report things more promptly and more fully. You should have told me at the time that Oliver wrote plays. Ugh, I can imagine them! Sickening plays. Problem themes shot through and through with the most refined ghastly comic relief. A Galsworthy one embodying his experiences in the General Strike. He was a scab, of course, in the strike – special leave from the Headmaster. It was the high spot of his career. Well, well! Things are breaking badly, Gwennie, I'm afraid. But we're not beaten yet. And certainly, Oliver as playwright and theatrical manager is a good laugh.'

'Honey, can't you warn Miss Edith what it means to us all if she marries Mr Oliver? It's not too late, is it?'

'No, Gwennie. No, no, no! It would be playing into Oliver's hands.'

It was clear now to Oliver that the story of Edna having phoned to say that she was about to have a baby, and the story of Edna having failed to have a baby because of an accident, and the story of Rose having said that Edna and Edith were identical twins, were all lies concocted by Mrs Trent to prevent him from marrying Edith. He wouldn't have believed her capable of it. Yet Jane couldn't be behind it. That would mean that she knew all about him and Edith, and yet if she had known she would obviously have had a row with Edith long ago. But she hadn't said a word.

Then Oliver thought: 'Perhaps it *was* all true about Edna. Perhaps Edith is telling lies just to keep me to my marriage with her. Perhaps she can't have children after all.'

He did not know what to think.

CHAPTER 12

PALFREY *v*. PRICE AND ANOR

IT was all reported at great length in the Press. We shall give, in a minute, a sequence of three extracts from three different newspapers. The outside view they give of the dispute, and of the three characters in the dispute, should be of assistance to the reader in arriving at an unprejudiced decision as to where, if anywhere, his or her sympathies should lie. It will be noticed that Messrs Harrow and Hazlitt are not longer joined as defendants with Oliver and Edith, and that the senior partner, Mr Ernest Harrow, actually gives evidence on Jane's behalf. The fact is, the firm made a separate peace with Jane before the issue of the writ and dropped out. That Jane was granted an interlocutory injunction against them in the first instance was due to a curious combination of circumstances.

On the afternoon of February 11th, Jane's lawyers, informed by her that the stamp was advertised for auction on the following afternoon, rang up Oliver at his flat, but got no reply. (He had gone out to a cinema.) Then they rang up Messrs. Harrow and Hazlitt and reported Jane's claim to the stamp. Normally this would have been quite enough to make them withdraw it from the auction, because they were an old-established firm and jealous of their reputation. But it happened that neither of the partners was in the office at the time and the senior clerk, who answered the phone, had a headache. Moreover, he was slightly deaf and one of those proud choleric men who refuse to admit the extent of their deafness and manage in ordinary conversation to supply the gaps in what the other person is saying by an intuitive reading of his face. On the phone, especially at a peak-hour when the wires are overloaded and audition is bad, they are apt to make remarkable mistakes. The senior clerk was now under the impression that the somewhat shrill-voiced person addressing him was the Mother Superior who was selling that collection of Tuscany stamps and had been on the phone already twice that day anxiously making sure that the auction would really take place. He had never liked nuns. He replied: 'No, no, no, no, no! Short of an earthquake, bombs from the air, or a universal pestilence or conflagration, there is, I assure you, no power in Heaven or Earth that can now prevent us from auctioning the property.' He rang off.

The lawyer was, not unnaturally, surprised at the unceremonious violence of this language. The next morning, having made a further unsuccessful attempt to get in touch with Oliver (who was out in the Park with his dog), he assured the judge to whom he applied for the injunction – in chambers – that the auctioneers refused to discuss the matter of withdrawal, and that Oliver appeared to be out of Town. Judges are usually chary of granting interlocutory injunctions *ex parte* without being well persuaded that a greater injustice would be likely to result from a refusal to grant them. Refusals are, in fact, not uncommon. But here the intransigence of the auctioneers (apparently acting on instructions from Oliver) and the strong *prima facie* case that the lawyer presented on Jane's behalf, and the urgency of the matter, combined to convince the judge that the application must be granted. It was even possible that Messrs. Harrow and Hazlitt were acting without instructions from Oliver, that they did not believe that an injunction could be obtained at such short notice, and that they intended to proceed with the auction, in the confidence of being paid their $12\frac{1}{2}$ per cent commission by Oliver, whatever the sequel. The judge reflected that if the sale took place the purchaser might be a foreign dealer who would perhaps leave the country with the stamp that same night; and it would be a costly and difficult task to recover it from him in a foreign court of law. But with the interlocutory injunction the *status quo* would be preserved during proceedings against Oliver.

Well, as we were saying, Messrs. Harrow and Hazlitt, who were surprised at the injunction, went to Jane's lawyer to inquire why it had been served. Of course, the senior clerk's mistake came to light at once and everyone thought it a good joke. Peace was immediately restored, and Jane's lawyer, who was a specialist in Imperial Russian stamps, struck up a firm friendship with Mr Harrow; and why not?

Nice people, solicitors. But barristers! The dreadful things they say in a public court!

The first extract is from an evening paper of October 15th, 1935. The sub-titles have been removed:

ANTIGUA 1d. PUCE
PIQUANT HIGH COURT CASE
Famous Actress-Manageress Claims Unique Stamp from Author Brother and Business Partner
FRAUD ALLEGED

Today in the High Court of Justice Mr Justice Hogtie was confronted with a judicial problem that might have baffled the legal acumen of a Solomon. Miss Jane Palfrey of the Burlington Theatre, w., where she directs the world-famous company known as 'Jane Palfrey Amalgamated', claimed from her brother, Mr Oliver St Simon Price, of Albion Mansions, Battersea, described as an author, and from Miss Edith Whitebillet, her business-partner, the already famous 'Antigua Penny Puce' postage-stamp, the value of which is estimated at anything from £7000 to £10,000. Miss Palfrey alleges that the stamp formed part of her share of a former joint-collection and that her brother converted it to his own use and offered it for sale by public auction at an Argent Street stamp-auction room on Feb. 12th last, fraudulently, without her consent and with intent to deprive her of it.

Mr Price insists that the stamp-collection of which Miss Palfrey claims that the stamp formed part was never held in common between them, but was his sole property. He states further that the stamp in question was never part of the collection and that he offered it for sale on behalf of Miss Edith Whitebillet, daughter of the late Sir Reginald Whitebillet, Bart., of the Whitebillet Shipping Company. Miss Whitebillet, a childhood friend of Mr Price's and Miss Palfrey's, has been associated with Miss Palfrey since 1930 in the management of the Burlington Theatre. Miss Palfrey's case is that an arrangement was recently entered into between herself and her brother for dividing the collection equally between them, and that, according to the method of partition agreed upon, the Antigua stamp would have fallen to her share had it been included in the album. She charges Mr Price with concealing the stamp and pretending ignorance both as to its whereabouts and as to its value.

Mr Antony Merlin, K.C. for Miss Palfrey, stated that in November, 1919, Miss Palfrey and Mr Price, then aged respectively eleven and twelve, entered into an informal partnership in a stamp-collection which had hitherto belonged to Mr Price.

Mr Justice Hogtie: Are they true brother and sister or children of different marriages?

Mr Merlin: True brother and sister.

Mr Justice Hogtie: Then is Miss Palfrey's name merely a stage name?

Mr Merlin: It is her legal name, my lord. It was changed from Price to Palfrey by deed-poll in 1929, the year that Miss Palfrey came of age. Palfrey was her mother's name.

Mr Merlin, continuing, stated that no account was kept of the value of the stamps contributed by each of the parties to the collection, but that by 1921, the date of the most recent additions, the estimated market value of the collection apart from the stamp under dispute was between £15 and £20. A large number of the latest acquisitions were made by the plaintiff, and the stamp under dispute was itself obtained by the plaintiff.

On Monday, September 17, 1934, the plaintiff met the defendant in a public picture-gallery where a picture entitled 'The Stamp Collectors' was being exhibited. Painted in 1920, it portrayed the plaintiff, the defendant and their father in a domestic scene centring in the stamp-album. The plaintiff then asked the defendant whether he still had their stamp-collection in his keeping. The defendant replied in disacknowledgement of the plaintiff's right to it, saying that it had long ago lapsed. The plaintiff insisted that this was not the case and wrote a letter to the defendant arranging for an amicable meeting at the defendant's flat at Albion Mansions, Battersea, ten days later. Each party should alternately choose and remove stamps from the collection, one stamp at a time, page by page, the album itself remaining in the defendant's possession. This meeting took place on Thursday, 27th of September. An album was produced by Mr Price similar to the original album and containing a collection of stamps apparently identical with the original collection. The plaintiff, who did not at the time realize that she was being deceived, allowed the defendant to make first choice. He chose a stamp from the first page of the album, marking his initials against it in pencil. The plaintiff then chose a stamp from the same page, removed it and initialled the vacancy created. The defendant then chose another stamp and once more pencilled his initials against it. This procedure was carried on from page to page, each page being exhausted before a new one was begun. When the last of the stamps of the United Kingdom section had been chosen, the same method of partition was applied to the British Colonies section, which occurred next. The first colony for which provision was made in the album was the Island of Antigua and the plaintiff immediately inquired for the brownish-purple (or puce) Antiguan stamp of one penny denomination and unusual design which she had sent him, attached to the original envelope, in November 1921, while he was a scholar at Charchester School. The defendant replied that he did not know where the stamp was; it had probably fallen out of the album at some time or other.

'It is an important link in my argument,' said Mr Merlin, 'that at this point Miss Palfrey deliberately missed a turn and so did not waive her right, under the partition agreement, to appropriate that stamp to her share. There were thirty-nine British stamps and only five Antiguan stamps: yet Mr Price, who had first choice of the British stamps and selected twenty of them as against his sister's nineteen, took three of these Antiguan stamps as against her two. It is plain that my client thus reserved her claim to the missing stamp, as her first choice in the Antigua section.'

Mr Merlin described how early in the February of this year Miss Palfrey heard by chance that the missing stamp was being offered for sale at Messrs. Harrow and Hazlitt's Argent Street Stamp-Auction Rooms. She experienced an unfortunate delay in obtaining an interlocutory injunction to stop the sale and it was only when the bidding had reached the extraordinarily high figure of £7,000 that the injunction could be served. He wished it to be clearly understood that his client was making no charge against Messrs. Harrow and Hazlitt's good faith in the matter.

Miss Palfrey appeared in a chestnut-coloured costume with a soft hat of a chestnut-lilac shade and a scarf of a soft silvery material. She described in her evidence how the stamp came to form part of the collection. She had permitted her brother to take the album with him to Charchester School in September 1921 to add to it by a process known as 'the swapping of duplicates', but he had in fact done nothing, while there, to contribute to its enlargement. She, on the other hand, had collected a number of stamps from her friends and sent them by post to her brother, who however wrote her a letter telling her that he was no longer interested in stamps, having 'put such things behind him' at his preparatory school. Among the stamps sent him was the Antigua rarity in question, recently given her, together with a few others, by Miss Edith White-billet, who had, she understood, obtained it from her father, the late Sir Reginald Whitebillet. She believed at the time that it was of great value.

Mr Merlin: What led you to suppose so?

Miss Palfrey then produced and read extracts from a re-markable letter which, she said, had been contained in the envelope to which the stamp was affixed. It was written in 1866 by a certain Captain Tom Young, commanding the steam-packet *Phoebe*, of the Whitebillet Line, which regularly con-veyed her Majesty's mails from Jamaica to the Leeward Islands, of which group Antigua forms part. In this letter Captain Young bids farewell to his brother, Fred, saying that his vessel has struck a rock half a mile from the shore and is break-ing up and that he is alone, awaiting death any minute. He recalls their happy youth together in the English countryside and hopes to meet again 'in the other land'. He writes that he is putting the letter in a bottle and consigning it to the mercy of the waves, having ensured that it will be forwarded, if found, by stamping it with a postage-stamp of a new consignment that he has in the safe in his cabin. 'It was this letter,' Miss Palfrey said, 'that suggested to me that the stamp might be valuable, as being the sole survivor of an entire issue of stamps. I searched for mention of it in a stamp-catalogue but, not finding it, concluded that no further stamps of that particular design had been printed and that therefore it must be unique. My brother's lack of interest, however, and my own youth turned my attention from the matter. But the division of the stamps brought it back to my mind. If he had not concealed the stamp from me, I should certainly have volunteered to share its value with him.'

The envelope, which was produced in court, was addressed to 'Mr Harry Young, last heard of in Canterbury Settlement' (New Zealand) 'in the care of Messrs. John Whitebillet and Sons, Parliament Street, Liverpool, England.'

Mr Merlin: In whose possession was the stamp-album between the years 1921 and 1934?

Miss Palfrey: In 1922 I also rather lost interest in the album and it was taken care of for us by our parents in our home at St Aidan's. At their death in 1930 my brother found it and took it away with him to London. I should not have permitted this, but I was in America at the time and on my return I was too busy with my professional duties to think of the matter. In 1934 it occurred to me that I might as well have my share of the collection before it was too late.

Miss Palfrey then described her visit to her brother's flat, the amicable partitioning of a collection of stamps which she assumed, from its extreme similarity, to be the collection in question, and her inquiries for the Antigua stamp, about which Mr Price professed to know nothing. She stated that although at the time she accepted in good faith that the album from which the stamps were taken was the original one, she now knew that it was a substitute, except for the cover and fly leaf, and that the stamps it contained were also substitutes for the originals.

Mr Philip Schreiner, K.C. for the defence: You suggest that inferior stamps were substituted by my client?

Miss Palfrey: No. Not necessarily inferior. But not the ones that had constituted the original collection. I noticed afterwards slight differences in tone and condition and in the position of the postmarks from the stamps I remembered as having formed our joint collection.

Mr Schreiner: I suggest that your memory was at fault in this matter, Miss Palfrey.

Miss Palfrey: No.

Mr Schreiner: I suggest further that in the year 1921 Miss Whitebillet did not give you the letter and stamped envelope in question, which was not hers to give, but merely lent you the letter to read as an exciting human document?

Miss Palfrey: It was a gift.

Mr Schreiner: I suggest, moreover, that you then said that the stamp would interest your brother, and asked permission to send it to him for an opinion as to value, and that Miss White-billet gave you permission?

Miss Palfrey: That is not so. Miss Whitebillet gave me the letter as a free gift and said that the stamp on the envelope was for the collection that my brother and I shared.

Mr Schreiner: When under the impression (which I shall show to have been an erroneous one) that you were being made this valuable gift, did not you inquire from what source Miss Whitebillet had obtained it?

Miss Palfrey: The envelope indicated that it had originally come from the Liverpool shipping office, but I asked no questions. I assumed that Sir Reginald, Miss Whitebillet's father, had said that she could have it. My father had similarly told me on several occasions that I could have stamps off old envelopes that I found in boxes of family papers in the attic.

Mr Schreiner: Surely only the stamps, not entire letters? Children are not given valuable historical documents to play with, are they?

Miss Palfrey: The historical value of the letter in question may not have struck Sir Reginald. If I considered the matter at all at the time I must have thought something like this: 'It's a letter that has been waiting for its addressee for over fifty years and Sir Reginald knows that it won't be claimed now, so he's let Edith (Miss Whitebillet) have it as a curiosity.'

Mr Schreiner: But you are aware now that Miss Whitebillet, whom you know to be a woman of the highest integrity, insists that the letter, envelope and stamp were only a loan to you?

Miss Palfrey: I am aware that this is the case that is being put forward.

Mr Schreiner: I put it to you that the collection was 'ours' to yourself and Mr Price in no more than a colloquial sense, as a child might refer to 'our' house, meaning merely the house it lived in with its parents?

Miss Palfrey: That is not so.

Mr Schreiner: I suggest that Mr Price merely allowed you for a short period to help him arrange the stamps.

Miss Palfrey: That is utterly untrue.

Mr Schreiner: In the face of the defence which my questions have indicated, do you still continue in your pretensions to the ownership of this stamp?

Miss Palfrey: I do. There is a proverb, common to many European languages, according to which to make a gift and then to recall it is as bad as, or worse than, stealing. And I cannot believe that Miss Whitebillet will give evidence on oath antedating her intervention in this dispute between my brother and myself to a day previous to September 17th, 1934. She had at the time not been in communication with Mr Price for a number of years. And if Mr Price says that the collection was not 'ours' in a joint-ownership of the most formal character, he will be committing perjury.

Mr Schreiner: I am to understand that you accuse your business partner of worse than stealing, and your brother of meditating perjury?

Miss Palfrey: Miss Whitebillet made a gift, and if she now recalls it after thirteen or fourteen years, I shall regard that as a morally reprehensible action. My brother, I am sorry to say, I do not regard as either a very truthful or a very honourable person.

The hearing was adjourned until tomorrow.

CHAPTER 13

PALFREY *v*. PRICE AND ANOR
(*Continued*)

From a morning paper of October 17th:

ANTIGUA PENNY PUCE
RESUMED HEARING
Miss Edith Whitebillet Faints in the Box
ANGRY OUTBURST BY MR PRICE

Yesterday before a crowded court the hearing of the case for the possession of the famous 'Antigua Penny Puce' postage stamp was resumed. . . . Mr Antony Merlin, K.C., the counsel for the plaintiff, called as his first witness today Mr Ernest Harrow, since 1904 a partner in the firm of Messrs. Harrow and Hazlitt, of the Argent Street Stamp-Auctions.

Mr Merlin: At what date did Mr Price first visit your firm in connexion with the sale of a stamp or stamps?

Mr Harrow: On Sept. 18th of last year. He asked us to value an album for him.

Mr Merlin (handing him an album): Was it this album?

Mr Harrow: No, but one similar. It was, like this, a Stanley Gibbons album of the 1916 edition.

– No, please retain it until I have finished my questions. Did Mr Price ask you to make an offer for the stamps that the album claimed as his (not this album) contained?

– No, he explained that he and a friend who had once collaborated in building up the collection were both anxious to have the album and had agreed that it should go to the one who made the highest bid for it over its market worth. He said that he had decided to let his friend have the album at a figure that would buy him a duplicate set of stamps to exactly replace the ones in the album, for starting a new collection for himself. We quoted a figure.

– Did Mr Price in fact give the order for these duplicates?

– Yes: on the following morning he called again and informed us that he had raised his friend's bid up to five pounds beyond the figure we had quoted. Would we therefore supply a duplicate set of stamps at the figure quoted and put them in another album which he brought us. We did so.

– Stamp for stamp?

– Yes.

– Did the Antigua penny puce stamp form part of the collection?

– No.

– Did he offer it for auction in your Sale Rooms as a separate item?

– Yes, in Christmas week, 1934.

– In what right did he profess to be dealing with it?

– As owner. He informed us that it had formed part of a collection belonging to his father, and when we inquired how it had come into his father's possession he said that his father had told him that he had exchanged it with a school-fellow for a pair of Indian clubs.

– It is a very valuable stamp?

– It is unique. I have been very much interested to learn its history in the course of this case. We had been able hitherto only to establish the fact of the sudden withdrawal of that issue on account of the feared explosive effect on public opinion, in Antigua, of the lighthouse incorporated in the design. It appears that numerous petitions for a lighthouse on that coast had been made to the proper authorities but without effect. We had always assumed that no stamp of that issue had survived even in an unused condition, still less that one had actually passed through the mails. As a result of the publicity given to the stamp at the auction of Feb. 12th the original copperplate subsequently came to light and is now in our Philatelic Museum. It had been scored across to prevent re-printing.

– Did the other album, which Mr Price brought to you in order to have the duplicate set of stamps inserted, contain other stamps?

– Yes, a small collection.

– Did Mr Price ask you to make an offer for these stamps?

– We offered him the sum of six pounds, which he accepted. We deducted this sum from our charge for supplying the duplicates.

Mr Merlin then asked dramatically: Is the album for which you supplied the duplicates the album that you are holding in your hand?

– Yes, this is it.

– Had it the pencilled initials O and J marked on the pages when you returned it to Mr Price with the duplicate set inserted?

– No, I do not think so.

Mr Justice Hogtie: What are you trying to prove?

Mr Merlin: That this is the duplicate album with which my client was tricked. She will be prepared to swear to the initials. It happened to come into her possession a few weeks after the fraud had been committed.

Cross-examined by Mr Schreiner, witness agreed that little difficulty had been experienced in finding exact duplicates for the stamps in the collection; in many cases they had been in better condition than the originals. The charge had been fifteen pounds, and Mr Price had paid punctually.

Mr Justice Hogtie turned over the leaves of the album attentively and made certain notes.

Mrs Trent, wardrobe mistress at the Burlington Theatre, a graceful grey-haired woman dressed in black, was the last witness called for the plaintiff. She stated that she had worked as a needlewoman at the house of the late Rev. Charles Price, Vicar of St Aidan's, between the years 1912 and 1929. His two children, the plaintiff and defendant, had jointly owned a stamp-album of similar appearance to the one that had been produced in court. It had originally belonged to Mr Price, but in the spring of the year 1919 Mr Price had agreed to share it with his sister, and she undertook to contribute to its enlargement according to her ability. There had been frequent quarrels about it between them. Mr Price was inclined to be domineering, and Miss Palfrey resented this. She had, on one occasion, Mrs Trent recalled, contributed 3s. 6d., a large sum for a child of not wealthy parents, for a packet of Central American stamps, and had written as far as Persia and Bolivia to obtain stamps of those countries from relatives.

Mr Schreiner (cross-examining): Mrs Trent, how long ago did you say this arrangement about the album took place?

Mrs Trent: It was in 1919, Sir. That would be just sixteen years ago.

Mr Schreiner: Isn't it a little remarkable that you should have so convenient a recollection of a bargain supposed to have been made between two children as long ago as all that?

Mrs Trent: Well, Sir, you see, Miss Jane – Miss Palfrey that is – persuaded Mr Price to come and say what they'd agreed in front of me and asked me to witness it. I'm afraid Mr Price wasn't always a very reliable young gentleman even then, Sir. (Laughter.)

Mr Schreiner: Never mind what you're afraid, Mrs Trent. Just try to answer my questions, will you?

Mr Merlin (to Mr Justice Hogtie): My friend asked for that one, my lord.

Mr Schreiner: Did Miss Palfrey lose interest in the album in 1920 and let Mr Price have sole charge of it, taking it with him to a school in Switzerland and from thence to Charchester School?

Mrs Trent: Mr Price lost interest in stamp-collecting before Miss Palfrey did. I remember a letter that he wrote to Miss Palfrey from Charchester, in November 1921, asking her to send no more stamps because they were 'soppy prep-school things.' (Laughter.)

Mr Schreiner: But Mr Price nevertheless inserted a number of stamps in the album during the following vacation?

Mrs Trent: I cannot remember.

Re-examined by Mr Merlin, Mrs Trent stated that she had a very clear recollection of the agreement to share the stamp-collection.

This closed the evidence for the plaintiff and the Court rose for lunch.

Upon the resumption of the hearing, Mr Philip Schreiner K.C. for the defence stated that Mr Price had begun the stamp-collection in question in December 1918 and that he had not at any time since then ceded or undertaken to cede any of his rights in the collection to his sister, the plaintiff, or to anyone else. The Antiguan stamp had never formed a part of this collection but had constituted a casual loan made to him in 1921 by Miss Whitebillet – a loan which, not realizing its immense value, he had omitted to return until August 1934, when he had been reminded of its existence by Miss White-billet and had immediately volunteered to sell it on her behalf, if it was worth selling. Miss Palfrey had on September 17th of the same year made a preposterous claim to joint ownership of the collection. A coolness had meanwhile arisen between them in consequence of a disagreement as to the disposal of certain effects of their father's, whose executor Mr Price was. Miss Palfrey had then made a claim to a half-share of the collection and suggested that it should forthwith be divided into two. To this suggestion Mr Price was, naturally, loath to accede. It was his own collection and he wished to keep it intact for his son, should he marry and have one. But Miss Palfrey was so insistent that for the sake of peace and from a sense of chivalry he pretended to agree, but resorted to an innocent subterfuge. He privately arranged with Messrs. Harrow and Hazlitt they they should fill an album with exact duplicates of his own stamps, half of which he then permitted her to remove as has been described. The Antiguan stamped envelope was not among these. But it would be a malicious and unwarrantable reflection on Mr Price's character to suggest that, even had the collection been jointly owned, he would have been acting dishonestly in withholding the stamp.

Mr Oliver Price, thick-set and fair-haired and bearing no marked resemblance to his famous sister, then gave evidence along the lines already indicated by his counsel. He stated that in August 1919 the plaintiff, his sister, had asked him to let her share his collection with him. He had replied that he would see whether she could 'pull her weight' and that, if she did so, at the end of a certain stated term he would consider her request. It was soon abundantly clear that, as many brothers before and since have found in the case of their sisters, Janey Price, as she then was, did not have the necessary philatelic temperament. She had no memory for varieties of stamps, injured certain valuable specimens by carelessness and would not agree to spend any money, as he himself conscientiously continued to do, on improving the collection. Her contributions were negligible and he was soon forced to inform her that he could not consent to share the collection with her. She did not renew her request that he should do so and did not make any claim to joint-ownership of the collection until so recently as September 17th, 1934. No ill construction could justly be put on the part that he had played in providing a set of duplicate stamps for his sister to choose from. She had been asserting an altogether preposterous claim and had said to him during their meeting at the gallery: 'We shall go through that album page by page, and I am going to watch your face carefully to see which stamps you most hope I won't take, and then I'm going to take them.' Her object had been merely to cause him distress of mind, and he had considered himself justified in outwitting her and retaining the original stamps, for which he felt a sentimental attachment that any stamp-collector would appreciate.

As for the Antiguan stamped envelope, it had originally come into his possession while a scholar of Charchester in the year 1921. Miss Whitebillet had lent it to him, sending it enclosed in a letter from his sister, as an object of possible interest. He had forgotten to return it to Miss Whitebillet, remaining oblivious of its very existence until June 1934, when Miss Whitebillet happened to ask him whether it was still in his possession. It had come from the papers of her father, the later Sir Reginald Whitebillet. He had replied that he probably still had it; and that it might, after all, have market value, because he had failed to trace it in an ordinary catalogue. Miss Whitebillet then asked him whether, if so, he would arrange to sell it by auction on behalf of her father's estate, of which she was sole executrix. He agreed, and Miss Whitebillet gave him the necessary authority in writing. This document was, he found, dated June 23rd, 1934.

Mr Schreiner: Were you to receive any commission from Miss Whitebillet on the sale of the Antiguan stamp?

Mr Price: Not a penny. Altogether I am considerably out of pocket in this business.

– Were you ever under the impression that Miss Whitebillet, in 1921, intended the stamp as a gift to your collection?

– Never. It was clearly not hers to give. As I say, I forgot to return it.

– When your sister inquired as to the whereabouts of the stamp how did you reply?

– Evasively. I had not thought that she would remember the existence of the stamp and I did not wish to complicate matters between her and her partner, Miss Whitebillet, who had asked me to sell the stamp for her. If Miss Whitebillet cared to remind my sister of the circumstances in which the stamp had accidentally become attached to my collection, she was at liberty to do so. My lips were sealed. An evasive reply was the only honourable one to make in the circumstances.

Mr Merlin then cross-examined the witness.

Mr Merlin: You have told the Court that you replied 'evasively' to your sister when she inquired after the Antiguan stamp. Would it not be truer to say that you told her a deliberate, calculated lie?

Mr Price: I object to that expression. I only wanted . . .

Mr Merlin: Never mind what you wanted. Kindly answer my question, did you tell your sister a deliberate lie, yes or no?

Mr Price was understood to answer the question in the affirmative.

Mr Merlin: Will you now explain why you also found it necessary to lie to Mr Harrow about the Antiguan stamp having been exchanged by your father for a pair of Indian clubs, and tell another cock and bull story about yourself and a fellow-owner having agreed to let the album go to the highest bidder?

Mr Price: I never said anything about Indian clubs.

Mr Merlin: Do you suggest Mr Harrow perjured himself when he told the Court that you did spin him that yarn?

Mr Price: He must have been confusing me with some other customer. How could I have invented such a story about my father? My father despised Indian clubs!

The Judge: Indeed! And why?

Mr Price: He was a golfer, my lord.

The Judge: I am a golfer too, but I do not despise Indian clubs. (Laughter.)

Mr Merlin: If you were aware of your father's misplaced scorn for those most useful adjuncts to health, it was a very plausible tale to invent. He was, according to you, getting rid of the Indian clubs, not purchasing them. In any event, did you tell Mr Harrow the truth?

Mr Price: I told him all that it was necessary for him to know in supplying the stamps I required. I was not on oath.

Mr Merlin: You were not on oath? Is it then your custom to tell any lie that comes into your head when you are not on oath?

Mr Price: It was none of his business.

Mr Merlin: Mr Price, do you ever speak the truth?

Mr Price: I'm speaking the truth now.

Mr Merlin: I'm sure we are all very grateful to you. (Laughter.)

Mr Justice Hogtie smilingly remarked that to expect constant truth from a novelist would be like expecting perfect credulity from a King's Counsel.

Mr Merlin (laughing): Very good, my lord! But there must be give and take. I am ready to yield my credulity to the spell of the romantic novel, which I understand is the defendant's *genre*, if he agrees to confine himself to the truth while I am cross-examining him. (Renewed laughter.)

Mr Merlin to Mr Price: Did you attach the cover and title-page of the original album to the duplicate album in order to give the impression that this was the original album?

– Yes.

– From whom did you obtain that duplicate album?

Mr Schreiner protested against the question but Mr Merlin said that he would show that it was relevant as to credit, as indicating the unscrupulous means employed by the defendant in perpetrating this fraud on his sister. The Judge allowed the question.

Mr Price: I got it from a Hammersmith schoolboy.

Mr Merlin: Did you pay him with a photograph?

– Yes.

– A photograph of your sister?

– Yes, my friend, and why not?

Mr Justice Hogtie (sternly): You must not call counsel your

'friend'. You will be good enough to restrain yourself and avoid being impudent in Court.

Mr Price: I am sorry, my lord. With great respect, I was under the impression that 'friends' of my counsel were also friends of mine.

There was a ripple of laughter in the back benches, which subsided instantly when the Judge threatened to clear the Court.

Mr Merlin: Was it a photograph that she had once presented to her mother, with an affectionate inscription?

– I did not notice the inscription. The photograph was included in the family papers left to me by my father.

Mr Merlin (producing the photograph): Was it this photograph?

– That, or one similar to it.

– It is the one that you sold to the boy Dormer. Do you recognize it now?

– I think I do.

Mr Merlin (triumphantly): Oh, indeed? By the inscription, I suppose? Certainly it is written in very bold handwriting.

– I said 'I think I do'; meaning that my memory of both the portrait and the inscription, if any, was vague.

– I suppose a convenient vagueness also made you forget your sister's standing rule that no autographed photograph of hers should be given to collectors? You were, of course, aware of this rule?

– I have seen or heard very little of my sister for a number of years, and am not an autograph-collector myself.

Mr Schreiner, re-examining: When you spoke to Miss Palfrey about the Antiguan stamp did you believe that she had any kind of valid claim to it whatsoever?

– I did not.

– Did you ever intend to defraud her of anything that was hers?

– Definitely not. On the contrary, I made her a gift of a number of stamps bought at considerable expense from Messrs Harrow and Hazlitt.

Miss Edith Whitebillet was called. She was dressed in a navy blue suit with a black fur collarette and a navy blue hat.

She appeared nervous. She stated that early in the year 1920 she had been asked by Miss Palfrey, her friend and neighbour, to see whether she could find any postage-stamps on old or foreign letters lying about the house to add to her brother's stamp-collection. She had supplied a number, removing them from their envelopes. The Antigua letter was an altogether different case. She had come across this among her father's papers and been extremely interested in the letter as a human document. She had shown it to Miss Palfrey, who had then said: 'The stamp is probably very valuable. Let us look it up in your cousin's catalogue.' They had done so and, not finding it recorded there, had sent it to Mr Price at Charchester for his opinion. She understood that Miss Palfrey had retained the letter, waiting for Mr Price to bring back the envelope with him at the Christmas vacation. By the time that Christmas came round, however, both Miss Palfrey, Mr Price and the witness had forgotten all about it: the letter had remained in Miss Palfrey's possession and the envelope and stamp in Mr Price's.

In June 1934, Miss Whitebillet said, she had accidentally met Mr Price in Regent's Park and they had talked about old times. The Antiguan stamp had been mentioned and Mr Price had volunteered to find out whether it had value and, if so, to sell it on behalf of the estate.

Mr Schreiner: Were you surprised when Mr Price on September the 28th, 1934 told you that Miss Palfrey now claimed that the stamp formed part of the collection?

– My partner's actions are so seldom foreseeable that I am never surprised, whatever she does. (Laughter.)

– Though linked to her by the strongest ties of affection and business you considered that Miss Palfrey was behaving in an overbearing and grasping way?

Mr Merlin: Really, my lord, need my learned friend lead his witnesses word for word? They appear to be competent enough to abuse my client without his assistance.

Mr Schreiner: I protest, my lord! The question was a perfectly proper one, and if my friend complains of abuse . . .

The Judge: I am afraid you overstepped the mark a little, Mr Schreiner, but I am sure you have no wish to offer Miss Palfrey any personal abuse?

Mr Schreiner: Certainly not, my lord. For Miss Palfrey, *as an actress*, I have always had the sincerest admiration ... Well, then, Miss Whitebillet, perhaps my learned friend will permit me to ask you this – did you consider Miss Palfrey's attitude justifiable?

– I didn't think it was very nice of her to try to make Oliver – Mr Price – give up half his collection to her, or to claim the stamp which I had given *him*, not her.

The Judge: I thought it was supposed to have been only a loan?

Mr Schreiner: My client uses the word 'given' loosely, I think. She means that she gave it to him for his opinion, not for possession.

Miss Whitebillet: Yes.

Mr Merlin: It would be so much more interesting if my friend would allow his witnesses to tell their own story, my lord.

The Judge: You must be very careful, Mr Schreiner.

Mr Schreiner: If your Lordship pleases.

Mr Merlin then cross-examined Miss Whitebillet.

– Were you not aware, in the years 1920 and 1921, that Miss Palfrey regarded the stamp-collection as belonging jointly to her and her brother and that her claim to joint ownership was allowed by the entire household?

– I always regarded it as Mr Price's collection.

– And the postage-stamps you found 'lying about the house', as you put it, were intended solely for Mr Price?

– Yes.

– Were you fond of Mr Price?

– I was much attached to him.

– At the time that you gave, or lent, or sent for inspection, the Antiguan stamp to Mr Price at Charchester, did you send any others?

– One or two.

– For his opinion on their value?

– As gifts.

– You specifically distinguished between them and the Antiguan stamp?

– I did not write to Mr Price directly. They were sent to him by Miss Palfrey. I do not know what she wrote to him.

– Why did you not send the stamps to him directly?

– It seemed more proper to send them through his sister.

– You did not wish to seem to be making advances to him? Miss Whitebillet's reply was inaudible.

– I suggest that you did in fact *give* the stamps to the jointly owned collection and that this story of the loan is an afterthought.

– No.

– I suggest that your recently renewed attachment to Mr Price has made you forget the loyalty and truth that you owe to Miss Palfrey with whom you have been living in trustful partnership for a number of years, and that you have coloured your evidence in a way calculated to strengthen Mr Price's affections.

– No, no!

– I suggest that you have, indeed, more than merely coloured your evidence, I suggest that you are deliberately prevaricating.

– Oh, no! Please!

– When were you first aware of the fraud practised by Mr Price on your partner in the matter of the substituted album?

– I didn't think it a fraud. The stamps she chose were of equal value, I understood, with the corresponding stamps in the original album. Mr Price did not tell me until after the auction, and then I thought it rather a joke. I thought Miss Palfrey had behaved meanly in raking up her old claim to half the collection.

– You now admit that she had an old-established claim to half the collection?

– A very shadowy sort of one. I never took it seriously.

– But rightly or wrongly, Miss Palfrey has, ever since 1919, treated and spoken of the collection as partly hers.

– I suppose so. It is not a subject that has come up very often since 1920.

– And she was and has been allowed to speak of it as hers?

– Well – yes – at least, *I* never contradicted her.

– Did Mr Price in your presence ever contradict Miss Palfrey when she spoke of it in this way? Now be careful, please, how you answer.

– I don't think he did. Mr Price was always for keeping the peace.

Mr Merlin (dryly): And no doubt anything else that could be kept, irrespective of ownership. Thank you, Miss Whitebillet. Now tell me this. We have seen your note dated the 23rd of June, 1934, purporting to authorize Mr Price's sale of the stamped envelope; when was that letter in fact written?

– On June 23rd, I suppose.

– You suppose? Are you in some doubt, then? Might it not have been written a little later, say in July or August?

Miss Whitebillet paused and then said: It must have been written on June 23rd if it was dated then.

– I put it to you that it was in fact written many months later, after the commencement of this action?

– No! No! I wrote it in June.

– Remember you are on oath, Miss Whitebillet. I put it to you that Mr Price extracted this stamp from the collection and ordered its sale without any prior authority from you, and that you wrote this note with a false date to be used for the purposes of the defence in this action?

– I wrote it in June, I say!

At this point Miss Whitebillet fainted and was carried out of court. When revived and brought back to continue her evidence she was permitted to answer questions seated.

Mr Merlin: You are your father's sole executrix?

– Yes.

– And principal legatee?

– I have a twin-sister: the estate was divided equally between us, apart from the business. That was formed into a limited company on my father's death in 1929. My sister and I held the shares. In 1932, in the slump, it was obliged to amalgamate with its competitors. There was the Clyde ship-building business as well, but we sold that in 1933 for almost nothing.

The Judge: Do you mean to say that the Whitebillet Shipping Company was never incorporated before 1929?

– No, my grandfather was prejudiced against limited companies and my father carried on the same policy.

– In October 1921 you extracted this letter without your father's knowledge or consent from his private papers?

– I was only a child. I didn't think I was doing any wrong.

– Where were these private papers kept?

– In the safe in his study.

– Was the safe left open?

– Must I answer that question?

– I am asking it.

– No, I forced it open with a skeleton key.

– Oh, indeed. And who supplied you with the key?

– I made it myself, my lord. I was only thirteen years old, at the time, and had been reading a book about a gentleman-cracksman named Raffles.

– I know it. It is by the late E. W. Hornung. I understand that it is frequently referred to by young offenders. You are, by the way, are you not, the Edith Whitebillet who occasionally contributes to the quarterly magazine, *Electrical Progress*?

– Yes, my lord, but not for some years now. I think January, 1930, was the last occasion.

– That was when I read an article of yours. Thank you, Miss Whitebillet. That will do. You may proceed, Mr Merlin.

Mr Merlin: To whom did your father leave his documents? To both of you, or to one of you only?

– To one of us.

– To yourself, in fact?

– Yes.

– So you are taking back a gift that you gave to Mr Price and Miss Palfrey, just because you now find it is more valuable than you thought at the time, and your lame excuse is that it was only a loan?

– It *was* only a loan, I tell you.

Mr Merlin: Miss Whitebillet, a final question. Are you now engaged to marry Mr Price?

At this point Mr Price rose and shouted loudly: 'Stop torturing the girl, you scoundrel! If you want to ask questions like that, ask me, like a gentleman.'

Once more sternly rebuked by the Judge and threatened with punishment for contempt of court, Mr Price subsided. Mr Merlin said, smiling urbanely: 'I have no further questions to ask this witness.'

The hearing was adjourned until today.

CHAPTER 14

PALFREY *v.* PRICE AND ANOR
(*Concluded*)

ANTIGUA PENNY PUCE
MISS JANE PALFREY LOSES CASE ON TECHNICALITY

The final scenes of this remarkable case were marked by intense excitement on the part of the public, but by no scene such as enlivened the proceedings on the second day of the hearing. Only one new witness was called by the defence, Mr Hazlitt, of Messrs Harrow and Hazlitt, the auctioneer under whose hammer the celebrated stamp came last February; and his evidence was not of exceptional interest.

Summing up the evidence for the defence, Mr Philip Schreiner, K.C., submitted that even were his Lordship disposed to accept the plaintiff's account of the joint ownership of the collection as a whole, she had wholly failed to establish her allegation that the stamped envelope in question formed any part of it.

Mr Antony Merlin, K.C., in a long closing speech vigorously attacked the evidence given for the defendants. 'I suggest to your Lordship,' he said 'that Miss Whitebillet is an hysterical and faithless woman who, in her infatuation for that worthless young man, is prepared to say anything that she believes will shield him from the public censure that his greed and fraudulence only too clearly merit; and that her evidence should, in consequence, be entirely disregarded. There could be no doubt on the evidence that the stamp-collection had in fact been a joint one.' Mr Merlin referred to the sober and unshaken testimony of the parties' old sewing-woman, Mrs Trent. Dealing with the Antiguan stamped envelope Mr Merlin suggested that the most natural explanation of what actually happened was that Sir Reginald Whitebillet, having no suspicion that the stamp had any extraordinary value, had given it, with others, to his daughter; and that she under the same impression had passed it on to the plaintiff. 'Is it conceivable,' he asked 'that if Miss Whitebillet had really, as she says now, regarded the transaction as a loan of a valuable article, she would have made no attempt to get it back until some thirteen years later?' The plaintiff's evidence on this point was clear, consistent, and, he submitted, credible; the defendants' contradictory and unconvincing. 'Can it be doubted for a moment that Miss Palfrey believed, and was given every reason to believe, that she was receiving the stamp as a gift?' It was impossible now to prove what had been Sir Reginald's intention with regard to the stamp, but could one reasonably accept Miss Whitebillet's uncorroborated evidence that this one stamp in particular had not been given to her, but had been stolen from her father's presumably burglar-proof safe with the aid of a miraculous home-made skeleton-key? Was not that a transparent and childish piece of invention? Could Miss Whitebillet plead her own theft from her father to excuse her fiancé's theft from his sister, her business partner? Was such a witness to be believed in anything?

Mr Justice Hogtie then gave judgement.

He said that a good deal of unnecessary personal feeling had been introduced into the case and that the issue, which was a relatively simple one, had been clouded by it. The question over which the learned counsel had exercised themselves most was whether the original stamp-collection was, in October, 1921 when the Antiguan stamped envelope first became attached to it, jointly owned by the defendant, Mr Price, and his sister, the plaintiff, or the sole property of the defendant. The evidence had been conflicting but the weight of testimony pointed to the plaintiff's joint-title having been generally acknowledged, and he was satisfied that the sharing agreement deposed to by the plaintiff and Mrs Trent had, in fact, been entered into. It was clear that in September 1934 the defendant had realized that the plaintiff had a just claim to half the stamps, and that he had acted in a most disingenuous manner in order to fob her off with a duplicate set.

'I am not altogether satisfied,' said his Lordship, 'with the accounts given of the circumstances in which, on June 23rd, 1934, Miss Whitebillet is said to have authorized the sale by auction of the Antiguan stamped envelope. There is, for example, a conflict of evidence as to whether the defendant volunteered to sell this envelope and stamp on Miss White-billet's behalf, or whether the suggestion was first made by Miss Whitebillet herself. But in the absence of proof that the authority is a later forgery I must accept it as evidence. I am, on the other hand, satisfied that the stamped envelope was not merely lent but freely given by Miss Whitebillet to the joint stamp-collection so far as it was within her power to give it, together with one or two other stamps, and added to the collection with a view to its permanent enrichment. Thus in September 1934 the plaintiff had a right to claim that the collection be partitioned between the defendant and herself. And I am satisfied that a binding agreement was entered upon between plaintiff and defendant for the partition of the original collection by the method of each party alternately choosing one stamp. I am satisfied that, had the Antiguan stamped envelope been shown in its proper position in the stamp-album, the plaintiff would have initialled it and that she did, in fact, appropriate it to herself. We have the evidence of the pencilled O's and J's in the duplicate album. I should therefore have had no hesitation in dismissing the points raised in defence and giving judgement for the plaintiff, had I been satisfied that the defendant, Miss Whitebillet, was, in 1921, in a position to carry out what I have no doubt was her intention, namely to vest the property in the stamps in Mr Price and his sister, the plaintiff. It appears, however, that at the time when she formed this intention and purported to carry it into execution she was, in fact, a mere wrongdoer in unlawful possession of the stamp, which she had feloniously extracted from her father's safe. I have not been able to accept Miss Whitebillet's evidence in its entirety, but upon this point I am satisfied: that she was speaking truthfully and that her memory was not at fault. Miss Whitebillet's remarkable experiments with remote control of mechanical figures were the subject of an article by her that I once read in a serious scientific journal and since the experiments described were carried on between the years 1923 and 1928, I see no inherent improbability in her manufacture in 1921 of a simple skeleton key. This stamp was not a mere separate foreign stamp that might have been given casually to a child; it was attached to an envelope containing a document of singular interest and, at one time, of great importance. The stamped envelope and the letter remained the property of Sir Reginald Whitebillet until upon his death in 1929 they vested in Miss Whitebillet as his executrix. It is not without reluctance that I allow Miss Whitebillet in effect to profit by her own fraud, but in the circumstances I am afraid I have no alternative. I therefore give judgement for the defendants. Possibly counsel may have something to submit in the matter of costs?'

Mr Merlin argued vigorously that as the case had been decided upon a technicality not raised in the pleadings and that the defence pleaded had failed, costs should be awarded to the plaintiff.

Mr Schreiner submitted that the plaintiff had failed to prove her case. She had alleged that the defendant, Mr. Price, had misappropriated her property; in his defence he had denied that the chattel in question was her property; she had failed to establish that it was, and ought to bear the costs of this action that she had wrongly brought.

Mr Justice Hogtie: I have heard with interest what counsel have had to say, and I have decided upon the proper course. The defendants did not plead that the stamped envelope and its contents had been removed from Sir Reginald Whitebillet's safe without his knowledge or consent, nor, so far as I am aware, did Miss Whitebillet ever inform Miss Palfrey of this significant fact. By suppressing until trial the one vital defect in her title she led Miss Palfrey into the reasonable belief that the stamped envelope was hers and in effect encouraged her to bring this action. In the circumstances I propose to exercise my discretion in the matter of costs, and shall make no order.'

The verdict was greeted with silence, and Miss Palfrey was cheered by a large crowd on emerging into the Strand. Miss Whitebillet left the Law Courts leaning upon Mr Price's arm. Mr Price was addressing her in animated tones. He refused to give his impression of the case to Press representatives.

CHAPTER 15

THE WEDDING

(At the Stefanssons'),
October 18th, 1935

Dear Jane,

I want you to congratulate Oliver and me. He and I are getting married tomorrow at an obscure Registry Office in the East End to avoid any fuss; but there's to be a reception at the Regina afterwards for just a few friends. At 3 o'clock. We are inviting the Company and Mrs Trent and Jenkins and Babraham and Adelaide, and Oliver joins me in hoping that you will let bygones be bygones and come too. It has all been a very childish business, we think, and Oliver says that an adult sense of humour ought to prevent us from carrying it on any further. He says that you and he and I ought to pull together in future, and if it is necessary to agree to disagree about certain small points, that should not be too much of a strain. But we both think that Slingsby is in bad taste, now that Oliver and I are getting married, and that he must be got rid of; and Oliver says that he'll talk over the question of the heirlooms with you if you like, but that there's no question of your having the Shepherd's Calendar or however you spell it: he's the writer of the family, and your mother would obviously have bequeathed it to him. But you can have the Madonna, which he says he doesn't admire: it's too severe for his taste.

My reason for not mentioning our marriage before this was that I thought you guessed and that I thought you disapproved, and surely I am old enough now to decide for myself? And it isn't a breach of contract either, because the contract says 'not until October 15th, 1935'. I hope you won't mind, but I shall be away on our honeymoon for a month. We are flying to Paris and then going on to the Château Country. The vintage will still be in progress, so it should be very interesting. I do hope Babraham will be able to carry on for me: you said that he was very efficient while I was in Africa, and I think he was a tiny bit disappointed when I returned and he had to go back into the publicity department. I feel rather mean going off before 'Apes and Peacocks' has got properly in its stride, but I feel you will forgive me, and when Oliver and I come back he and I will run my side of the show together more efficiently than I have done by myself. Oliver, by the way, has a perfectly lovely play which I want us to put on in the Spring. I think it is really *excellent*, but of course Oliver doesn't know much about exits and entrances and things, so perhaps a few slight alterations will be called for, and I'm sure he won't mind if you make suggestions.

As for that stamp, you must have known, of course, long ago, that it was me for whom Oliver was selling it, but as you said nothing to me, I said nothing to you. It was an unpleasant topic, anyway. The fact was that I *did* think that you were being rather mean to Oliver, and also I had no right to *give* it you originally, and anyway it was Oliver's collection more than yours; and also it would have been unfair to Edna. When I sell it again I shall give Edna half the money, and Oliver a third and you a sixth: just to show that I'm not being mean. Is that all right?

I do want everything to turn out well between us three, because you know I love you both so very much and it hurts me terribly when you quarrel with Oliver – over nothing at all. Oliver never says anything unkind about you. I think he is more puzzled than angry at your persecution of him.

If I see you tomorrow afternoon at the Regina I shall assume it is going to be all right between us all, and I shall be so happy.

Love,

Edith

Jane showed The Emu the letter. 'What do you think of that, Emu?'

He shook his head. 'Bad.'

'Couldn't be worse?'

'Impossible. He's got her. Look here, this is a funny thing, she's taken to making Greek d's instead of English ones; but now and then she relapses. I seem to remember that that tripe I read in green ink about bailiwicks and such was all Greek d's.'

'Sharp-eyed Emu. A bad sign indeed. It was the first thing I noticed, too. And then the crossings-out, where he's insisted on her changing things she'd written. Well? Do you think I ought to kiss and be friends now? Be careful how you answer.'

'Careful be hanged, cousin! Speaking straight from my heart, like a Russian, I tell you here and now that if that bum, your brother, comes to work at the Burlington even in the most subordinate capacity imaginable, I move out. And you?'

She smiled at him approvingly. 'It's ingenious of Oliver,

though. He has let Edith write this smeary let's-be-friends letter, with no possible basis of real friendship to support it, and put the whole burden of being nasty on me. Pretends that *they* are the injured party. And knows perfectly well that I wouldn't stand for his being about in the same building as myself, but that I can't legally prevent Edith from engaging whatever assistants she pleases in her side of the show. And that if he were about I'd have to abandon Slingsby because I couldn't have my partner's husband stalking about the theatre and scattering natural Slingsbyisms like coppers.'

The Emu said: 'Oh, I don't know. Everyone knows Slingsby, but very few people know Oliver. They would only think that Oliver was imitating Slingsby.'

Jane said: 'No. Ruthless as I am in anything that concerns Oliver, it wouldn't be good publicity for me. If Oliver came, Slingsby would have to go. But Slingsby is not going. No, Emu, Mrs Trent guessed his game weeks ago. He wants to make Edith buy me out, and for the two of them to take over the whole show. Oliver has views on the drama and a quite diseased self-assurance. I believe that he actually thinks he is capable of taking my place himself.'

The Emu stared. 'Not really? Not him? That's rich!'

'Rich indeed! And, as a matter of fact, I may decide to let him have his way. It may be my wedding present to him. If I do, it will bring him about as much pleasure as the shirt of Nessus brought Hercules . . .'

'I was brought up in the back-blocks,' he reassured her, 'but I can guess that one. The other fellow's shirt was a bit snug under the arms.'

'It positively ate into his flesh,' Jane agreed. 'Or, to come down to modern times, as much pleasure as Oliver himself got from the gift of a certain packet of Central Americans, assorted, 3/6, mentioned in Court by Mrs Trent. But I can count on you in all things, Emu?'

'To the death. Tell me, Jane: Edith was just lying about that stamp having been only a loan, wasn't she?'

'Yes. And she as good as admits it in the letter. I didn't expect her to lie. It makes things easier for me now, in a way.

Releases me from the obligations of old friendship, and all that sort of thing.'

'What are my instructions?'

'You shall have them in writing as soon as I have made a short address to the Company. My course of action will depend on their response.

> I'll see what stuff their loyalty is made:
> Whether 'tis loyalty to the death, like thine,
> Or that infected loyalty of the buskin –
> To the next pay day.'

She summoned them all to her office. 'Ladies and gentlemen of the Green Room, I have bad news for you. Before I say a word I demand an assurance from you that you will not breathe a word on the subject that I am about to broach to a living soul unless or until I give you leave.'

They all gave their words of honour, for what they were each worth.

Jane continued: 'My partner, Miss Whitebillet, has an equal voice with me in the management of this theatre, and owns by far the larger block of shares in the company, her financial contribution having been much greater than mine. Hitherto, Miss Whitebillet and I have seen eye to eye, but an event has occurred which threatens to destroy this harmony. Miss Whitebillet is getting married tomorrow to a Mr Price, against whom I have just brought an unsuccessful action for fraud, and whom she proposes to intrude into the management. I have known Mr Price for a number of years – and can assure you that he is an impossible associate in any business. You will understand what I mean when I inform you that when Miss Whitebillet asked him what he would like as a wedding present from her, he replied: "The death of Owen Slingsby!" Miss Whitebillet, in her infatuation, seems to have granted Mr Price this abominable gift; without consulting either Mr Slingsby himself or me, Mr Slingsby's creator. Now what do you think of that?'

There were groans and hoots. Owen Slingsby paled, but Doris flung her arms around him: 'You'll always be Owen Slingsby to me, no matter what happens.' Even J. C. Neanderthal was touched by this. He said that for his colleague Owen Slingsby, the actor, he had as much esteem as he had dislike for Owen Slingsby, the man; and that if Owen Slingsby, the actor, were condemned to death he, for his part, was ready (always with Miss Palfrey's permission) to brave the ultimate mystery too and follow him into the blackness of abolishment; and that this was neither braggadocio nor Quixotry, but his clear duty.

The others would have made similar avowals, but Jane was anxious to get to the point. She said: 'Ladies and gentlemen, you have not, I see, forgotten who it was who created you. In return you have offered me an unwavering and, at times, an almost religious loyalty, which I appreciate more than you are perhaps aware. You have, apart from occasional lapses, done worthily, and I confess I am proud of you. But as I created you, so also I have the power to destroy you. It is a power of which I should be very loath to avail myself, and if you come out well from the test to which I propose to subject you, you may regard yourselves as more or less permanently saved. But first, my children, you must drink the hemlock cup and eat the bitter arsenic sandwich.'

They wondered at her words, at a loss whether they were expected to laugh or look grave.

'Tomorrow morning you will be given your orders. On the stage tonight I expect you to surpass yourselves. (Last night you were a bit off colour.) A number of superstitious accidents will occur in the course of the evening's performance. The Marquess will report them to the omen-greedy Press and I expect you, when interviewed, to confirm them circumstantially, and also to complain tomorrow morning of confused and frightful dreams. Fairy, remember that your mother was from the West Highlands, and, please, in your emotion, relapse into broad Scots and confess to feeling gey fey and to having met your weird in the wings while waiting for your call.'

'Whit wad ane weir-r-rd be, Miss Palfrey?' Fairy asked dutifully in broad, if synthetic, Scots.

'Someone *exactly* like yourself, only different, who gives you a meaning look and passes on.'

'And whit wad thot blink seegnify, Miss Palfrey?'

'You shudder to think.'

'Och, ay. And whit wad gey fey be?'

'Southrons would laugh at you if you told them.'

'Verra weel, Miss Palfrey.'

They went away, murmuring uncomfortably, but taking their leave of Jane with due ceremony.

The Emu came in. 'About half a dozen news-hawks wanting to see you about the trial. I told them that you were busy but that your message was that you were pleased with the consideration of the Judge, and that somehow you felt that the last chapter of the story had not yet been written. I also hinted at the marriage, rather discreetly. I then ordered them away. But they wouldn't go.'

'Good, Emu. Tell them that there's a big story about to break, and to phone after the show and again tomorrow morning.'

The morning papers were full of the verdict, and all carried Miss Jane Palfrey's subsequent 'smiling remark' that the last chapter of the story had not yet been written. Another paragraph described the extraordinary events at the Burlington that night – signs that would make even the least superstitious quail, 'and actors are a notoriously superstitious profession'. Practically every mirror in the theatre had been shattered in a series of unrelated accidents, a large piece of scenery had fallen on J. C. Neanderthal in the last act, nearly knocking him unconscious, a white bird had tapped for admittance at the window of the principal dressing-room, and three cross-eyed women had been seen drinking gin together in a corner of the Bar.

Fairy Bunstead was interviewed. She was reported to have relapsed, in her emotion, into broad Scots, and to have said: 'A amna supersteetious, ye ken, but ma mither cam frae the Hielands, ye ken. Och, ye laddies may well speer whilk sorrt o' ill feelings A hod in they cauld wings yestreen! A was confronted by a pairfectly gashtlie veesion – a pairson exoctly like tae mysel', thof wi' a wee bit beardie an' ass's lugs, wha coost me a seegnificant blink an' swiddered on. A felt sae gey fey that A coud hairdly stond. A tairned sae white as a muckerkin. Aiblins 'twas ma weirrrrrd!' ('Our representative questioned Miss Bunstead as to the meaning of "sae gey fey", and she replied that she shuddered to think what Southrons would say if they knew.')

Not quite word-perfect, but atmospheric and good enough for the Press. The caption was: HOODOO HAUNTINGS IN WEST END THEATRE.

It had been an unfortunate idea of Oliver's to avoid publicity by getting married at an East End registry office. The East End is not so far away as all that. If reporters and cameramen wish to swoop down on any criminal or social event that takes place there, it is not, when you come to think of it, more than a couple of bow-shots and biscuit toss or two from Fleet Street. The Emu put them on the scent, the various East End registry offices were questioned by phone, and Bethnal Green owned up. Except for one conscientious but drink-sodden reporter who had been too long at the job and, trying to get a start of the others, chartered a plane and flew to Gretna Green, all were there at the bridal hour.

The Bethnal Greeners realized at once that something was up, but nobody seemed to know exactly who it was who was getting spliced. The Emu, disguised in a turban and sandals, was telling people that it was Mr Owen Slingsby, the actor, marrying the daughter of the King of Montenegro against the wishes of her Royal father; he was supposed to be her Montenegrin cook. He distributed confetti and rice among the children. It was all quite orderly at first, so the police did not move the crowd on. When Oliver and Edith drew up in a taxi, telling it to wait, they looked rather alarmed at the crowd. Oliver then made the mistake of using threatening language to a reporter who buttonholed him. (Never threaten the Press. The Press always has the last word.)

A registry ceremony does not take long, but long enough, when a large crowd has already gathered outside, to give time for a still larger one to swarm up; and, as Oliver and Edith emerged and darted for their taxi, the rice flew into their faces like hail. Taxis are rare in Bethnal Green, so when the driver tried to start up his engine and failed and told them that it was a big-end gone and advised them to get out and walk to the nearest Tube station – he was really very sorry, on such an occasion – what else could they do? It was a rough passage. Confetti and camera-men, rice and reporters, all the way. A smart young Greener managed to pin a placard on Oliver's back, 'JUST MARRIED', which kept the fun going, and a mixed orchestra of concertina, comb and biscuit-tin drum marched in front.

'Crude, but necessary,' The Emu explained to Jane afterwards. 'We had to begin early on the task of sapping Oliver's morale. He's tough, but I think we did fairly well. Edith took it all as a great joke at first, except when the little boys shouted 'Hurrah for Slingsby and Mrs Slingsby.' She didn't like that. Oliver's face was penny puce. They were both in pretty bad shape by the time they reached the Tube station. It was a new sort of confetti I'd found – Coney Island burr-confetti, that has to be picked from one's clothes piece by piece. . . . No, they didn't see me.'

They arrived late at the Regina. This was because of the confetti, which they had stopped somewhere to pick off. But they might have spared themselves the trouble. Another large crowd, also armed with rice and burr-confetti, greeted them at the hotel. A new batch of reporters rushed forward to congratulate them on their marriage and to ask them to confirm a rumour that they were honeymooning in Antigua. Oliver struck a reporter a blow on the chest and in the resulting struggle someone knocked off Oliver's hat and squirted white paint from a spray-gun over his hair. Nobody ever knew who did this.

The Emu arrived correctly dressed at the reception, with a gardenia in his button-hole. Adelaide came with him. And Mrs Trent and Jenkins too. But not many friends had been able to attend at such absurdly short notice – it had all been done by telephone or telegram on the previous day. Apart from people connected with the Burlington, and Edna (whom he recognized by her likeness to Edith) The Emu could not identify more than three or four of the guests. Among these, however, was Algernon Hoyland who hailed him, 'Hullo, what do you think of all this? Deep fellow, old Oliver, eh? Never let on until the very last minute. Pretty girl, the bride, too. Know her, by any chance?'

The Emu said severely: 'I am a friend of the bride's. I am not personally acquainted with the bridegroom. I am not even personally acquainted with you, sir.'

Hoyland said: 'Oh yes you are, don't you remember me? I'm Hoyland. We met in Oliver's rooms.'

'Case of mistaken identity, Mr – I didn't catch your name – and, by the way, speaking as a friend of the bride's, I deplore her choice in bridegrooms.' (That ought to choke him off.)

Hoyland looked incredulous, so The Emu turned on his heel. 'Who's that gentleman, do you know?' Hoyland asked a neighbour, who happened to be Jenkins.

'That's the Marquess of Babraham, sir. He's a distant cousin of the bridegroom and connected with the bride in her theatrical work.'

Hoyland was still unsatisfied, and not being a travelled man misunderstood The Emu's back-block accent. He managed to catch Oliver disengaged. 'Who's that semi-Cockney over there, with the long legs, who calls himself a Marquess?'

'Don't know him from Adam. Probably a reporter in disguise.' And Oliver bustled off. Hoyland gave it up.

Edith was worried. She kept looking towards the door in the hope of seeing Jane. She asked The Emu whether Jane had said anything about coming, but he shook his head.

'Jane told me nothing,' he said, and hurried off to avoid being introduced to Oliver.

Edith brightened up when the doorman announced: 'The Ladies and Gentlemen of the Burlington Theatre,' and in trooped the whole Company. They offered their congratulations to Edith with unaffected insincerity and said that Miss Palfrey sent her apologies – she had a severe headache. They insisted on being presented to Oliver, whom they plied with offensive compliments on his good luck in making so splendid a match. Owen Slingsby, who had been well schooled in his part that morning, pumped Oliver's hand up and down and wished him lots and lots of children, all boys and all taking after him. 'I have taken the liberty of bringing you a wedding present,' he said, 'and I hope you will not be offended. Seven little stamp-albums with a 5s. packet of 200 Colonials, all different, in each. Just to give 'em a start, you know. And seven little boxes of gummed hinges. And seven little pairs of tweezers.'

The Company then broke into tinkling laughter and moved away in a body, Slingsby leading them with the rolling walk that had been borrowed for him from Oliver.

Suddenly Leonora uttered a shriek and, in the frightened hush that followed, exclaimed: 'Oh, do you see that waiter? He was in my dream last night. And so was that pot of ferns! And so was that sofa! It's all coming back now. Oh!'

J. C. Neanderthal told her to pull herself together. 'You can't behave in public like that!'

'O *can't* I!' she cried. 'It's fearful. I'm getting out of here.' The others held her back (while J. C. Neanderthal apologized to the bridegroom for his wife's hysteria) and sat her forcibly at a table in an alcove, where they poured champagne down her throat. The guests already seated there, friends of Oliver's, cleared out in embarrassment and the whole Company sat down and started hammering on the table ill-manneredly, calling for sandwiches and more champagne.

Oliver lost his temper and strode towards them. 'Behave yourselves,' he bawled, 'or I'll chuck you out.' Edith darted after him and put a restraining hand on his shoulder. 'Noll, darling, it's only their joke.'

The five men filed forward submissively, removed coats and waistcoats, pulled out their shirt-tails, and knelt down on the floor in a row. 'We be five burghers of Calais who lay our lives at your feet, my liege King,' chanted The Squire. 'But if peradventure, damn it all, your gracious Queen, the sweet Lady Eleanor, shall take pity and misericord on this our hapless plight . . .'

'Imbeciles!' said Oliver, and was forced to join in the burst of laughter that rose all around him.

'Come and have a drink with us, Happy Man,' giggled Nuda, squirming her hips. She was dressed in a close-fitting flesh-coloured satin, and had a rose between her teeth.

'No, thanks,' said Oliver shortly.

Slingsby rose and waved his arms: 'Listen, everyone! All folk who journey through this here bailiwick of Sloshpot must first blooming well drink the health of my Lord the Bridegroom: in mead, be they poor; in good Rhine wine, be they of the better sort.'

Oliver started as if he had been stung. He turned savagely on Edith: 'So you're against me too, are you? You make fun of me in front of everyone. I allow you to read my novel before it's in proper shape and you put bits of it into the mouth of this lunatic . . .'

Fortunately there was too much noise going on for anyone to hear exactly what Oliver was saying, and Edith's denials of the charge seemed so genuine and indignant that he did not press it. But he had not showed his novel to a soul but Edith, not even to Algernon Hoyland. Obviously it was Edith. Who else could it be unless . . . of course. Jane. That day she had been at his flat. She had slipped in while he was downstairs borrowing Hoyland's teapot and must have had a quick rummage through his private papers – typical sporting behaviour on Jane's part – and found some sheets of his novel and memorized that phrase. He was apologizing gruffly to Edith when the waiter brought caviare sandwiches to the table where the Company were now sitting soberly, making brittle small talk. Each seized a sandwich, each thrust it simultaneously into his or her mouth, and chewed vigorously. The silence was broken by Doris.

'Tastes bitter to me.'

The Squire said: 'Far be it for me to cast aspersions on the hospitality of our good friends, Mr and Mrs Wedding Bells, but if *this* be caviare, then I'm no General.' He laughed hollowly.

It was Horace Faithfull who first complained of burning pains in his stomach (he was the character who always played butlers or clergymen, and whom we have not hitherto had occasion to mention particularly). Roger Handsome was soon writhing on the floor and groaning, and plump! down went Madame Blanche beside him, screaming 'murder! murder!' in a strangled voice. The Squire, both hands clutched to his stomach, cried, 'A doctor! An ambulance! Urgent! Oh!' But the Emu had already dashed to the telephone and was speaking in rapid tones. 'Yes, the Regina. Case of poisoning. About twelve guests affected so far. Better send ambulances for twenty. Hurry!'

A doctor pushed his way through the crowd and was soon attending the sufferers behind screens in an adjoining room. He was not a real doctor, but The Emu knew that nobody would ask him to show his diploma or whatever it is that gives doctors a right to save people's lives. The ambulances (which Jane had borrowed from Elstree where a hospital picture had just been filmed) came clanging up within four minutes.

The sensation outside, when the crowd learned who the victims were, was indescribable, especially as the afternoon papers were already on the streets with a sensational account of the events at Bethnal Green. The police were obliged to join hands and strain obliquely backwards against the crowd, in order to keep a clear gangway between the Hotel steps and the ambulances. There were concerted groans of pity and indignation as stretcher after stretcher came lurching down the steps, a gauze cloth over each sufferer's face.

The final editions carried the whole story. A sudden marriage had been celebrated between Mr Oliver Price, a novelist, brother of Miss Palfrey, the well-known actress, and Miss Edith Whitebillet, daughter, etc., etc., who was associated with Miss Palfrey in the management of the Burlington Theatre. Miss Palfrey had attended neither the marriage ceremony nor the reception, but the entire Burlington Company (Jane Palfrey Amalgamated) had been present at the latter function. Champagne and sandwiches were served, and after partaking of both, Roger Handsome and Horace Faithfull, members of the Company, had complained of severe pains. The rest of the Company had also been taken ill, one by one. First-aid had been administered immediately by Doctor Adams, a fellow-guest, and ambulances summoned by telephone. The condition of Mr Owen Slingsby, Miss Nuda Elkan and Col. Julius Squire ('The Squire') was stated to be grave; and that of Miss Fairy Bunstead, Major J. C. Neanderthal, Miss Leonora Laydie (Mrs J. C. Neanderthal), Miss Doris Edwards, Mr Roger Handsome, Madame Ada Blanche, and Mr Horace Faithfull, critical.

Neither Mr nor Mrs Price would make any statement or confirm the rumour that they were spending their honeymoon on the island of Antigua, from which the famous postage-stamp . . .

Miss Jane Palfrey appeared greatly distressed and stated that in view of 'this terrible catastrophe' performances of *Apes and Peacocks* would be indefinitely suspended, and the money refunded to the ticket-holders.

It was this last announcement that astounded everyone. It had been freely said that the poisoning was a far-fetched practical joke, intended merely as publicity. But what sort of publicity was it that suddenly closed the theatre at the beginning of what promised to be a very successful run, and disappointed thousands of playgoers? And what connexion had 'this terrible catastrophe' with the Antigua Penny Puce trial that had ended yesterday in a victory for the bridegroom and his bride?

CHAPTER 16

THE PALFREY HEIRLOOMS

WHEN the reception had broken up in confusion, Edith said to Oliver: 'We must see Jane. This is like a nightmare. It's persecution. We've got to stop it or she'll go on. We've got to have a straight talk with her and find out what she wants of us!'

'I'll talk to her with a hatchet, but with nothing else,' Oliver replied in an awful voice.

'O Oliver, please, please be sensible and kind and help to straighten it all out. We can't go off to France tonight leaving things in this mess. Just as a matter of business, even, I have to see Jane. The fact is, I was too confident that everything would be all right. I should really have given her a week's notice about my going off for so long – it's in the contract – because it wasn't a case of illness. She can sue me for breach of contract. You simply must come with me and talk things over. I can't face Jane alone.'

'Oh, all right,' said Oliver, '*I'm* not afraid of her. But mind you, I won't be responsible for what I say to her.'

They went through the kitchen of the Regina to avoid the crowds and took a taxi to the theatre; but it was empty. They phoned Jane's flat, but she wasn't there. Then Edith called up the Hostel where the Company lived and, when she gave her name, was told by someone, probably Adelaide, to hang on for a moment. Then Jane's voice: 'Oh, is that you, Edith? I suppose I ought to congratulate you on your marriage. But it's not easy for me to strike a properly enthusiastic note at the moment. I'm feeling pretty low. They're all shockingly ill. Lips purple and puffy, froth on the tongue and ghastly breathing. The poor old Squire may peg out any minute and Fairy isn't much better. Were any other of your guests affected?'

'Can Oliver and I speak to you?'

'Is it important? I'm a sort of hospital matron now. I don't know if I can spare the time. I thought you were going off to France.'

'We want to see you first to talk things over.'

'Where are you?'

'At the theatre.'

'Right. It's so painful here – please stay where you are. I'll be with you in five minutes. Adelaide has everything in control. She's wonderful in an emergency.'

While they were waiting at the theatre, with nothing to do and little to say, Oliver pulled the original manuscript of his novel from the bag he had with him – all the rest of their luggage was already at Victoria Station – to confirm his suspicion against Jane in regard to it. It was his habit, every morning, when he started work, to write the date in the margin as an encouragement to himself. He aimed at twelve hundred words a day; which meant about seven thousand a week, because he did not work on Sundays – an old scruple. (Ten weeks at twelve hundred a day – seventy thousand, roughly, + ten more weeks to polish = about five months.) But it had taken him about three times as long, polishing and polishing. The day Jane came, he remembered, was September 27th a year ago. . . . But that was impossible! He'd not got nearly so far as the bailiff of Hochschloss by then. Hochschloss occurred for the first time in January. That passage . . . Yes, here it was, under the date Feb. 12th – the day of the auction.

He turned to Edith. 'Edith,' he said, 'I find you've been double-crossing me after all. It couldn't have been Jane who got that sentence out of my book. When she was at my flat it wasn't yet written. It was *you*, and nobody else!'

'Don't be ridiculous, Oliver. Really, I mean to say! What sort of person do you take me for?'

'Well, whoever else could have done it? Tell me that.'

'I refuse to be put in the dock, like this. Work out your own theory. It wasn't me, and that's all that matters.'

Oliver's eyes flashed. 'Oh, is it. Suppose we wash out this marriage altogether. It's not been consummated; there's still time.'

Edith began to cry. 'O Noll, I didn't mean to say that. But I *did* think you were being unjust. I swear it wasn't me. Wasn't there a first draft, or something of that chapter that Jane could have seen when she came?'

Jane arrived at this moment.

Jane said: Hello, you two! I can give you exactly twenty minutes, no more. I can't leave my people. Their respiration is getting worse and worse every moment.'

Oliver tried a scornful laugh, but Jane and Edith both disregarded it.

Jane asked: 'Well, what have you to say?'

Oliver shouted: 'I want to know what the Hell the game is. Trying to make fools of me and Edith, eh? But only hurting your own reputation, really. You're kicking against the stamp verdict, I suppose. It was a fair trial, wasn't it? Why don't you appeal, if you didn't like it?'

'Oh, *please*, darling!' wailed Edith, pulling at his sleeve.

'The game,' said Jane, 'is this, as I see it. You two have been playing a sort of amatory Puss-in-the-Corner behind my back for months. Of course, love is a privileged thing, but there are decent limits even in love. You've overstepped all the limits, Edith. Condoned a wilful theft of Oliver's and perjured yourself on his behalf, and now you're skipping off with him to France and breaking your contract with me. I don't blame Oliver's theft on his being in love. He's not in love. And if you don't know that, *he* does. That's the first thing I have to say. The next is that you, Oliver, have always been a crook, but Edith had always been perfectly straight with me until you got hold of her.'

Here Oliver began bawling something about football boots and sabotage; so Jane stopped talking until he had finished and then went on quietly.

'I am sorry, Edith, that you've allowed yourself to be taken in by him and involved in his lies. I want to know whether you're going to stick by him now. If you do, that's the end between you and me. And the end of the Burlington, so far as I'm concerned. It's a valuable property – far more valuable than when we took over the lease and there's still thirty-five years to run, so I foresee no money loss for either of us if we sell out. Or, if you prefer to hang on to it, you can buy my interest at the price provided for in the agreement: it is proportioned to our average net profit for the three years previous to the transaction. I have a notion that Oliver wants to wear an astrakhan collar to his overcoat, that's why I mention it.'

Edith said miserably: 'O Jane, darling, *can't* we all be friends? I love you both so much. *Why* can't we all be friends?'

Jane said: Because – don't you see? – it doesn't work. Oliver is a thief and a liar. He won't even contradict me when I tell him that he's not in love with you.'

'It's beneath my notice,' said Oliver, 'and I'll trouble you to leave the subject alone.'

But Jane went on: 'You see, poor Edith, he's decoyed you into marrying him, partly because he couldn't marry Edna and because you're the next best thing, and partly to spite me and break our partnership, and partly for your money, and partly because you're someone whom he thinks he'll be able to boss – as he couldn't succeed in bossing me when I was his kid sister.'

Oliver blustered: 'Boss! That's rich. Who's been bossing Edith and making a slave of her for the last ten years or so? And who grabbed all Edith's money as soon as her father died and invested it in a theatre, for her own glorification? And who talks of spite? Spite, indeed! You're the most spiteful . . .'

'Please control your spittle,' said Jane, drawing back a step.

Edith made another despairing appeal for peace. 'O darlings, *do* be calm and keep your sense of humour. All this fuss over a wretched little brownish-purple –'

'Puce,' Oliver corrected.

' – p . . . p . . . postage-stamp,' wept Edith.

Jane dried Edith's eyes compassionately with a clean pocket handkerchief. 'The stamp was not important until Oliver made it so. But I'm not unreasonable, my dear. If Oliver returns me the stamp, as a token of repentance and future good behaviour, and with it the Palfrey heirlooms except the ones I told him he could keep; and if you renounce the idea of giving Oliver any part in the management of the Burlington (which I couldn't stand); and if you promise to take him in hand generally and make an honest man of him – well, then, Edith, I can be friends with you again and you can introduce him to me as your husband and, forgetting that he was ever my brother, I'll see what can be done.'

'Come on, Edith, don't talk to her, she's mad!' growled Oliver, yanking Edith by the arm.

'Good-bye, Jane,' sobbed Edith, 'It's no good, you see.'

'Good-bye, Edith,' said Jane unsteadily. 'And if you're ever in trouble, come to me. And when you do come, I expect to hear either that you have already got rid of him by murder or divorce, or that you want my advice on how to get rid of him by divorce or murder.'

'You see, it's useless to go on jabbering,' Oliver said with a triumphant grin. 'Edith's mine now, in spite of all your sinister deceits and shifts. And I think it will be a long, long time before you hear from her again except on legal business.'

He was wrong. Edith rang up Jane from Newhaven a few hours later. She was incoherent in her distress. 'Oliver's left me. Or else he's been killed. I don't know which. He's nowhere on the train.'

Jane asked: 'Weren't you together then?'

'No. He was wearing a grey beard and green spectacles, and sitting in another carriage from me. To put reporters off the scent. I had the hand-luggage with me. I was disguised too. I wasn't wearing my glasses and I had borrowed a baby from a woman in the compartment. One reporter went along the compartments asking: 'Excuse me, is Mrs Price here? and several others peeped inquisitively in, but none spotted me. Then the train moved out. When we were clear of London I gave back the baby and put on my glasses and went along to the other carriage. But Oliver wasn't there. I could remember the carriage, but I couldn't remember which compartment it was. He was nowhere. Do you think he could have committed suicide out of a window?'

'No, I'm afraid not, Edith. He's not the suicide sort. . . . I mean, I'm afraid it's worse: either he's left you, or else he's been arrested for something. Perhaps for poisoning the wedding guests. Perhaps for bigamy.'

'O, Jane, you *are* cruel.'

'You don't expect me to regret any accident that happens to Oliver, do you! I was perfectly explicit on that point this afternoon, wasn't I?'

'O, Jane, *do* you know where he is?'

'Yes, I do, as it happens. Roughly, that is.'

'*Where?*'

'In custody.'

'O, Jane . . . it isn't . . . it isn't really bigamy, it it?'

'No, only theft this time. And resisting arrest. But I'm afraid he'll get off. He's gone down on his knees to the owner of the stolen goods, and the fellow's soft-hearted and so the charge will probably be dropped. And, so far as I can make it out, it wasn't direct theft, only receiving. He'll be on the boat-train tomorrow morning, I expect. So that's that. You haven't asked after the invalids yet. Their respiration . . .'

'O, Jane, it's *not* funny!' Edith protested.

'The Devil it's not!' And Jane rang off.

Oliver had been arrested at the news-stand by a certain Inspector Marvell, while buying an evening paper. 'Excuse me, are you Mr Oliver Price?'

Oliver waited for his change before answering. Then he said, 'No, blast you!' and walked towards the carriage.

The Inspector tugged off Oliver's beard. 'It will save you embarrassment if you come with me quietly, Mr Price. I have certain questions to ask you.'

Oliver made some scornful rejoinder and attempted to slug the presumed reporter in the eye. Inspector Marvell collared him low and Oliver went down with a crash. It was two or three minutes before he recovered partial consciousness and by that time Inspector Marvell had walked him off and put him into a taxi. 'Rochester Row Police Station' Oliver vaguely heard him tell the driver. The Inspector had done his best to have Edith found, but she did not appear to be on the train.

Oliver was less groggy by the time he reached the police station and able to answer questions intelligently.

'You are Mr Oliver Price?'

'Yes.'

'Of 27, Albion Mansions, Battersea?'

'Yes, and I wish to protest against this arrest. What am I charged with?'

'You are not as yet under arrest. You are only being asked to co-operate with us in the recovery of certain stolen goods. If you refuse to co-operate you will immediately be put under arrest and charged with receiving these goods, knowing them to be stolen.'

'It's a plant. What stolen goods?'

'It is we who are interrogating you, not you us, Mr Price. We advise you to pipe down a bit. It doesn't do you any good in the long run to throw your weight about.'

'But this is inhuman. On my honeymoon journey! My wife left stranded on the train!'

'You should not have tried to strike Inspector Marvell, Mr Price, and all would have been well. Now tell me, the lady you have just married was a Miss Edith Whitebillet, wasn't she?'

'Don't you read your papers?'

'Any more of your lip and you'll be charged with assaulting a police officer and rushed off to the cells.'

'All right, then, yes, she was.'

'Are you aware that your bride walks in her sleep and has kleptomaniac tendencies when in that condition?'

'No, that's news to me.'

'We are putting it charitably, Mr Price. If that were so, and if your intended wife had come to you and said, 'See here, I am in an embarrassing position. I have just returned from a week-end at a country house with some things that aren't really mine. Will you please return them for me? I must have taken them in my sleep,' then you might have behaved like a gentleman and said, 'yes, my dear. I'll send them back in such a way that the theft won't be traced to you.' And then you might have kept them locked in a box, intending to send them back but not quite sure how to set about it. We are putting it charitably, mind, Mr Price. Now don't interrupt, please! If you agree that this is what occurred and return the abstracted goods to the owner of the country house, who is a proper gentleman and doesn't like a fuss, well then, there'll be no prosecution. If on the contrary . . .'

'It's the most ridiculous story I heard in my life,' cried Oliver.

'You do not therefore acknowledge that you have in your possession goods abstracted from Babraham Castle in Christmas week, 1934?'

Oliver choked. 'I'm ready to sign an affidavit to that effect.'

'Better not commit anything to writing, Mr Price, without the advice of your solicitor. And now, perhaps you will accompany Inspector Marvell to Albion Mansions and show him over your flat. He has a search warrant. Have you your keys? If not, I am afraid we may have to force the lock.'

Oliver tried again: 'This is a damnable plot. It's my sister, Miss Jane Palfrey, who's behind this, isn't it? I admit that I have certain things in my possession – pictures, ornaments and a couple of books – that used to belong to Babraham Castle, but that was years and years ago. They were left to me in 1930 by my mother, who was the daughter of the seventh Marquess. We had them at home.'

'If you can prove that, Mr Price, it will alter the look of things considerably. So they were specifically mentioned in your mother's will?'

'No, not exactly.'

'Could you prove that they had been in the possession of your family for many years? Have you witnesses that they were displayed in your home?'

'They weren't displayed.'

'What, not even the pictures weren't? Nobody saw them besides yourself and your mother?'

'And my father. My father is dead too.'

The Superintendent clicked his tongue sympathetically. 'Too bad. Well, you'd better go along with the Inspector and we'll have a look at the things and compare them with the list which the Marquess has given me.'

They were back at the station within half an hour. The various objects were laid on the table, still in their cases and wrappings.

'Here you see!' said Oliver, unwrapping the *Shepheardes Calender*. 'Look at the date of this newspaper – April 20th, 1930. That was when I inherited it from my mother. That proves it.'

'Not altogether logical, Mr Price. The only thing that the newspaper proves is that the book was not wrapped up in that newspaper *previously* to April 20th, 1930. It might have been wrapped up in it at any subsequent date. First, let's check the list. Silver pyx, that must be this. Illuminated *Book of Hours* –

here. Ivory Madonna – here. Rowlandson prints, two. Dutch oil painting attributed to the younger Breughel, three – one, two, three. O.K. Spenser's *Sh-Sh* – looks like *Shepherd's Calender*. This it? Yes. But, hey, twenty-seven enamelled snuff-boxes and fifty-two Greek silver, and eighteen Greek gold coins. What about that lot?'

'I haven't got them.'

'Where are they?'

'Sold, I'm afraid.'

'Whom to?'

'I don't know. My mother sold them.'

'But you say your mother died in 1930. Yet the loss was reported last December. That proves, Mr Price, that you are not being frank with us.'

Oliver sneered. 'You are not altogether logical, Superintendent. The only thing that has been proved is that the loss did not take place *subsequent* to last December. It might have taken place at any previous date.'

The Superintendent was annoyed. 'You'll have to account for these coins and snuff-boxes, I'm afraid, Mr Price.'

'I never saw them in my life and it'll puzzle you to prove that I did.'

'Would you care to see the Marquess of Babraham?'

'I would. I'll tell him to his face that it's a trumped-up charge.'

'My advice, Mr Price, is to be reasonable. His Lordship does not wish to charge you, on account of your being a grandson of the late Marquess; and he says that he respects your gentlemanliness in not giving away your bride's unfortunate abstraction of the goods and will be satisfied with their return in good condition. You will note that the proceedings so far have been extremely informal. You have not been warned that anything you say may be used as evidence against you. You have not been charged. You are, let me repeat, merely assisting us in an investigation. The goods, with a few exceptions, have been found in your possession. Inspector Marvell is a witness to that. No doubt you will assist us to recover the remainder. You will then be a free man. If you prefer to assert your innocence you will be formally charged with receiving goods

T – G

known to be stolen and Mrs Price will also be charged with the more serious crime of larceny.'

The Emu entered. 'You are Mr Price? I was at your wedding reception this afternoon by your wife's invitation. I'm sorry this has happened. I don't want it to go any further. Of course, I quite understand your motives in hanging on to the stuff. Wouldn't want to give away the name of the person who pinched it; and a bit awkward, sending it back. Still, honesty's the best policy, and so on.'

'How did you know I had the things?'

'Oh, a friend of mine lives below you. He came up one day to borrow some cigarettes, found the door open, saw you handling the goods and put two and two together. He slipped away before you were aware that he was there. It was the pyx that caught his attention. He recognized it as a practically priceless object.'

'Hoyland! That sneaky ink-slinger?'

'An honest man, a friend of mine, and, I think, a very promising writer.'

'Look here, Lord Babraham. This is a framed charge and you know it. I believe that my sister Jane is behind all this. These things have been in my family's possession for thirty years. They were all Palfrey heirlooms that came to me from my mother, and I'll defy you to prove to the contrary.'

The Emu took up the *Shepheardes Calender*. 'When I succeeded to the title,' he said slowly, 'I decided, as soon as I could spare the time, to recatalogue the library at Babraham Castle: it had been allowed to get into a bit of a confusion in the course of the previous eighty years. I had new book-plates engraved, and by 1934 the whole thing was in order again. Look here! "Tiberius 3.D." The book-cases are named after the Roman emperors. "Tiberius 3.D." is the shelf reference.'

The Superintendent examined the book-plate and said sternly to Oliver: 'Do you wish to be charged? Look at this! 'Babraham Castle Library. Tiberius 3.D. August 1934. F.ff. Librarian.''

Oliver goggled at the book-plate.

'Do you wish to be charged?'

Oliver's defiant manner collapsed. 'No, Inspector, if Lord

Babraham will be content with the return of these things. But I'm afraid I haven't got the coins and snuff-boxes. I never had them. My mother . . .'

'It would be wiser and more filial to leave your mother out of it at this stage, Price,' said The Emu severely. 'Your mother died in 1930.'

'I'm sorry,' said Oliver meekly. 'It was silly of me to mention her.'

Emu and the Superintendent exchanged merry glances.

'I am much obliged to you, Superintendent,' The Emu said, 'for the very delicate way in which you have handled this inquiry. The man Price is not, I believe, wholly bad. He was acting in what he believed to be a gentlemanly way. I shall not prosecute either him or his wife, and I prefer not to press the matter of the snuff-boxes or the coins. I am a rich man. Coins and snuff-boxes have no great interest for me. Now, if I may be allowed to pay for the expenses of the inquiry – taxis, telephones, time, etc. ? No ? Oh, but I insist! A police charity then ? Yes ? Delighted. Police Athletic Sports Fund ? Police Orphanage ?'

He wrote out a cheque for twenty-five pounds and shook hands all round. 'I'll send for this stuff tomorrow.'

Oliver asked doubtfully: 'Am I free to go now ?'

Yes, he was free to go. But it was late now and he did not know where Edith was. So he decided to return to Battersea for the night. The Emu gave him a lift there in his car, for which he was extremely grateful, not realizing why the offer had been made. The Emu was, as a matter of fact, making sure that Oliver should not realize on emerging into the street the gross deception practised upon him. For he had not, indeed, been in Rochester Row Police Station at all; but in the offices of the Kookaburra Wool Company, a few doors off, which an Australian pal had allowed The Emu to convert for the occasion into a convincing setting to Jane's carefully rehearsed little play. Inspector Marvell was no policeman really: he was Alfred Williams, the Burlington assistant electrician. And the Superintendent was Mr Kinch, the stage prompter, and the constables were two other theatre employees on whose discretion Jane could count. Oliver had been so easily taken in because he had a guilty conscience in the matter of the heir-looms; and the bang on his head helped to muddle him nicely. Besides, everyone is secretly afraid of policemen: one needs no Dr Parmesan to account for *that* neurosis.

The most delicate part of the game had been Oliver's capture, and this could only be worked, even by a man of Alfred Williams' coolness and remarkably policeman-like bearing, with the help of a diversion. The diversion that Jane provided was a quarrel between a husband running off to France and a wife who complained that she was being left penniless: by the time the husband had been persuaded by the genuine policeman on duty to hand over some alimony and avoid further scandal, Oliver had been safely marched off the platform. It was only afterwards that Jane and The Emu paused to consider how extremely risky it had been. 'If I were a Catholic,' Jane said, 'I should now burn several hundredweight of candles to Saint Crispin, or someone. That's the worst of being born a Protestant.'

'I always light a big bonfire,' said The Emu. 'I shall light one tonight in my garden and send off a rocket or two, perhaps.'

'Oh, Emu, you can't do that! What would people say! With the whole company on their death-beds!'

'I don't know how I came to suggest such a thing,' he said in such a remorseful tone that Jane's heart went suddenly out to him. Edith's defection had advanced The Emu, she suddenly realized, into the position of the best friend she had.

So Oliver slept in his bachelor bed again that night and early in the morning Edith, who had returned to Town by car, rang him up, and they met for breakfast in her hotel.

Naturally Edith and Oliver had a lot to tell each other. Oliver said: 'I can't sue them, that's the devil of it! Because, by returning the things in the presence of witnesses, I admitted that I had no legal right to hang on to them. Only a moral right, which I couldn't press, because appearances were so heavily against me. How the deuce that book-plate was planted there beats me. It wasn't done last night, because the book wasn't even unwrapped until they opened it at the police station. And I had always kept the trunk they were in locked. It must have been Hoyland, acting for Jane and the Marquess. He must have broken into my rooms when I was away at St Aidan's with a skeleton key or something . . .'

'Have you seen the paper this morning? Jane says that the Company has survived the night, but their condition is still critical and that, even if they live, it will be a long time before they can return to their professional duties.'

'I can't understand the newspapers printing such rot. They must know the whole thing is a hoax.'

'Well, it isn't, in a way. If Jane lets them die, it means that she's going to retire from the stage. Tell me, Noll darling, what are we going to do about the Theatre? Shall we sell out?'

'That's just what Jane wants. She hasn't let the Company die, because she thinks that you'll decide to sell. Then she'll buy up your interest, and start again on her own. Babraham will back her.'

'So what do you propose?'

'Take her at her word and hang on, of course. Buy her out. It's the chance of a lifetime. I've always wanted to stage Shakespeare as he should be staged, and Restoration comedy, and the best eighteenth-century stuff, and Wilde. And dramatize Joyce and D. H. Lawrence – a lot can be decently acted that can't be decently read. A real literary theatre. Jane may joke about astrakhan collars, but I'll make a jolly sight better manager than she did. I mean, I'll stage things really worth staging.'

Edith said: 'The best thing, then, is to rent the theatre for a few months until we know where we are.' She would have preferred to sell out, being tired of the theatrical business and wanting to get back to science. But Oliver seemed so excited and so confident that she humoured him. Besides, there was his play. A really lovely play. It ought to be given a chance.

'I'll write a note to my lawyers immediately,' she said, 'telling them of our decision.'

'Do. The sooner we fix things up, the less the waste. The theatre is lying idle now: it might be rented at once. But isn't this going to interfere with our honeymoon?'

'Not at all. My lawyer has power of attorney for me. And the price and everything is provided for in my contract with Jane. He'll fix it all up while we're in France.'

At the boat-train, again avoiding camera-men and reporters, Oliver was accosted by a Special Messenger with a large packet in his hands. 'Are you Mr Price, and will you please sign a receipt for this?'

'What is it?'

'I don't know, sir. I was told it was a wedding present, and to handle it carefully.'

Oliver signed, doubtfully, and took the packet. He and Edith had reserved an entire first-class compartment for themselves. As the train moved out Edith untied the string. 'O look, Oliver, pictures! And what's this in the corrugated-paper packet? A queer little white statue! Looks Chinese, or Red Indian or something.'

They came with a note, 'Mr and Mrs O. Price, with the sincerest wishes of the Marquess of Babraham, on the occasion of their wedding.'

For Jane had always told Oliver that what she wanted was the pyx, the *Shepheardes Calender* and the *Book of Hours*, and that he could have the Dutch pictures, the Rowlandsons and the Madonna – which were more in his line.

'Curse her,' he said mildly, relieved it was nothing worse.

'We've got to lug them all over France with us and go through agonies at the Customs.'

'Perhaps Jane decided at the last moment to be friends,' Edith said, 'and didn't think of the nuisance they'd be.'

'The hell she didn't!'

CHAPTER 17

JANE LEAVES THE THEATRE

It was a tribute to the thoroughness of Jane's inspirational method that several of the Company had, by a sort of auto-poisoning, contrived to make themselves seriously ill, and the remainder dangerously so. The puffy purple lips, the froth on the tongue and the laboured breathing were all forthcoming and required real trained nurses, which contributed to the illusion and aggravated the symptoms. Jane was alarmed at the success of her plan and called in a couple of well-known genuine doctors, one of them being Sir Thomas Medoc, a Court physician, whose bulletins were communicated to the press and jolted the public into the view that the poisoned sandwiches had not been a hoax after all.

Jane received the letter from Edith's lawyers and was at last able to do something for her sufferers. She went from bed to bed and asked each of them in turn whether, now that the Burlington was passing into other hands and she had decided not to try and lease another theatre, they would prefer to die, or whether they would care to recover and come with her into the motion-picture industry. They all chose life, so gradually the bulletins improved and after a few days they were all stated to be out of danger.

Jane did not have enough capital to build her own picture-studios and, though she could have got several financiers to put her up for it, she liked none of them well enough to wish to be under any obligation to him. Picture-making, she knew, was worse than the theatre. Money-backers were always jogging the producer's elbow and telling him what to do; and demanding that their protégés, male and female, be made into stars. Finally, The Emu said: 'Look here, Jane, what about me? Won't you let me finance you? I've got bags of money and I'll not jog your elbow or expect you to feature all my friends. I haven't any friends, you see.'

'Oh? What about Adelaide? Wouldn't she insist on taking the celluloid path to Marchionesshood?'

'Adelaide a Marchioness? Who told you that one?'

'Nobody. But I thought it was foregone.'

'Indeed not. For three reasons. A, she wouldn't make a good one. One has to be careful in appointing Marchionesses as in appointing Bishops. B, she's fixed up already. She's going to marry a young airman whom she's known for years. He's just off to beat the Round-the-World flying record. I'm backing him, for Adelaide's sake. Bought him the latest thing in planes. C – I forget C.'

'Adelaide's airman isn't a boy called Dormer, is he, by any chance?'

'That's right. Oh, yes, of course, you'd know of him. He's the chap who swapped the stamp-album with your brother, isn't he? He's a mechanical genius, and only discovered it about twelve months ago.'

'You're not sick at heart about Adelaide and him, are you, Emu?' Jane asked sympathetically.

'No indeed. You see . . . there's C.'

'But you have forgotten C.'

'True. But not irrecoverably. I've promised myself not to remember it until somehow I've got hold of something that somebody wants. Jane, what do you think me good for? Much? Little?'

'My opinion of you improves every day. You are really thoughtful, really intelligent, and quite nice-looking. And I think I know that something that somebody wants that you want to get hold of somehow.'

'I wonder if we're thinking of the same thing.'

'I expect we are. Is it a very small and very silly something that means a lot to me?' Jane asked, amused.

'Yes.'

'You propose that it should provide a test?'

'Yes. C to be discussed between you and me only if the test is passed.'

'Agreed,' Jane said, looking very pleased.

'Then C won't come as too much of a shock.'

'And even if you fail, Emu . . . Because it seems a pretty tough test.'

'Don't cramp my form,' he pleaded.

Jane said: 'I wonder what sort of children Edith and Oliver will have. Awful?'

'Not necessarily. There's a decent strain in the Whitebillet family.'

'The Whitebillet strain won't have much of a chance against the Price. The Price strain is dreadfully dominant. You should see all my paternal first cousins! Three sets of them. Slingsbys to a man – even the women!'

'But the Palfrey strain isn't exactly recessive. The offspring might have the luck to take after your mother.'

'Yes, you'd have loved my mother,' said Jane. 'She once emptied a jug of water over my father as an act of general criticism. He had done nothing in particular to offend her. He thought she had gone mad, and she wouldn't explain why she had done it. That was when I was about six years old. They drifted apart after that, as the saying is.'

'My father was queer too,' said The Emu. 'He used to go about in a straw hat without a crown in Australia's hottest sun. And fall suddenly melancholy over nothing. I didn't realize until I came over here what an aristocratic sign that scarecrow hat of his was. . . . He married my mother because she was the best-tempered, most solidly built, most insensitive woman in the whole island of Tasmania. Dutch origin. You should see my young sisters. You can drive pins into them and they just giggle. Legs like milk-churns,' he added, glancing affectionately at his own slim ones. 'But you'd have loved my father. Over-bred, like your mother, and the best man on a bucking brumby I ever saw.'

'It's a great experience for me, Emu, to feel sympathetic towards my relatives. And if your sisters don't mind having legs like milk-churns, everyone's happy.'

'They love it,' said The Emu.

So everything was settled. Jane and The Emu went into partnership and while the studios were being built began learning their job practically at Elstree and picking up good camera-men and technicians. *Apes and Peacocks* was filmed and was quite a success; but Jane knew that she could do much better next time, when the Company had learned to accommodate itself more spontaneously to screen technique.

Oliver and Edith came back from their honeymoon and there was a good deal in the Press about the Burlington being destined as a permanent home for classical drama; but when Jane happened to pass Oliver in Bond Street one day he was not yet wearing his astrakhan collar.

Harold Dormer flew half-way round the world, beating several records, but then crashed; so Adelaide had to go half-way round the world to nurse and marry him. The reason for her switching from The Emu to him was that, being a sensible girl, she soon realized that her ambition of becoming his marchioness was sordid – because impossible. And when Harold took up flying he became romantically interesting. After he recovered from his accident The Emu gave him a bigger, faster and more dangerous plane still, as a wedding present. Harold and Adelaide stepped into it one day for a non-stop flight from San Francisco to Tierra del Fuego. They got killed, somewhere in the Andes, but they were together, and in love, and going at two hundred and fifty at the time, so the general effect was gay rather than gloomy. All this happened a good deal later, however.

One day in November (1935) The Emu met Algernon Hoyland. Hoyland told him of a scene on the stairs at Albion Mansions, where the lift was still out of order, or out of order again. Hoyland going downstairs one evening had met Oliver coming up. Oliver had behaved in an extraordinary way, shouting threats and actually aiming a blow at him. Hoyland did not know in the least what it was all about and shot back into his room, where he stood a sort of siege, Oliver hammering on the door and demanding admittance. Hoyland had no telephone, and anyway it would have been an awful business to bring the police into it. A long story, but the climax was that he remembered the fire-escape; and when he returned the next morning he had seen Oliver's furniture being carried out and loaded in a furniture van, so he had gone away again, and come back in the afternoon, and not seen Oliver since.

'Hoyland,' said The Emu, 'let us sponge these memories off the slate, and in future avoid the company of all Prices. And I want to say this: if you ever have any bright idea for a film scenario, bung it across to us, and if it's not absolute punk

I'll see whether I can get my partner interested in it. No promise, observe: only an open mind and an open heart when Algernon Hoyland's name appears on a script.' Curiously enough, Hoyland sent us along something quite good, which Jane decided to use.

The next event of importance to be recorded in this short and rather scrappy chapter is that Mrs Trent had a letter from Edith. It said that she was very well, considering that she was having a baby. Edna was away in India, tiger-shooting with Freddy, and she was feeling rather lonely. Would Mrs Trent come to see her? Oliver had gone off by himself to finish a play. She showed Jane the letter.

'Miss Edith sounds a little unhappy,' said Mrs Trent.

'Miss Edith has made her own bed and now she must lie in it and mother her litter of little Slingsbys. She's beyond my sympathy now. But I think you ought to go and see her.'

Mrs Trent sighed. 'We were very fond of Miss Edith once.'

Jane unexpectedly began to cry, but turned her back so that Mrs Trent should not notice.

Oliver published his novel. He had to pay to get it published and was grossly over-charged and, in spite of a large additional sum that the publishers demanded for advertising, only sold forty-five copies in England and seven in Canada. It is always a mystery in such cases who the forty-five buyers are. 'Probably,' Jane thought – Miss Hapless' sister, in the publisher's office, had given Miss Hapless the figures, and she had passed them on to Jane – 'forty-five old ladies who come very slowly into forty-five book-shops exactly at closing time and say very slowly to the forty-five assistants: "Please, young man, I want a nice interesting book of the kind that won't keep me awake at night. None of your nasty murders or detective tales. Rather old-fashioned, if possible." And the forty-five assistants reply: "We have the very thing for you, Ma'am. *A Session of the Diet*, by O. Price. It's one long yawn. Bill, wrap this lady up a *Session* and look sharp! It's gone closing time already, we'll have the cops in. That will be seven shillings and sixpence, Ma'am, thank you, Ma'am."'

So long as Oliver retained the A P P, as we may now call the Antigua penny puce stamp for short, Jane felt conscientiously obliged to keep the war active. She knew the literary editor of one of the leading Sunday papers and said to him one day: 'I have a young friend who is interested in historical fiction and is a bit hard up. Could you possibly find him a book or two to review?'

'Send him along to the office and tell him to pick out what he fancies,' replied the Literary Editor warmly. 'We like specialists.'

So The Emu strolled along to the office, picked up *A Session of the Diet*, by Oliver Price, and two other historical novels, and then spent four days at the Institute of Medieval Studies looking up minor historical points. He located fourteen anachronisms. Jane read the book too and found seven faults in grammar and three textual contradictions. Not much of a harvest really. An average drama of real life contains just as many anachronisms, hundreds of grammatical faults and a textual contradiction every two or three minutes. But fourteen anachronisms, seven glaring grammatical faults, and three flat textual contradictions look pretty bad when listed in a review under the heading: 'History, Fiction – and Hash.' Jane had an instinct against anonymous abuse, so the review was signed by Owen Slingsby. It spoilt a Sunday breakfast for Oliver.

Owen Slingsby had been writing *Confessions of a Cad*, his autobiographical first novel. Many of the milder confessions were ones that Oliver too would have made, had he been of a confessional nature, but even these were made to read a little worse than human. Some were quite apocryphal. But in the chapters headed 'Browsing among Private Diaries', 'I Get a Weak Heart', 'I Commit Perjury', 'I Poison my Wedding Guests', there was enough flavouring of fiction with fact to make the tale wholly plausible. Before it was published, early in 1936, Jane consulted a lawyer, a personal friend of hers, who was a specialist in libel. He made a few suggestions.

'The Mr X, some of whose actions are, you state, paralleled in this book, will not in my opinion be likely to sue if you modify the passages I have lightly marked in pencil in the margin. In order to establish a course of action Mr X would have to allege and prove that he was the person caricatured. Since

you assure us that there is no geographical or other evidence
that would tend to associate him with the hero of your story,
and the parallels are only in behaviour, not in description,
name or setting, and also not of a sort that Mr X would be
tempted to press in a public court, my opinion is that Mr
Slingsby will incur little practical risk in publishing.'

Enclosed with this letter, which was typed, was an unsigned
manuscript note:

My Dear Jane,

As you may be aware, we are specialists in literary libel and, for
our sins, many prominent authors are clients of ours. A pretty
murky crowd. Since the case of *Hulton* v. *Jones* which, decided in
the House of Lords fifteen years ago, established that *where there is
evidence that persons acquainted with the plaintiff might reasonably believe
him to be the person referred to and reflected upon in a work of fiction, it is
immaterial that the writer never intended to refer to him, or, indeed, that
he has hitherto been unaware of his existence,* we have always advised our
authors to avoid the portrayal of purely fictitious characters. The
safest method is the one that appears to have been followed in this
novel: to portray an actual character with a careful alteration of
scene and circumstances and at the same time to reveal such detailed
knowledge of some discreditable passage, or passages, in his life
that he will not be tempted to present himself in court as that
character's counterpart! But all this is 'under the hat'.

Michael

This was, in our opinion, somewhat rash advice for a self-
styled expert in libel. Suppose you, a writer, have a hold over
a Mr X and spitefully model your not-so-fictitious character
'Gregory Garboyle' upon him. This Gregory Garboyle may
still by chance be identified as an accidental Mr G. Garboyle
of Streatham Common, or somewhere, just as easily as if he
were wholly fictitious; and aha! where are you? Your assertion,
if you dare to make it, that your Gregory Garboyle is a representation of your friend Mr X, is no stronger than an assertion that he is a mere creature of your fancy. For, though you
have a practical defence against Mr X's getting nasty (the fact
that he may have committed some of the crimes and follies
recorded in your book), you have no legal defence against this
accidental Garboyle of Streatham; £1,000 is what that joke
will cost you. And costs. It will not even have been sufficient to

assure yourself that no Gregory Garboyle appears in the London Telephone Directory. The fellow is always careful to have no phone, and lies in wait like a spider.

However, in this case, 'Michael' was right. Mr X, or Oliver, had to bite the bullet. The *Confessions*, which was a hurried collaboration between Jane and Algernon Hoyland, sold so well, so well, so very well, that even a few booksellers found time to read it in their annual holiday (which they take in the summer, usually at Ostend) to see what it was all about. But what was there to see? Booksellers are always a little resentful of best-sellers, even though they could not possibly live without them. Booksellers stand for sound literature; best-sellers are manifestly unsound. Mr Jacob, of the well-known City firm of Jacob and Jackson, talking one day to his partner, Mr Jackson, on the sands at Ostend, expressed himself with a vigour that only a foreign climate and sea-air would ever have tempted him to use. 'Take the *Confessions of a Cad*, now: it will not *live*, it is not wholesome, it is not humorous, it is not well written, it does not depict decent characters, and yet it ran away with the whole Spring season! That's the devil of it. We'd have been in the red without that book, Jackson. It paid for our passages out here. It's paid for this new Panama tile of mine. It's going to pay for a small flutter at the Casino tonight. I tell you, Jackson, I feel – I feel like a fancy man living off the immoral earnings of a woman of a certain class.'

'Dickens,' said Jackson sleepily. 'Dickens, Bulwer Lytton, Scott. And the Bible, of course. That's what I was brought up on. All sound stuff. And *Three Men in a Boat*. Funniest book ever written, to my mind.'

There the conversation tailed off. But Oliver, who was at Ostend getting local colour for a play and who overheard that much, felt very grateful for it. It is pleasant to feel that one has the booksellers on one's side and, by implication, posterity. Speaking of posterity, his son would soon be born and learning to read at his mother's knee. But this is getting ahead of the story. By the time Reginald was born – a very ordinary little boy, obviously a Price, but with the additional handicap of short sight and a gloomy scientific habit of mind – and able to spell out unsmilingly 'The cat sat on the mat but the ox sat in its box', the story, but for a short final incident which will appear in the last pages, was as good as over.

This has been a tidying-up to prevent either uncertainty as to what happened to any of the minor characters, or curiosity as to the subsidiary activities of the major characters; or anti-climax.

We are still in November, 1935, when Oliver published *A Session of the Diet*, and the next day of real significance to the story (the nub of which, we must again point out, is the bitter struggle between Jane and Oliver for the possession of the Antigua penny puce, or A P P, at present in Oliver's hands, or Edith's, which was now the same thing) was December 4th of that year. It was then that, after having journeyed to a Philatelic Exhibition at Florence (heavily insured) and been greatly admired by many thousands of philatelic pilgrims from all parts of the world, the A P P returned to London and was once more announced for public auction by Messrs Harrow and Hazlitt, of the Argent Street Stamp-Auctions.

CHAPTER 18

ODDY BELLS

THE APP was now far more than the rarest stamp in the world and the heroine and sole survivor of a classical shipwreck. The case of *Palfrey v. Price*, the eventful marriage of Oliver and Edith, Jane's retirement from the Burlington Theatre, had together invested the APP with a romantic penumbra that brought press representatives to the second auction from as far away as Turkey and Latin America.

When the APP was once more entrusted to them for sale by auction, Messrs Harrow and Hazlitt broke with a lengthy tradition. They decided to accept Mr and Mrs Price's generous offer and to move for the occasion from their intimate Argent Street premises: staging the auction, instead, at the Burlington Theatre, with movie-cameras, microphones, spot-lighting, and a considerable radio hook-up. By an ingenious device (thought out by Edith) each stamp as it came under the hammer would be immediately reflected in magnification on a large screen above the auctioneer's head. A postage stamp nearly six feet high cannot but look impressive – the sort of stamp, as Oliver put it, that would take a letter all the way from the G.P.O. London to the planet Mercury. It was to be a very special auction, restricted to individual stamps, or blocks of stamps, of extreme rarity. Meanwhile Messrs Harrow and Hazlitt circularized their clients all over the British Isles, Europe and the world; if these had been holding back rarities from the market, December 4th was a golden opportunity to sell them and there would be no extra charge for the elaborate arrangements that were being made to ensure success.

The theatre idea was wholly Oliver's. His notion was to publicize both his control of the theatre from which he had succeeded in evicting his sister, and his control of the APP. This time the only conclusion to the bidding would be the victory of the bidder with the longest purse. 'Irrespective of colour, religion, race or character,' he joked to Edith. 'Even Jane will be allowed to bid if she is so desperately keen on getting it: "*Madame P., qui désirait plus que tout autre chose un timbre-poste puce, pour la gloire de sa collection philatélique.*"' He had a complimentary ticket sent to Jane, to tease her, reserving a place for her at one of the baize tables on the stage.

The Emu said to Jane, when she showed it to him: 'A ringside seat? That's just what I want. May I have it? Success now stares me in the face.'

'O Emu, what are you going to do? Are you going to barrack the auctioneer? No? Are you going to shoot the stamp out of his hand with a pistol? No? Are you going to stampede the audience with a cry of Fire? No? Then what's on? You've got that bush-ranger look in your eye. I like it, but are you sure that you're not going to gaol for the sake of the stamp and C.?'

'That depends on my female accomplice.'

'Ha! Do I know her?'

'No.'

'Is she nice?'

'Not very.'

'Young?'

'Twenty-sevenish.'

'Professional crook?'

'Oh, no. Honest bourgeois stock and a fellow-countrywoman of mine.'

'How did you find her?'

'I advertised in the *Christian Science Monitor*, and she replied from Manchester. Christian Science is strong there.'

'You're not an X.S., are you, by any chance?'

'Me? No! But then, you see, I'm never ill.'

'Then why a Christian Scientist?'

'They have nerves of steel and foreheads of brass. I'd rather have a confirmed Christian Scientist at my side in an emergency than, than – than almost anyone,' he finished lamely. 'I was going to say a Metropolitan policeman, but probably most of them are Christian Scientists too. The movement's spreading. What do *you* think of Christian Science, Jane?'

'Meaning, I'm not to question you further?'

'Meaning exactly that, please.'

'Well, at least tell me her name.'

'Mildred Young.'

Jane had to be content with this. If she had thought very hard she might have worked it out, but in Christian Science, as in Communism, there are no speculative vistas; flood-lit foreground and all foggy behind.

And yet The Emu was telling the truth. He had indeed secured the services of Mildred Young by advertising in the *Christian Science Monitor*; and he had advertised there because an obliging elderly man at a petrol-filling station near Oxford had told him that she had once refused to have her tonsils removed.

This is the story. The Emu had the letter to Brother Fred and he also had the 'Save Will Young' broadsheet, and he lost no time in cleaning up the clues contained in them. Starting from the assumption that the Duke of Marlborough's Yeomanry must have been quartered somewhere in the neighbourhood of Blenheim Palace, near Oxford (which was as far as Edith had got), he drove out there one sunny morning in his car by way of Windsor, Marlow, Abingdon and Oxford, and drank a glass of beer at 'The Bear' at Woodstock, not far from the Palace gates. He addressed an intelligent looking farmer at the bar: 'Excuse me, sir, may I ask you a question of local history? Are the words "ducket", "stank", and "red-leg" used in this neighbourhood?'

'Eh?'

The Emu repeated his question amid a general hush.

'Well, sir, I won't disguise the fact that there's some terrible expressions used hereabouts at Election times. "Red-leg", "black-leg", "black-and-blue-leg"; "ducket", "kicket", "smashet"; not to mention "stink", "stank", and "stunk".'

The laughter that this facetious retort excited lasted for three or four minutes, with renewed bursts while it was explained to the barman who had missed it, a deaf man, and two new customers.

It is to the credit of The Emu that he managed to laugh too. It was his Australian upbringing. 'Well, you certainly had me there. What I really meant to ask you was this: Are there any moors in this neighbourhood? I'm looking out for a moor.'

'Moors? None that I've met. But a gentleman from the Workers' Educational Association at Oxford was lecturing here last week and he said that the *Morris*-dances that used to be danced here when I was a boy was in reality *Moorish* dances, brought here by the Moors from Africa.'

'What's Moors, Farmer Tompkins? Black men, ain't they?' someone asked.

'Black men, the lecturer said.'

'Then if the gentleman is looking out for black men he's not far to go. I'm a Black Man myself. I'm Oddy-born.'

The Emu strode over to the Black Man: 'What's yours? A double whisky?'

The Black Man looked embarrassed, but said that he didn't mind if he did.

'Tell me about Oddy,' said The Emu, sitting down beside him. 'What's Oddy?'

'Oddy's what the old people call Oddington. I've not been there since I was a nipper,' said the Black Man, 'but it's still standing they tell me. A little village, a matter of eight miles from here. 'Tother side of Kidlington.'

'Any red-legs in that neighbourhood?'

'Red-legs? Ay, come to think of it, that's what we used to call them birds in the marsh. A bit shy, they were. I never saw one close.'

'Why are you called Black Men, if I may ask?'

'That I don't know. We marsh-men have always been called Black Men. We're created different from the rest of the world. You can always tell a Black Man by the build of his chest, and other signs.'

The Emu remembered the webbed feet and involuntarily glanced at the Black Man's boots. But all he asked was: 'Ever heard of an Oddy family called Young?'

The Black Man considered. 'I was only a nipper. No, can't say as I have.'

'Ever heard that Oddy bells were supposed to ring out a particular tune?'

'Ay, that's right. Oddy bells always ring: "Hang Sam Gomme, Save Will Young."'

'What was that story? Who was Sam Gomme?'

'I've heard tell he was a carpenter and a spy. And Will Young he was a hero. But that's all I recollect.'

'Black Man, here's a ten-shilling note for your courtesy. "Ducket" and "stank" can wait for another day.'

But a thirsty labourer earned a drink by defining stank as the Oxfordshire for 'weir'. 'There's a stank not far from Oddington, where the Ray runs into the Cherwell.'

The Emu drove at speed to Kidlington and from there was directed to Oddington. He stopped at a small village a mile or two short of his destination. He found he needed petrol. A distinguished-looking elderly man came out of the Post Office and offered him the choice of three pumps.

'Excuse me, is this the way to Oddington?' The Emu asked while his tank was being filled.

'Yes, sir, it's the way by the map, but I fear you'll not get there in your car. The road's flooded over to a depth of four feet in places, I'm told.'

'Isn't there a way round?'

'That'll be flooded too. Chorlton and Oddington are standing out of the floods like islands.'

'How do the villagers manage?'

'Oh, they're all right sir. Otmoor men have webbed feet, as the popular saying is.'

The Emu did not need to go to Oddington after all, because Mr Steel, the distinguished-looking elderly man, told him all he wanted to know. He appeared to be the local historian, as well as the postmaster and custodian of three petrol pumps and a telephone. He said: 'So you wish to know why the Oddington bells ring "Hang Sam Gomme, and save Will Young"? If you care to step into the office, I'll try to spare a minute to tell you the story. ... Well, then, Oddington is one of the seven Otmoor Parishes. Otmoor is a large marshy moor, lying yonder, which is subject to floods at this season of the year. Until the beginning of last century it had common land on which the Web-footed Men, or Black Men as they are also called, used to pasture great flocks of white, web-footed geese. They claimed that they held this right from time immemorial. Then the big landowners, who were the political leaders in South Oxon, took it into their heads to enclose Otmoor and

turn it into wheat-growing land. The Duke of Marlborough
and the Earl of Abingdon were at the head of this movement.
Naturally, the men of the Otmoor parishes objected and, no
sooner were hedges fixed to enclose it, than out they swarmed
by night and broke them down with bill-hooks and scythes.'

'And duckets,' put in The Emu.

'Duckets too, as you say. Do you see that glass-fronted
building there to the left of your car? That's where Lord
Churchill's troop of yeomanry (the Duke of Marlborough's
son, you know) was stationed during the disturbances. And
do you see that lad passing now? That's young Fisher Beckley.
His great-grandfather played a part in the story I'm telling you.
The Yeomanry went riding out to Otmoor on the information
of a carpenter of Oddington by the name of Sam Gomme.
That was the sixth of September, in the year 1830. They caught
the men of Otmoor in the act of destroying fences. The Captain,
who was a JP, read the Riot Act, but the mob wouldn't budge,
so they seized a couple of score of 'em, and brought 'em along
in wagons to Oxford Gaol. Now, the Fisher Beckley of the
time (there's always a Fisher Beckley in this village) was up the
River Ray fishing and when he saw what was happening he
rowed pretty rapidly down the river to "The Swan", facing
the bridge at the end of this street. There he jumped out and
into the skittle alley and told the farmers who were drinking
there what was happening. One of them took horse and
galloped to Oxford.

'Now, as luck would have it, it was the day of St Giles' Fair
and the country-folk for miles around were assembled in St
Giles' in their thousands. (That's in front of St John's College,
where the Woodstock and Banbury roads branch out of the
City). The farmer spread the word round that the Otmoor
men were arrested for asserting their grazing rights on the
common, and by the time the wagons arrived with the prisoners
the mob was well roused. "Otmoor for Ever", was the cry
they took up, and, St Giles' being cobbled at that time, not
asphalted, you can imagine that the soldiers were given a warm
welcome. At the corner of Beaumont Street, where the Ran-
dolph Hotel is now standing, the fighting was fiercest and the
Yeomanry were overpowered and disarmed. The prisoners all

escaped. The mob collared a few of them and trussed 'em up, the same as the Otmoor men had been, and dragged 'em in front of the Mayor of Oxford; who was in a pretty good fright, I imagine, and made all sorts of promises that he didn't intend to keep.

'Will Young and a fellow by the name of Cooper were the ringleaders on Otmoor, and of course as soon as the Fair was over and the country-people had dispersed the Yeomanry came in stronger force than before to seize them; they had no difficulty in making the arrests. Everyone said that Young and Cooper would hang and everyone blamed it on Sam Gomme, the Earl of Abingdon's spy, and Sam Gomme had to ask for special protection from the military. But it all ended fairly happily. Not a man was hanged or even transported. The longest sentence inflicted was three or four months. The Otmoor men lost, because they lost their right of free grazing for their geese, which was the only profitable stock for marsh-land, and the landowners lost, because in spite of their draining and diking the greater part of Otmoor remained a marsh and always will remain so. About the only gainer was the Church. The parsons were given tidy little slices of glebe land to make them preach obedience and contentment to their flocks.'

'And Will Young? What happened to him? Are there any of his descendants about?'

'Well, curious that you should ask me that. About a matter of ten, or maybe twelve years ago an Australian lady came here and wanted to buy or lease a house in the neighbourhood. She was the daughter of a nephew of Will Young who had become a free settler in Australia because he couldn't any longer make a living on Otmoor. Her father had prospered and married in his old age and she had come to England to see Oddington, of which her father had often talked when she was a girl. Well, she took a fancy to Otmoor and so did her daughter, and I believe they were in treaty with the Reverend Barter, our Rector, who is also Rector of Noke (that's another Otmoor parish about a mile from here), for him to lease or sell them Noke Rectory. It fell through somehow, because they couldn't agree about a price, so they went off and some time later another gentleman took the Rectory. I heard from someone that the lady had died. I wasn't altogether surprised, because she had some serious complaint and refused to see a doctor. Her daughter, Miss Mildred, was the same. She was a pretty girl of seventeen or so. She was always having trouble with her tonsils, but she wouldn't *dream* of having them out, she said, because it was all error to imagine that tonsils could be poisonous.'

The Emu asked: 'You don't happen to have any forwarding address that would find the daughter?'

'I'm afraid not, sir. They stayed at the "Swan", but the inn has changed landlords since then, so it won't be much use asking there whether they left an address. Nor, come to think of it, will it be any good asking the Reverend Barter for an address, because he came to me once to ask if I could put him in touch with the lady again, and I couldn't.'

So the Emu had no option but to advertise in the *Christian Science Monitor*: MILDRED YOUNG – If Mildred Young, whose Mother, in 1923, attempted to lease or buy NOKE RECTORY, Oxfordshire, applies to Messrs Hennington and Paul, Solicitors, Ledger House, Gray's Inn Road, she will hear SOMETHING TO HER ADVANTAGE.

'If only the tonsils haven't carried her off,' he thought, 'or converted her to a faith in surgery.'

But they had not. She answered by return of post, writing on notepaper headed 'The Christian Science Reading Room, Fallowfield, Manchester', and The Emu went straight up to Manchester to interview her and strike a bargain. He found her a bit sticky, and had to allow himself to be almost converted to her faith before he could persuade her to do what he wanted.

CHAPTER 19

THE SECOND AUCTION

PHILATELY is an aspect of Western culture that (it will be acknowledged by even the most fanatical stamp-lovers) has affected the teeming millions of the East considerably less than football, radio, the cinema, ice-cream. Yet the Rajahs of India, the Lamas of Tibet, the Mandarins of China, the Generals and Vice-Elder Statesmen of Japan, the Princes of Burma, Siam and Annam and the feudal chiefs of the rich East India Islands, are, as a rule, passionate devotees of the craft. So many of them have had European tutors when young; and the tutoring of Oriental nobility and royalty somehow always goes with stamp-collecting; as financial advising to Oriental nobility and royalty somehow always goes with botany. This preamble is to account for the presence, at this second auction, of the Maharaja of Ophistan and of Li Feng, the Chinese war-lord. The Maharaja of Ophistan, said to own the finest collection of stamps East of Suez, had come to London for the Empire Table-Tennis Championship. He was not competing, because he was too stout now, but he had been India's Number One table-tennis player in his time, and if there was one thing that he enjoyed watching it was really good table-tennis. Indians take to the game naturally. Their wrists are so supple and their eyes swivel so. Li Feng, also said to own the finest collection of stamps East of Suez, was in London buying anti-aircraft guns and trying to raise a ninety-million yen loan in the City. Li Feng and the Maharaja both applied for and were granted stage-boxes at the Burlington.

Strange, that our so trivial story should knot together the four corners of the earth. Rural and metropolitan England; Australia, natal land of The Emu, of Adelaide, of the supposititious Mildred Young; Bolivia, where Cousin Eric was mining engineer and bought the stamps some of which went into 'our' collection; Cuba, where Dr Parmesan studied the occurrency of nystagmus among sugar-workers and bought his tobacco-making machine; the United States, where Jane was touring at the time of her parents' deaths; Persia, where stamp-sending Aunt Nellie was married to someone at the British Legation; Antigua – fatal name; and now Northern China and Ophistan; to say nothing of Newfoundland, Tuscany, Puerto Rico, Barbados and other philatelic ports of origin. The universality of the stamp-album as a symbol of domestic war between brother and sister is partly responsible for this geographic breadth. For instance, the Maharaja of Ophistan's succession to the throne and to the immense revenues of Ophistan had been directly due to a quarrel between his elder brother, the heir-apparent, and his elder sister. A Mr O'Gorman, who had been tutor to the Royal Princes in that enlightened state, had, on his departure, tactlessly presented the stamp-album over which they had all spent so many hours together to the elder prince alone. The princess was jealous and introduced a small specimen of the jessur (*Daboia Russellii*), a beautifully marked and highly poisonous, viperine snake, into the spine of the album. . . . Li Feng too, who had been educated at a Missionary School at Shanghai, had once had a beautiful sister, Chao Wuniang, who was educated at a Catholic seminary at Hankow. Both grew up with Western notions, but one morning at dawn, after a bitter all-night dispute about a family stamp-album, of which each wished to be the guardian, Chao Wuniang draped herself with pink convolvulus and drowned herself in the family well. She left a short valedictory poem on the well-head, which has become something of a modern classic in China; but, being written in terms of wet sleeves, widowed mandarin-drakes and deserted ferry-boats, it supplies no data for our better understanding of the world-wide stamp-album problem.

Other boxes at the Burlington were occupied by a Pittsburgh steel tycoon, members of the French and British aristocracy, and the Ambassador of a large South American republic; the stalls were filled with rich private collectors, and the general public crammed the rest of the house. The stage was set with an auctioneer's rostrum and long baize-covered tables reserved for members of the Royal Philatelic Society and a few favoured guests of Oliver's and Edith's. The dealers were placed on either side of the stage on tiers of benches covered with bottle-green cloth. The portrait of Sir Rowland Hill had been brought along, to make everyone feel at home. The girls in green uniform had been supplied with green stockings and shoes, and when the curtain rose on the scene, 'Uncle' Hazlitt was discovered to be wearing evening dress and the dealers to have substituted silk hats for bowlers.

It will not be necessary to name all the lesser rarities that were bid for before the lot of the evening came under the hammer. Among them was a Spanish 1851 *dos reales* blue, unused, which, being an error of colour, fetched £1500. And a pair of 1901 Pan-American 2 cents black and carmine-red, with the centre (a picture of a railway train) printed upside down, also unused, and in glorious condition. It went for £700. These were big game, though not in the same class as the APP, and contributed greatly to the afternoon's enjoyment. Both lots went to America and in each case there was warm applause at the fall of the hammer, while the orchestra played the first few bars of the *Star-spangled Banner*. James Reilly Meugh had bought the first of them on behalf of a New England museum, and the second on behalf of the Boy Patriots' League, as a birthday present for the President. He rose and bowed and thanked the house for its fine sporting instincts. 'You Britishers sure are grand losers!'

Tea came, and tea went, untasted as ever, and the long-awaited moment drew near.

Lot 49, the penultimate lot, was a Hawaiian Islands 1851 'Missionary' stamp, 2 cents blue, of type 2, used, but a superlative copy, the cancellation being unusually light. Sir Arthur Gamm secured this for £3200, and the orchestra played *The British Grenadiers*, Mr Meugh proving by his vigorous applause that Americans could be grand losers too. Sir Arthur rose from his seat at the head of the table to repeated calls for 'speech' and said: 'Thank you, ladies and gentlemen. Thank you very much indeed. I shall be brief. I have left my hundred-volume collection of postage-stamps to the British Museum, and I hope when I am dead that you will all frequently come and visit it, and remember me. This is likely to be soon, because my medical adviser has warned me that my heart is in no condition to attend these auctions, and yet habit is habit, and I cannot tear myself from them.' Sir Arthur was breathing heavily and his face had a most unhealthy look. Everyone noticed it.

There was a roll of drums and the spot-light switched from Sir Arthur to Hazlitt. Hazlitt was going to make a speech too. Hazlitt was making a speech.

'Your Highness, Your Excellency, Ladies and Gentlemen. This is the last lot of an, I think you will agree with me, extremely interesting and indeed historic evening. It has marked an epoch in the quiet course of philately. Never has so distinguished and select a gathering of stamp-lovers assembled to pay homage to so distinguished and select a gathering of stamps.

'Our respected friend, Sir Arthur Gamm (cheers), the dean of Philately, recently confided to us in a letter which he has permitted me to quote: "The days of spectacular discoveries are, of course, over: but little fish are sweet." While bowing to Sir Arthur's pre-eminence as an authority on our great art, I must, if he will forgive me, challenge so pessimistic a view. Spectacular discoveries are still occurring. Let Lot 50 be my witness. Already in the eighties and again in the nineties of last century it was said that the stream had been well fished, that the twenty-pounders had all been hooked and only the little fish left to reward piscatorial patience. But wrongly. Every now and then, if I may vary the metaphor, some thrust of the archaeologist's spade, some chance broaching of an age-sealed store of documents, or some other freakish turn of philatelic fortune justifies our faith that the future may hold finds as great as, or greater than, those known to the past. Moreover, philately is *living* history. All the historic stamps were not minted in the dim Early Victorian Age! By no means. Little fish grow up. They wax fat. We have seen the phenomenon tonight of a pair of twentieth-century stamps changing hands for no less than seven hundred pounds. And, in twenty years' time, I warrant you, the same pair will be worth three times that very handsome sum. Every year the number of philatelists increases. The demand for rare stamps exceeds the supply. There is no need to control the market by the destruction or holding back of supplies as is done in the pearl and diamond trades. . . . Stocks are indeed running low. Prices are mounting . . .

'Lot 50. The rarest and most beautiful stamp in the world. The Venus de Milo of Philately. The unique Antigua, one penny, purple-brown, 1866, which has already become enshrined in the public heart under the unphilatelic but expressive *nom de guerre* of "Antigua Penny Puce". Let the nickname stand as a tribute to greatness. Queen Elizabeth was content to be known to her loyal subjects as "Queen Bess", as her Royal father thought it no shame to be "King Harry". I have the great honour to offer you Antigua Penny Puce. Your Highness, your Excellency, Ladies and Gentlemen, what will you bid?'

There was an incident in the course of this speech which caused a ripple of laughter, but to which nobody paid any serious attention. A proud little green girl was making her formal trip down the narrow gangway between the green baize tables, displaying the APP to the house before putting it into the enlarging machine. A tall young man, seated halfway down the left-hand table, happened to tilt his chair back and stretch out his long arms and legs in a luxurious yawn. The girl tripped over his feet and went down on her face with a little scream. The young man uttered a cry of apology, dived under the table, picked up the girl, brushed her carefully, rescued the fallen envelope and restored it to her undamaged. He was recognized as the Marquess of Babraham. And we may as well say at once that the stamped envelope that he handed back to her was not a substitute, but the original. There are no forgeries in this story.

'May I start the bidding at two thousand pounds?'

'Now they're off!' Oliver whispered excitedly to Edith, from his seat in the front row of stalls.

Many people wanted to be able to boast afterwards that they had bid for the stamp, even though the narrowness of their purses made purchase out of the question. The constant flutter of handkerchiefs from the stalls, and even the upper circle, until the four thousand mark was reached was a testimony to the irresistible seductiveness of the stamp. By five thousand it was easier to see who were the real bidders. By six thousand there were only four left. But at six thousand five hundred, two new champions stepped into the ring – Sir Arthur Gamm and James Reilly Meugh.

Up and up the price went, while the great coloured enlargement of the stamp glowed and flickered on the screen above the auctioneer's head. The seven thousand mark was passed, to a burst of applause.

'Eight thousand,' barked Mr Meugh, with an air of finality. Sir Arthur was now his only opponent, but a redoubtable one.

Sir Arthur had come to buy the Antigua penny puce. There must be no mistake this time. He had just realized on a block of valuable armament shares, and could dare to go as high as £7500, or £8000 – or £8500, even, if the worst came to the worst. 'Money no object,' as the big businessmen say. He had hardly enjoyed a moment's peace since February 12th, the day of the previous auction, either waking or sleeping. She even haunted his dreams. Usually she was a lady with the Young Queen's features, dressed in an old-fashioned purple-brown figured bombazine dress and red morocco slippers. She would be walking swiftly and soundlessly down a hotel corridor across his path, always from right to left, always in profile. He would dash forward out of his bedroom and fling himself at her feet, but, damnation take it! miss her by yards every time; and wake up sweating. Or else she was the stamp itself, and he had bought her, for a mere one shilling and sixpence, in a little shop in Brighton, and he was feeling absolutely ecstatic in his possession of her. She had become detached from her envelope now and he was, oh so delicately, supplying her with a gummed hinge, and, oh so tenderly, sticking her (oddly enough) in the exact centre of the title page of his very first stamp-album – the one he had brought with him to Christ's Hospital in 1876 when he went there as a bluecoat boy on the nomination of the Worshipful Company of Fishmongers. He was ten years old again, in his first school uniform. The yellow stockings tickled his legs. Then suddenly there would be a frightening smell of scorching and he would watch her sink, burning like acid, through the page, through the whole album, through tablecloth and table and, swoop! there she would fly with a whir of wings out of the open window into an illimitable, rainy landscape, streaked with poplar trees and telegraph poles! High blood-pressure dreams. Yet he was most careful on his diet these days.

He pressed his right hand to his heart, which was paining him. With his left hand he signalled another fifty pounds.

'One hundred.'

'And fifty.'

'Two hundred.'

'And fifty.'

£8,300 was James Reilly Meugh's limit. 'You've got me licked,' he cried huskily. 'I can't stand the pace.'

'And fifty.'

Hazlitt chanted: 'Lot 50. The sum of eight thousand three hundred pounds is offered. Going at eight thousand three hundred pounds . . .'

Complete silence. Everyone sat frozen. Then a sharp movement from the Royal Box – the Maharaja of Ophistan spreading out his hand in a princely gesture.

Hazlitt was embarrassed. Was it a bid? his respectful glance inquired.

It was.

£8,400.

'And fifty.' Sir Arthur's face was ghastly.

'Five hundred.'

'And fifty.' It was Sir Arthur's last bid. He slumped forward in his seat, uttering a deep groan. Two attendants rushed forward and carried him out into the foyer. There was calls for a doctor and a moment of great emotion. Sir Arthur was already dead by the time the doctor was found, but the audience knew nothing of this until they heard it over the radio later in their homes.

'Six hundred,' offered the remorseless Maharaja. He was reflecting that the sceptre of Ophistan was topped with the largest and most valuable diamond in the world. He would in a moment be the owner of the rarest and most valuable postage-stamp in the world. He would lay it between two thin panes of rock-crystal and fix it at the sceptre's base. He would have been prepared to go up to ten, twelve, fifteen thousand pounds for this prize.

'Six hundred.'

'The end,' Hazlitt said to himself. 'The end,' Oliver whispered to Edith. And 'The end,' The Emu muttered miserably to himself. For Mildred Young had clearly let him down.

Yet Mildred had not let him down. She had only been delayed on her journey from Manchester by a thick fog. She was already hurrying towards the theatre in a taxi. Nor was it yet the end. The Maharaja was not the only bidder left. There was Li Feng, the Chinese war-lord. Li Feng had held his fire until now, for reasons of Face.

He considered that he had lost Face by not having been specifically included in Hazlitt's speech. 'Your Highness' had been for the Maharaja, 'Your Excellency' had been for the Ambassador. Was Li Feng, likewise a box-holder, the greatest power in Northern China, and of sixty-four generations of pure Manchu princely blood, to be reckoned in with the mob on the stage and in the body of the house, under the vulgar heading 'Ladies and Gentlemen'? Face had been lost. Face must be retrieved.

'For the third time, going at eight thousand six hundred pounds . . .'

The hammer was hovering for a final descent when Li Feng spoke: 'Him no havee. Me takee.' He used pidgin English to show his contempt for the proceedings. Pidgin is the language of trade.

The Maharaja bristled. His aide-de-camp announced, 'His Royal Highness does not wish to brawl with this Chinese gentleman. He bids nine thousand pounds, and hopes to end matters at a stroke. There is no bottom to the Maharaja's purse.'

Li Feng smiled nastily. 'Me makee tly.' He crooked his finger.

'And fifty,' reported Hazlitt.

The Maharaja smiled that cold Rajput smile that suggests elephants with jewelled howdahs and heavy golden anklets.

'Ten thousand pounds,' the aide-de-camp interpreted.

Li Feng's opium taxes alone brought him in a million Chinese dollars yearly. He could go up to a hundred thousand pounds without feeling it. The pig-trough tax brought in twice that sum. And he had high hopes of a million more from the ancestor-tax that he had just imposed. 'And fiftee,' he pidgined.

The Maharaja's smile grew uglier. 'Who *is* that funny little chop-chop man?' he inquired in cultured accents of nobody in particular. 'Let us call his bluff. Let us try him with fifteen thousand.'

'Likee havee?' jeered Li Feng, crooking his finger again, and then followed the one insult that a table-tennis enthusiast can never forgive: 'Playee ping-pong?'

The Maharaja flushed darkly and whispered into his aide-de-camp's ear, who disappeared from the box and presently reappeared on the stage. He whispered his message to Hazlitt. Hazlitt nodded; he must go to any figure to get the stamp for the Maharaja.

'I am bid sixteen thousand,' he said briskly.

'Going, going . . .'

'Makee hundled pound eachee time. No stoppee till loof falle,' Li Feng said in his bird-like voice.

It was a farcical position in which Hazlitt now found himself. He had instructions to make bid against bid without limit.

'I am bid sixteen thousand, I am bid one hundred, I am bid seventeen thousand, I am bid one hundred,' he said dryly.

Two thousand pairs of eyes switched backwards and forwards from right-hand box to left-hand box. No sign of weakening in either the Maharaja or Li Feng. Rajput pride, Chinese Face. The irresistible force coming into contact with the immovable post. What resulted? Perpetual motion?

No motion is perpetual. Mildred's taxi stopped at the stage door. Alfred Williams, the assistant electrician, was there to meet her.

'Am I too late?' she gasped.

'Hurry, Miss, hurry!' said Alfred Williams.

Mildred hurried. She ran. She reached the wings just as Hazlitt was saying, 'I am bid one hundred and thirty-five thousand pounds. I am bid one hundred pounds!' in the voice of someone trying to put himself to sleep by counting imaginary sheep jumping over a gate.

She marched forward, a confident figure in a rather common-looking grey coat and skirt, a fox wrap and a hat like anyone else's. The APP was still lying on the enlarging plate behind Hazlitt's rostrum. She took it up and the gigantic image immediately vanished from the screen. Hazlitt did not notice; it was behind him.

'And I am bid one hundred and thirty-six thousand pounds. And I am bid one hundred pounds.'

Mildred came up to him and said, in the matter-of-fact tones that a hotel guest uses to a porter when claiming a letter from the rack: 'I think this is mine.'

'Madam?'

'My letter.'

'Madam, you are mistaken, kindly replace that envelope at once! There is no letter inside it, and it is not your property. And I am bid one hundred and thirty-seven thousand pounds.'

She drew the letter out: 'Your mistake, not mine, Mr Auctioneer. Look, it's on the same paper and in the same handwriting as the envelope. It's *my* letter and *my* envelope and *my* postage-stamp.'

She handed Hazlitt the letter and as he examined it in some confusion of mind, she ducked behind his rostrum and walked calmly away with the envelope.

It was just as she reached the wings that Alfred Williams, at a signal from The Emu, blew the main fuse of the electric lighting system and plunged the theatre into darkness. Of the jumble of mixed exclamations that convulsed the house only four need be disentangled: two angry indignant cries, and two gentle sighs of pure relief. The cries of 'Stop her!' and 'Stop thief!' emanated respectively from Hazlitt and Oliver. Of the sighs, one must be attributed to Li Feng, his Face saved; one to the Maharaja of Ophistan, his pride preserved.

Mildred got safely away, under cover of darkness and Alfred Williams' guidance, while The Emu made a covert raid on Hazlitt's rostrum, felt about it until he found the letter, pocketed it and returned to his seat undetected.

Alfred Williams, when questioned later, said that the black-out had been due to a mouse that had somehow managed to find its way into the switch-box. That went down well – people like to think that one little mouse can plunge a whole theatre into darkness. And he had the corpse to show; for The Emu was thorough.

CHAPTER 20

A FLAW IN THE TITLE

'No,' said The Emu, in reply to Jane's anxious questionings. 'Only a blown fuse, and I had to trip up a little girl in green. Not real rough-house stuff.'

'Emu,' said Jane, pressing the envelope to her bosom, 'we can now speak plainly. You have made my quarrel your own, and you have apparently performed an impossible task! If what you say is true, then – C!'

'Jane!'

'No, no, Emu! Keep your ground. First, we must be sure that this is to be no short-lived triumph, with prison gates yawning for you and me at the end of it.'

'No need to worry,' he beamed. 'Everything is in apple-pie order. Mildred has deeded her rights in it to you. It was un-questionably Mildred's property as the legatee of the Harry Young whose name is on it. I had to cable to Australia to check up on the inheritance dope, but she's the girl all right.'

'What did you pay her for the stamp?'

'Nothing! I put it to her this way. "I have a document, a letter, which will help to procure you a legacy of twenty thousand pounds and all I want in return for giving you the same is the stamped envelope in which the letter is contained. I collect rare stamps." You remember that the letter indicated Brother Fred and his heirs as the legatees of certain moneys left in care of Messrs Whitebillet? Well, the moneys were still there, I found, and compound interest for seventy years had brought them up to twenty thousand pounds. Ne'er the less a Tidy Sum. But Mildred deserves all that and more. The "more" is that I'll pay all her legal expenses for recovering it; but I have spoken to the firm's solicitors – they happen also to be mine – and they say that they will advise the firm not to dispute the claim.'

'But are you sure Mildred has a right to the stamp? Isn't there a statute of limitations, or something, to prevent her from claiming possession? Seventy years is a long time.'

'I see that I must now give you a brief sketch of the legal view of possession. It wasn't made altogether clear in the case of *Palfrey* v. *Price*. Certain salient points were not pressed. But I was studying for the Bar in Australia, so I am perfectly competent to give you the whole lay-out. First, did you know that there was a difference in Law between *possession* and *ownership*, and that the *right to possession* is a third conception?'

'Well?'

'Well, possession is, roughly actual, physical control, with the intention of exercising it, and may be either rightful or wrongful. The Law protects possession, whether rightful or wrongful, by granting remedies in respect of its arbitrary disturbance. If I take away your umbrella without leave, you continue to own it, though I possess it. You have a right of action against me for taking it, of which you may or may not choose to avail yourself. But I also have a right of action against anyone in the world, except you or your agents, who interferes with my possession by taking the umbrella away from me. In such a case the new thief would have *possession*, I should have a *right to possession* against him, and you would have *ownership*. After you have acquiesced in my wrong for six years the Law takes away its remedy of an action, but the umbrella is still yours. You have what is called "a right without a remedy". The umbrella is then in rather a peculiar position; I am *almost* its owner, in that no one can by legal action get it away from me, and I can myself recover it by legal action from anyone, except *you*, who takes it away from me. But if you chance to see it in a rack somewhere and take it back then I have no action against you, because, despite the loss of your remedy, you never lost the property in it but remained the owner. Further, by recovering possession, you have restored yourself to your original position and if I manage to take the umbrella away from you again you will have a new action for this new wrong and will continue to have it for a further six years. This odd position has never, so far as I know, been laid down authoritatively in a reported case, but it is supported by the text-book writers and is generally believed to be correct. All clear so far?'

'Transparent, Emu. You talk like Blackstone himself. You

mean that the stamp was Mildred's as the legatee, and that the Whitebillets won a right of wrongful possession to it by its not being claimed; and that then Oliver and I, by keeping it in our stamp-album, won a right of wrongful possession; and that the only possible person who could claim it from us was Mildred, but that she wouldn't have had any chance to maintain her claim to it in a Court of Law unless she had happened to find it lying about somewhere and gone away with it in her handbag.'

'Exactly. Ownership without possession or remedy is a barren right and can only acquire value in combination with physical grab and run. This Mildred has effected, with my aid and that of your old friend Alfred Williams. (Alfred Williams must be rewarded. He must be given a big job at the studios.) And Edith now has no right to possession. For Mildred, having ownership *and* possession, has deeded her title to you.'

'You said something about tripping up a little girl in green.'

'Oh yes, she was carrying the envelope, poor child. My only chance to get at it for a bit of sleight-of-hand. She wasn't hurt. I slipped her half a crown, so *she* didn't mind.'

'Explain.'

'I had consulted my solicitor, who agreed with me that a letter and an envelope, once the former's insertion in the latter has been officially solemnized by a postmark, form a single marriage-like unit. He agreed that Mildred had a right to possession of both envelope and letter. But he felt that her title might be somewhat obscured by the fact that the letter, after thirteen years' estrangement from its envelope, had started a new phase of its existence as your property; whereas the envelope had now been awarded to Edith. It might simplify matters, and conform the authenticity of the envelope as the one originally intended for Mildred's grandfather, if it could have its letter restored to it. I did not agree that this would make a halfpennyworth of difference, but what a lawyer thinks a judge may think too, and I was taking no chances. So I hastily performed the remarriage ceremony under cover of the table. And certainly the letter's being inside startled Hazlitt out of his self-possession and gave Mildred the five seconds she needed for her getaway.'

'So the stamp's absolutely and unchallengeably mine?'

'Yes.'

'Emu, you are my Lancelot, Galahad, and all the Scarlet Pimpernels in the world in one.'

So they were married in Christmas week, and all was jollity at the wedding and there were no poisoned sandwiches, and they invited Oliver and Edith, who didn't come. Everyone else did, who was anyone. Li Feng came and brought a charming wedding present – a complete set of Gilbert and Sullivan gramophone records – and the Maharaja came and brought a charming wedding present – a complete set of the Classical French dramatists in a crimson morocco binding. And the Brazilian Ambassador. . . . But never mind the wedding presents. Everyone congratulated the new Marchioness on her possession of the Antigua Penny Puce and everyone thought that Oliver was scored off and stamped upon to extinction and would never dare to raise his head in a Court of Law ever again.

Nevertheless on New Year's Eve, as Jane went down the steps of her house to where a Packard was waiting to take her and The Emu to a ball, a bright-looking youngster came forward shyly and offered her something. He had a fountain pen ready. 'Please are you Jane Palfrey?'

'I don't sign autographs,' she replied patiently, 'especially with green fountain pens.'

'I know, your Ladyship,' he said. 'I wouldn't have the cheek. It's not autographs. Please read this. And may I trouble you to compare the copy with the original?'

So she took what he pressed into her hands.

In the High Court of Justice.   1935. – P. – No. 510

KING'S BENCH DIVISION.

Between Edith Whitebillet Price, *Plaintiff*

and

Mavis Jongh, *otherwise* Mildred Young, and Jane Palfrey, Marchioness of Babraham, *Defendants*

𝕲𝖊𝖔𝖗𝖌𝖊 𝖙𝖍𝖊 𝕱𝖎𝖋𝖙𝖍 by the Grace of God, of Great Britain, Ireland, and the British Dominions beyond the Seas, King, Defender of the Faith, To

Jane Palfrey, Marchioness of Babraham and Baroness Blancaster

of 31, Cocked Hat Street, Mayfair
in the County of London

WE COMMAND YOU, That within Eight Days after the Service of this Writ on you, inclusive of the day of such Service, you do cause an Appearance to be entered for you in an Action at the Suit of

Edith Whitebillet Price, wife of Oliver Palfrey St Simon Price,
And take Notice, that in default of your so doing, the Plaintiff may proceed therein, and Judgement may be given in your absence.

𝖂𝖎𝖙𝖓𝖊𝖘𝖘, Douglas McGarel, Viscount Hailsham, Lord High Chancellor of Great Britain, the thirtieth day of December, in the year of Our Lord One thousand nine hundred and thirty-five.

THE PLAINTIFF'S CLAIM is for ...

Jane was genuinely surprised when she turned over and found that what the plaintiff was complaining about was the conversion of a chattel, to wit, a postage-stamp, in colour, brown-purple, of the face value of one penny, issued and cancelled by the postmaster of the Island of Antigua in the year of Our Lord 1866.

She called The Emu out of the car, where he had been waiting for her. 'Read this.'

He read it, and bit his lip. 'It's bluff. They've not a leg to stand on.'

The youth left Jane the copy and endorsed the original with the green fountain pen. He said good night in an apologetic voice. They did not reply and went slowly back into the house to talk things over.

Jane said, 'Henry' (she called him that now when she remembered), 'does this mean that Oliver wins the last round? They wouldn't dream of taking action unless they had some sort of case.'

He looked worried. 'I can't think what the point is. Unless ... unless ...'

'Unless what?'

'Unless they are disputing Mildred's title to the *stamp* as opposed to the letter or envelope.'

'But surely a stamp is part of the family unit of letter and envelope, isn't it? A sort of child?'

'Normally, yes. But what it may be is that since old Captain Tom Young never paid for the stamp he, as it were, purloined it. And it remains the property of the Antigua Post Office. I did think of this at the time of the trial, only it seemed so fantastic.'

'But they postmarked it. They clearly accepted his right to the stamp.'

'No, they only agreed to convey the letter, which wasn't even sufficiently stamped. I'm afraid that they may still be the lawful owners.'

'Pooh. It can't be that. Remember what you told me about the six years. They could only have legal ownership without possession or remedy. And that's a barren right and can only acquire value in combination with physical grab and run. We can prevent the Antigua Postmaster from grabbing the stamp simply by keeping it in my private safe. If he tries any tricks he can be charged with breaking and entering. Obviously he won't. And Edith can't sue on the Postmaster's behalf any more than she can on her own. She is remediless. The Postmaster is remediless. He, or his predecessors in office, acquiesced in the original misappropriation in 1866 and lost remedy in 1872.'

Emu shook his head mournfully. 'Yes, that's all very well. But . . .'

'There can't be a "but" in the case.'

'Suppose they have hit on this idea? The "but" would be that until 1942 Edith has a right to sue you for disturbance of her possession (wrongful but genuine possession) of the stamp, which is *owned* by the Antigua Postal authorities. The letter and envelope are Mildred's and she had a right to take them back – Edith won't dispute that. But: old Captain Young never owned the stamp, so he could not have transferred the title of ownership to his brother and his brother's heirs. The stamp would continue to be *owned* by the Antigua Post Office. But the *possessor*

until the other day was Edith. She has a right to claim the
protection of the Law against anyone but the true owner.'

'You mean Oliver's got us on a technical point?'

'He may have.'

'Emu, you've let me down. You're no good after all. I've
lost all faith in you. If Oliver wins this, it'll never be the same
between you and me again, not so long as we live.' She was
white with vexation.

He said, 'Well, my dear, if that postage-stamp means more
to you than I do –'

'And if it does?'

He continued with perfect good nature, ' – I shall damned
well see to it that Oliver doesn't get it away from you.'

Jane sobbed: 'O Emu, forgive me. I didn't mean that, really.
But it *is* awful for me, isn't it? That unmentionable Oliver,
laughing and laughing at me and Edith snuggling in his arms –
Edith who used to be my very best friend! And we were so
sure that it was all right about the stamp!'

He said: 'We're not beaten yet. There must be a loophole.
And we'll find it. Our position is strong in one respect. We have
present possession. It is always difficult to shake that.'

So Jane and he went on to the Ball, and even enjoyed themselves; and the next day consulted their lawyers, who said
that if the Prices took the line that Mildred had a title to the
envelope and the letter but none to the stamp, because it had
originally been misappropriated, and could prove the misappropriation by the letter, then the case was lost. Unfortunately
the letter had already been printed verbatim in a Sunday
paper.

'Find a loophole,' Jane ordered.

Something that looked like one was found.

CHAPTER 21

PRICE *v.* YOUNG AND ANOR

THE following account of the proceedings appeared in a
Sunday paper on April 26th, 1936:

THE ANTIGUA PENNY PUCE AGAIN
MRS OLIVER PRICE SUES MARQUESS AND MARCHIONESS OF BABRAHAM AND FORMER FUN FAIR ARTIST

Last autumn's *cause célèbre* in which Miss Jane Palfrey, now the
Marchioness of Babraham, sued her brother Mr Oliver Price,
a rising author, and her theatrical partner Miss Edith Whitebillet, for the famous 'Antigua Penny Puce' postage-stamp had
an equally momentous sequel in the Courts yesterday when
Miss Whitebillet, now Mrs Oliver Price, sued the Marchioness
of Babraham, her husband the Marquess, and Miss Mildred
Young of Fallowfield, Manchester, described as a secretary,
for the same now notorious property.

It will be remembered how by a daring coup last December
the stamp was spirited away while it was actually being
auctioned and when the bidding had reached the unprecedented
and astonishing figure of £137,000. It is claimed that Miss
Young, *alias* Mavis Jongh, who was revealed yesterday as the
mysterious figure who walked off with the stamp under the very
nose of the auctioneer, Mr Hazlitt, was the true owner of the
stamp, as heiress of the person to whom it was originally posted.
It is further stated that the Marchioness of Babraham, in whose
possession the stamp now rests, has since purchased it from
her. The price is not revealed. Miss Young is an Australian
and it was to her grandfather that a poignant letter bearing the
unique stamp was addressed seventy years ago by her grand-
uncle, a sea captain, and cast away in a bottle from a sinking
ship off the coast of Antigua.

A sensation was caused when Mr Philip Schreiner, K.C.,
rose and, on behalf of the plaintiff, submitted that on the pleadings no defence to the action was disclosed. He asked for

immediate judgement. Mr Schreiner argued that even were the defendants to prove all their allegations they would only have established their title to the envelope to which the stamp was affixed, and not to the stamp itself.

Mr Justice Hogtie ruled that the matter must be argued, but expressed the opinion that Mr Schreiner's point was a weighty one which he would hope to see fully dealt with by Counsel.

Mr Schreiner then submitted that, on the pleadings, the burden of proving this case rested upon the defendants. His Lordship assented and directed that they should begin.

Opening, therefore, for the defence, Mr Antony Merlin, K.C., told how in the Spring of 1866 the letter, the subject of this action, had been addressed by the doomed sea captain to his brother Fred Young, of Oddington, Oxfordshire, an early emigrant to the Antipodes; how it had been found by some person unknown among the wreckage on the shore and sent through the post to the shipowners in England, in whose care it was directed. He described the fruitless efforts that had been made to trace the captain's brother, who was then a resident of Norfolk Island and out of the reach of the newspapers advertising for him; and how on the failure of these efforts the letter, together with certain substantial moneys due to the ill-fated captain and certain of his personal effects, had been faithfully kept by successive generations of Whitebillets awaiting a claimant, and gradually forgotten.

Mr Merlin then revealed the remarkable circumstances in which the Marquess of Babraham, himself an Australian by birth and early upbringing, had traced the descendant and sole successor in title to the original addressee: the present defendant, Miss Mildred Young. He explained that Miss Young, having by lapse of time lost her right to recover the letter from the plaintiff by action at law – by what means it had come into her hands was a question into which he did not now propose to delve – was nevertheless still its lawful owner. She had resolved to recover possession of her property by the somewhat unusual but perfectly lawful method of peaceful recaption, and had indeed effected this on the stage of the Burlington Theatre during an auction of stamps.

Mr Merlin added that Miss Young's claim to be the living

representative of her grand-uncle and grandfather had, after close investigation, been freely acknowledged by the White-billet, Thunderbottom and Spanish Main Shipping Company, Ltd. – the present owners of the old Whitebillet line – and that the long-dead sea captain's property had now been, very properly, handed over to her. In recognition of the Marquess's assistance in regaining her family's property, and for a further nominal money consideration, Miss Young had recently by deed transferred all her rights in the stamp to the Marchioness of Babraham.

Dealing with the point raised so dramatically by Mr Schreiner at the beginning of the trial, Mr Merlin argued that the stamp could not be distinguished from the letter. They were part and parcel of one another and inseparable.

Mr Justice Hogtie: Very many years ago it was my practice to hold the envelopes that I had been given from foreign letters, or that I had retrieved from the waste-paper basket, to a jet of steam from the kitchen kettle. This is not a procedure that finds favour with modern stamp-collectors, I understand, who maintain that the action of the steam injures the surface of many ill-printed but valuable specimens. Nevertheless, if my memory does not betray me after a lapse of some sixty years, I found the stamps to be readily separable from the envelopes – or 'covers' as I believe they are technically known to the philatelically initiated. (Laughter.)

Mr Merlin: Physically separable, my lord, but . . .

Mr Schreiner: My lord, I am only claiming a physical stamp and shall be content to leave my learned friend all the spiritual consolation his client is able to pick up. (Laughter.)

Mr Merlin: What I was going to submit, my lord, was that envelope and stamp constitute one single piece of property, as surely as they did in the era prior to the introduction of the adhesive postage-stamp, or as they do now in the case of those post-paid envelopes employed by large business firms; and that, although one can undoubtedly tear the physical object to pieces, the title to it as a whole is indivisible.

Mr Justice Hogtie: Is it not divisible in this way, Mr Merlin? Assuming the notepaper to have been the property of Captain Young when the letter was written and by him transferred to Miss Young's grandfather, does it not appear that the stamp was clearly not his at all? It seems to me that the stamp may be in a very different position from the envelope.

Mr Merlin: There may or may not have been defects in Captain Young's title to the stamp, or indeed to the notepaper and ink – these may have been the property of the Company – but he was indubitably in possession of the letter as a whole, including the stamp, in prior possession to the plaintiff, and I propose, with your Lordship's leave, to establish that his rights, imperfect though they may have been, but yet superior to any rights of the plaintiff, have descended to the defendants in this action.

Mr Merlin proceeded to develop an abstruse legal argument far above the heads of the fashionable crowd thronging Mr Justice Hogtie's court, and to cite a number of decided cases and ancient authorities. Evidence was next called of Miss Mildred Young's ancestry and Miss Young herself appeared, a tall striking-looking woman wearing a silver-fox coat, a Russian cap of the same valuable fur, and several rings that sparkled at every movement of her expressive hands. She gave evidence in proof of her identity as successor in title to her grandfather in respect of the letter addressed to him.

Mr Schreiner (cross-examining): You are an Australian by birth?

Miss Young: I am.

– And a faith-healer?

– A Christian Science practitioner. Not a licensed one, I'm afraid. I mean, I am on my own.

– You mean you are a quack?

– Not at all: I have never taken a theology course, but I practise according to books.

– You do it as a profitable hobby?

– No, to do good. I charge no fees.

– But if people care to pay you, they can?

– Mrs Eddy laid it down that one shouldn't refuse money offered in that way if one needed money.

– In fact, you make a living by it?

– It helps.

– When did you come to this country?

– In 1923 first, with my mother. I returned to Australia two years later and came here again in 1930 by myself.

– You were living in very humble circumstances in Australia, I understand, between 1925 and 1930?

– I had a bit of a struggle towards the end.

– Some of the ways in which you managed to support life during these years were a bit questionable, were they not?

– You may question me about them if you wish.

– I propose to do so. You were employed in a Sydney Fun Fair?

– For a time.

– Did you pose there as a Starving Woman?

– It was not a pose. My doctor advised starvation as a cure for an intestinal complaint from which he said I suffered.

– Your doctor? Were you not a Christian Scientist at this period?

– Not a very strong one, I am afraid. And fasting did not seem to go against the tenets of our faith. The Founder fasted too.

– I do not wish to hurt your religious susceptibilities, Miss Young, but surely the Founder of your religion did not exhibit herself at a Fun Fair?

– I was not referring to Mrs Eddy; I was referring to Our Saviour.

Mr Schreiner appeared somewhat confused by this reply.

– Did you also pretend to tell fortunes?

– No, I read characters. That is a very different thing.

– You were once, however, in this country charged with pretending to tell fortunes in a Fun Fair at Blackpool?

– I was not prosecuted. I did not tell fortunes.

– You mean that the fortunes you professed to tell were all humbug?

– I mean that I knew fortune telling was illegal.

– You were a knowing sort of girl, were you?

– All Australian girls are pretty wide-awake, and I had learned to be very careful not to overstep the limits of character-reading. I did not make any reference to future events that defects of character might lead to, even if I clearly foresaw them.

– I see. Well, it was while fortune-telling, or character reading as you prefer to call it, at Blackpool that you came into contact with your late employer, Mr John Guffey Brownsea of Blackburn, a retired mill-owner?

Mr Merlin: I protest, my lord, this sort of questioning is absolutely irrelevant to the case. Need my learned friend extract Miss Young's entire autobiography from her?

Mr Schreiner: It is relevant as to credit, my lord.

Mr Justice Hogtie allowed the question to be put.

Miss Young: Yes, he was greatly impressed with a warning I gave him about defects of his character. He engaged me as his secretary.

Mr Schreiner: Paying you five pounds a week?

– Yes.

– For about an hour's work a day?

– Sometimes it was much more.

– You converted him to Christian Science?

– He came to see the truth through quiet talks with me.

– Mr Brownsea took a great fancy to you and made you valuable presents of clothes and jewels?

– Not so valuable as all that. And I was privileged to do a lot for Mr Brownsea in return.

– What sort of things?

– I helped him to keep from drinking. He was a drunkard.

– Mrs Brownsea did not take so great a fancy to you as her husband did?

– She disapproved of my religious views and seemed to wish him to return to error.

– And did he do so?

– I am sorry to say that owing to what I regarded as her malpractice and to a mistaken notion of duty on his part, he did backslide a little.

– He died of acute alcoholism, in fact, in 1934?

– He passed over.

– I am asking you whether he died? Cannot you speak plain English?

– I do not use the word you use. It is a wrong word.

– Well, before 'passing over' as you call it, he did not *pass over* your name when attaching two codicils to his will?

– No, he left me a legacy.

– Of £5000?

– Yes.

– In the name by which he knew you – Mavis Jongh?

– That is right.

– At the same time he left £2000 to a female contortionist, one Patty Fahy, to whom you had introduced him at the Blackpool Fun Fair?

– He met her at Morecambe first. Miss Fahy was a respectable girl, and Mr Brownsea was actuated by the most generous motives. He wished to give her a start in a business where she would not be exposed to unpleasant staring. She had always longed for a little sweet and tobacconist shop.

– Never mind about Fahy's secret longings. He left her £2000.

– Yes.

– The will was disputed by the widow?

– Yes.

– And overthrown?

– Yes.

– It was proved that you had used undue influence on Mr Brownsea?

– I did not. I never mentioned wills to him. There was a prejudice against us as Fun Fair artists.

– But that was the decision of the Court?

Miss Young assented.

Mr Schreiner was understood to remark in an aside, 'We are coming to it now.' He then said to Miss Young: I put it to you that you are by profession what is vulgarly known as a 'gold-digger'?

Miss Young was seen to colour: No, nor do I make a profession of what is vulgarly known as 'digging up dirt'. (Loud laughter.)

Mr Justice Hogtie: Be careful, Miss Young. You must answer only what you are asked and you must keep your temper.

Miss Young: I am sorry, my lord. I forgot where I was. I regarded the question and the manner as offensive. With all respect, this gentleman's manner is sometimes such that, if he were to use it to me outside this court, I should be tempted to slap his face.

The Judge: That is not at all a proper way to speak. You are still forgetting where you are.

Mr Schreiner (in suavely ironical tones): I am sorry, Miss Young, if I have failed to treat you as the *grande dame* that you profess to be, but we lawyers aim at getting the truth without undue circumlocution. We are no respecters of silver-fox and diamonds. Now tell me: who first informed you that you were the heiress of Captain Tom Young who died in 1866?

– The Marquess of Babraham.

– You were totally unaware of the relationship beforehand?

– My mother had mentioned a grand-uncle, Tom Young, who had been a sea captain, but only in connexion with a story of a fight with a Polar bear on an icefloe. She did not know what had eventually become of him.

– Who sent to Australia for copies of the birth and marriage certificates and other documents that have been handed in in an alleged proof of your ancestry?

– The Marquess of Babraham's lawyers undertook the business for me.

– I put it to you that you are not really Mildred Young, the delicately nurtured girl who is known to have come to England in 1923 on a pleasure tour with her wealthy mother, and who suffered then from a so serious affection of the throat that her family physician anticipated her early death – which may indeed have since taken place, for all the evidence that can be found to the contrary – but one Mavis Jongh, a person of doubtful antecedents, who was never in England before 1930?

– Mavis Jongh was my professional name. I am the Mildred Young you mean.

– I suggest that you are an impostor who last year, in response to an advertisement inserted in a newspaper by Lord Babraham or some member of his entourage, offered for a fee to impersonate the missing, perhaps dead, woman?

– That is a ridiculous lie. Mildred Young did not pass over. I am still alive. We lost all our money, that was all, and my mother passed over, not me, and I was left alone. I had to provide for myself somehow, in spite of my delicate nurture as you call it, and there was a bad slump in Australia at the time.

– Indeed? And the affection of the throat?

– I never had an affection of the throat.

– Are you aware that the Mildred Young who came to England in 1923 had seriously poisoned tonsils and refused to have them operated upon?

– There was a Doctor Baring-Naylor at the village where we stayed. He was materialistically-minded and said that I should have my tonsils out. I was only a girl then, but I was steadfast in my faith and the error faded away. I have testified to this cure in several Churches of Christ Scientist. There must be hundreds of witnesses.

– It has been said that it was through the medium of a Christian Science newspaper that you came in contact with Lord Babraham?

– That is so.

– Did you convert him to your faith?

– No.

– Did you try?

– We discussed religious questions. We are forbidden to *try* to convert people by forcing our opinions on them. The demand must come from themselves first. The Marquess was anxious to see the light.

– In the intervals of these discussions, in the course of which the Marquess professed such anxiety for his salvation from materialistic error, did he suborn you to make a barefaced raid on Mrs Price's property?

– He told me that it was my stamp and that it would be auctioned at the Burlington Theatre on a certain afternoon. So I came and fetched it away, that was all.

– I put it to you that he gave you detailed instructions as to how you should make a felonious raid on the stamp?

– It was not felonious. I went in and appeared openly on the stage.

– He instructed you at least how to *enter* the Theatre in a covert manner?

– I knew that I could not gain easy access to the stage except by the stage-door, so I got in there by showing the

Marquess's card. He had left the card at my lodgings when he visited me at Manchester. It was my own idea to use it.

– Then you told a lie to get admittance?

– I do not tell lies.

– Oh, I see. Then clearly the doorkeeper had orders to admit you?

– I do not know what orders he had. I showed him the card and was told that the Marquess was on the stage. I went up, saw the stamp, took it and walked off.

– Under cover of a black-out that you had been promised would be engineered?

– The black-out surprised me.

– You regarded it as an answer to prayer, perhaps?

– I did not pray for it.

– That was not the first time you had engaged in an affair of the same sort, was it?

– I do not know what you mean.

– Let me put it more plainly then. Were you ever arrested for shop-lifting in a Manchester draper stores?

– Yes, mistakenly.

– You mean they did not find the lace on you?

– I had not taken it.

Mr Merlin subsequently re-examined Miss Young. He elicited the information that the shop-lifting charge had been brought by a person describing himself as a private detective to her landlady but to herself as a patient in need of Christian Science treatment. Under both these descriptions he had made lengthy inquiries into her antecedents. This was a month after Miss Young's recaption of the stamp. The 'detective' one day accompanied her to the Tot End Universal Stores at Manchester, where he raised an alarm, charging her with stealing lace and conveying it to an accomplice, but subsequently failed to appear as a witness in the police court. The case was dismissed and the Stores made a full apology in writing to Miss Young, which she was generous enough to accept. Mr Justice Hogtie remarked that the matter looked very suspicious, and expressed a hope that the 'detective' could be laid by the heels. On the face of it, this seemed a disgraceful plot against a friendless and innocent young woman.

Mr Schreiner then stated that he proposed to call no evidence for the plaintiffs, but would submit that the defendants had established no defence at law to their high-handed removal of an extremely valuable piece of property from the plaintiff's possession. While it might be presumed that the notepaper had been Captain Young's property, any such presumption in the case of the stamp was overborne by the undeniable fact – already clarified by the letter itself, the text of which had been published in a Sunday newspaper with the authority of the Marchioness of Babraham – that the stamp was the property of somebody else. This 'somebody else' might be the Antiguan Post Office, or perhaps the insurers of the *Phoebe*, the wrecked ship; but what was pertinent was that the stamp (though in a moment of such cataclysmic emergency as would no doubt exonerate the Captain's memory from moral censure) had been illegally appropriated by Captain Tom Young and never to this day paid for.

But before Mr Schreiner had proceeded with his legal argument the Court rose, being adjourned until tomorrow.

'Henry!' Jane said, as they were going out, 'What odd playmates you do choose!'

'You mean Mildred? Mildred's all right. She's a good sort. I apologize for her appearance today, but you must remember that female defendants in a difficult position always without exception dress like sirens. To soften the Judge's heart. And also Mildred's had a rotten life for the last year or two and the moment she was actually paid her legacy, it was natural for her to rush out and spend a thousand or so of it on furs and sparklers.'

'I'd have done the same.'

'Besides, Schreiner's cross-examination gave an absolutely grotesque impression of her life. I'd prefer to be in the dock on a murder charge with Schreiner prosecuting, than in the witness-box in a simple case like this with Schreiner cross-examining.'

'Why?'

'Because in a civil case, with which I might have nothing directly to do, he could turn up my whole past in all its

innocently atrocious detail, with the excuse that he was showing me to be an unreliable witness, whereas in a murder case
where I was the accused, the main exhibit, he would not even
be allowed to mention a string of previous convictions against
me on the same charge. English juridical humour.'

'I must say,' said Jane thoughtfully, 'that I wouldn't like
to have *my* past dug up by him. Folly's Resurrections wouldn't
have sounded very strawberry-leaf in Court. And then again
the clothes I didn't wear when I was the original Nuda; and
once in my Doris Edwards days I pushed a man over a cliff.
I don't think I told you that one. He was a rich Greek, and
tried to make love to me on top of Beachy Head.'

'You can't pull an Australian's leg.'

'It's Heaven's truth. But fortunately only Heaven was my
witness. It was several yards from the top but I gave him a
shove that he went staggering down the shelving bank in his
pointed-toed yellow patent-leather shoes and couldn't pull
up in time. His name was Themistocles and he came from
Alexandria and he was stinkingly rich. I have avoided that
neighbourhood ever since.'

'Anything else on your mind?'

'I got expelled from my School of Dramatic Art at the age of
eighteen or so for having a bad influence on the younger girls.
That could have been made to sound awful. Oliver knew about
it. I suppose it was only his Public School honour that restrained him from divulging it to Mr Schreiner at the first
trial. By the way, while in Manchester did you meet Fahy, the
respectable female contortionist?'

'Am I on oath?'

'Yes.'

'Then I did. I couldn't avoid it. She and Mildred were
always about together.'

'Did she try to convert you to contortionism?'

'Yes. But – with great respect – please don't ask me another
thing or there'll be proceedings in another Division.'

There was a consultation that evening. Things looked none
too good, Mr Merlin said. He did not think that the Judge had
been convinced by his arguments. (And indeed his raising of

the point of the inseparability of cover and stamp had been most unfortunate. It is an undeniable fact that the modern philatelic trend is actually to separate cover and stamp, in order to prevent a gradual oxidization of the latter by acids contained in the paper of the former. A conservative neglect of this simple precaution has, it is alleged, reduced many of the British Museum classics to a deplorable condition. 'They resemble,' as Sir Arthur Gamm pronounced shortly before his death, 'penny-packet stamps exposed too long in the side-window of a suburban stationer's.')

'You mean we're going to lose?' Jane asked.

'I am none too confident, your Ladyship.'

Then The Emu spoke. 'There's still a hope. That fellow Schreiner gave me an idea. I must be an awful fool, but it had never occurred to me before. I believe that I know who's the real owner of the stamp, and it isn't the Antigua Post Office, and it isn't Messrs John Whitebillet and Sons, or their heirs or assigns.'

'Who is it, Henry? Quick!'

'Patience! I'm waiting for confirmation. I phoned my lawyer half an hour ago to look it up for me. I'll say nothing . . .'

The telephone fortunately rang at that moment, and he went across the room and took down the receiver.

'Yes, Babraham speaking, Hullo! Hullo! Yes, you're sure that's right? Coastal and Marine is the name? Yes. Yes. What date? 1871? Excellent. Excellent. Good-bye.'

'*Emu!* Who is it? Tell me! Who's the owner?'

'Me,' said the Emu simply. 'Which is to say – you.'

CHAPTER 22

MY BEASTLY, BEASTLY BROTHER

THE next day Mr Merlin arose in Court to announce an important change in the position, and begged leave from Mr Justice Hogtie to adjourn the trial and amend the pleadings, subject to his client paying all the costs of the case theretofore incurred.

The plaintiff's counsel (Mr Schreiner) naturally opposed this plea with all the eloquence at his disposal. He felt confident of victory as the pleadings were now framed, and it will be clear to observant readers how much depended on immediate victory. If Edith now succeeded in legally regaining possession of the stamp, leaving Jane to bring a new action for its recovery (the only alternative to a grant of leave to amend proceedings), where would Jane be? Jane would be nowhere. Jane's new rights (which we shall soon define), being defensive only, would no longer be of any avail. The formal grounds of objection brought forward by Mr Schreiner were that Jane was seeking to plead a title to the stamp which was not in her when she unlawfully took possession of the stamp unlawfully seized by Mildred Young.

Mr Justice Hogtie, however, overruled this objection, granted the application and adjourned the case. The legal possibilities intrigued him.

The explanation of all this was that The Emu while in Liverpool, helping Mildred to recover her legacy, had been given access to the papers relating to the wreck of the *Phoebe*, and had noticed that all risks had been fully covered by an insurance company – 'The Coastal and Marine'. The name had seemed vaguely familiar to him, but he could not remember in what connexion. And it was only during the hearing of the case that it had been brought home to him that, since the *Phoebe* had been fully insured, the claim for the lost cargo must have been subsequently settled, and that the cargo included the consignment of stamps, and that therefore the APP, as survivor of the wreck, had become the property of the insurance

company, and that the insurance company was the Coastal
and Marine which . . .

Yes, among the property in which The Emu had succeeded
the sixth Marquess, Jane's grandfather, was one of apparently
small value – the recoverable assets of the Coastal and Marine
Insurance Company which, at the winding up of the firm in
1871, following a run of bad luck, he had bought for a trifle
from his fellow creditors. The office buildings in Upper
Thames Street were handsome ones, and there were some bad
debts that he thought might not be so bad as the directors
had pretended them to be. The *Phoebe* claim had been settled in
October 1867. The receipt survived.

All this was fully confirmed by The Emu's lawyers, and
Jane bought all rights in the APP from him at the formal
price of half a crown.

Edith's lawyers were informed of this transaction and,
realizing that her case was now hopeless, advised her to withdraw.

Edith withdrew. The Marchioness of Babraham was thus
left as the legal owner of letter, envelope and stamp, and it
was inconceivable that any further claimant to any of these
properties could now appear. None did.

Then is this not the end of the story? Not quite.

By the time that the second High Court action came on for
hearing Oliver and Edith had started their reign at the Burlington. The less said about this the better, because now that
Jane has won the APP for her very own, is happily married to
her rich, handsome, intelligent and sympathetic cousin, and
promises to make a great success of her venture in the motion-
picture industry, it seems rather unfair to emphasize the spectacular failure of Oliver's theatrical plays. He had no sense of
what the theatre-going public wanted, he tried to bully his
actors and actresses, he did not spend enough money on advertising, he staged his own plays. The longest run he ever had for
a play was a fortnight, and the profession, being notoriously
superstitious, concluded that there was a hoodoo on the
theatre and boycotted it.

Edith's health gave way and that was a good excuse for selling out. They sold out. They lost a lot of money on the deal. Jane took over the lease of the Burlington, turned it into a glamorous picture-house.

Edith's boy was born, and, a year and a half later, a girl. Then she was seriously injured in some electrical experiment she was making. Oliver was away in Constantinople at the time, getting material for another novel. As a matter of fact, he and Edith did not get on at all well together.

Edith, under morphine, kept calling for Jane. Jane was sent for and, when she heard that Oliver was out of England, went at once.

The doctor told Jane: 'I'm afraid Mrs Price is not going to live. If she does, she'll never walk again. But she's not to know that.'

Jane came softly into the darkened room.

'Is that you, Jane?'

'Yes, Edith, darling. You *are* a silly goose to get hurt. But they say there's nothing much wrong with you. Only shock.'

'They're wrong. I'm not going to live. That's why I sent for you. If I were going to live, I'd not have dared.'

'You mustn't talk like that, darling.'

'I must. Jane, do you forgive me? I've been wanting to ask you that ever so long – since my boy was born, in fact.'

'What for? For Oliver? Nonsense! I wouldn't have come, if I hadn't forgiven you. Have you forgiven *me*?'

'What for? For trying to keep me from marrying Oliver? If only you'd succeeded!'

'What! O, I *am* so sorry. Hasn't he treated you well?'

'No. He never cared for me, at all. I found out that too late. He really wanted Edna. But Edna wasn't to be had and he got his revenge on you by marrying me. And my money was useful, of course. And as soon as my little boy was born he started being perfectly beastly. Our failure at the Burlington was what got under his skin. And do you know what's going to happen now?'

'Tell me, poor Edith.'

'I'm going to die. And Edna is divorcing Freddy. You know the sort of thing that happens in India. And Freddy drinks like a fish, too, and he's gambled nearly all her money away for her on the Stock Exchange. So Edna will come and look after my children – she loves children – and within a year from now Oliver will marry his deceased wife's sister.'

'Rot, darling! First thing, you won't die. Second, nobody but you would ever be idiot enough to fall in love with Oliver.'

'No, honest! I know very well that she's with Oliver at Constantinople now, helping him to dig out stuff for his next novel. I think she was fond of him all along, but ashamed of it.'

'I don't understand women!'

'How's the Company getting on? How's Nuda? I liked her the best, I think. And J. C. Neanderthal. And Madame Blanche. Give them all my love. Even . . .'

'Even Owen Slingsby?'

'Yes, all of them. We had great fun together. . . . Jane!'

'Yes, dear!'

'Do you remember when I was a girl you used to set me little scientific problems to work out? It was such fun. It kept me happy until I saw you again. Would it be a bother?'

'You want a problem now?'

Edith nodded.

So Jane said: 'Let me see. What do I need? At the moment all I need is an umbrella. I hate umbrellas, they make one look so shabby. Edith, design me a dignified umbrella. That weighs nothing, tucks away in a purse, can't be blown inside out, can't tear, and can't get lost. Will that do as a problem?'

'It'll last me all night, thank you, dear Jane. There's no expense limit in the making, is there?'

'No. You see, only one umbrella is needed. For me. Or rather two, one for me and one for you. I don't want anyone else but you to have one like it.'

The nurse came in and said that it was time for Jane to go. So Jane kissed Edith and Edith said she felt happy now.

'I'll come first thing in the morning,' Jane said.

Edith died that night and next morning the nurse showed Jane an unfinished design scribbled on the fly-leaf of Oliver's last novel, which had been lying by her bedside. Under it was written: 'Umbrella with love from Edith. XX.'

The nurse said: 'Poor Mrs Price was delirious. She made me promise to tell you that the principle of your new umbrella was helium gas. She said that without that she couldn't get the necessary rigidity in a thing small enough to fit into a handbag and weighing nothing. It's queer the notions that some patients get when they're just crossing over.'

So Oliver married Edna. Jane and The Emu were invited to the wedding but did not attend. Jane said, 'I suppose that it's not for nothing that Edith and Edna were twins. It looks as if they were identicals, after all. The same unaccountable chemistry of the heart.' And certainly Edna had no children by Oliver, and certainly this cannot have been Oliver's fault.

It will have been noticed that we have already passed out of 1936 and are confidently flying into the future. Edith's little girl has not yet been born, even, as this goes to press. The legitimacy of such overshooting of the date has long been debated. On May 10th, 1813, for example, Miss Charlotte Clavering wrote to Miss Susan Ferrier with whom she was collaborating in a novel: 'Now I have a doubt to propose. Is it allowable to write of events which must happen at a time yet to come? Because you lay the mother's history, as I conjecture, in about this last seven or eight years; then the daughter's history will reach at least nineteen years beyond. This does not shock me in the least, but I don't know what other people might say to it, as it has no parallel.' But Time had corrected the fault by the year 1852, and Time can be trusted to correct this too. By 1949 or so, all will be comfortably passed.

It is June, 1949 and Jane, still a young woman and looking well and handsome (but dressed in fashions that 1936–7 would consider unfortunately Wellsian), is walking in Kensington Gardens. It is still recognizably Kensington Gardens, though new flower-beds full of remarkable Himalayan flowers have appeared (some new scientific triumph over the climate?) and there is no distant rumble and screech of traffic from outside, only the occasional swish of things through the air, high up, too quick for the eye to see. And a feathery sky-line – the roof-gardens of luxury hotels. Nursemaids with perambulators still – but these are crazy-looking things with legs, not wheels,

built in the shape of animals, walking along most realistically
and controlled by the nurse's voice only. It must be fun to be a
nurse in 1949. There are still Guardsmen about, dressed in
scarlet, and switching the air with their changeless swagger
canes. One of them, a pleasant-faced young corporal of the
Coldstreamers, is talking to a trim young Afternoon Air
nurse on a bench under a chestnut tree. The nurse is wearing a
small diamond nose-ring and has dark-green topiated hair.
The chestnut trees are dwarfed by a semi-circular wooden
trellis some sixty feet high, up which climb creepers with stems
like the rubber hoses one uses in dock-fires. They appear to be
the familiar morning-glory (*Ipomaca*) artificially giganticized
and perfumed, and the blooms, electric blue and pillar-box
red, are the size of tea-trays. Horrible things in themselves,
but quite ornamental in a public park. On the top of the trellis,
at each end, is anchored a beehive. The bees, which, we gather
from the Corporal's chatter, are of the stingless sort, though
bumble-bee sized, are kept busy. For these flowers (which, for
some reason or other, he calls ' Stosias ' – we suppose that they
have to be called *something*) literally drip with honey, as in
legends of the Golden Age. However, nobody pays much
attention to them, so they have probably been on display for a
year or two at least. The nose-rings, by the way, are universal
and look quite nice, once you get accustomed to the notion.
Jane has a beauty, of star-sapphires.

The nurse's charge is a pretty girl of eleven or twelve years
old. She has long fingers, a delicate profile, parti-coloured hair
and a springy walk. She wanders away from the tree and meets
Jane.

'Bored?' Jane asks, kindly.

'Stiff. I've got nothing to do but brood,' answers the little
girl in precise tones.

'What about?'

'It's my beastly, beastly brother and his hateful stamp-
album.'

Jane stares. 'What's your name, my dear?'

'Sarah. Sarah Whitebillet Palfrey Price.'

'You unlucky creature! I might have guessed. Isn't your
brother called Reginald?'

'Yes. He's older than me and such a pig. How did you know about him?'

'Your mother was my best friend for years.'

'Was she? Then why don't you come and see us?'

'I quarrelled with your father.'

Sarah laughs. '*I* quarrelled with Father, too, this morning. Over that hateful stamp-album.'

'Tell me,' Jane says, 'everything about it. But first I want to know: are you aware that you have an Aunt Jane? Do they ever talk about her?'

'No. Have I really? Is she nice?'

'Your father doesn't think so.'

'Oh, Father! Father doesn't think *I'm* nice, either. He gets furious when I practise dancing. I have to do it on the sly. And then Reggie is such a sneak.'

'About that stamp-album, Sarah.'

'Oh, yes. Father gave it to Reggie on his twelfth birthday. He preached a sort of sermon over it. He said it was his own stamp album when he was a boy and he kept it carefully ever since to give it to Reggie when he was old enough. And he told Reggie that I mustn't ever, ever poke my nose into it or have anything whatsoever to do with it, because it's entirely Reggie's, and girls don't understand stamps, and that it's worth pounds and pounds. Reggie's been unbearable ever since. He says: "You're only a girl and I have a stamp-album worth pounds and pounds, and you're not to come near it *ever*, and if you do I'll tell Father."'

'Sounds a bad life,' Jane muses. 'Is he one of those round-shouldered, burly boys who tell lies and pull their sister's hair?'

'Yes, that's Reggie. Only he'll be pretty careful about pulling my hair now. The last time I threw a pot of gum at him and it stickied his hair and face beautifully. Besides, he wears glasses; I can always break his glasses, accidentally on purpose.'

'Yes, it's a good trick. *I* remember once breaking someone's glasses, accidently on purpose. I suppose Reggie's going to Charchester next year?'

'Yes. He's down for it. Father was there.'

'And you?'

'I'm going to run away as soon as I've got enough money. I'm saving up already. I'm going to be a dancer. You'll not tell them, will you? Promise?'

'I promise most solemnly, Sarah. Tell me about your quarrel with your father.'

'Oh, I only told him that if he made the stamp-album a sort of out-of-bounds secret place for Reggie and him, then I'd jolly well make Reggie wish he'd never had a twelfth birthday. And I declared war on Father himself. This morning I got up early and stole two pages of the new novel he's writing. I stuck them in the Encyclopedia – the *Lord-Mumps* volume. He's not missed them yet. It'll be fun when he does. He goes quite mad when he even mislays his tobacco pouch. I've hidden that, too, now. I've rolled it up in a pair of his winter socks.'

Jane gazed admiringly at Sarah. 'Will you be about here next Sunday?'

'Every afternoon except Tuesdays and Fridays, when I have music lessons.'

'Look out for me then.'

They met the next Sunday. Jane had a parcel with her. 'This is for you,' she said.

Sarah opened it. It was the Stanley Gibbons stamp-album that had once belonged to young Harold Dormer. The stamps it contained were, Jane told her, an exact duplication of the stamps in Reggie's album, with another ten pounds' worth of new stamps that Jane had commissioned Messrs Harrow and Hazlitt to add to them to bring the collection up to date.

Sarah said: 'I suppose you're my Aunt Jane, aren't you? When I run away from home, what's your address?'

The next day a letter came for Sarah. It was not her birthday, so Reggie and the nurse were both surprised. 'Open it, Sarah! Why don't you open it?'

'I must have my breakfast first,' Sarah replied.

She took the letter away with her unopened and locked herself in her bedroom to read it at leisure.

It ran:

June 21, 1949
Big Five Banking Corporation,
Trustee Dept.,

Telev. City, 9191

Madam,

We beg to inform you that we are holding for you until your sixteenth birthday a unique postage-stamp known as 'The Antigua penny puce, or purple-brown, 1866', that has this day been conveyed to you by deed at the order of your paternal aunt, the Marchioness of Babraham, D.B.E. Your aunt desires that it be sold on your sole behalf by public auction under arrangements that we shall ourselves make on your informing us that your sixteenth birthday has been attained; and that you devote the moneys so realized to opening a credit account with us. The one provision attached to the gift is that you do not meanwhile cede your rights in the stamp, in whole or in part, either directly or indirectly, to any male member of the Price family. Assuring you of our services we remain, dear Madam,

Yours obediently,
V. Ramage,
per pro B.F.B.C.
Trustee Department

Sarah hid the letter in a secret drawer that she had discovered in the writing desk left to her by her mother. When Reggie said: 'What was your letter? Let's see!' she answered calmly: 'It was only a letter from my bank. No business of yours.'

Reggie was playing football that afternoon. In the evening when he came back he found her, with a pair of tweezers in one hand and a little pile of stamps in the other, bent over an album at the schoolroom table. He gave a howl of rage and dismay and tried to snatch it from her. She hung on to it. He pulled her hair. She dug the tweezers into his leg. He hit her in the face. She bit his thumb as hard as she could. He howled. Oliver and Edna came rushing in.

Oliver bellowed, 'How *dare* you take Reginald's album after I told you expressly that I forbade you to touch it?'

Sarah said in an injured voice: 'Reggie's album, Father? This isn't Reggie's album. It's mine. It's a much better one than Reggie's, and it's mine.'

Sarah showed him the fly-leaf; 'Sarah with much love from herself. June 20th, 1949.'

'She bit me, Father!' Reggie howled. 'Punish her!'

Oliver caught up the album and gave it a long, searching look.

Jane! Always Jane!

*

Yes, the stamps (you may rest assured) were fairly priced: some of them might well have fetched even more – that 1851 2-soldi brick red Tuscan gem, for instance. As for the true legal position of the Antigua Penny Puce – who knows? We are dealing here with a very unusual and complicated state of affairs and in such circumstances it is seldom possible to say that the Law is thus and thus: it is upon the uncertainty of the Law that the legal profession thrives (if at all). In any case we have satisfied ourselves that the newspaper reports quoted give a fair enough account of both the trials that occur in this book, and if the Judge perhaps gave a wrong decision in the first of these, well – with the greatest respect – judges sometimes do.